Fall I Want

By Lyra Parish

VALENTINE TEXAS
Bless Your Heart
Spill the Sweet Tea
Butter My Biscuit
Smooth as Whiskey
Fixing to Be Mine
Hold Your Horses

BILLIONAIRE SITUATION SERIES
The Wife Situation
The Friend Situation
The Boss Situation
The Bodyguard Situation
The Hookup Situation

VERY MERRY SERIES
A Very Merry Mistake
A Very Merry Nanny
A Very Merry Enemy

STANDALONES
Fall I Want

Fall I Want

THE COZY CREEK COLLECTION

LYRA PARISH

An Imprint of HarperCollins*Publishers*

FALL I WANT. Copyright © 2024 by Lyra Parish. Bonus scene copyright © 2025 by Lyra Parish. All rights reserved. Printed in the United States of America. No part of this book may be used or reproduced in any manner whatsoever without written permission except in the case of brief quotations embodied in critical articles and reviews. For information, address HarperCollins Publishers, 195 Broadway, New York, NY 10007.

HarperCollins books may be purchased for educational, business, or sales promotional use. For information, please email the Special Markets Department at SPsales@harpercollins.com.

Originally published as *Fall I Want* in the United States in 2024 by Lyra Parish.

Interior text design by Diahann Sturge-Campbell

Nature autumn background © ecco/Stock.Adobe.com

Library of Congress Cataloging-in-Publication Data has been applied for.

ISBN 978-0-06-345177-3

25 26 27 28 29 LBC 5 4 3 2 1

To my loving husband.
Thank you for inspiring me every single day.

CONTENT WARNING

Loss of a parent (discussed)
Depression (discussed)

This is a happy-go-lucky book with lots of love, laughter, and magical autumn vibes. However, after I lost my dad I didn't realize how much I needed this warning. If you're like me and are suffering or have suffered through grief, I'm sending you TONS of big warm hugs.

PLAYLIST

... Ready For It? // Taylor Swift
Espresso // Sabrina Carpenter
Cursed Romantics // Maude Latour
September // Earth, Wind & Fire
One of the Girls // The Weeknd, JENNIE, Lily-Rose Depp
favorite // Isabel LaRosa
Dispose of Me // Omar Apollo
Stardust // Zayn
Rich Girl // Daryl Hall & John Oates
Linger // Royel Otis
Think I'm in Love with You // Chris Stapleton, Dua Lipa
Can't Help Falling in Love // Vitamin String Quartet
The Alchemy // Taylor Swift

In the middle of the night, in my dreams
I know I'm gonna be with you
—Taylor Swift, ". . . Ready For It"

CHAPTER 1

Autumn

I'm three steps from the office when the bell above the main door of Cozy Coffee sounds. I pause, realizing I forgot to lock it after I entered. My heart rate doesn't increase, but I spot a clear path to the emergency exit in case someone is being nefarious.

The two very full glasses of cheap wine I drank before bed and the fantasy that ripped me from dreamland haven't done me any favors this morning. I might as well be a zombie because my brain isn't functioning yet.

"*Autumn!*" my best friend, Julie, yells in her motherly tone from across the building. Thankfully, she's not a murderer. Not that I was concerned. Cozy Hollow is safe, and most people don't even lock the doors to their homes.

I flick on the overhead light and set my keys on the desk.

As I look around the tiny room with its single exposed redbrick wall, I realize how disappointed younger me would be knowing we're working the same job I had at sixteen. The only difference is now I have the fun title of Assistant Manager, thanks to Julie's parents, who promoted us both.

Back then, I believed I'd become an inspirational story: barista turned mega best-selling author. I went to a prestigious university for undergrad and received a master's degree in fine arts from another. As it stands, I graduated nearly a decade ago and have nothing to show for it.

By my thirties, I was supposed to be thriving, but my creative well is bone dry and has been since the breakup from Hell.

"What if I were a robber?" Julie scolds as her chunky-heeled boots clunk against the hardwood floor.

As soon as September first rolls around she pulls those vintage, dark leather Doc Martens from her closet. They have a distinct sound when she walks.

Less than a minute later, my bestie greets me at the doorway wearing a serious expression and stares at me. Her bright red hair is twisted into a low bun, and her spider headband matches her dangly earrings. When the Halloween accessories appear, I know my favorite season has officially arrived. Autumn isn't just my name; it's my entire personality 365 days out of the year.

"What?" I finally ask.

"You know better, Autie. Considering you devour slasher movies like you'll croak next week, you'd think you'd be aware of the risks."

"At this point, I'd welcome *any* adventure to break me out of the monotony of my so-called life."

I'm not even Bill Murray in that 90s movie *Groundhog Day*; I'm in an oblivious, non-supporting role stuck in a loop. My soon-to-be psychologist sister believes it's one of my cycles and has given me solid advice, but nothing has worked. I'm broken and boring.

"You should be careful what you wish for," she warns. "Words carry power. You of all people know that."

"I'm not into the superstitious stuff," I remind her, or maybe I'm just trying to convince myself.

"You say that, but you won't walk under a ladder, and you've complained about that bad luck mirror you broke for two years."

She's right. Maybe I'm a *little* superstitious. It's better to be safe than sorry, right? While it's annoying that she's almost always right, she knows me better than I know myself and I wouldn't trade her for the world.

I bend down and type in the code to the safe. The door clicks open, I remove the money drawers and then count them down to ensure we have the correct starting bankroll.

"Sometimes I worry about you." She sets her coffin-shaped purse on the desk next to my keys.

"This is Cozy Hollow, Jules." I don't explain further because she's memorized the safety statistics.

"Yeah, and you've always heard people on TV say *I never thought it would happen here.* It only takes one bad pumpkin to ruin the whole damn patch. You're too trusting, and your situational awareness is lacking. Did you even notice me on your walk to work this morning? I trailed you the entire time."

She tucks a tube of dark brown lipstick into her back pocket then waits for my answer. "You *never* saw me," she finally says, not needing confirmation.

She's been overprotective of me and Blaire, like a big sister, for as long as we've known each other. Not to mention she is a year older than us both. However, her paranoia about being kidnapped is why her parents enrolled her in karate lessons in second grade. They thought she would grow out of it. She hasn't.

Pretty girls going missing in neighboring small towns kept her up at night for years. Nothing like that has or will ever happen in Cozy Hollow.

"Don't worry about me, bestie. On my walks here in the early morning, I always have this." I pick up my key chain, showing her the pepper spray in its orange and black bedazzled case. It sparkles under the overhead light.

"At least I'll sleep better knowing you're protected." She's being sincere.

"Good. I'm fine. I promise. And who knows? Maybe I'll find a strong man to walk me to and from work every day."

"I hope so," she says.

"Hate to change the subject, but guess who visited me last night?" I singsong.

"Oh, Mr. Dreamy?" She grins wide.

It's the nickname I've given the tall man with dark, messy hair who has haunted me like a ghost in my dreams for thirteen years. It's a good omen when Mr. Dreamy arrives. It usually means something *big* is about to happen, something life changing.

"Tell me everything." She plops onto the office desk and swings her feet as I count the loose coins, stacking them in tens.

My expression softens and I replay it in my mind like a movie. "We made out, a lot."

"Of course," she says, because that's typical when I have dreams about him.

"He told me to be patient a little longer and that it will work out. Oh, and he called me Pumpkin in that deep growl of his." I sigh. "Then I asked the stupid question and was jerked awake."

Anytime I have a dream about this mystery man, I ask him if it's real, and it pushes me awake. When I woke up this morning, my heart was pounding hard in my chest. I tried to close my eyes and fall back into the fantasy, but it was useless.

"I hope he's real," she says. "Because whoever you date next will have some big fictitious shoes to fill. Your subconscious has created the perfect man for you, and I'm not sure anyone can live up to him."

I laugh. "Honestly, I feel the same."

I have a journal where I've scribbled down my Mr. Dreamy dreams. Because he swept me off my feet each time, I planned to put the scenes in a future romance book. At least I will one day, when I go back to it.

"Maybe you should write about Mr. Dreamy and trash what you wrote when you were with *Sebastard*. I'm convinced you can't finish your novel because the story reminds you of him."

"I don't think that's the reason," I admit, but he *is* responsible for stunting my creativity.

"Hmph." Julie was never and will never be a fan of my ex, Sebastian. If he crawled back tomorrow, apologized for everything he did and admitted he was a cheating bastard while kissing the ground I walked on, she'd still dislike him. After the first time they met, she said he was a sleazy fuck boy. Her first impression of someone has never been wrong.

"I'm not writing anymore, Jules. At least not right now. You know that." I squeeze past her and move through the storage area to the front counter.

"You should. You're wasting all that talent."

It's a valid opinion because I've always let her read everything I've written, from my teenage poems to short stories about butterflies. I've left her on the cliffhanger of a lifetime, and she's been upset I won't finish it because she loved the characters. She's more invested in the story than I am.

Julie follows behind me, flicking on the main lights. The hums of the multiple espresso machines fill the quiet room. It's the only time they can be heard.

As I slide the cash drawer into the register and flick on the computer, Julie whips us up two strong shots. Taking them together before our shift for the day has been one of our traditions for over a decade. "You made me promise I wouldn't let you give up."

"We're back on that again? Come on."

"I had a repeat reminder to bother you all day about it. Sorry, but you knew what you signed up for when you asked me to remind you about how bad you wanted this."

"I appreciate the monthly nudges, but I'm not ready."

I used to be a hopeless romantic, now I'm just hopeless.

"Disagree. Authors who write thrillers with serial killers don't murder to legitimize their story. Watch some romcoms or porn, maybe both? Get the emotional aspects with one and the physical with the other."

Scents of freshly brewed coffee waft through the large space.

"I've tried it all. I have the literary version of erectile dysfunction. I don't believe *everlasting* love exists, and it's kind of a requirement. Happily ever afters and all that. How do I create when the magic is gone?"

"Start small, like a haiku," Julie says, grinning.

"Are you serious?" I ask.

Julie moves to the junk drawer where we keep extra pens and notebooks. Back in the day, it's where the phone books were kept. She finds a small leather-bound book and flips through it.

"It's blank," she says, handing it to me. "One per day. Your theme is love. You can do that."

I look down at the Moleskine notebook that's the size of my palm and stare at it like it might bite me.

"Kids write haikus. Unless you don't think you can? Scared?" Julie reaches for it and I shove it into my apron pocket.

"You're using reverse psychology," I tell her. "Don't forget who I grew up with."

"Out of the Three Musketeers, you were always going to be the famous one. I'll run the coffee shop when my parents retire, and Blaire will be selling love spells online and crafting cute jewelry in a cottage away from everyone. You're the only one of us in the position to write a mega bestseller, get feature films, be on billboards, and travel around the world. You promised me a red-carpet affair."

The fairy tale I used to share still makes me smile. "I had tons of ambitions, Jules, like getting married by thirty. We're going on four years beyond that. If I've learned anything, it's that we don't always get what we want in life, and that's okay. I will fully support your coffee house dreams and Blaire's obsession with witchy cottage core."

"I'm grateful you didn't marry that scumbag. And then have his children. Ew." She shakes the thought away as I grab the sanitizer pail and fill it full. Years ago, I wished on every star for that to happen.

I wring out the fresh towel, then wipe down the counter.

"Right now, my love life is the punch line. I can't even get a random hookup. I've visited Bookers several times over the summer, hoping some single tourist would take me back to the town inn and rail me. The only free drink I got was the water I ordered from the bartender."

Bookers is a local pub that's packed with tourists and regulars, regardless of what season or time of the day it is. It's the place to hang out in Cozy Hollow.

She snickers. "I could always hook you up with my brother."

"He's very much not my type." I glance up at the oversized clock on the wall, knowing Blaire will arrive within the next twenty minutes.

"Ah, right. Almost forgot. You go for total jerks who need their mouths taped shut in public settings."

"I just require him to be attractive, a few years older, and not be local. Which seems to be *way* too much to ask because, as it stands, I'm practically a virgin again."

She laughs and checks the amount of milk, half-and-half, and whipped cream we have in the lower fridge under our station.

I can pinpoint the moment when my life changed.

"Honestly, I should've been more careful with that mirror. How will I survive five more years of bad luck?"

"Here we go again," she says with a snicker. "I don't want to hear the story about how it shattered on the pavement and you cut your hand. You're not cursed."

"How else would you explain my situation? I'm thirty-three going on thirty-four and if a penis comes anywhere near my vag, it might actually bark and growl. Shit, it might bite. I swear there is a tiny No Trespassing sign hanging on my *mons pubis*."

"Autie," she says, laughing.

"You'd think I'd have a revolving door of men I'd never have to see again considering how many people visit this town. I should have a bazillion numbers in my phone. I even downloaded a dating app and didn't match with a single person. Not one."

"Because you have a certain type, and they usually aren't on apps trying to get laid."

"Next full moon, I'm stripping out of my clothes and saying Beetlejuice three times, hoping he's desperate. Beetlejuice, Jules. He hangs out in a fucking graveyard and has gross as hell teeth. That's where I am. I'm so sex deprived I'd let Beet—"

"Don't say it. But also, I can't with you," she says, smiling. "A guy tried to pick you up last week when we had margaritas. You literally rejected him."

"He tried too hard. It's supposed to happen naturally and I should at least want it."

"Your problem is you're secretly searching for forever."

I'm not afraid of falling in love. My biggest fear is being alone. I've learned that if I don't give anyone a chance, then they can't leave me.

She stocks cups and lids.

"Would still like to spice things up in my life," I say, and my thoughts drift back to Mr. Dreamy.

"What conversation did I just walk into?" Blaire asks, looking between us as she walks behind the counter. Her bracelets jingle with each step forward. She gives a magical vibe with her black hair, purple lipstick, and sharp-winged eyeliner. Her matching glittery eyeshadow sparkles when she turns her head. "What are we spicing up?"

"My love life," I explain, but she knows that I've been in a dry spell, too.

Blaire chuckles. "You're too intimidating. Most guys can't talk to someone who looks like you. And the ones who can . . . they're typically trouble or ex-Olympian skiers with tiny dicks."

I snicker and they high-five. "Sebastian wasn't that small."

Blaire rolls her eyes and holds out her pinkie. "I witnessed it with my own eyeballs."

"Average is perfectly fine," I say.

They both glare at me. Neither ever understood what I saw in him. Sebastian was my rat boy ex. We all have one, right?

When Blaire grabs an apron and ties it around her waist, I notice her black cat earrings with dangly tail and paws.

"I want a pair of those," Julie says, stealing the words out of my mouth as she carries a few gallons of milk to the extra storage fridge. "I would wear the *fuck* out of those."

"Guess it's an F-bomb day?" I ask with a brow lifted.

"Every day is."

I shake my head. "Two dollars of your tips are going into the fuck jar. It's too early for all that."

While Julie can do whatever she wants, last month her parents ripped us a new one over our inappropriate language. Apparently, the pastor overheard one of our "rowdy conversations," as they labeled it. We're convinced his hearing aids were in spy mode. The two of us were practically whispering. The *fuck jar* was created, and it's covered the expenses for several margarita days.

When the store is ready for the morning rush, I glance out the wall of glass, noticing the line of regulars that's already formed. The sidewalk outside of Cozy Coffee is one of the hot gossip spots and one reason I'm convinced so many show up weekly. Or it could be our kick-ass java. Probably both.

"Food is almost done," Blaire says as she enters from the back. "Five more minutes."

Sweetness wafts through the air, and though we make chocolate croissants every day, it never gets old. I glance out the window, seeing the sky has brightened as Blaire sets fresh vases of flowers on each table.

"I'll be happy when we can light the fireplace," Julie says, placing a few decorative pumpkins on the mantel. It's not officially autumn yet. Honestly, everyone is lucky she doesn't start with the spooky decorations on July fifth.

The timer rings from the back and I run to grab the pastries. With two mitts, I slide the trays from the commercial oven and carry them to the front. Once they're put away, it's time to open. Julie goes to the door and unlocks it. The early morning chatter fills the space, and every person is smiling as they enter.

"Ready to rock this?" I ask.

"Yep," they say in unison.

Blaire moves to the cash register and I move to one espresso machine. "It's a great day to have a Cozy Coffee. Welcome in, everyone," she says with a wide smile, like it's a grand opening.

Soon, the printer is spitting out orders and we make drinks like bartenders. Most other shifts run with more people, but Julie and I can predict each other's movements and we're efficient baristas. For the first hour, we nonstop set drinks at the end of the counter. No one waits longer than four minutes. It's an art and why this place has continued to stay in business for eighty years straight.

I pull the next order from the machine and immediately snicker, then show it to Julie.

She shakes her head. "Glad it's you and not me."

While I have a degree in literature, I trained at one of the most prestigious coffee shops in the country when I was in undergrad. Making a ristretto shot is nothing, all the finance men in the city drank them, but it's also a dickhead drink nine times out of ten.

I go to a manual machine, knowing I need a precise amount of liquid. After finely grinding the beans, I carefully tamp the powdered grounds. Soon after, the espresso drips from the metal tips and it looks like a thick honey. The crema on top is perfect. This cup is a ten out of ten and whoever Alexander is, hopefully they're impressed.

I check the name on the side of the short cup and move to the end of the counter. "Ristretto for Alexander."

When I glance up, his deep ocean-colored eyes are on me and my mouth slightly parts. The pulse in my neck increases and I nearly lose my ability to speak. My temperature rises and I forget how to breathe as my eyes scan down his tall, muscular body. The sleeves of his stark white dress shirt stick to his carved biceps. The cuffs are rolled to his elbows and his navy-blue suit pants sit perfectly on his waist. He's clean-cut like he should be on a yacht sipping dirty martinis with his swimsuit-model girlfriend.

I force a friendly smile and search for words as he approaches because he shouldn't exist.

Mr. Dreamy.

My palms grow sweaty as he stares at me. Everyone and everything fades away and in that moment, it's the two of us. I clear my throat and glance back down at his name. "Alex?"

"*Alexander,*" he corrects, his voice deep and smooth just like the ristretto I prepared. He pauses, and his gaze wanders from my eyes to my lips then back up again. This man is trouble, and not intimidated by me whatsoever.

I'm frozen in place.

"Do . . ." He stops speaking with his head tilted. There's a flash of recognition from him. Or am I imagining it?

He's too familiar. He shouldn't exist. The voice is the same one I've heard in my dreams a handful of times. A chill runs down my spine.

"Do I know you?" he finally asks.

"I don't think so." I'm breathless as I push the cup toward him. His fingers brush against mine and electricity swarms between us. My skin feels singed where we connected.

I pull away as he places his perfect lips to the rim and drinks. I expect him to smile, maybe even give a compliment. In my fantasy, he'd call me a good girl.

Instead, he scowls.

"No." He sets the cup on the counter, breathing out. "This isn't right."

My brows furrow, because that's not what he's supposed to say. "Excuse *me*?"

"This is made *incorrectly*. Apologies, but it tastes like total shit."

My mouth falls open and Julie walks past me carrying two cups in her hand. "Peter. Two vanilla lattes for Peter."

She notices my disdain.

"I'll remake it for you," I offer. "Please? I'd love to make sure you're one hundred percent satisfied."

He shakes his head and narrows his eyes. "Did you make *this* one?"

"Yes. I—"

"No, I'd rather not. I'll try anything once, even disastrous coffee. However, I cannot handle that atrocity twice." He glances down at my name tag, and I see the ghost of that sexy as fuck smirk playing on his lips. *"Autumn."*

He meets my gaze for a few more seconds then leaves, shaking his head.

Julie's eyes are wide and her jaw is on the floor. "Who was that?"

The cup sits on the edge of the counter where he left it. I pick it up, remove the lid, then swirl it around. The crema still floats on top and the warmth of it seeps into my fingertips.

"Alexander. Mr. Ristretto Shot, and he *hated* it." I take a sip of the hot liquid. "What an asshole. I made this perfect."

I glance at the door.

Julie just shakes her head.

"What a dickhead," I say between gritted teeth, in case anyone is being nosy, and we move back to our espresso machines.

"By the looks of him, he ruins days for a living. Any man who wears navy slacks with brown shoes does. Don't let him get under your skin. The day just started." She pats me on the shoulder, knowing how proud I am of my barista skills. Right now, it's the only thing I'm good at, other than running half marathons.

I try my best to shake it off. I've dealt with men like him before, the rude, attractive ones who only drink beans that come from civet poop. Kopi Luwak is the most expensive coffee in the world and something we'd never have here.

If that's what he wants, he's shit out of luck. Literally.

"He must have a terrible palate. Poor guy." The delicious chocolate notes of the ristretto dance on my tongue. "Some people will always be miserable."

"We'll probably never see him again," she says with a snicker. "He looks like he's staying at the resort."

"Good. Hope he enjoys the gross shit water they have up the mountain."

Fifteen minutes pass and I can't shake the feeling that man left me with. "This will sound ridiculous, but when I met his eyes, I thought—"

"He was Mr. Dreamy? I noticed he matched the description you've given me over the years."

I nervously chuckle. "I think I need a vacation."

"Shit, me too. Somewhere tropical, though. I'm not picky."

"Would be a dream," I tell her, but I'm still bothered.

Fucking Alex. And yes, I'm shortening his name because I can.

Maybe my dreams were really a warning to stay away from the tall, attractive man with messy hair and deep blue eyes.

"What the hell was that?" Blaire asks as she grabs some extra napkins for someone.

"He better not come in here again," I mutter to her.

"Or what? You'll ask for his number?" Blaire teases. She must've noticed how I looked at him. Did everyone?

I furrow my brows as I steam milk.

"There was a connection. I saw it." Julie squirts pumpkin-flavored syrup and caramel in a cup.

"Forgot to mention I did love spells for both of you during the full moon last week." Blaire pulls a few pastries and places them on plates.

I glance at her.

"You asked me to! Honestly, I think you *begged*."

"Oh, right. Almost forgot about that. Granted, I had an entire bottle of wine that night. No regrets. I hope I don't ruin your love spell streak."

"Nah, you won't." She snickers. "But if it works, you owe me. And if one of them is rich, like that man, I'll take a cottage in the woods."

I burst into laughter. "Sorry, but Alex looks like the type of man who will *never* be pleased."

"But you'd try," Blaire says. "I would."

"Humph." I carry the decaf mocha to the end of the counter, but I'm laughing. I won't let that douchebag take me down.

"Good morning, Mrs. Mooney," I say. She's wearing a cream-colored sweater with an embroidered pumpkin on the front that sparkles. I love it. "I thought autumn didn't officially start until September twenty-second?"

"You, of all people, know the falliday season begins when the first leaf turns yellow. Will you be attending the ball this year?" she asks as she removes the lid and pours extra milk from the condiment bar into her cup.

"If I can find a Prince Charming to accompany me, I'll be there." It's the type of party you attend as a couple, otherwise it's awkward because all the singles are grouped up.

The ladies in my mother's book club have always acted as my fairy godmothers. They all have delicious grandsons and nephews but have *never* delivered on their hookup promises. I haven't been to the fall ball in two years, and everyone has noticed.

"I'll get the witches together and we'll light a love spell candle for you at our next meeting."

"Oh, that would be outstanding." I placate her. This town is full of witchy old women. Blaire will be like them one day. Hell, she already is.

"I just need to know who, dear," she says, placing the lid back on her coffee. She takes a sip and grins.

"Like, his name?" I almost laugh, knowing I have nothing.

"Yep, just tell me the last person who made your heart flutter."

"Alex," Julie says from behind me with a giggle. "That's the name."

"Got it. And his last name?"

"She's joking," I explain, but my cheeks heat at the thought. Mrs. Mooney notices.

Her kind expression doesn't change. "Do you believe in magic?"

"Not anymore." I haven't since my heart was broken.

"I'll ask you the same question in exactly one month." She winks, then leaves.

Julie looks at me with a raised brow. "I fucking love this time of year because everyone gets so fucking weird."

"That was two in one sentence." I laugh, meeting her eyes as she pulls several dollars from her tips and puts them in the fuck jar that's on the counter behind us.

"Do you feel that?" I ask Julie as the air sparks around me. An unexplainable electrical current streams through my body, causing my arm hairs to stand on end. I rub my hand over the goosebumps on my skin. Something happened between me and that beautiful bastard. The attraction is undeniable.

She grins. "Maybe love is in the air? Maybe you just captured lightning in a bottle."

"Pfft. Yeah right." I pull the tiny notebook from my pocket and write my first haiku.

> *What's that in the air?*
> *Love is out of the question.*
> *This feels like a prank.*

Julie glances at it. "Good one."

"Yeah." I grin. "I thought so."

She lifts her hand and I give her a high five. "Glad to see you're writing something."

CHAPTER 2

Alexander

I exit the coffee shop and hold back a grin as I travel down the sidewalk toward my Jeep. This is the first time I've felt a tiny spark of anything in six dreadful months. Depression has threatened to take hold, and when I slipped into a darker place, I left the city without regret or apology.

Some may even say I ran from my issues, but they can assume whatever they want. They do regardless of my actions. But for once, I put myself first, something I've forgotten how to do until now.

A flyer with the community-scheduled activities for October flaps against one of the black vintage streetlights that line the sidewalk around the town square. I slide my phone from my pocket and snap a photo. Maybe I'll attend a few, considering my schedule is almost completely clear from now until January.

I swallow down the hint of ristretto that still lingers on my tongue and my mind wanders back to Autumn.

She was too damn pretty with her long lashes, plump lips, and need to please. As soon as my gaze drifted to her, I stopped. That woman captured my breath, leaving me speechless.

At first sight, I knew I was doomed. That's why I'll avoid that coffee shop from now on.

When she said my name and her chestnut-brown eyes finally met mine, it was like I'd known her for an eternity.

Our fingers brushed together and something sizzled between us.

I saw it in her expression. Her eyes softened as she focused on me like we were old friends or past lovers. Familiarity danced around us. And here I am, intrigued, almost consumed by her.

My phone buzzes and distracts me from my thoughts about Autumn.

I glance down at the screen and see it's Roxie, my publicist. I'm tempted to reject her call, but I don't because I have some business to handle before I fall off the planet.

"Alexander," I answer, my eyes scanning the flyer again as I commit the upcoming events to memory.

"I stopped by your penthouse to drop off the suit for your television interview tonight and the front desk told me you weren't there," Roxie says. "Will you be returning soon?"

Sometimes, silence is the only answer.

"Hello?" she asks, growing frustrated. She's worked with my family for the last two decades and has been tasked with keeping me and my sister Harper's images cleaner than most celebrities and pop stars. We had a fantastic twenty-year run; however, my reputation is in ashes after my ex burned it to the ground with twisted truths.

"I'm not taking part in this," I firmly state, taking back my power.

I glance up at the mountains in the distance. They called, and I answered. Nothing or no one can convince me to return to Manhattan.

"Excuse me? Did you say you weren't doing the interview?" Roxie clears her throat. And it's not lost on me that I've been difficult to work with, but I've always followed instructions and stayed hidden in plain sight.

"I didn't stutter." I stroll down the sidewalk, watching leaves rustle across the pavement.

A group of workers hammer together the wooden structure that will be used for the pumpkin patch that's opening in two weeks. That flyer has already come in handy.

"We had a plan. You agreed, and we promptly signed a contract with the network. This was three months ago. Everyone wants you to break your silence and tell your side of the story. Not to mention, your father donated a lot of money for you to have a prime-time segment. They booted the president of the United States for you."

"Really sorry about that. I've thought it over, and I changed my mind. Unfortunately, I won't be participating." I'm firm with my decision.

Sitting in a studio with cameras in my face as I spit out well-rehearsed answers to pre-written questions isn't my style. And it never will be. "The world can believe what they want. They can believe her."

"This isn't about anyone other than you," she says. "And your reputation."

"Please tell me what part of 'I won't be fucking doing it' is difficult to understand."

"Maybe I can set up an online intervi—"

"Absolutely not. I won't perform like a puppet, and I will no longer be used as a pawn. This is a publicity stunt, Roxie. Seems like you and my father constructed this spotlight to increase the business's bottom line during the holiday season. I'm choosing to believe you wouldn't be that stupid or assume I was. My eyes are wide fucking open."

No one will control me.

Not my ex. Not my father. And not fucking her.

"Unbelievable. You're off-script, and we all know that's bad for business," she sneers.

My father had plenty of scandals in his twenties and thirties, and it nearly sent my grandfather into an early grave.

To avoid his karma, my father spent ridiculous amounts of

money to ensure Harper and I never experienced what he did. The overprotectiveness worked. A few months ago, the dramatized docuseries of our lives was released and we were put on every popular network's radar. My ex took center stage, stealing the spotlight by showing our private text conversations. Each one was taken out of context.

Overnight, I became the man in millions of women's fantasies. I have no safe spaces except here in Cozy Hollow. I hope.

"Do the fucking interview."

"My life isn't a movie. Got it, *Roxane*?" I use her full name because she hates it.

"Are you okay?" she asks.

I almost laugh because it's been months since I've been okay, but no one notices until I fuck up their itinerary. "Are *you*? Me skipping that hour-long spotlight tonight saved your goddamn job. Take this as a verbal warning. Treat me this way again, and I will fire you on the spot."

"Your father hired me."

"And you don't think I can dismiss you? You're not that naïve. Now, if you treasure being employed by me, continue sweeping the Internet for the bullshit that's not true. I'll reach out to you. Not the other way around. My life has been painted as something it's not, thanks to your instructions."

She says something else and I end the call. I'm over the conversation and exhausted by the nonstop need to make the world believe I'm perfect. I'm not and never will be.

Roxane and my father are worried about the rumors. Eventually, my truth will be heard, but I won't be the one telling it. Everyone will figure it out.

The problem with liars is they can't keep their stories straight. They're too busy weaving together their tall tales that the wires cross. Celine believes she's won the war, not realizing she's setting up her own downfall. What she did destroyed me at my core.

My nostrils flare. I'm angry at the world, and I'm bitter.

A few minutes later, my phone rings, and I see my sister's name. I answer.

"If Roxie told you to call me, it's not happening. *Leave. Me. Alone,*" I say, shaking my head.

"Ew. You're *rude,*" Harper says. "What are you talking about?"

"Sorry. I know how she likes to loop you into the bullshit sometimes."

"Something I should know about?"

I clear my throat. "I'm not doing the interview tonight."

"Uh." Her voice goes up an octave. "But I thought yo—"

"I want to disappear for a few months."

She bursts into laughter. "Hilarious that you actually believe you can *disappear.*"

"Okay, that's enough," I say, clenching my jaw as I unlock the Jeep with the four-wheel drive I purchased and had delivered to the airport this morning.

Now, she's wheezing.

"I will end this call," I warn as I take the top off the Jeep. Now that the sun is out, I want to soak it in.

"Wait," she continues, still laughing at me. "Did you forget who you are?"

"Goodbye." I contemplate hanging up, but I would never do that to her. My sister is kind, even if she's outspoken.

"No, no, please don't. But I want to remind you, I predicted all of this."

I roll my eyes. "Don't start with the psychic thing again, okay?"

"Have you met her yet? The woman who will stop you in your tracks and steal your breath away with one glance?"

Goosebumps trail over my arms because I remember the vision Harper had about my life almost two years ago. Everything she's said has happened in the correct order.

"Harp." I sigh.

"You saw her, didn't you?" She laughs. "I'm excited for you."

"Stop." I don't want to entertain it anymore.

"Did you go to Cozy Hollow?" She grows silent. "To see if Hollow Manor feels like home?"

"Sometimes you're annoying," I mutter. It was a part of her prophecy, too. But it was the only place that felt right when I knew I needed to leave. My mother loved visiting Cozy Hollow. And I did too, when I was younger.

Before I was born, my father built a ski resort on top of the mountain as a gift to my mom, along with allowing her to design her dream home. After my mother passed away, I inherited the manor, but I've refused to visit since she's been gone. It was always too hard, until now. Having my life in shambles makes being back here not seem as hard.

I finally feel ready to face this place and the memories attached to it.

This town embodies everything my mother loved in the fall and winter. I want to experience that magic again.

"Please promise me you won't be a recluse in that big house."

"I can't do that," I tell her.

"Make some friends or something. Enjoy the festivities."

The thought makes me chuckle. "Because I'm incredibly approachable."

"You can be when you want to be. Mom would want you to at least do the pumpkin patch a few times. Only weirdos go alone."

She's right. My mother wouldn't want me to be holed up in Hollow Manor by myself, not when there are fall festivities in town.

"Are you attending Dad's wedding?" She abruptly changes the subject.

"Not sure."

My father has been single since my mother passed away when I was fifteen. Now, he's marrying my ex–best friend's mother. It would be rude for me to ask which of us they'd like in attendance, so I've planned to skip. It won't be a problem if I'm not there.

"You can't be serious."

"I'm not committing," I admit, glancing at the cloudy sky and seeing sunrays burst through the fluffy clouds. "You know Celine will be there, and I'm not ready to see her with Nicolas yet."

"But Dad asked you to be his best man."

"Yeah, there is that." I think about how strained our relationship has been this year.

"What's your plan, then? Driving to your dark castle and hiding away for the winter?"

"You tell me since you've already predicted it all," I snap back.

"We both know your future wife will be with you."

"Okay, well, since you have the answers, did you want to discuss anything else?"

"No. I was checking on you because I got this strange feeling and it made me pause," she says. "Like, ten or fifteen minutes ago."

The moment I met Autumn.

I ignore that fact, though.

"I'm fine. I need space. A lot has happened in a short amount of time. I can't pretend everything is perfect anymore. I want to find solace in Cozy Hollow, just like Mom did."

"It's impossible to run from your problems. They always follow you."

"I know, but at least I can deal with them how I want without the pressures from the outside world. Mom always said fresh air and mountains can fix anything. I came to see if she was right."

After I finish putting the top down, I climb behind the steering wheel and put on my seat belt. "I'll check in with you."

"Okay. Is the town hosting those events like they used to?"

"Yep. I took a picture of the flyer. I'll text it to you so you can be jealous." I grin, thinking about the time my mother insisted we enjoy the celebrations every weekend as a family. I say family, but it was only the three of us—her, Harper, and me. My dad was too busy working, but he stopped in when he could. Those months we spent together are ones I'll cherish for the rest of my life.

"Maybe I'll crash your pity party for one," my sister says.

"Please don't." I crank the engine. "Is that all?"

"I guess so."

"Great. I love you, sis. Stay out of trouble," I tell her.

"Yeah, you too," she says, and the call ends.

I lock my phone and pull onto Main Street. I take the block around the town square. At the stop sign, I switch the radio to the local station that plays only oldies. The nostalgia of being here nearly takes me under, and the tension in my neck slightly releases.

Tourists walk the streets and I can smell the sweet scent of homemade crêpes on the grill of one of the food trucks sitting outside of the park.

Ten minutes later, I pull onto the twisty road to the ski resort.

At the halfway mark, I turn off onto a private drive that's cut out between the forest. I stop at the reader and slide my card against it. The iron gate clicks and automatically slides open. Once I'm through it, I wait for it to lock closed before leaving. The last thing I need are tourists from the resort and Cozy Hollow rolling up on me.

My heart pounds hard in my chest as I take the paved single-track road that slowly winds its way through the woods as I climb the mountain. It's been a long time since I've been here and I think back to old memories. When the large gothic house comes into view, I smile. The driveway wraps in front of the house and leads to the garage in the back. I click the sensor that's already programmed in my Jeep and drive in.

I step through the backyard, and it's exactly how I remember it, with Mom's butterfly garden and the greenhouse full of flowers she grew. The property has been maintained weekly, even though no one has visited for twenty years. When I was given the keys, I had no desire to come back to Cozy Hollow. I wasn't ready to be here, but after the shit I've been through this year, I am.

It's the only place I can escape.

The back door is unlocked, and I step inside. The cathedral ceilings and the large windows allow the sun to leak in. When I turn, my eyes scan over the long counter lined with bar stools. I think about Mom and the homemade pumpkin cinnamon rolls she made us every Saturday morning. The countless breakfasts we ate and the coffee she'd let us drink.

I smile as I'm transported back and close my eyes, almost imagining the laughter in the kitchen. My father couldn't be with us from August to December, so it was just Harper and me with her. My sister and I were pissed that we wouldn't be returning to boarding school for the semester.

Instead, my mother had hired a private teacher to go through our lessons. It felt like a prison, but we didn't know the reality of the situation yet. She wanted to make memories in one of her favorite places in the world before she started chemo.

When I open my eyes, my jaw is clenched tight and I try to relax.

I check the fridge and the pantry. Both are stocked full of food, per my instructions. I'm impressed by how fast my request was met.

I walk through the living room, glancing at the gigantic fireplace, unlock the front door, and step onto the porch that wraps in an L-shape, giving a view of the Rockies in the distance. The black rocking chairs are still in the same place they were. It's almost as if no time has passed at all.

It's a perfect day and the mountains are visible. I inhale the fresh mountain air, unpacking all the shit I've been harboring for far too long. Once I'm back inside, I take the wide stairs that lead to the top floor, hoping that when I leave here in January, I'll be a different man.

My hand glides up the smooth, hand-carved railing, which is adorned with whimsical embellishments. It's the small details in this house, the tiny things most people don't pay attention to. Mom had her own style, and every square foot is her. Each room in the house is quirky in its own way. I could never change it because this property is the only place where my mother's presence and personality haven't been erased.

It doesn't feel like home yet, but it will. My sister confidently predicted it.

CHAPTER 3

Autumn

My phone buzzes on the nightstand next to my bed and wakes me from the nap I had to take after work today. Despite being nothing out of the ordinary, the morning shift felt harder than usual.

The text messages pour in from Julie. I sit up, shaking the grogginess that's threatening to take over. While I love napping, I try not to go for over an hour or I'll be up all night.

Julie
Did your headache go away?

Julie
Still going for a run?

Julie
Don't sleep too long or you're gonna feel like shit tomorrow!

She knows me well.

Autumn
I'm up five minutes early because of you. And yes, I'm going running. I need to clear my head.

Julie
Alex still under your skin?

Autumn
Who?

Julie
Nice try.

He has been lingering in the back of my mind for the last two weeks. I know I said I never wanted to see his chiseled face again, but I search for him in crowds. With a single glance, that man buried his asshole self into me, and I can't shake it. I can't shake him because he's the man of my dreams in the goddamn flesh.

But he was a jerk and lied about my coffee. I don't understand why and I want to know.

I grab the little notebook Julie gave me and have successfully written a haiku per day, noticing Alex has taken center stage. Fuck, I'm doomed.

> *He's under my skin*
> *Haunting me like a damn ghost.*
> *Floating in my mind.*

I slide out of bed and put on my workout clothes. After I shove my phone into the deep pocket of my leggings, I stretch. This is the only time my mind is clear, and I need it.

Once my earbuds are in, I wrap the bear spray holster around my waist and leave. Whoever invented this running belt is a genius. I've only had to draw it once while out in the early morning.

Music floats out the wide-open glass doors of Vinyl Vibes, a new and used record shop I live above. It smells like lavender incense and old paper. Classic cars slowly cruise the main drag with their windows down. The locals love being outside in September, especially as the temperatures continue to fall.

I cross the street toward the trail, watching leaves rustle across the sidewalk. After the breakup, I cried every day as I ran. Then, one day, no more tears fell. But sometimes I pushed so hard my body wanted to break as much as my heart. Running told me I was still alive. I knew I'd survive when I felt like dying.

Once I'm at the base of the mountain, I start my smartwatch. If I keep a steady pace, I'll be home well before dark.

It's two miles each way, and I do this three to five days per week. It makes me feel good, a mental reset of sorts.

My feet are light under my body and I keep my focus forward. I won't stop until I'm at the top, breathing in the clean air and taking in the view from the lookout. At night, it's a typical make-out spot.

With little effort, I pick up my pace, passing a few walkers on the wide path. At the halfway mark, the trail turns into a single track that weaves through the dense forest. The cool autumn breeze brushes against my cheeks as I listen to my kick-ass playlist packed with up-tempo songs.

I push harder, wanting my thoughts to vanish. It's almost like I'm in a trance as my attention skirts over the rays of sunlight reflecting through the branches, painting the ground.

An hour and fifteen minutes later, after an uphill run, I'm at the top of the lookout with burning lungs. I stand with my hands resting on my head, taking in the view of the distant mountains and gondolas that are carrying people to the resort. Some dark clouds loom to the west, but they might dissipate before making it here.

As I try to cool down, a few tourists stop me.

"Excuse me, can you take our picture?"

"Sure," I tell them as the woman hands me her phone.

There's a sign that shows the elevation at the lookout point and the three of them stand beside it. They look exhausted. I remember the first time I hiked up it at eleven years old. I thought my heart would explode because it's a constant uphill climb. Going down is easier.

I take several pictures in different orientations for them then hand her phone back to her.

"Thank you," the lady says, and I give her a smile. When I glance over the woman's shoulder, a flicker in the distance pulls my attention away.

"No problem! Have fun!" Then I focus upward.

The lights are glowing in Hollow Manor, the black mansion that's rumored to be haunted by a woman and her two children. All murdered by their father, who disappeared soon after. It's eerie to see the house lit up. The yellow lights in the windows are like eyes.

I stare for a few seconds then blink hard to confirm I'm not imagining it.

In my younger years, I was obsessed with the lore of Hollow Manor and researched the place until I was blue in the face. I tried to find as much information as possible but always fell short. Many locals believe the owners of the ski resort covered up the truth because they were related to the family. I'm unsure if any of that is true.

What I know is the house and land have been registered to a management company since it was built. The yard is always landscaped and the driveway is shoveled and cleared during the winter months, even though no vehicles have ever been seen coming or going. Not even maintenance workers or lawn care. It's a mystery.

Maybe the ghosts maintain it? The thought makes me laugh.

The ski lift gives a perfect view of the property, and I've always been drawn to it with its black exterior and high-pitched roofs, not to mention the eggplant-purple door.

I move closer behind the lookout informational sign and glance at the game trail that leads up to the house. It's a steep climb, one

I haven't taken in over a decade. However, it doesn't seem over-grown.

When we were teenagers, we'd hike up, drink tequila from the bottle, then dare someone to run up to the house and twist the doorknob. Each time I've done it, the door has always been locked, but I'd secretly hoped that it wouldn't be.

The inside is a mystery to everyone and the dark curtains are usually drawn tight. Over the years, there have been pictures of the front of the house with a female figure standing in the upper window posted in our town gossip group on social media. I've never seen such things though.

As I turn around, I take in how many people are nearby. There are a lot because it's one of the best places to see the seasons changing. At least I know if something happened, I could blow my rescue whistle for help.

I walk past some tourists snapping selfies of themselves with the yellow leaves shimmering in the breeze. The single-track trail leading up to the house looks well maintained, and it makes me wonder if the younger generation kept the tradition going.

After one quick glance at my watch and the time, I know I can make it to the top and back down here in forty-five minutes and be home by dark.

Nostalgia mixed with nosiness is a dangerous combination, but it takes hold and I make my way up. It's steeper than I remember, or maybe age has caught up with me. My heart rate increases, but it's great for endurance.

When I get there, I stop and stare at the house. I feel nineteen again. I'd come home from college for Halloween. We snuck up here and it made me homesick.

After moving away for undergrad and experiencing the city life, I decided I always want to live in Cozy Hollow. I don't want to be anywhere else in the world. This is home.

I pull my phone out of my pocket and open my camera, taking another picture. Seeing I have cell service, which is a miracle, I send it to Julie. The message hangs for a few seconds, and when hope is lost, it shows the delivery receipt at the bottom.

"She got it," I say, checking my watch and laughing.

When I see her text bubble pop up, I wait with bated breath for her words to come in.

Julie
Are the lights on?

Autumn
Yes.

Julie
Maybe it's the ghost of the Hollow family.

Autumn
I'm going to check the door. See if it's unlocked.

Julie
What if someone is there?

Autumn
I'll introduce myself and ask them a million questions about the house and will finally solve the mystery of who owns it.

Julie
What if some weird man captures you and takes you to his dungeon? What will I tell the police?

Autumn

If you don't hear from me in three
hours, call the authorities, okay?

After it is delivered, my cell service drops.

Shit.

As I hold my phone up to the sky, I step out from the overhead canopy and search for one bar. When I look up over the peak, dark clouds move in. Random storms aren't uncommon at this altitude and I've been rained on more times than I can count, but this wasn't predicted. I have no rain gear with me.

Double shit.

Thunder roars in the distance and I look down at my watch. Sunset is in three hours. Sprinkles fall and I have one minute to decide. I can head down the mountain right now and potentially get soaked or wait it out on the porch of the house for thirty minutes.

I choose the less risky option because the last thing I need is to chafe.

The house sits in a clearing of bright green Bermuda that's mowed like a golf course. It has the best view of the gondolas and ski resort, and I stroll down the paved driveway that circles to the back of the house. My heart rate is calm as I cross the soft grass and take the wide cement steps. The gaslit lanterns flicker, and the moment I'm under the covered porch, the bottom falls out of the sky.

Calmly, I reach for the doorknob I've twisted countless times over the years. When I turn it, the latch clicks and my adrenaline spikes. I stand frozen in place.

Then I glance around, searching for cameras just to make sure nothing has been installed. I suck in a deep breath, knowing that I have to enter or curiosity will haunt me for the rest of my life.

I shouldn't. I know I shouldn't.

Every warning bell blares in my head, but I ignore them. After a deep breath, I slowly open the door and enter. A gasp escapes me as I look up at the tall, dark ceilings and long windows that line the fifteen-foot walls. Sunrays float across the wooden floor as rain splashes against the glass. A sweet cinnamon aroma fills the space and I don't know what I expected to find here. Maybe a pile of skeletons? Regardless, it wasn't this.

I tiptoe and laugh at myself, moving to a normal stride. It's so quiet my ears ring from the silence. If I yelled, my voice would echo back. Vintage images of the moon and stars are hung on the gray walls, a dark chandelier hangs from above, and I look up at the black marble staircase that belongs in a palace.

I take my phone from my pocket and snap a picture because Julie will never believe me. I make my way to the second floor, noticing the intricate embellishments carved into the handrail. At the top, I look both ways down a long, wide hallway with more chandeliers and more tall windows.

I take pause, staring outside, noticing the view.

"Wow," I whisper.

Several closed doors pique my interest, so I start at the opposite end. I reach for the handle and enter a magnificent room full of bookshelves filled from ceiling to floor. To my right is a light switch and I flick it. Dim golden yellow light splashes across the space. It reminds me of the New York Public Library with its dark wooden walls and shelves.

On one side is a gigantic fireplace and a comfy couch.

I walk to the shelf closest to me and my eyes scan up and down the spines. Many are classics, and the genres range from fairy tales to horror.

"Who do you belong to?" I whisper, moving around the perimeter, wanting to read every title and mentally catalog each one.

It's a collector's haven. A secret special edition collection hidden inside of a haunted house. It's a perfect space.

As I move forward, a firm hand grasps my wrist, pulling me backward and adding enough pressure to keep me locked in place.

I don't struggle. I've learned to stay calm in situations like this, but my mind is a tangled mess. This is a worst-case scenario, and the only person who remotely knows where I am is Julie. Maybe she will call the police when she hasn't heard from me in three hours.

"What in the fuck are you doing here?" The deep growl is low in my ear. I can't see behind me, but I also don't look.

"I'm sorry." I keep my voice flat.

"Explain yourself," he growls, and I understand how dangerous this is. But his scent surrounds me and he smells so damn good, like fresh mountain air. Only fuckboys smell like this.

"I was curious and the door—"

"Why are you here?" Now he's angry.

My breath hitches and he finally lets me go. Seconds later, I pull the bear spray from the pack around my waist and unarm the safety. When I turn, I hold the can upward and meet Alex's deep blue eyes.

He crosses his arms over his broad chest, almost daring me to discharge.

My mouth slightly parts, but I can't find the words to speak. His presence sucks the air from the room, especially from my lungs.

"*Autumn*," he says, matter-of-factly, like he knows me.

Spraying it inside the house would be bad for both of us.

"Not *you*," I whisper, but the truth is I've wanted to see him. I've wished for it.

"The feeling is more than mutual." His jaw clenches.

The only explanation for this is I'm still asleep. My alarm hasn't gone off yet and I never went for my run. Right?

There is no way I'm in Hollow Manor standing in front of the douchebag that has plagued me for two weeks.

"Is this real?" I finally ask. When I say that in my dreams, my subconscious always wakes me up.

"More like a goddamn nightmare," he snaps, and I'm not ripped away, but this time I wish I were.

His stony gaze stares through me like I'm invisible.

A few more seconds pass as he studies me. I holster the bear spray and glance away from him.

This man is my curse, with his high cheekbones, chiseled jaw, and bad attitude. Alex has haunted me since the moment he stormed out of Cozy Coffee.

For once, I should've listened to my best friend and not turned that knob. Or maybe I'm supposed to be here. Everything happens for a reason, right?

"You shouldn't fucking be here."

CHAPTER 4

Alexander

*A*utumn stares at me like I stole her voice.

"Did you forget how to speak?" I ask, surprised she's standing in my house. I've somehow avoided the coffee shop for two weeks, even though I've been tempted to visit again just to make sure she was real.

When she entered the library, she didn't see me sitting in the room's corner reading. For a few minutes, I watched her eyes scan over the books. Weirdly, I'd been thinking about her, and then she waltzed into the room. It was like she was summoned.

The athletic clothes fit her like a second skin and leave no room for the imagination.

"I'm very sorry," she mutters. "I wasn't trying to— Wait, do you live here?"

I narrow my eyes. "You're not in a position to ask me any goddamn questions. I should have you arrested then file charges for breaking and entering."

"I broke nothing. The door was unlocked. Since it was raining I—"

"I'm calling the chief of police," I say, turning to exit the library.

It's one of my favorite rooms in the house, the place I spent most of my time when I was a teenager, filled with my favorites.

Autumn scoffs and follows behind me. She keeps up with my long stride. "Please don't do that. We can discuss this like adults."

I stop walking and she crashes into the back of me. I turn and glare at her. "You're trespassing. *No one* should be in this house other than me."

"Fine. Good luck here. It's haunted," she says, glancing up at the high ceilings like she expects a ghost to pop out, then tries to skirt past me, but I grab onto her.

"Excuse me?" My face almost breaks into a smile, but I force it away. She's too damn adorable.

"A family was murdered within these walls," she says with a serious expression. "Didn't anyone warn you about Hollow Manor?"

I shake my head at the ridiculousness. My mother and father built this house and have been the only owners and residents. Sure, it's been vacant for a long while, but if a ghost is haunting the space, it's my mom. She would've loved the thought of that.

Autumn exhales and glances out the window. The rain has subsided but the dark clouds roll overhead.

"Will you pretty please let me leave now?"

"What are you willing to trade?" I ask, keeping my grasp on her wrist. "I don't grant favors."

"And I don't give IOUs," she states.

I stare at her, wondering if I've finally met my match. My sister predicted it, after all. "Do you know who I am?"

"All I know about you is you're a liar," she says.

"Excuse me?" For a moment, I wonder if she knows who I am, and if she watched the docuseries about me.

"You shit on my ristretto. I tasted it after you left and I know it was perfect."

Ah. Maybe this woman is my match.

"Interesting."

"Why does everyone keep saying that to me?"

"Because it is."

"Tell me why you lied."

I let go of her, refusing to confirm anything, and move down the stairs. It takes all of my strength not to smile, because I know from this single encounter she will be the end of me.

She follows behind me, and having her here is too convenient. When my feet hit the bottom step, I walk into the kitchen and open the fridge. I pull a beer from the door and pop off the cap.

"Do you make it a habit of walking into strangers' homes?" I ask, taking a sip.

She blinks up at me and I think I could paint her face with my eyes closed. "Does it matter?"

"Wow. So you're a liability," I state.

Autumn gives me the dirtiest look. "Frame it however you want. You don't know how many times I've turned the knob to that door and it's never opened. No way I was turning back."

"How many?"

My question shocks her. She doesn't know how to respond to me, and that's okay, most people don't. I was raised to be direct. We can blame my father for that, and for breaking me from being intimidated. I bow to no one.

"At least twenty," she says. "This place has been a mystery for so long."

"And you'll keep it to yourself. No one needs to know."

"If you let me leave, I promise I won't tell a soul."

"I should make an example out of you," I warn. "Then if anyone else has the audacity to enter, maybe they'll think twice about it. What if I'd have drawn a weapon? Or attacked you?"

"I have bear spray."

"You and I both know I had you pinned. I could've done whatever the fuck I wanted and no one would know. I could've made you disappear. I still can."

"Disappearing doesn't sound so bad," she says, and it reminds me of the conversation I had with my sister recently. "But my best friend knows where I am, and if I don't text her back before dark, she'll report me as missing, this being the last place I was."

Maybe the two of us aren't so different. I glance up at the window, noticing the rain has subsided.

"Tell me why you lied," she says.

The attraction is intoxicating, and when I meet her eyes, poison bubbles in my blood. "You won't let it go."

"No, absolutely not."

"Tell me why you can't accept that it tasted like shit?" I state, taking a long pull of my beer.

"I thought someone like you, with your tailored pants and designer shoes, would've had a more refined palate and appreciated the greater things in life. I guess not," she says. Her phone buzzes in her leggings pocket. "That's probably my boyfriend checking on me."

"Fuck him. Right now, you're *my* entertainment, Autumn."

She swallows hard.

"Now." I cross my ankles, leaning against the counter. "We're negotiating."

"Negotiating?"

"Yes, do you know what that word means?"

She scoffs. "You're an asshole."

"Thank you." I give her a sarcastic grin. I'm glad she believes that's who I am. It's best for both of us if she stays away from me. Broken people break people, and I don't want to do that to her or anyone.

"What can I offer the man who clearly has everything?" She lifts her arms and glances around the space.

My eyes rake from her eyes to her mouth and I study how her

tongue darts out and licks her plump lips. The connection streaming between us is undeniable.

"I want an IOU," I state, matter-of-factly, testing her boundaries.

"I already told you, I don't give those," she says, staying firm in her decision.

"And that's exactly why I want one. I want to be your exception." I pull my phone from my pocket and unlock it. Then I scroll through my contacts and click on the person I'm searching for.

"Mr. Alexander," he says.

Her face contorts.

"Hi, Jerry. How are you, sir?"

He has been the chief of police for the past thirty years. All I'd have to do is snap my fingers and Autumn would be picked up in a patrol car, handcuffed, and put in jail for the night. Everyone would hear about it because the locals are in each other's business.

"Fantastic. I was given word that you'd be staying until January. Is that correct?"

"Yes, sir. That's right. So, I wanted to chat with you about something . . ."

"Okay," she whispers. "Fine. You have an IOU. *Fucking asshole*," she seethes.

"I'd love to have lunch one day while I'm in town," I say.

"That would be great. Please let me know when you're available," he tells me.

"I will. Thank you. Have a good evening."

I hang up and stare at her with a smirk.

"Your name is Alex Alexander?"

"You can call me whatever you'd like."

"Are you trying to make me hate you?" she asks.

"Actually, yes," I say, placing my hand on her shoulder and leading her to the door. "It will make this a lot easier."

I look up at the sky, then glance down at my watch, knowing she has an hour and a half before darkness falls.

"Wait," I say, gently pulling her back toward me. Her eyes focus on my mouth then slide up to my eyes. "Give me your phone."

I don't know why she does, but she hands it over to me unlocked. I program my number into her contacts. "Text me so we can discuss what I want."

"And if I don't?" she asks, stepping onto the porch.

"Oh, you will." I'm firm.

"Is that your IOU?"

"Not quite, sweetheart. You owe me much more than a shitty text."

She narrows her eyes at me and I see defiance sparkling. Autumn opens her mouth, but I slam the door in her face. Then I force myself to walk away from her.

The universe has a fucked-up personality.

Three Days Later

I WAKE UP gasping and sit up, rubbing my hand over my face. The scruff has taken over, but that's what happens when I don't shave for a week. Being off the grid, away from the city, away from responsibility, has been good for my soul. Maybe by the end of the year I'll feel even more like myself than I did before. One can hope.

I reach over to the empty side of the bed and run my hand across the cold sheets. I'm relieved after the dream I had about the brown-eyed girl with a snarky fucking attitude.

The sun climbs over the mountain peaks in the distance. One habit I haven't broken yet is waking up early. Since I've been in Colorado, I've not slept in.

I place my feet on the floor, then go take a shower. As the warm stream rolls over my body, Autumn is on my mind. She hasn't texted me. That woman is a dangerous combination of everything I want, but this is a game of cat and mouse that I can't play.

An espresso machine sits on the counter and I look in the pantry for the medium roast coffee beans. Since I arrived, I've drunk black tea each morning on the balcony, but I finished the box yesterday. I move containers around and realize there isn't a drip of caffeine in this place. If I don't rectify that, I'll have a headache by noon.

So I grab my keys and leave. Leaving the comforts of my home wasn't in my plan for today.

I slowly drive down the mountain, passing a few bicyclists. I wave at them, knowing how hard it is. This road is steep as fuck.

The parking lot for the grocery store is full and I make a mental note not to come this early in the morning again. Once I'm inside, I find the correct aisle and glance over the bleak selection. There are only grounds, and unfortunately my machine will not take that.

A woman with salt-and-pepper hair walks by me. She stops and grabs a container. "You look confused."

"I need whole beans," I say, glancing at her.

"Oh, sweetie, you'll need to visit Cozy Coffee. They're the only establishment in town that carries them. They worked out a deal with the owner of the store. Cozy won't sell grounds and the grocery store won't sell beans."

Of course. Smart, though.

"Do you like their beans?"

"They're the best in the country," she says. "Try the dark roast. It's fantastic."

"Thanks for the recommendation."

"Oh, if you're ever tempted to take a chance on the coffee at Cozy Hollow Confectionary, don't. All the locals know it's awful."

"I will keep that in mind." Instinctively I look at my watch and see it's just past seven.

"Anyway, honey. Good luck. The line was wrapped around the building five minutes ago."

"Thanks for the heads-up and the luck," I say with a grin. "I'll probably need it."

I walk several blocks until I meet up with those waiting for a cup of Cozy. Briefly, I contemplate going back to the store and grabbing some tea, then calling it a day.

However, someone still owes me a text so maybe seeing my face will remind her of that IOU she gave me.

When I enter, it's as if Autumn can feel my eyes on her; she turns her head toward me, like I commanded her to notice me, or maybe she felt my presence.

A crack of lightning snaps between us and she sharply inhales.

Why am I constantly being led to her? Even when I don't want to be.

The silent conversation continues for a few more desperate seconds, and I'm the one to force my attention away.

This needs to stop before she becomes the wind in my sails.

Ten minutes later, I'm in front of the cash register speaking to Blaire. It feels like déjà vu as she gives me a warm smile.

However, I notice how she shoots glances toward Autumn. I glance at the other woman's name tag—Julie—and I catch a whiff of the sweet aroma of sugar and bread as she passes by carrying a tray of chocolate croissants.

Julie's green eyes meet mine and she bursts into laughter. "Alex. Good to see you again. Street clothes today? Wow, I didn't recognize you."

I grin, and it's easy to romanticize living in Cozy Hollow permanently. No place in the world has friendlier people.

By how Autumn's friends are gawking, I assume they've talked about me.

While it shouldn't please me, it absolutely fucking does.

I'm happy to be the center of their conversation, but I keep my jaw locked tight, not giving any of them a reaction.

Blaire clears her throat. "Your regular order?"

I meet her eyes, noticing her witch earrings. Her confidence is palpable. "You remember what I had two and a half weeks ago?"

"No one in this building will ever forget Mr. Ristretto."

"I love to hear it. May I also order a slice of pumpkin bread and a pound of Colombian whole beans?"

"Ah, I'm sorry. We just sold out of pumpkin bread," she says. "What about a chocolate croissant?"

"No, thanks," I tell her.

"Apologies, it's super limited. Maybe tomorrow?"

"Maybe." I lean in and lower my voice, ridiculously aware that Autumn is listening. "And can I request someone other than *her* make my drink?"

"Sure thing," Blaire says, typing something into the computer. Blaire places a bag of beans into a paper sack, handing it to me.

After I swipe my card, the sticker prints out on the machine. I think I hear Autumn scoff as I move to the opposite side of the dining room and wait. While I pretend to be reading something, I glance up at her, and our eyes meet.

She immediately looks away. And even though the magnetic force begs me forward, my feet stay planted in place and I unlock my phone, scrolling through social media to keep my mind busy.

A couple of minutes later, my name is called.

"Ristretto for Alex," Julie says.

I lock my phone and put it in my pocket.

Julie hands me the cup and I remove the lid, then swirl it around, studying the crema on top. Then I take a sip. She waits with bated breath and so does Autumn, even if she pretends like she doesn't care.

"This is perfect." I lift the cup and smile. "Thanks."

"You're welcome." Julie bursts into laughter when Autumn groans.

I push open the door, allowing the next person in line into the building, then leave with my coffee beans in tow.

This time, it's much harder to hold back my smile as I pass the wall of windows that line the sidewalk, but I manage. I'm a pro at a poker face. Having Autumn as my special project is very fucking tempting. It's something to think about.

CHAPTER 5

Autumn

*W*hen our shift is over, the three of us walk to Bookers to grab a few adult beverages before going our separate ways for the day.

The long bar top stretches the length of the place. Booths line the walls, and tables and chairs are spaced perfectly in the dining room. Large TVs take up most of the space between the floor and ceiling. In the back, there's a game room that gets rowdy on the weekends when the sun sets. This is one of the few establishments that stays packed no matter the season. The food and drinks are great and so is the service.

Blaire leads us across the room toward an empty booth and we slide into it.

"Need menus?" a server asks but knows better. We visit often and Julie's curse jar always pays for it. Those morning shift fucks have come in handy.

"Nah, we're having strawberry margaritas for lunch," I say with a laugh. I have leftovers at home that I don't want to waste.

"Frozen or on the rocks?"

"Half and half with sugar," I say. "I'd like a shot of Patrón on the side."

"Oh, it's gonna be like that." Julie's eyebrow quirks upward and they order the same.

When we're alone, I glance between my two best friends, who sit across from me. They're wearing shit-eating grins.

"Why are you both looking at me like that?"

"What happened at Hollow Manor four days ago?" Blaire bluntly asks, leaning forward and interlocking her fingers together.

"Not much." I shrug, knowing I can't talk about it. It would lead to the IOU and the number that was added to my contacts. Not to mention the text message I haven't sent just because he wants me to. I've recently learned that I like to please people, but on my terms.

Julie and I haven't talked about the incident and I've successfully avoided the conversation. After Alex showed up in the coffee shop this morning, I should've predicted they'd want to discuss it.

"If you hadn't texted me when you did, I would've called the police. I think we deserve to know the truth. You've been weird as fuck."

"September" by Earth, Wind & Fire plays on the radio and I'm sure I'll hear it at least a thousand more times this season.

"Why does this strangely feel like an interrogation?" It could be the light that's hanging over our table, or maybe it's how my friends are glaring at me.

Our drinks are set in front of us, and I immediately knock the shot back to loosen up. I want to change the subject, but they won't allow it. They're too committed, but this is the only exciting thing that has happened to any of us in far too long.

"Because it is. You've been weird, not like yourself lately," Blaire says, swirling her straw around and mixing her margarita together.

"I know." I inhale deeply. That man is to blame. I know it and so do they. He pushes me off-axis.

"Tell us." Blaire lowers her voice to an almost whisper. Julie nods.

I trust them with my life and know they'll take this information with them to the grave. "I'm sorry, I promised I wouldn't discuss it."

"Can we guess?" Julie asks, glancing at Blaire. They know I won't break my word, but they also know I suck at lying.

"No," I say. They can read me too easily and know how to back me into a corner.

Julie rests her chin on her hand and stares at me. "If I had to guess, I'd say Mr. Dreamy was at Hollow Manor."

"Pfft." I tuck my lips inside my mouth and avoid her gaze.

"Holy shit," Blaire whispers. "Alex *lives* there?"

My face burns and I gulp down more of my drink. Ordering margaritas on an empty stomach was a terrible decision, but we did it anyway.

"Did you go inside?" Blaire asks, and I cover my face.

"Fuck. Was he pissed?" Julie asks.

I stay quiet, remembering how he grabbed me with his strength and pinned me in place. His touch made every inch of my body spring to life. Having his hot breath on my skin and hearing his deep voice in my ear was exhilarating.

"No wonder he looked at you like that today," Julie says.

I try to ignore her words but I know what she's referring to.

When our eyes met earlier, the intensity nearly pulled me under and it took all the strength I had to look away from him. I refused to steal another glance because it was too much.

The confidence he exudes isn't like anything I've ever experienced. It's like he knows exactly what he wants and will get it, no matter what. And being attracted to a man who carries himself that way says more about me than him.

"He looks at you like he plans to unravel you," Blaire says.

Shit, I guess she saw it too.

Julie nods in agreement, glancing past me. "Speaking of, he's co—"

"Come on, guys. You're as bad as the fairy godmothers. He's an asshole. Rude. Orders prick drinks. Total dickhead. And if I never had to see him again, great."

Julie makes a face and opens her mouth, but I hold up my hand and continue. The tequila has worked its way through my bloodstream.

"Men like him are used to getting whatever they want and never have to work for anything in their life. I'm tired of it, to be honest. And don't you dare try to tell me how hot he is. Maybe he is, but it doesn't erase his shitty attitude. As soon as he speaks, it's a complete turnoff. I'm sure he enjoys it when women fall to their knees for him, but I refuse." I lick the sugar from the rim.

Julie nervously chuckles and the energy in the room undeniably changes. When I look up at my friends, they aren't paying attention to me, but to whoever is *behind* me.

I close my eyes tight and shake my head.

He takes a step forward and stands at the edge of the booth. I immediately smell his cologne, his skin, everything about him. His brown hair is messy, and he's wearing the same faded Beatles T-shirt that he had on earlier.

"I'd love to hear more about how women fall to their knees for me," he says, amusement in his tone.

"No," I say, not daring to meet his eyes because it gives him too much control over me. No way I'm drowning in those baby blues again.

"Please, join us," Blaire and Julie offer in unison.

I glare at them as Alex sits beside me in the booth, scooting his warm body against mine. I don't move, so we sit closer than I'd like.

"Thanks for the invite," he states, sweetly.

My temperature rises and I blame the margarita swimming through my bloodstream, but deep down, I know it's him.

"Don't try to win over my friends," I say, twirling my straw around in the empty glass. He shouldn't be here right now, not when these drinks were supposed to help me forget he exists.

"I don't have to *try*," he says with a cocky-as-fuck attitude. The server offers him a menu, but he doesn't take it. "I placed a to-go for Alexander."

"Sure, I'll check on that for you. Would you like a drink while you wait?"

"I'll have what they're having, and let's have another round for the table."

"With the extra shot of tequila?" the server asks.

I nod, wanting to numb whatever is swimming inside of me.

"One for everyone," he announces, and she walks away.

When I'm not able to take his closeness any longer, I scoot away, creating much-needed space. I can't sit that close to him, I'll internally combust. It's short-lived because he moves toward me, not allowing me to escape him that easily.

Asshole.

Honestly, I could use five more drinks now that he's here.

When the fresh margaritas arrive, I gulp down my shot, not waiting for anyone else.

Julie and Blaire are giddy as they glance at us. They don't have to say anything, we've been friends long enough for me to know what they're thinking.

"Stop," I say, not wanting them to play matchmaker. I don't need the extra pressure. This beautiful bastard has already put enough on me by *forcing* an IOU out of me.

"Did you tell your friends how you broke into my house and gave yourself a tour?" Alex asks in his velvety voice, glancing at me.

Julie's and Blaire's eyes widen, their assumptions confirmed.

I remember how tightly he held me against him. I swallow hard and so does he, as if he's replaying it too.

"Actually, she said she couldn't talk about it," Julie tells him.

I kept my promise to him, even though I don't believe he deserves it.

I groan. "He left the door unlocked."

Blaire meets Alex's gaze. "You know that house is haunted, right?"

"Autumn warned me. How many ghosts are there again?"

"Three," Julie confirms. "Apparently, what happened there was horrific."

"Yeah, and I vaguely recall the boy and girl who lived there," I admit. My blood feels as if it's bubbling. "I met them one year at the pumpkin patch."

"How long ago was that?" Alex asks.

"Over twenty years. I was ten going on eleven," I say.

It's what started my obsession with Hollow Manor. Sometimes I think I imagined meeting them.

He narrows his eyes and we stay locked in a trance together.

Julie clears her throat and I glance at her, realizing I was lost in him. Damn it.

I change the subject. "So did anything happen last night during the new moon? Apparently, that's when spirits haunt."

"The only peculiar thing that happened since I've arrived at Cozy Hollow was finding you inside my house," he says, taking his tequila shot. He licks the rim and places the lime between his lips. I've never been so jealous of a fruit in my whole life. I try to pretend he doesn't exist.

"I'm surprised you didn't have her arrested," Julie mutters, watching him. She's trying to unlock him as she studies his mannerisms. After this meeting, I'll get her full opinion on him because she is never wrong about anyone.

"Autumn convinced me I shouldn't," he tells her.

"How'd she do that?" Blaire asks.

He glances at me. "By being herself."

"Aww," Julie says, and I shake my head.

"He's playing games. Don't fall for it." I'm not wowed by his ability to woo them. It's obvious he's been trained to be charming, especially with looks like his.

Beautiful people are not caged by the same rules. It's clear Alex writes and plays by his own.

"You wound me," he says. His arm brushes against mine, causing goosebumps to pepper my skin. Each time he gently grazes my skin, a spark of electricity jolts through me. There isn't enough room to escape him. He made sure of that.

The server pulls his attention away and hands him food in a paper bag.

"Everything they order on my bill, please. Would anyone like anything else? Another round?" Alex asks everyone.

Julie and Blaire shake their heads.

"I'll have mine on a separate check, please."

"No, not necessary," Alex insists. "I will tip you very well if you ignore her request."

They exchange a smile and she walks away grinning. He's naturally charismatic without even trying, like he commands rooms for a living. It's not lost on me that he has that effect on those he comes in contact with. Even me.

Alex's focus is back on me. "I'd like to talk to you."

"No thanks," I tell him.

"We were just heading out," Blaire offers, and Julie agrees as they chug their drinks.

"Thanks, Alex. So nice to see you again," Julie tells him, glancing at me.

I sigh as they slide out of the booth. "I hate it when y'all do this. You're seriously leaving me?"

"Yep, we'll see you in the morning." Julie shoots him a wink and I shake my head.

"You're both traitors," I mutter.

"Text us," Blaire says to me, then glances back at Alex. "Join us anytime."

"The invitation is appreciated," Alex offers, then they walk away.

Once we're alone, he shifts his body toward me with a brow lifted. I swear he sees straight through me.

"You're feisty as fuck," he says.

"Tequila," I tell him, knowing the liquid courage has set in.

"I do want to speak to you," he admits. "I was serious about that."

"Not in here. I need fresh air."

"Sure," he says. The server returns with the bill. Alex signs the slip then he stands, allowing me out so I can lead the way.

When we're outside, I inhale the sweet scents of the churro food truck that's parked across the street. It makes my mouth water.

We step to the side of the entrance and I turn to him. "I'm not fooled by you."

He studies me. "Oh, you think this is an act?"

"Absolutely. The fake charming thing. I can see your true colors, Alex Alexander."

He chuckles. "Yeah? What color am I?"

"Your aura is red like fire. A raging flame," I state, without missing a beat. "I'm convinced you're the damn devil."

"A flame? That's interesting." A bark of laughter releases from him and I hate his perfect smile. It makes him look younger, carefree, even. It's light and contagious and he nearly breaks me. I have to stay annoyed with him. Right?

"May I drive you home?" he asks.

"No, thank you. I live a few blocks away," I say, shoving my hands into my pockets.

"May I walk with you?"

"Why?" I glance at him, needing to escape his presence.

"Because this conversation isn't over. You never texted me." He sounds disappointed.

"I find it hilarious that you thought I would, like you can tell me what to do. You get *one* IOU, Alex. *One*. If you want to use it on me texting you, I'll do it right now so we can end this game. Then you can bounce back to living in a world where I don't exist."

"We're past that," he confirms. His words are confident, like he knows something I don't.

I look at him like he's insane.

"What are you afraid of?" He narrows his eyes. He's serious.

"Pfft." I try to blow him off.

His expression doesn't change and my heart rate ticks upward.

The door to Bookers swings open and a few regulars from the coffee shop pass by. Some of them slow and I know they're listening. This conversation shouldn't take place here. The last thing I need is for rumors about me and him to spread around town. Several people already noticed he joined us for drinks and sat with me. Not to mention our little exchange at the coffee shop weeks ago.

"Not here. Come on," I say, and he follows. We walk across the street and he unlocks his Jeep with wide tires. It's a dream on wheels. He sets his paper bag of food on the passenger seat, then returns to me.

I lead him to a sitting area that overlooks the pumpkin patch, which will open this weekend for the first official day of autumn. He sits next to me and his leg touches mine. He relaxes and places his arm around the back of the bench like he doesn't have a worry in the world as he watches people.

"Why are you so determined to be close?" The smell of his soap and cologne pulls me under.

"I enjoy watching your heart rate increase," he admits.

Denying it is impossible. I wish he didn't notice what he does to me.

When his fingers brush against the outside of my arm, I stop breathing. My body betrays me. I remind myself that he's rude and men like him are used to playing games.

Alex stares out into the open field.

The grass was cut this morning and the fresh scent lingers in the air.

Five minutes pass and I wait for him to start the conversation, but he doesn't.

I turn to him, wanting to get this over with so I can go home. "What does the man who has everything want from little ole me?"

"Friendship."

It's the last thing on earth I thought he'd say. Laughter escapes me and bounces off the building across the way. I glance at Alex, waiting for the punch line, but he's not smiling.

My heart lurches forward, and it's not lost on me that, at this moment, I'm the asshole.

CHAPTER 6

Alexander

I guess considering how I've acted toward her each time we've been together, I'd believe it was a joke as well.

She notices my blank expression and her smile fades.

I glance away and focus on the chilly breeze against my cheeks. My very expensive therapist, the one I've seen online weekly since the breakup, has given me different tips to gain control when my anxiety threatens to take over. The one that seems to work the best is the *five, four, three, two, one* method.

Five things I can see: grass, trees, mountains, pumpkins, a woman walking her dog.

Four things I can hear: the wind blowing through the leaves, a few birds chirping, a couple in the distance chatting, a car zooming by.

Three things I can touch: the wood on the bench, my jeans, the soft fabric of my T-shirt.

Two things I can smell: the light hint of Autumn's perfume and the scent of freshly cut grass.

One thing I can taste: the sweet and sour from the margarita I had at Bookers.

A sliver of relief floods over me and I want to relax. I need to, but I don't remember the last time there wasn't an elephant sitting on my chest. I was so accustomed to having control of every aspect of my life that this feeling has thrown me off.

The silence draws on between us and people pass but no one looks in our direction.

I remove my arm from the back of the bench seat and create the space she wanted five minutes ago.

Right now, I need to escape.

Autumn clears her throat and moves toward me. It's the first time she's taken initiative, but I don't want her pity attention.

"I've offended you," she says, placing her hand on top of mine and squeezing. Her fingertips on me are comforting. "I'm sorry. Laughing was cruel. I didn't realize you were seri—"

I avoid her gaze. "It's okay. You don't have to apologize. I deserve it."

"You *don't* deserve that." She shakes her head. "There's no scoreboard with us."

At the moment, I see her at her core and know she has a kind heart.

If she continues to touch me, I won't be able to concentrate, so I slide my hand from under hers. "It's lonely being me. I don't expect you to understand."

"Loneliness doesn't care who you are," she says, her voice calm. "I laughed because I was shocked. I'm sure a man like you can be-friend anyone in Cozy Hollow, but you chose *me*. I don't get why. I make shitty coffee and break into people's homes."

She has a few freckles scattered across her nose and cheeks. A light breeze blows through her hair.

"You interest me."

She smiles. "I'm boring. Trust me."

"I thought—" I stop and shake my head. "I thought there was a connection between us. It sounds stupid. Maybe I imagined it."

It wouldn't be the first time, but I hope it's the last. Time to bury the shard of ego I have left and move on.

She swallows hard. "I work the morning shift, run the short trails in the evenings, and drink boxed wine while I watch slasher films. Every day is exactly the same. What's interesting about that?"

I don't respond because she's too busy trying to convince herself we'd be terrible friends. But I'll take her words at face value. If I've learned anything from my shitty breakup, it's that there is truth to people's words, especially the ones they speak about themselves.

I thought there was something between us. Silence lingers, and when our eyes meet again, that odd sense of déjà vu creeps in. She glances away.

Have we lived this life together before? I can't shake that feeling.

"I should go," I finally say as the awkwardness chokes me.

I stand, avoiding her gaze, not wanting to be swallowed whole by her. I'll never beg or take time to convince someone to be friends with me. "I'll see you later."

"Alex," she whispers, but there is nothing more to say.

I shove my hands into my pockets and walk away. I took a chance, and it didn't work out. It happens to the best of us. Trying is what matters. At least I can tell Harper I put myself out there and it won't be a lie.

It was presumptuous of me to think Autumn would want anything to do with me, especially after the hard time I've given her. First impressions are everything, and I blew it purposely as a protection mechanism.

When my feet hit the sidewalk that leads to my Jeep, I don't look back. It's one thing I won't do anymore. We're strangers and we should probably stay that way.

It will make leaving Cozy Hollow easier. Harper's prophecy was wrong.

I drive toward one of my favorite lookouts that gives the perfect bird's-eye view of the small town. I grab my bag of food and sit on the hood eating it.

A butterfly floats in front of me and I shake my head.

"Thanks, Mom," I say. She always told me she'd visit me in butterfly flutters. Sometimes, when I'm alone, I'll talk to her, hoping that she can hear me. "Bringing her into my life is your doing. I know it."

The monarch circles me a few times before flying away. In a way, it feels like a sign.

I grab my phone and take a picture of the scenery. By some miracle, I have phone service, but sometimes at this altitude it's easier to reach the cell tower from the resort.

I send my sister a picture of the yellow and orange leaves coating the mountainside.

Harper
Wow. It's peaceful. I'm hella jelly.

She sends me a text of the New York skyline. Her drawing pencils are splayed across the desk beside a coffee cup.

My sister is the vice president at Harp, an incredible company that's co-owned by her and Billie Calloway. Instead of working for the family business, they both chased their passion. Now, she and her best friend are kicking ass and taking names, traveling the world and changing fashion.

I'm happy for her and jealous. She's living her dream.

Alexander
I tried to make a new friend.

Harper
I knew you would. You're likable.

Alexander
I said I tried. It didn't work out.

Harper
It's already over?

I stare at the view, my eyes scanning over the rolling hills as I replay the conversation Autumn and I had.

> **Alexander**
> I don't want to talk about it. She's stubborn.

> **Harper**
> Wait. SHE?! Tell me everything.

I realize my fatal mistake.

> **Alexander**
> Sorry to be a disappointment, but there is nothing to discuss.

> **Alexander**
> I have doubts. I may leave Cozy Hollow and fly to London instead.

> **Harper**
> You're attracted to her.

> **Alexander**
> I'm not having this discussion with my little sister. It's fucking weird.

> **Harper**
> I need to meet her and make sure she's the one. All the others I've met, I knew within ten seconds they weren't for you.

Alexander
Great, I'd like to avoid walking
red flags from now on.

Harper
Deal. And if I don't approve?

Alexander
I won't propose.

Harper
Oooh! I can't wait to pick out the
perfect sister-in-law for me.

Alexander
As long as you're happy.

My sister knows I'm not currently searching for a romantic relationship, even if she predicted I'd fall in love here. I'm convinced it would take someone very special to break this curse.

I set my phone on the hood and finish eating. Afterward, I place my hands behind my head and watch the clouds float across the sky while breathing in the fresh mountain air. For once, I want to live and experience the life I've missed out on. I have to stop mourning a life I've never had and change the one I have. I crave things money can't buy—*happiness and true love*.

Yellow leaves fall from the trees and it pulls my attention away. In a month, winter winds will carry the first sprinkle of powder. Being here for the first snowfall is one thing I'm looking forward to experiencing this year.

I close my eyes as the sun warms my skin and I sprint through happy memories. Loss is deeply rooted inside of me and I'm afraid it's tethered to my heart. Life would be easier if I were the heartless bastard people believe I am.

I'm okay with the rumors. It stopped me from having to entertain people I never liked but dealt with because of the company I kept. I'm exhausted from floating through the world as a ghost of myself, but there is no escaping reality when my close relationships are braided so tightly together.

I sit upright, sucking in a lungful of fresh air before taking the long road home.

Time slips away from me, and two hours later, I drive through the gate at Hollow Manor. I continue down the paved driveway. It's smoother than the washboarded roads I've traveled down today. The tires roll on the pavement like I'm driving on glass.

When I pass the house, I notice something hanging on the front door.

I park in the garage, close it, then walk straight to the front porch. A plastic bag is looped on the knob and I remove it. Once inside, I set it on the counter, pulling out something wrapped in brown paper. A note is tucked under the ribbon that's tied in a cute bow.

I pull it out, skeptical.

My eyes scan over the neat handwriting on the orange stationery.

Alex,

I thought you could use some pumpkin bread to cheer you up since you seemed sad. So I made you a loaf using my family's secret recipe. You'll never get a slice during the season if you keep showing up to Cozy Coffee after seven. :)

I know you said not to apologize, but I won't sleep at night knowing I hurt you. I'm truly sorry.

I will always take accountability for my actions because it's what <u>friends</u> and good people do.

Your new BFF,
Autumn

A smile slides over my lips.

Friends. I read over the word and say it out loud. I untie the bow that's wrapped around the brick of bread. It's still warm. Scents of sweet pumpkin and sugar fill the room, and I move to the front door to scan the woods for her, wishing she would've stayed.

Had I come straight here instead of taking the long road home, I'd have been here. We could've talked. I regret that now.

Once I'm back inside, I take a quick picture of the perfect loaf and text it to my sister.

Harper
Let me guess, your new friend delivered that?

Alexander
Actually, yes.

Harper
How does it feel to be God's favorite?

Alexander
Pretty damn good.

I grab a knife and cut a small piece from it. It's moist and tastes similar to how I remember my mom's.

CHAPTER 7

Autumn

Earlier

I watch him walk away with his eyes focused forward and my conscience berates me for not stopping him.

After my last breakup, I told myself I'd chase no one who walked away from me again. Today, he tested that. I'm proud of staying true, but damn, I feel terrible. Alex wanted to escape from me. I felt that.

Five minutes later, his Jeep passes in the distance and it fades behind the buildings.

I pull out my phone and text our group chat called the Sanderson Sisters.

Autumn
Welp, that went horribly. I'm
pretty sure he hates me.

Blaire
Huh? No way.

Julie
????

Autumn
He said he wanted to be friends,
and I laughed AT him.

Blaire
Oh no.

Julie
Eek!

Autumn
Yeah, he revoked his words then left.

Julie
You didn't stop him?

Autumn
No. I owe him an apology.

Blaire
This isn't over yet.

Julie
You'll see him again. It will all work out.

Autumn
Sigh.

I sit on the park bench for thirty more minutes with my back pressed against the wood. When my stomach growls from hunger, I walk the few blocks home and warm up the leftover chicken that's in my fridge.

No matter how hard I try, I can't shake the hurt behind his gaze that I caused.

Since I was a kid, I've been ridiculously aware of the energy in rooms and of people's auras. When I felt his shift, I knew I'd fucked up. I'm not a cruel person, he just caught me off guard, something he's good at.

After I finish eating, I call my little sister, Winter, because I need to talk this out.

Next year, she will complete her residency and will officially be able to open her own practice. She's currently living in Southern California, loving the sunshine even if she texts me about how much she misses the mountains. That smarty-pants has always given me the most logical advice without emotion, especially in situations like this.

If it weren't for her talking me through my breakup with Sebastian, I'm not sure where I would be right now.

"Autumn!" she answers with a laugh. Chatter and laughter fills the background.

"Is it a bad time?"

"No, not at all, what's going on? Everything okay at home?"

"Oh yeah, all is great. Mom still asks me when I'm going to date again and hasn't stopped."

She laughs.

"I need some sisterly advice because I'm overthinking again."

"You sound tortured," she says, then tells her friends she'll be back. I imagine her on the beach, having a cocktail on a Wednesday afternoon.

"If you offended someone you don't really know and wanted to apologize, what would you do?"

She chuckles. "Who'd you offend?"

"An out-of-towner. He asked me to be his friend and I laughed. It was very rude."

"He?"

She hangs up, and before I can react, I get a FaceTime call. I answer and my sister is grinning. It's easier for her to read my body language when she can see me.

"Tell me more about him."

I explain all the details from the moment he entered the shop to him refusing my coffee to wanting to befriend me.

"He sounds like he's fighting demons. Maybe he wanted to offend you to push you away but realized that's impossible because you're actually a good person?"

"Doubt that."

"Why?"

"Because how would he know that? We've spoken to one another twice."

"Your demeanor gives you away. He mentioned he felt a connection with you. Did you feel the same way?"

"Yes." I sigh, knowing I can't lie to her, not when she's staring at me, analyzing me.

"Why are you afraid of becoming his friend?" Her brows are lifted.

I shake my head. "He asked me what I was afraid of too."

"Well?"

"Seems like a waste of time, doesn't it?"

"Sounds like your fear of abandonment is taking hold again. Alex is not your ex. You barely know this man."

I clear my throat. "I left one thing out. He looks exactly like Mr. Dreamy."

Now her mouth falls open as she studies me. "Now that's a plot twist I wasn't expecting."

"Yeah," I whisper. "In the flesh."

"Sister to sister, I'm not telling you to be a yes man, but what's the worst that could happen? What if he *is* the man of your dreams?"

I groan.

"Or you could make a new friend and keep in touch with things like . . ." She gasps. "The Internet."

"You better not treat your clients like this." I huff.

"Oh, I absolutely will be truthful. I want to understand your fears of befriending people, especially men. I think this would be good for you. Take it day by day with no expectations. Who knows? Maybe he'll be the one, just like Mr. Dreamy."

What sucks is that she's right.

"I know what I have to do," I say.

"Perfect. Keep me updated?"

"I will. Love you. Thank you!"

"Love you! Good luck. I hope to meet him at Christmas."

"I'm sure Mom would support that. It would be nice to have us all together."

"I'm going to try. Bye!"

I end the call and move to the kitchen, pulling out the flour, baking soda, baking powder, and salt. I made fresh pumpkin purée at the beginning of the week. During the season, I always have it in my fridge, waiting for me on reserve.

After I preheat the oven, I mix the dry ingredients together then beat the eggs and butter. Once it's incorporated, I pour the batter into my loaf pan then bake it for seventy minutes. As I wait, I turn on some music and tidy my apartment, lost in my thoughts.

My sister is right. I have abandonment issues. Other than Julie and Blaire, allowing people into my life has backfired, so why should I even try? This could be a catastrophe, or it could be incredible. I guess it's a flip of a coin.

While the bread cools, I dress in my running clothes and wrap the loaf in some paper, tying a ribbon around it before I write him a note. I shove it in my backpack then tighten the straps.

Then I grab the notebook with all the haikus.

You drive me crazy
Buried deep under my skin
Let's see where it goes.

I jog up the mountainside trail at a faster pace than usual. No one can be sad while eating still-warm homemade pumpkin bread. It's impossible.

Making a new friend wasn't on my bingo card this year, but maybe we both need this. While I still don't believe I'm the best choice, sometimes the universe works in mysterious ways. Walking away from him at this point isn't an option. That much is true.

Being with him today feels like a hazy dream, and it's still going.

Once I'm at the top of the mountain, staring at Hollow Manor, I step out of the woods and walk across the soft grass. The sun shines up above as I approach the porch, then check the door. It's locked.

He's lucky because I would've walked inside and yelled his name, made my presence known.

Instead, I ring the doorbell and wait for him to answer. Five minutes pass.

Before I allow myself to think the worst and create an avoidance scenario that he may not deserve, I walk to the driveway, noticing the garage is open and empty.

Alex isn't home.

A breath of relief escapes me because I'd assumed the worse. It's something I have to stop doing. He deserves a fair chance.

I remove my backpack from my shoulders and pull out the plastic bag with the pumpkin bread and note inside. I tie it on his door and leave.

An hour and a half later, I climb the stairs to my loft and kick off my shoes, then walk to the shower. My place still smells like sweet sugar and I wish I had made a loaf for myself. He got the first one of the season. Lucky guy.

After I bathe, I wrap my hair in a towel then open the large window, allowing the fresh air in.

The light sound of music plays from Vinyl Vibes and chatter from tourists fill the streets.

I sit at the bench seat with big fluffy pillows that I turned into a reading nook last year. In the evenings, before the sun sets, I'm always here watching people while drinking cheap rosé. It's my favorite wind-down time.

My breathing slows as my eyes scan up the mountainside and I see Hollow Manor in the distance, hoping Alex found my gift and note. It's not like he could call me even if he did. Then I remember I never texted him.

I grab my phone and click on his name.

Alexander

Then I type out a message.

> **Autumn**
> Hi. It's me, Autumn.

Boring.

I delete it and shake my head, realizing I care what he thinks. *I care. Shit!*

> **Autumn**
> Hi, it's your new friend. Now you have my number. I left you pumpkin bread!

Lame.

I delete it and move to the last conversation I had with Julie.

> **Autumn**
> Do you think I should text Alex?

Julie

Yes and make it ridiculously flirty.;)

Autumn

He needs a friend, Jules. That's it.

I can't get that sad expression on his face out of my head.

Julie

Tell him you were thinking about him
and thought you'd send a text just
in case he was doing the same.

Autumn

You and I have two totally different personalities.
I could never come off that strong.

Julie

I'm the extrovert to your introvert. But I
know you, babe. You're probably sitting at
your nook staring at that haunted house
on the hill while daydreaming about him.
Who wouldn't? That man is gorgeous.

Sometimes I hate how well she knows me.

Autumn

Jules.

I move my focus back to the street, watching the passersby down
below. The tourists have already arrived. Not surprising, considering the official first day of autumn is this weekend. It's when most

of the fall festivities kick off and they last through October 31, then the town transforms into a winter wonderland that could be the set of a movie.

Julie
Next up, you'll be baking him pumpkin bread.

My brows furrow. How could she know?

Autumn
Huh?

Julie
Think about every man you've ever had a crush on and fell madly in love with. What do they have in common?

Autumn
They were all tall with dark hair. Muscles.

Julie
No. The relationship has ALWAYS started with pumpkin bread and has since we were teenagers! It's a dead giveaway, almost like an omen. Or maybe it's one of your cycles. Fuck, for all I know you've been putting a love potion inside of it.

I stand and pace the small space, replaying it all. Shit. *Shit!*

"Autumn!" I hear someone yell from the street, and I move to the window.

When I see Blaire, I let out a relieved sigh. She's carrying several reusable grocery bags and they're packed full. The leaves of a celery stalk stick out of the top of the one that's swung over her shoulder.

Seeing her in passing is normal since she lives a few blocks away above the antique shop at the corner. She has a better view of the town square from her place than I do, and it's much bigger. After the breakup, she convinced me to move close to Main Street and I don't regret it.

"What are you doing?" she asks with concern in her tone.

"Melting down," I admit.

"I can see that." She nervously chuckles. "Or you're trying to get more steps after your six-mile run? It's one or the other, and based on the look on your face, I'd be willing to bet it's a meltdown."

I groan and plop back down in my seat, leaning my head against the wall with my eyes closed.

"Do you want me to come up? I have some time to chat."

I focus on her. "Just tell me this one thing: When you think about me and pumpkin bread, what comes to mind?"

"Easy. Love." She laughs.

My eyes widen and I place my face in my hands.

"Holy shit. You made him a love loaf!" She's giddy and hops around in a circle as tourists walk past her. "Yay!"

"*Oh, my God!* You have a nickname for it? I cannot do this. This is how it starts. This is how it always starts. He just needs a friend. That's it!"

"Hey, don't worry about it." She keeps her tone soft as she sets down her bags, giving her arm a rest. "You're cursed, remember? Or maybe he's the man who will help you break it?"

"This cannot be happening."

She lifts her grocery sacks to her shoulders. "I'm coming up."

"No, no. I'll be fine. But can you keep this to yourself? Please?"

"Sure. Now, get out of your head. What's the worst that could happen? You've got this!" She smiles and waltzes into the crowd. "I'm so jealous," she yells back toward me.

I let out a calm breath, wishing I knew pumpkin bread was a tell. I just wanted to cheer him up, but even now, I don't know if I did. He could've trashed my love loaf.

After another minute of being lost in my head, I pick up my phone and click on his contact again. Counting down from three to one, I type the first thing that comes to mind and press send.

Autumn

Hey, this is my number!

Thirty minutes pass and I don't receive a text back. I watch the sun fade on the horizon, and when the streetlights cast warm rays on the ground, I close the window and bring down the blinds.

I light a few candles and turn on a lamp. As I cook dinner and drink a glass of wine, my cell buzzes on the counter. I pop a sautéed mushroom into my mouth and glance down at the screen.

Alex Alexander
Message Received

My heart does a somersault and I take a pause, sitting in it.

It's been years since I've felt that rush of excitement travel through my body and I'm scared shitless.

I read his text.

Alex

And what should I program
you into my phone as?

I glance up at what I sent, noticing I didn't say my name.

Autumn
How many random people have
you given your number to?

Alex
Hm. Several.

Autumn
Really?

My brows furrow.

Alex
Just one very stubborn woman.

A smile dances across my lips.

Alex
Thanks for the pumpkin bread.

Autumn
I can't wait for you to try it.

Alex
I already did. It's the best I've ever had.

I take a sip of wine, rereading his last text, realizing I'm smiling as I lean against the counter while I cook. Chatting with him is easy. *Too easy.* I imagine him standing in his kitchen in that T-shirt with messy hair, wearing a cute little smirk.

Before I can reply, the fire alarm screams out in protest.

It startles me and I drop my phone onto the tile floor. Instead of picking it up, I remove the pan from the heat and flick on the box fan I keep plugged in for this very reason and open the window again. The ventilation is awful in this small space. I've set it off by boiling water, so it doesn't take much.

I stand on a stool and use the handle of my broom to press in the button on the smoke detector to make the high-pitched squeal stop. It double beeps, then turns off. I move my food from the skillet onto a plate. Thankfully, it's still edible.

The chicken breast, spinach, and roasted tomatoes smell heavenly. My cell is still face down on the floor and I pick it up, only to find my screen is shattered.

"Shit," I hiss, feeling it vibrate but unable to read what it says. So, I do the only thing I can think of and use voice command. This is the third device I've broken this year.

"Send a text to Alex Alexander."

It talks back. "What would you like to say?"

"I'm not ignoring you. I'm really clumsy and dropped my phone again. The screen is shattered. I hope it's not a bad omen. Anyway, have a good night." I command it to send.

After a few seconds, it vibrates with a text I can't read. When I don't respond, my phone rings. Out of habit, I click where the button to answer would be and am surprised it works.

"Hello?"

"Hi. Um. Did you mean to text me?"

"Yes," I say, sitting on my loveseat and setting my plate of food on the old coffee table I rescued from the landfill. Silence fills the space. It's awkward when I don't know what to say. "I shattered my screen so I can't read your texts. I used voice command to explain the situation."

He clears his throat and chuckles. "It says: 'I'm not boring you.

I'm really horny and dropped my panties again. I hope it's not a bad omen. Anyway, have a good night.'"

My phone did me so dirty, and my cheeks heat from embarrassment. "I did not say that, I swear."

"Do you have plans this weekend?"

"Let me check my schedule." Instead, I take a bite of food, knowing my calendar is free from now until eternity. "I'm available."

"Can you reserve Friday night and Saturday for your new best friend?"

A smile takes hold. "Be careful using the term *best friend* around Julie and Blaire."

"Noted." He pauses. "I want to hang out with you."

My heart races. "I'm extremely boring."

"Perfect because I was just thinking about how I could use more *boring* in my life."

"Okay." I grin, setting my fork down. "This weekend is yours."

"Great. We're going to have a lot of fun."

"I look forward to it," I say, truthfully. "Good night."

"Sweet dreams."

He ends the call, which is great because I wouldn't be able to with a shattered screen.

September has already been a whirlwind and I have a feeling we're just getting started. I just hope I'm not making the biggest mistake of my life and setting myself up for heartbreak. It's too early to tell.

CHAPTER 8

Alexander

I wake up without an alarm and sit up to see the sun rising through the windows that stretch across the wall of the main bedroom. A balcony large enough for entertaining runs the length of the room and wraps around one side of the house. Since I arrived, I have not once drawn the curtains. Every day I'm here, I plan to enjoy the view.

Instead of staying in bed, I get up and open the glass door then step outside to watch the sun rise over the mountains. A chill rushes over me and I shiver, but take it in. Bright bursts of pink, orange, and yellow whip across the sky. My phone buzzes on my nightstand and I ignore it. Who the fuck is calling me this early, anyway?

Then I remember the time difference and know it's later in New York. However, I won't be pulled away from this view.

I sit on one of the Adirondack chairs and place my feet on the railing. It's cold, but it makes me feel alive as I watch the fog drift over the peaks. With a logical mind, I'm ready to tackle my day of nothing. My agenda is blank and the schedule is cleared until January.

After nearly three weeks of being here, it's sinking in that I'm free to do whatever the fuck I want. It's empowering and has me reconsidering everything in my life. Especially the future.

Once the sun has fully risen, I go inside and grab my phone. It's a missed call from my father. Not today. Instead, I get dressed and go downstairs.

Golden rays fill the space and I glance around, replaying old memories of sitting on the floor in front of the fireplace and the snow falling outside. Mom loved the Christmas tree in the room's corner, but it was ridiculously tall. We had to take turns climbing up and down a twelve-foot ladder to decorate it.

This house is like a time capsule, preserved how my mother kept it, and being here makes me feel closer to her. Harper was right.

The mantel is filled with silver photo frames that contain pictures taken during the five months we were here all those years ago. I'm drawn to them, my eyes scanning over the precious moments she didn't want us to ever forget. It's not lost on me that she was close to my age now. She never saw forty.

I set the coffee beans on the counter, knowing I could make a cup, but opt for fresh air. Before I can talk myself out of it, I snatch the keys off the countertop and leave, wanting to see Autumn.

The early morning quietness will never get old and it's something I crave.

With the top down, I slide a pair of sunglasses on and take the road that leads down the mountainside. Fifteen minutes later, I'm cruising down Main Street noticing how the crowd has continuously doubled in size thanks to the festivities this weekend. The town will stay packed through Valentine's Day.

I find a spot four blocks away and snag it. As I head toward Cozy Coffee, my phone buzzes in my pocket. I pull it out, see it's my father again, and decline the call, turning it off. When I arrive at the coffee shop, I find the end of the line and wait patiently, but it goes fast.

The three women work efficiently and I'm amazed they can handle this crowd on their own. Ethics and skill allow it. The kiosk in the ski resort is full of fucking amateurs.

When I enter, my eyes meet Autumn's and she grins wide before focusing back on steaming milk. A few stolen glances later and I step up to the counter to order.

Blaire laughs. "Becoming a regular while you're in town?"

"I'm thinking about it," I tell her. "How many days in a row until I've earned my title?"

"By my standards, if I see you more than once a week, you're already there," she says. "So the usual or do you want to spice it up this morning?"

"The usual," I playfully say. "If you remember."

"Barista preference?" She smirks.

I lick my lips. "No, but if it's Autumn, please tell her not to fuck it up this time."

She types something into the computer.

"Noted." Blaire lifts a brow. "Pumpkin bread?"

I meet her eyes. "I think you know I don't need any today."

Blaire laughs, and it's confirmed. "Three seventy-five."

"Is it possible for me to pay for everyone who's behind me?"

She meets my eyes then glances at the line that's still wrapped around the building. Cozy Coffee is the only gourmet establishment in town, so it doesn't surprise me.

"Seriously?" she asks, and I can see her doing the calculation of it in her head. "That's a lot."

"Yeah." I grab my wallet from my back pocket and pull out five hundred dollars. "Use this until it's gone. My treat for your regulars."

"Are you sure?" she asks.

"Absolutely," I tell her, and she grabs the crisp bills from my hand. Her mouth falls open as she looks down at it, then I slip more into their tip jar. Julie and Autumn keep glancing in our direction.

"I want to put some magic into the world and make someone's day better."

She shakes her head. "Clever. I knew you weren't an asshole."

"Oh, I am. But I can be nice too."

Blaire grins. "Okay, I think you might've just become my new favorite regular."

"A title I'll *happily* take," I say.

Blaire submits my order and seconds later, the printer that's located three feet away spits out a sticker. Autumn rips it off and reads it as Julie stands behind her chuckling. When I pass in front of the espresso machines, I steal a glance at Autumn.

That's when I notice her long dark hair is pulled back into a thick braid. Loose strands fall around her face as she looks up at me. I don't stop to chat even though I'm tempted.

I really just want to be friends. That's it.

I stand beside the condiment station where the extra milk and napkins are kept and patiently wait. Every table in the building is taken with people actually talking to one another as they drink their coffee. It's almost shocking to see. Back in New York, most would be buried in their laptops or phones, unaware that there is an entire world around them.

My thoughts travel back to my father, knowing he's called me twice today. I don't know what he could want, other than to make sure I'll be at his wedding. If it were leaked that I didn't show, it would be a scandal.

Autumn moves to the end of the counter, carrying my drink. Her tongue darts out and she licks her plump mauve lips.

"Ristretto for Alex," she says sweetly, meeting my eyes.

I take three steps forward, noticing her earrings—they're black cats with dangly legs and paws.

"Cute," I tell her, sliding my gaze from her eyes to her mouth. She hands the cup to me and our fingers brush together, just as they did the first time I ordered. My heart pounds a little harder.

"Blaire made them," she says.

"I wasn't talking about the earrings," I say, low enough for only her to hear, and her cheeks heat.

"Please taste your ristretto and let me know if it's up to your standards." Her brow is popped and it's flirty.

"Hm." I read the side. The sticker says: *He's all yours, Autie. Ristretto.*

No mention of her not fucking it up.

"I'm all yours?"

"Blaire is facetious. Do you know what that word means?"

"Of course I do."

She quickly recovers. "They're playing matchmaker because of you."

"Me?" I question. "I've done nothing."

"You exist," she whispers. "That's all it takes."

Maybe she seems familiar because I see shards of myself in her.

I place the rim to my lips and sip the hot liquid caffeine, tasting the thick crema. "It's perfect. *Very good.*"

Her heart rate ticks rapidly in her neck. I think Autumn likes to be praised. My jaw clenches and I breathe in deeply, noticing her friends glancing between us.

"You should text me," I say.

"My screen is cracked," she reminds me.

"Oh, that's right."

"You should call me," she snaps back. If I push, she pulls, and we dance this dance, but I can tell she doesn't chase anyone. A woman like her doesn't have to.

"Should I call you Autie?" I say her nickname out loud. It's adorable.

"Actually, you should call her Pumpkin," Julie says, nudging Autumn in the side.

She turns to me. "No. No, do *not* call me that."

I chuckle, gripping the warm cup. Her cheeks are bright red.

"Have a good day, *Pumpkin*." It comes out in a deep gruff and she chews on the corner of her lip.

"You too," she whispers as I turn and walk toward the door.

"What the fuck was that?" I hear Julie mutter, and I laugh. As I leave and pass in front of the windows, I steal a glance at her, but she was already watching me.

I swirl the shot of coffee, hoping it will cool faster, and shoot it down, throwing the cup away. At the end of the block, I wait behind a crowd of people, lost in my thoughts. As I pass the windows of a store, I realize it's full of electronics. I back up and enter.

"Hi. Do you sell phones?" I ask the woman who greets me.

She walks me over to a counter in the corner of the open space.

"All these are smart. What kind are you searching for?"

"The latest and greatest."

She pulls the new iPhone box from a locked cabinet and sets it on the counter. "Can get a discount on it if you sign up for a new plan."

"No thanks. It's unlocked, right?"

"Yes, it is," she says. "When you turn it on, it will ask you to activate it. Want any accessories?"

"Do you have any cases and maybe a screen protector so it won't shatter?"

I'm led to a wall covered from floor to ceiling in every accessory a person could ever dream of. When my eyes land on the one with a pumpkin on it, I grab it.

"Add whatever else you think I might need," I offer.

She grabs a few extra things, but not much. Once I finish paying, I return to the coffee shop with the plastic sack swinging in one hand. When I enter, Autumn tilts her head at me, surprised. I skirt past the line and move toward her espresso machine.

"Everything okay?" She stops what she's doing and seems genuinely concerned.

I hand her the bag. "This is for you."

She glances inside. "Alex. I can't accept this."

"You need a new one so you can text instead of talking. Seems you don't like it much."

She narrows her eyes. "You noticed?"

"I'll text you," I say, tapping the counter, willingly attempting to learn more about her. It starts with me, right here, right now. "It's a gift."

"Okay," she whispers. "Thanks."

"You're welcome."

This time, when I leave the coffee shop, I don't look back, but know her eyes are locked on me.

CHAPTER 9

Autumn

*W*hat just happened?" Julie asks as she follows close behind me. My body is on fire as I move through the storage area toward the office with the bag in my hand. Once inside, I set it on the desk and stare at it.

We have orders out the ass to make, and customers are flooding in, but I can't concentrate on anything else right now. I have to step away and clear my mind.

"Well?"

"He gifted me this." I point at it, shocked because no one has ever given me anything so expensive.

She glances inside.

"Wow." Julie pulls out the brand-new iPhone box. "Rose gold. Largest storage. Did you give him a handy we don't know about?"

"Hell no. I treated him like shit and then apologized the best I could. I don't think I can accept this," I tell her.

She places her hand on my shoulder. "Why not?"

"I don't want him to think he needs to buy my friendship. I also don't want to be love bombed."

"He can slap my butt and call me Pumpkin." Julie snickers. "Look. Maybe gifting expensive things is his love language, just like how baking pumpkin bread is yours." She shoots me a wink.

"You have a point." I shake my head and groan.

"Wait, *did* you make him pumpkin bread?"

"Ugh." I won't be able to deny it to her face. I thought I'd have more time to spill the news. "Yes."

"I knew it!"

"What's wrong with me?" I whine.

"Nothing. You're just really predictable. I seriously told Blaire yesterday that you were gonna bake that man a love loaf." Julie chuckles and sets a screen protector, extra-long charging cord, and a pumpkin case on the desk. "Mr. Dreamy is totally into you and he has a sense of humor, *Pumpkin*," she teases.

Hearing him say it gave my heart palpitations. I wished for and wanted him to exist. And he does.

"He's being nice," I explain. "Too nice."

"And recently, he was a total dickhead."

"Exactly. That's proof things between us are escalating. We went from annoyed strangers to friends," I mutter. He's been buried under my skin since the moment our eyes met.

"First comes love," she singsongs.

"What do you think about him? Your honest opinion."

Julie is never wrong about anyone I've ever befriended or dated. She was dead-on about Sebastian, and the jerk I was with in college.

"I think deep down Alex is a good guy and has a good heart. But it's clear to me that he's going through some shit," she says. "We just have to figure out what that is."

I sigh. "I can't fix him."

"Maybe he can fix you." She waggles her brows. "And you'll be writing in no time."

"I've kept up with my daily haikus. All love themed as assigned."

A wide smile fills her face and she squeals. "He *is* your inspo. Oh my fucking God!"

"Hello? Are you kidding me?" Blaire yells from the doorway to the storage area. "Want me to handle it all alone? We're getting majorly backed up."

Julie pops her head out of the office. "Sorry! We're coming. Just crisis avoiding."

We jog to the front where the line quickly moves. Half the dining room waits for their order, but no one seems upset.

"I need to tell you both something," Blaire says behind Julie as we work the hell out of the espresso machines. "Alex gave me five hundred bucks to pay for everyone's order who walked in and then he tipped us the same amount."

"Are you kidding?" Julie's voice goes up an octave.

"Why would he do that?" I ask, glancing between them.

"He said he wanted to put some magic into the world." Blaire shrugs. "I've been telling everyone it's their lucky day. Our tip jar has been stuffed full three times."

"Gotta be truthful, I fucking like him," Julie states. *"A lot."*

"Next you'll be planning our wedding." I shake my head as Blaire returns to the register wearing a bright smile.

"Who says I'm not right now? I get to be your maid of honor. You were my best friend before Blaire moved here!"

I bump her with my hip as I slap a lid on a vanilla cinnamon latte.

"I heard that. We'll play paper, rock, scissors for it," Blaire says.

They've fought over who'll get the position since we were teenagers. If I ever get married, I'll have two, I guess. It's a choice I can't make.

Julie and I work as fast as possible, apologizing to those who may have waited a little longer, and offer them a free chocolate croissant. They're all happy and in a good mood because it's their lucky day. Not one person complained or cared.

The rest of the day flies by and it's like I blink and our shift is over.

Blaire and Julie finish restocking and I rebalance the register, then sign off on completed midday duties. Tracy, another supervisor, asks for an update of where everything is. I fill her in as Blaire grabs our tip jar and the other two that are full. Several twenties fall onto the floor.

Tracy's eyes widen. "Damn. How'd you manage that?"

"We flashed our boobs to every customer," Julie explains. "Works every time. Coffee and cleavage."

I roll my eyes. "Someone gifted a lot of drinks to customers, who reciprocated with tips," I explain.

Tracy laughs. "That's it. I'm putting in a request to switch to the morning shift because all the cool shit happens to the three of you."

"Today was magical," Julie explains, glancing at me. Alex accomplished his goal and put some magic into the world.

After I wrap up my mini meeting with Tracy, I meet Blaire and Julie in the office where they're grabbing their things.

Blaire glances at the bag and sees the phone and accessories. "He hooked you up. Smart for him to get you a non-destructible lifetime guarantee screen protector considering this is the third one you've destroyed this year. Gonna make it a quarterly habit?"

"I hope not. We'll see if this one lasts until December. If I keep it," I add.

"Accept the gift with an appreciative thank-you," Blaire says. "Damn, you'd never make it as a sugar baby."

Julie chuckles and slides her coffin-shaped purse over her shoulder. "I'd let him spoil me."

"God, me too. Can we trade places? He's actually hilarious. I told him I thought he was an asshole, and he said he was, but he's nice sometimes, too. I dunno. He seems genuine. Also, did anyone else notice the diamond-encrusted Rolex he sported today? He's wearing a two-hundred-and-fifty-thousand-dollar watch around town like he picked it up at the souvenir shop on the corner."

My eyes widen because Blaire knows her jewelry. Since we were teenagers, she's been obsessed with making and designing it.

Julie is speechless.

"Yeah. When I saw it this morning, I nearly shit my pants. I'd researched those watches a few months ago, so it took everything not to grab his wrist and look at it up close. No way it was a knockoff. They're too easy to spot."

"So he's *rich* rich. Now I don't feel so bad about my phone. Or the tips," I say. "That's like five bucks to us."

They burst into laughter.

"I *really* love this for you," Julie says.

Blaire nods. "Please date this man."

"We're *just* friends." I sit at the desk and drop my head against my arms as a chill runs up my spine. "Strangers, if I'm honest."

"That's how most relationships start," Blaire says.

"I'm doomed, aren't I?"

"Or maybe you're destined," Julie offers as we leave together.

As soon as our feet hit the pavement, I take the lead in front of them. I round the corner of the building, and crash into a brick wall. Or so I thought. When I turn my focus forward, strong hands are steadying me. I meet his blue eyes and my mouth falls open as he smiles.

"Alex," I whisper.

"Sorry," he mutters. "I was trying to catch you after your shift. Not literally, though."

"We'll see you two later," Julie says, pulling Blaire away. They're giggling like teenagers as they turn in the opposite direction.

"Sorry," I say, noticing how close we are with his firm grasp still on me.

"Don't be." He lets me go. "Will you join me for dinner at Bookers at eight?"

I laugh. "Tonight?"

"Yes. If you're busy—"

"I'm not." I smile. "It would be fun."

He glances down at his watch, the one that costs a quarter of a million dollars, then his phone rings.

"I'm sorry, but I've got to take this. I've been avoiding this call all day. I'll see you tonight?" His voice is honey.

"Perfect."

He grins and answers. I walk away, but before he's out of sight, I turn and glance back at him. As he crosses the street, he turns his head and our eyes meet. I tuck my lips inside my mouth and continue forward toward my place.

Did he catch me or was it the other way around?

When I get home, I eat a quick turkey wrap then unbox the new phone, powering on my old one. I put on the screen protector and case, hoping it will make it last longer than three months. The pumpkin case was a nice touch considering I have a feeling it's now become my new nickname. I'm not complaining though. Secretly, he can call me Pumpkin any day of the week.

As my data transfers over, I move to my closet and skim over my clothes.

I slide a dress from the hanger and decide against it, then pull out a purple slouchy sweater and a pair of jeans. This is dinner with a friend, not a date. The last thing I want to do is give off the wrong impression. But I do want to solve him like a puzzle, even if he's already three steps ahead of me.

I grab my poem book and write. Lately, I've been jotting them down as soon as he comes to mind. Alex has me feeling things I haven't felt in years.

> *There you are again*
> *Thoughts of you keep haunting me.*
> *How can you be real?*

As I breathe out, I replay the moment we crashed together and how close his lips were to my mouth. I wonder how they would feel pressed against mine.

The new phone dings and it snaps me back to reality. I swipe through my photos to ensure I'm not missing anything. I scroll back a few years and stop at a photo of me and Sebastian at the resort. He's smiling wide and one of his gloved hands gives a thumbs-up while the other is wrapped around me. The year prior, we met on the lifts and I thought it was love—maybe more like lust—at first sight.

When things were good with us, they were *really* good. The highest of highs came with the lowest of lows.

A notification pops up at the top of the screen. When I see Alex's name, I grin and click on it.

Alex
Please text me your address so I can walk with you to dinner.

Autumn
1313 Pumpkin Crossing Drive, Apt 2.
I'm upstairs from Vinyl Vibes.

Alex
Thanks. See you soon!

I scroll up and read the previous messages that synced from our conversation. My cheeks heat reading the jacked-up text my voice command sent.

I'm not boring you. I'm really horny and dropped my panties again. I hope it's not a bad omen. Anyway, have a good night.

Then I see his skull emoji reply. Maybe he has a sense of humor.

For the rest of the day, I sit at my nook and devour a thriller I picked up a few days ago. My brain is quiet, even if thoughts of Alex slip in every once in a while. When I randomly glance up at the edge of the mountain, my eyes scan over to Hollow Manor. How is it possible he lives in that house? Too many things keep pulling us together.

An hour before he's set to pick me up, I shower and get dressed. As I finish putting on my lipstick, there's a knock at my door.

As soon as he sees me, he smiles. "Hi."

"Hello." My eyes slide from his eyes to his mouth, down the light gray button-up shirt that's tucked into black slacks that fit his body perfectly. Then I notice he's holding a bouquet. Just for me.

"They're called coneflowers," he says, handing them to me. Our fingers brush together.

I immediately inhale their sweet scent. "They're gorgeous. Thanks."

"You're welcome," he says.

"I should keep these here. Oh, come in."

Alex follows behind and I allow him to enter. The door closes and seeing him standing there throws me off. I'm tempted to ask if it's real, but I don't want to wake up if it's not.

"What?" he asks curiously.

"Nothing at all." I move to my kitchen and pull a vase from the cabinet. I drop an aspirin in the bottom, then fill it with water. My fingers brush against the silk ribbon as I untie it and put the bright red flowers inside. "When we're *actually* friends, remind me to tell you why I was looking at you like that. Right now, it would be a little too awkward."

He chuckles, tucking his hands into his pockets. "I look forward to learning why. It's the same expression you had when you handed me my coffee. It's a flash of recognition. Tell me, Pumpkin, what is it I remind you of?"

I try to hold back a smile as I lift the vase onto the windowsill, knowing my heart rate is ticking. I'm sure he noticed that too. "Ah yeah, you're halfway there. One day I'll tell you. And when I do, promise me you'll find it adorable."

"Okay," he says, and our eyes lock for a moment too long before he breaks the contact to glance around my space. "It feels like home here. Cozy. Comfortable. Not at all haunted."

"Oh, good. Glad to learn I'm clear of ghosts, considering you're an expert now," I say, happy for the subject change.

He chuckles. "Shall we go?"

I nod and we make our way outside.

As we travel down the sidewalk, our arms brush together. "Have you always lived here?"

"I moved to New York for school, then Europe for almost three years while I got my master's degree."

"Impressive. What's your profession?"

I glance over at him. "I dreamed of being an author."

"Just dreamed?" he asks, meeting my eyes.

"I can't write anymore," I say.

I wait for him to push, to ask me more questions, but he doesn't.

"What about you?"

He grins. "I guess you could say I'm in hospitality and tourism. But I'm not in Cozy Hollow for that. My time here is a vacation, not business related at all," he admits, reaching for the door of Bookers and holding it open for me. Alex follows behind me with his fingers softly pressed against my back, staying close. The lights are lowered after the sun sets and the room glows golden.

I slide into one of my favorite booths away from the crowd, giving us some privacy so we can speak freely without being over-heard. Alex sits in front of me and the leather-bound menus are passed to us. "May I grab you a whiskey or a margarita?"

It's busy tonight, but nothing out of the normal for this time of the year.

Alex glances at me, allowing me to order first.

"I'd like to start with a water," I say, glancing down at the menu full of autumn-inspired brews.

"I'll do the same," Alex says.

The server walks away and I twist the menu around so he can see what they have on tap.

"Pumpkin beer?" he asks with a brow popped.

"It's an Oktoberfest thing one microbrewery outside of town makes each year. It's actually great. One of my favorites."

He watches me with his fingers interlocked. I hold back a smile, focusing back on the list of drinks. I don't mind being the center of his attention, but it makes me nervous.

"You're intense," I say, not looking at him.

"I've been told that before," he states.

The server sets our drinks down. "Want a few minutes?"

I nod, meeting his gaze, and she leaves us.

"Thanks again for the phone."

"So you're keeping it?" One of his brows arches.

"Huh?" There is no way he knows about the conversation I had with Julie and Blaire earlier. "How'd you kn—"

He smirks, glancing at the appetizer list. "I can easily read you."

I mutter, "I'm usually not that easy to figure out."

"That's tragic for you, then. Guess those games you like to play won't work on me." He flips the page like he's reading a magazine.

"Excuse me?"

He meets my eyes. "I feel like I know you. I can look at you and know exactly what you're thinking. And I shouldn't."

"No, you can't," I say, but I wonder if he can.

He closes the menu. "You feel the invisible tug. I know you do. It's written on your face."

My throat goes dry. I nervously grab at my water and clumsily knock it over. I stand, somehow avoiding getting wet, and Alex grabs the stack of napkins, using them to stop it from leaking over on his side.

"You can sit right here." He pats beside him.

I look around for someone to help with this mess before embarrassment takes over, but the restaurant is busy.

I move next to him, scooting close, blocking him against the wall like he did to me. It's like a lifetime has passed since the moment he walked into that coffee shop.

"You didn't have to make a mess to be close," he says, moving my hair over my shoulder. His fingertips brush against my neck and a gasp escapes me.

"You're right," I blurt out. "I do feel it."

"I know," he says, but before we can continue this conversation, my attention is being ripped away by a familiar voice calling my name.

When I turn, I see dark eyes and messy sun-bleached hair.

"Sebastian?" My voice goes up an octave. He's the last person I expected to see here.

"Hey, Autie." He gives me his boyish grin, the one that used to reduce me to a puddle on the floor, but it oddly doesn't work. "I was hoping to see you."

"Aren't you supposed to be in Canada?" I ask, realizing I'm actually immune to him, like the blindfold has been removed.

"I'm back. I couldn't stay away from Cozy Hollow . . . or you," he explains, smiling. "I've missed you."

"Uh." I grow uncomfortable.

Alex clears his throat, bringing the attention to himself. Sebastian briefly narrows his eyes, then ignores his existence and focuses back on me.

"How do you know Zane?" His voice is accusatory and he sounds angry.

I glance at Alex, confused, and feel his entire demeanor shift. His jaw locks tight and he might rip Sebastian's throat out if he says another word.

"Are you together?" Sebastian asks. I don't appreciate his tone. Or the way he's interrupting our dinner, like I owe him five minutes of my time.

"Actually, we are," I confidently say, glancing at Alex, meeting his eyes and begging him to play along. If he really can read me, it needs to be right now. A second later, he wraps his arm around me, brushing his fingers against my arm. "Happily," I add.

"Best decision of my life," Alex says, tucking loose strands of hair behind my ear. It's the perfect touch.

Then he glares at Sebastian directly in the eye and speaks. "And I'm going to marry her one day."

I chuckle. "Oh, really?"

"Absolutely," he states. He's too damn good at lying, because for a brief second, I believe him. But then I remember—just friends. He's doing me a solid favor and I will owe him one after this.

When I turn back to Sebastian, the color drains from his face. His reaction is one of the most satisfying things I've witnessed in two fucking years. Even though it's a lie, telling it was one hundred percent worth it.

CHAPTER 10

Zane

*A*utumn leans against me like I'll keep her safe, and in this moment, I absolutely will.

"Can we talk soon?" Sebastian lowers his voice and asks her, keeping his gaze on her.

"Fuck no," I say, not giving her the chance to answer. "She doesn't want to speak to you."

"Autumn can speak for herself," he seethes, glancing back at her.

"No thank you," she states. "I have nothing to discuss with you. *We* wanted to see other people, right? I've moved on. Clearly."

"With Zane Alexander?" He pretends like I'm not here. "You haven't. Trust me."

"You know what I just realized?" Autumn laughs at him. "Had you not broken up with me, Zane and I would've never met. Wow. Appreciate that *so* much."

The sarcasm is fucking harsh, but I don't blame her acting this way toward an ex, especially him. But I also realize exactly what she said, and damn, I want to hear my first name come from her lips again.

"I've tried texting you since the beginning of the month." Sebastian's voice softens. "Did you change your number?"

"I blocked you," she snaps. "The day *you* ended it."

"That's what I'd like to discuss with you," he says with sad eyes, nearly pleading.

"Holmes." I bark out his last name in the same way I used to when we were on the slopes together. Autumn tenses, realizing I know her ex. The thought of her ever being with him makes me sick to my goddamn stomach. "I don't like the way you're speaking to my fucking *girlfriend*."

His jaw clenches tight and I glare at him.

She interlocks her fingers with mine and I kiss her knuckles, smelling her sweet perfume that smells like the flowers I picked. "You let me go, Bastian. You didn't expect me to wait for you, did you? That's ridiculous."

I have to admit, it was harsh as fuck.

His mouth opens and closes, then he narrows his eyes at me before walking away.

"Do you two know each other?" She's pissed.

"Yes," I say, picking up my water and taking a sip. Fuck him for ruining my perfect night with her.

"*Zane Alexander?*"

"Shh. Not too loud," I whisper.

"I'm confused."

"That's my name." I hold out my hand toward her and she takes it. "Most call me Alexander. You call me Alex."

"Nice to officially meet you, *Zane fucking Alexander*." She lets me go. "Why did you lie to me?"

"To protect myself."

"From who?"

"The public," I say. "Do you know who I am?"

"No," she says, and she tries to scoot out of the booth, but I wrap my arm around her hip, keeping her next to me. "I have no reason to lie to you. I planned to tell you tonight so you could fully understand who you're hanging out with. You deserve the truth."

Relief washes over me when she relaxes.

"My name is highly recognizable if you're into celebrity gossip."

"I'm not." She shrugs, still completely unimpressed by me, and I fucking love it.

"My family owns the resort on the mountain and many others across the world."

"Oh," she says, and makes a face.

"Tell me why you had that reaction."

"I just don't agree with everything they do."

I pick up my water and take a sip. "Something we can agree on. I'm here on vacation, but I'm willing to listen to any of your suggestions."

That makes her smile.

"I didn't want our friendship to be built on a lie or for you to be blindsided. I can see I failed and I'm sorry about that."

"I get it."

"No excuse. I can't stand liars, almost as much as I can't stand Sebastian Holmes."

Her lips slightly part when I say his name. "How do you know him?"

"We used to snowboard together."

The server walks over and sees the water and ice everywhere.

"Oh no, did you spill any on you?" She glances over us.

"No, no, we're fine. But, I think I'd like a double shot of tequila with salt and a lime," Autumn says.

"Make it two," I add.

"Sure, I'll have someone clean up this mess and get those drinks."

When we're alone again, she turns back to me. "I dated him for six years of my life. Often, I think I gave him my best years."

My nostrils flare as I study her, because he's a known fuckboy and always has been. Autumn deserves better.

She shakes her head like she can read my mind. "He broke me. I haven–"

We're interrupted by a few people mopping the spill and wiping the table with dry cloths. I'm tempted to ask everyone to leave us, but they make quick work of it. Both of us wait patiently to be left alone and I regret coming here. I should've cooked her a nice meal, but I wanted her to be comfortable. Bookers is safe and public, and doesn't give off the wrong impression.

Our tequila is set in front of us.

"You told him we were dating," I say as her eyes sparkle.

"I shouldn't have done that, but it slipped. Thank you for rescuing me. I didn't want it to seem like I've not moved on."

"Have you?" I ask.

"I'm trying," she says, picking up her shot.

I grab mine. "We should toast to us."

For a second, she hesitates, then smiles. "To us."

We clink the edges of our glasses together and salt falls onto the table. We shoot the tequila back, lick the rim, then bite the juicy lime. Autumn does a little wiggle and I can tell she's lost in her head.

"I haven't been with anyone since him," she blurts out. "You're actually the first man I've even been to dinner with."

"I'm sorry you had an awful experience." I want to apologize for everything that stupid fuck did to her, but I don't say that out loud.

I remember when Sebastian broke up with his girlfriend and moved to our Canadian location to teach.

The silence lingers.

"Do you still love him?" I shake my head. "Apologies. You don't have to answer that."

"No, it's fine," she says, tracing the rim of the glass with her finger. "Love and hate, two powerful emotions, and I've felt both for him over the years. When I saw him again, I thought I'd have a different reaction."

I nod, listening. "Was it a good one?"

"No." Autumn moves to the other side of the booth so we can

chat with one another more easily. I miss her closeness but prefer being able to look into her eyes.

The server returns to take our order.

"Want to share a platter of nachos?" Autumn asks.

"Sure," I say. "Two more shots."

When we have our second round, we toast to us again and slide our glasses to the edge of the table.

"How long are you here?"

"Until the first week of January. I'll be gone for a week in October, maybe. I haven't decided yet," I say. "My father is getting remarried."

She tilts her head at me. "Oh."

"It's complicated."

She doesn't push me to say anything else, which I appreciate. I'll eventually tell her, I want to.

Twenty minutes later, a gigantic platter of loaded tortilla chips is set in front of us with two small plates.

"What happens after January?"

"I don't know," I say truthfully. "I'm undecided about a lot of things in my life."

"Does it scare you not knowing what the future holds?"

"Somewhat," I admit. "I'm used to having my life scheduled. Right now, my publicist and father believe I'm off-script."

She moves some food onto her plate. "Interesting choice of words."

"I thought so too."

"Is your life scripted?"

When I glance up, I see Sebastian heading toward us again carrying a bag of food. "Give me your hand."

"Huh?"

I reach forward, interlocking our fingers, and rub my thumb against hers. Immediately, she leans forward and smiles, understanding. Sebastian walks past us and meets Autumn's eyes then keeps going. I don't pull away and neither does she.

"I'm sorry for putting you in this position," she says as I keep her hand in mine.

"You say it like you're a burden," I mutter, letting her go. "You're not."

A blush hits her cheeks.

"I've never seen him so jealous," she mutters. "It's almost like he cared."

"If the roles were reversed, I'd have realized how much I fucked up when I saw you with me. He should've never let you go. Now he understands that."

"I wasn't perfect in our relationship," she admits.

"No one is. Sometimes we date people who bring out the best in us, sometimes they bring out the worst." I pick up a chip with beef and sour cream and pop it into my mouth. "The goal is to avoid the latter."

"Are you dating someone?" she asks.

"Other than you?" I shoot her a wink. "No. My ex broke me too."

"Seems like we have a lot in common," she says.

"Maybe too much."

After we finish eating, I pay the bill and Autumn and I leave. As we walk down the street, I grab her hand and smile.

"Good call. He could be watching us right now," she says, then holds my hand a little tighter. "You know, my life would be easier if people thought I was dating someone."

"Is that the tequila talking?"

She shakes her head. "My parents, my friends, the fairy godmothers, everyone in my life wants me to move on from Sebastian and I haven't. Having you close would clear me from putting myself out there, at least until the new year."

I'll do whatever I have to in order to stop that from happening.

"Do you want to negotiate?" I ask with a brow popped.

"That word again." The warm glow of the streetlamp gives me the perfect view of her.

"If I go to my father's wedding in two weeks, I'll need a date for the ten days I'm there," I breathe out. "My ex will be there and I'd love to give her a taste of the same medicine we delivered to Sebastian. She's made my life hell for six months and everyone is also convinced I'll never move on. Be my girlfriend, let me propose, and have them eating out of our palms. In exchange, I'll play boyfriend until you say stop."

"Okay, and what happens when we don't get married?"

I shrug. "We'll just say it didn't work out, like the others."

"Others? How many times have you been engaged?"

"Twice. Both mistakes."

"Oh," she says. "I'm sorry."

"I'm not," I state, because I would've never met her.

"So, I have two weeks to get to know you well enough that the idea of us being together is at least believable?"

"Yep, and I have nothing to hide from you, so ask me anything, anytime."

"You might regret saying that." She chuckles then grows quiet. "This deal is unfair. I'm spending a week with you, and you have to hang out with me for months."

"Trust me, it's more than equal. You haven't been around my family and acquaintances. Do you want time to think about it?"

She tilts her head at me, like she's thinking about it. "No. I need a little adventure in my life and I'm curious what yours is like. Are you sure you won't regret wasting your third engagement on me?"

This makes me laugh. "Nah. No one really expects me to get married, anyway. I'm hard to please, apparently."

She smiles. "Same."

"Oh, I forgot to mention that it's being held at our private island resort in the Caribbean. We'll have a villa close to the water and there will be plenty of beach time between events."

Her mouth falls open. "I'm getting a much better deal."

"Do you have your passport?"

"Of course I do."

"Perfect. So, what do you say?" I ask.

She holds out her hand and we shake on it.

"No backing out," she warns.

"Never." A grin fills my face as I lift her knuckles to my lips and kiss them. "I finally met my equal."

"Funny, because I was thinking the same thing."

"With that being said." Autumn pulls her hand away. "We should probably make some sort of rules to protect ourselves."

"We can discuss it tomorrow night."

People pass us on the sidewalk as we stand outside of her place. I overhear their chatter about the pumpkin patch and having apple cider.

"I'm glad I found you," I say to her, looking forward to the day when we're no longer strangers. It's easy to imagine a whole life with her.

"You say it like I was lost."

"You were." The mood grows slightly serious and I have the urge to kiss her when she looks up at me like that. The same look she gave me the first time we met and back in her apartment. I want to know what she sees when she wears that expression. I have to know.

"I should go," I whisper, placing my hand on her shoulder, stopping whatever could happen.

"Yeah," she says, and we both instinctively take a step away from one another, then laugh.

The connection is deeper than I'd imagined it could be. "Good night," I say.

"Good night," she tells me, then walks up the stairs to her loft. Before walking in, she smiles.

The black cloud that's been hanging over me temporarily disappears.

Roxie was wrong. I'm not off-script, I'm currently writing it.

Finally, I'm in control.

CHAPTER 11

Autumn

I'm up before my alarm sounds.

I turn it off before the high-pitched song scares the shit out of me. As I do that, a notification flashes across the screen.

Alex Alexander
Message Received

Before I do anything, I change his contact to Zane Alexander, then I go to his message. It's a voice note.

"Good morning, Pumpkin. Since you want to get to know me, I thought each day after I wake up, I'll share a few fun facts with you until you're caught up with all things about me. My birthday is on September twenty-second and I'm turning thirty-eight. This is also my favorite season. What about you?"

The roughness in his tone is sexy, but I push those thoughts away.

I click the button and record a message for him.

"Good morning. I've never sent messages like this before so bear with me. My birthday is on October thirty-first and fall is my favorite too. Winter is a strong second. How'd you sleep last night? See any ghosts? I hope you have a good day. Tonight, I'm yours, right? I think your name was on my calendar for today and tomorrow. I'm excited to spend your birthday with you. Maybe it will be a new tradition."

I climb out of bed and jump in the shower, needing to wake up. I turn on my music and step under the hot stream. It pounds against my skin and I stand there until the water turns cold.

After I'm finished, I wrap a towel around my hair and my body and see I have another message.

"No ghosts, unless I can count the thoughts of you. Also, I think my name is on your calendar for eternity." He clears his throat and lowers his voice. "Anyway, I hope you have an incredible day. I'll see you soon. Oh, also, if you want to keep calling me Alex, you can. However, I love it when you say my name, too."

When I pass the mirror, I realize I'm smiling. I take two steps backward and look at myself, wondering if it's believable that the two of us could be together.

I click the button to record.

"I don't think you're supposed to flirt with your friends."

Send.

He laughs at the beginning. "Better get used to it. You've got two weeks to prepare."

I slide on a pair of comfy jeans and a T-shirt, then head to work. One thing I love about working at Cozy Coffee is we're not required to wear a uniform.

My feet hit the sidewalk and I have a pep to my step as I move to the beat of "Here Comes the Sun." Ironically, that ball of fire hasn't risen yet and won't for an hour and a half.

Mornings aren't my favorite, but I've learned to appreciate them. There's something beautiful about experiencing the stillness before the flowers bloom and birds start chirping. It's proof of new beginnings. After what I've been through, a restart on life is something I can get on board with.

Then I remember Sebastian is back in town and panic. As soon as I see Blaire and Julie this morning, I will need an emergency girl meeting to fill them in on last night.

I unlock my phone and send Zane a text message.

Autumn

What am I supposed to tell my friends? They'll ask questions.

Zane

Share whatever you'd like.
If you trust them, I do.

As I cross the street, the crisp autumn breeze kisses my cheeks and I shiver. I wrap my arms around my body and enjoy it because I've been waiting for summer to end since before it started. I'm tempted to dance in the streets, alone, in the glow of the lamps that are programmed to cut off when the sun rises. But I keep my excitement to myself.

Right now, it's in the lower forties. This weekend, at night, it's supposed to get down into the thirties. I'm looking forward to it.

The upbeat music blares through my earbuds, and the Beatles are what I need to help wake me up.

Less than ten minutes later, I approach the wall of tall windows at the front of the coffee shop. Similar storefronts stretch the entire length of Main Street.

All week, I've daydreamed as I've watched couples and families on vacation enjoy my hometown. Sometimes I wonder what it would be like to experience it as an outsider during these months. I've heard it's more magical than Salem, but I'll never be able to fully compare it.

After I unlock the door, I slip inside and remember to turn the deadbolt this time.

"Locked," I whisper, continuing to the office so I can start my morning duties.

The layout of the room hasn't changed since it opened eighty years ago. I'm convinced I could navigate the space with my eyes closed. Might have to test that theory soon.

As I walk through the small kitchen where we bake our pastries, the bell above the door rings.

"Great job!" Julie hollers, and she's humming something. As I count down the registers, she joins me in the office.

"Well?"

"Well, what?" I ask, moving to the front with the money drawers in tow.

She follows behind me. "How'd dinner go with Alex?"

"It was fun. Did you know Sebastian is back?"

Julie is usually on top of the town gossip, even though most of it doesn't include anyone our age.

"No. Ugh. Right when everything is going great! *Sebastard* is like a cockroach. Just when you think they've been eradicated, they come back stronger."

"He said he wants to talk to me about us."

She flicks on the machines then glares at me. Her annoyance level rises anytime we discuss him.

"I told him no. He also believes me and Alex are dating."

Her brow pops up. She's intrigued. "Really?"

"And we'll probably keep that lie going until the end of the year."

"Oh, my God. It's the look."

I roll my eyes, trying to ignore her as I turn on the registers. She makes the drip brew, shaking her head, but she's smiling.

Eventually, Blaire knocks on the door and waves at us.

When I allow her in, she immediately grins. "Whoa. It's the look."

"Did you plan to say this to me today?"

"So, you saw it too?" Blaire glances at Julie. "It's unmistakable."

"What does that even mean?" I sigh. "We didn't have sex! I know it's not *that* look."

"It's the *fuck it I'm falling in love* look," Julie says.

"No," I whisper.

"Sebastian is back," Julie mutters as Blaire checks the dining room and wipes down a few tables.

"What the fuck?" Her voice rises an octave, and it echoes through the empty room.

"He said he couldn't stay away from here or me," I explain as Blaire groans.

"In better news, Autumn and Alex are official," Julie says.

"What?!" Blaire questions.

"We're *fake* dating. I lied, and Alex played along flawlessly. And his name isn't Alex," I blurt out. "Promise to keep it to yourself."

They wait with bated breath.

"He's Zane Alexander."

Julie gasps and drops the metal cream container in her hands. Luckily, the lid was on and screwed tight, so just a tiny drop spills. The loud noise startles me.

"A complete documentary about his family was released a few months ago. He's elusive, super secretive, and doesn't befriend anyone."

I shrug. "I don't know if that's true. We became fast friends."

Blaire is almost speechless. "The Rolex makes more sense now. He's a fucking billionaire. Like, old money. Vanderbilts. Calloways. Alexanders. I cannot believe this."

My palms grow sweaty.

"You're dating Zane Alexander. Holy shit!" Julie laughs and gives me a high five.

"When one of us gets a sugar daddy, we all win," Blaire says, repeating the hilarious thing we've said to each other since we were old enough to drive. It's ridiculous.

"We're *just* friends trying to scare off my ex," I say as we continue working. "You both know Sebastian won't stop. Boundaries don't exist for him."

"Rat boy is very stubborn," Julie says.

"You're right," Blaire agrees. "Guess that means Alex is not only your dream man, but your knight in shining armor."

At six on the dot, I move to unlock the door, seeing Zane is the first in line. He's holding another bouquet of hand-picked flowers with a black ribbon tied around the stems and hands it to me.

"Thank you," I say, glancing down at the peach-colored roses.

"Morning," he says, placing a kiss on my cheek. I reach up and instinctively run my fingers up the side of his neck. He pulls away, meeting my eyes before walking past me to the register.

Mr. Henry, one of our regulars, waggles his brows at me as he enters. One of the fairy godmothers, Mrs. Blanchard, gives me a wink. A smile takes over and I try to push it away as the dining room fills with customers.

Zane chats with Blaire and I set the flowers in a vase on the shelf for everyone to enjoy.

The order prints out and on the side it says: *Your boyfriend. Large. Order: Surprise him with your yummy goodness.*

I glare at Blaire and she snickers as I make him my favorite drink—a mocha with homemade whip. I prepare it as if I'd be drinking it and only hope that he enjoys it. Not sure I can be friends with someone who despises what I love.

Two minutes later, I walk to the edge of the counter and say his name. He pushes off the wall and stalks toward me wearing a small smile.

"Alex," I whisper, handing his cup to him, and our fingers brush together.

He twists it around and reads what Blaire wrote on the side and chuckles.

"Don't say a word," I warn.

"That's no way to treat your boyfriend."

"You two are super cute," Julie says between us, encouraging it.

Before I can say anything, my attention is pulled away by Sebastian entering. Zane spots him too.

"Please, meet me outside," Zane says.

"Right now?" I ask.

"Yes." We hold a silent conversation and I turn to Julie. "I'll be back."

"Okay." She glances at Sebastian. I walk around the counter and Zane holds his hand out toward me. I take it and he leads me past Sebastian, outside, to the edge of the sidewalk.

Then he takes one step forward, leaning in and whispers in my ear, "May I kiss you?"

My body burns with anticipation because I know a kiss never lies. I study him and nod, giving him all the permission he needs. His large hand rests softly on my cheek and his mouth gently slides across mine. I grab his shirt with my fist and our tongues slide together. It's explosive, instant fireworks. He tastes like spearmint and smells like fresh mountain air.

It shouldn't feel like this. It shouldn't feel like home. It shouldn't feel like I want to do this again and again and again. But it does. My body buzzes and the sensation nearly brings me to my knees as the kiss deepens further. I whimper against him and I'm lost in this moment. Nothing else in the world matters.

As if Zane realizes we've gone too far, he gently pulls away, his swollen lips hovering above mine as he fists my hair.

"It wasn't supposed to be like that," he whispers, placing his fingers on my chin, forcing me to look into his eyes, and I drown.

"I know," I say.

He takes a step back, creating much-needed space. We crossed a line, one we probably shouldn't have, even if we've walked it finely so far.

"See you tonight, Pumpkin," he says.

"Yes," I say, surprised I can even form words because I'm pretty sure he stole my soul when our lips touched.

Zane shoots me a wink and chuckles. "Perfect coffee, babe."

He raises his cup, then walks away. I watch him, stunned, and when I come back to reality and turn around, I realize the entire coffee shop witnessed our first kiss. Immediately, I tuck my hair behind my ears and walk in.

Julie and Blaire smile wide as the room bursts into applause and encouragement from regulars.

"Marry that man," a woman yells from the back, and I laugh.

As I pass my ex, I realize Zane was sending an obvious message—I'm with him. Fake or not, I think Sebastian understands that now.

"What the fuck was that?" Julie asks after I wash my hands and return to my espresso machine.

"Zane just cursed me."

"You were already cursed, remember?" She's confused, but she doesn't know the turmoil that's swarming inside of me.

When Sebastian walks up to the register, I hear him ask about the flowers.

"Oh, Autumn's boyfriend brought those for her this morning," Blaire says. "He's thoughtful. Anyway, how have you been?"

They hold a pleasant conversation and I glare at Julie.

"What am I supposed to do?" I ask between gritted teeth.

"Ignore him like he ignored you before he broke up with you."

"You're smart," I say, needing the reminder. My cheeks still burn and my body continues to buzz. I'm floating on cloud nine and shouldn't be.

The sticker pops up on the printer and Julie takes it.

I read what Blaire wrote.

Sea Biscuit. Medium Mocha.

Julie snickers. "I've got it."

When he passes the espresso machine, I keep my eyes down, focusing on the dark liquid pouring from the spout. Julie hurries and makes his coffee and calls his name with zero enthusiasm.

"Hey, Jules," he says to her as she hands him his cup.

"It's Julie," she corrects. Her nickname is reserved for her friends only.

"Right. Anyway, thanks."

He leaves the coffee shop and doesn't look back. Julie returns to my side.

"That kiss was passionate as hell. What did it feel like?"

My body is still singing. "Like . . . magic."

CHAPTER 12

Zane

I force myself to walk away from Autumn, stunned by the intensity of her lips against mine. She tasted like sugar, spice, and everything nice. While I kissed her to prove a point to her stupid-as-fuck ex, it made me realize the connection we have is much deeper than I originally suspected. There is no explanation for it.

But when she grabbed on to me, deepening the kiss, something that's stayed dormant for a lifetime ignited deep inside me. Overpowering emotions streamed between us, and I swear she cast a spell on me.

I replay all that she's shared with me, mentally cataloging facts about her, but I need to know more. I want to know everything about her: what makes her happy or excited, her favorite foods, and her favorite color. I want to know Autumn at her core.

When I'm finally home, I go upstairs to the office my father insisted be built in the house so he could work from this location when my mother wanted to escape. My eyes slide across the desk and the oversized windows that face the resort. The sunlight floods in, but I turn on the lights to better see the space. I move forward to sit in the high-backed executive chair and pick up the silver frame, noticing the picture of the four of us at the Winter Olympics. At that point in my life, I dreamed about joining the U.S. Team and was on my way to becoming one of the top snowboarders in the world.

I let out a deep breath and tuck the framed photo into the drawer. Then I notice a folded note with my name on it. When I open it, I see my mother's perfect handwriting.

My sweet boy,

I know you'll discover this after I'm gone, but I've decided I'm leaving this house to you when that time comes because you love being here. I wonder when you'll find it, though. How old will you be? What is your life like? Are you happy? I hope you're visiting Cozy Hollow because you are, not because you need healing. However, know the mountain air can cure anything. Well, almost anything, though it certainly cannot cure cancer. (It's a joke. It's okay to laugh.)

I love you so, so much. You are strong, and you have such a beautiful heart. Yes, I'm taking full credit for raising you to be kind, polite, and caring. Yes, you are every single one of those things. I hope by now you're able to take a compliment.

Right now, you're only fifteen years old, and I know I won't live to see you turn sixteen. It hurts knowing I won't be here to watch you become a man or fall in love or have a family. I often smile when I imagine the future, knowing you'll accomplish greatness. You work hard and put your full self into all that you do. I am proud of you.

Out of everything that has come with my diagnosis, understanding that my time is running out is the most difficult one to comprehend. Time. It doesn't matter how many numbers are in anyone's bank account, because it's the only thing money can't buy us more of. I've tried to cherish the passing seconds with you and Harper this season, and I have.

I know you find all the pictures I took annoying; however, I think you'll appreciate them now. But please, don't be sad for me. Know that when I leave this earth, I'll go with a happy and grateful heart, because the day you were born, every one of my dreams became a reality.

You made me a mom, something I didn't know was possible. And I'll live forever through you and Harper. Knowing that brings me joy.

Zane, I've had this conversation with you several times before, but I need you to promise that you'll always be true to yourself and will follow your heart. It will never guide you wrong.

The weight of the world doesn't matter, all that does is how you spend your life. I know the pressures of the business and who you are have already taken their toll. None of it matters. You are an Alexander, but most of all, you are my son.

You have the power to do whatever you want in life, so choose what makes you happy. Take more risks. Dance in the rain. Swim in the sea. Ski off-trail. Love with your full heart. Magic is in the moment. Magic is all around us. I hope you can still find it.

Never forget who you are, but don't let it define your every move in your life, either. Or I swear I'll come back and haunt you. (You are supposed to laugh here too.)

I will always be with you, my son. I'll visit you in butterfly flutters. I promise.

Love you for eternity,
Mom

P.S. Since you've always loved a scavenger hunt, know thirteen notes hide in different places in the house. You'll discover them when you need them the most. What number is this? If I had to guess, I'd say the first.

My jaw is tight as a few tears stream down my cheeks and splash onto the soft cream paper. Now, I'm able to smile recalling the memories we had, but it took years. Grief changes a person; no child should have to heal from that. *Ever.* I tuck the letter back into the top drawer, flick off the lights, and leave the house because the air inside feels too thick.

As I stand on the back porch, I close my eyes and breathe deep.

My phone vibrates, and I'm thankful. Right now, I need the distraction.

Autumn
Dress code tonight?

A smile touches my lips.

Zane
We'll be outdoors. Meet you at 6:45.

Autumn
And I've figured out what we're doing based on one text.

Zane

A pumpkin patch for my pumpkin.

She pulls me out of my spiral, and thoughts of her twirl and dance in my mind for the rest of the day. I count down the minutes to when I'll see her again.

AT SIX, I drive down the mountain. The Jeep is topless and I'm thankful I wore a light jacket. The pumpkin patch opens this evening at seven and the mayor is giving a speech with a champagne toast. My goal is to attend as many events as possible. I came to Cozy Hollow to live a little and to relax.

By some miracle, I find a place to park. I hop out and walk the three blocks toward Autumn's apartment. The sidewalks are busy with tourists, so I keep my eyes focused forward and my mind wanders to Autumn.

I've tried to forget her hot breath on my mouth or how her tongue twisted against mine as emotions poured through me. She grabbed on to me for dear life as we fell into the abyss together. Neither of us was in control and we couldn't save ourselves.

I take the stairs leading up to her apartment and knock on her door.

"Who's there?" she asks on the other side and I swear I hear her laugh.

I lean in. "Your boyfriend."

A minute later, the door swings open and out walks Autumn wearing tight jeans and an orange sweater that shows a peek of her tummy. Her dark wavy hair is down and her brown eyes pull me in.

"Wow, you're . . . *gorgeous,*" I say, watching her tongue dart out and lick her red lips.

She leans against the door frame. "Thanks. Are you sure I'm dressed okay? You look like you're going on a date."

"Wait, this isn't a date?" I'm wearing a dress shirt and suit pants, nothing out of the ordinary.

"Uh, I—"

"I'm *joking.*" I find it cute that I make her nervous. "Shall we go?"

I hold out my hand and she takes it without hesitation. Once we're on the sidewalk, we fall in line with the crowd that is funneling in toward the middle of the town. If I close my eyes, it's almost easy to pretend I'm in New York with the chatter drifting on the breeze.

"What are you thinking about?" she asks, glancing over at me.

"My life," I say.

Just as she's about to say something, a man walks up. He mutters something to her and she stills beside me.

"Actually, no, I don't think my boyfriend would appreciate that very much," Autumn says, moving closer to me.

Leaning forward, I meet his gaze. It's like he didn't see me. "Yeah, and I don't share."

"Sorry, man. Didn't mean any disrespect," he says, sizing me up after his beady eyes slide over her. I move her to my opposite side, putting myself between them.

"None taken," I tell him coldly and wrap my arm around Autumn, protecting her.

"Thank you," she whispers as we walk away.

I lean in and speak loud enough for her to hear. "I don't want anyone ever looking at you like that again."

"I don't either." She holds my waist, hooking her finger in my belt loop. She's warm against me and her hair smells like sweet red apples. Autumn might be the end of me.

A part of me wonders if I should stop this before we get in too deep, but while we're still strangers, I don't know if I can walk away from her now. There are too many invisible links keeping me cuffed to her.

Autumn guides me over to a vacant bench as we wait for the festivities to begin. She sits first and I join her, resting my arm on the back of the seat. She scoots in close, and to anyone watching, they'd assume we were together.

I'm allowing her to call the shots, to make the moves. She's in control.

"When you kissed me earlier, why did you say it wasn't supposed to feel like that?"

Has she been thinking about it as much as I have?

The mayor walks onto the stage and grabs the microphone before clearing her throat. "Welcome, people and friends of Cozy Hollow! Are you ready for one of the best pumpkin patches in the world?"

The crowd goes wild.

"At the stroke of midnight, it will officially be autumn!" the mayor continues.

"Tell me," Autumn whispers, returning her attention to me. "Please."

I turn my focus on her and everything around us disappears. "Only if you tell me why you looked at me that way last night."

She cocks her head. "Ah, it's like that?"

"A secret for a secret."

Autumn chuckles and we watch a group of kids marching up on the stage carrying pumpkin cutouts. They burst out into song and I chuckle.

Autumn bumps her body against mine as high-pitched voices scream the lyrics with all their hearts. "What, they didn't teach you a pumpkin anthem to welcome in the season?"

"Not quite." Boarding school wasn't fun. It required pristine uniforms and the best behavior.

I don't think I've ever been as carefree as I am right now.

Once they're finished, the mayor returns and taps on the microphone. "Please enjoy yourselves during this time, stay safe, and don't forget to shop local."

The crowd erupts into thunderous applause and themed music plays through the speakers strategically placed around the park. When I try to stand, Autumn takes my hand and pulls me back to her.

"This conversation isn't over." She closes her eyes and keeps them closed as she nervously smiles. "I just need to blurt it out."

I chuckle, waiting for her answer.

"I've had dreams about you," she rushes.

"What?" I stare at her until her long eyelashes flutter open. Her heart rate ticks in her neck and her breathing grows ragged.

A moment later, she meets my gaze, chewing on that plump bottom lip I tasted earlier.

"For thirteen years, I've dreamed about a man who looks and sounds like you." She pauses. "Okay, this is where you're supposed to find it adorable. You promised."

"Sorry." I shake my head, realizing my sister's prophecy has officially freaked me the fuck out. "I do. I swear. But I don't know what to say."

"Imagine how I feel," she says. "You're a figment of my imagination; every time I'm with you, it feels like I'm losing it."

I laugh. "I'm literally the man of your dreams?"

She sucks in a deep breath and whispers, "He said he'd find me. So, seeing you . . ."

Autumn doesn't finish her sentence.

I can't take my eyes off her as her wavy hair blows in the cool breeze. The smells of cider and sweet bread float in the air. Not to mention the electricity that surrounds us.

"Tell me your secret," she says.

I lick my lips and glance down at hers. Then I lean in and whisper in her ear, "Kissing you felt like magic."

CHAPTER 13

Autumn

$H$is hot breath is on my neck and a chill rushes down my spine. I'm sure I'm imagining things. This man has to be in my head, scanning through my thoughts. It's the only explanation.

"How did you know?" I ask as he pulls away from me. I'm dreaming, right? However, I can clearly see Zane's beautiful face and bright blue eyes. Lately, it's been the only way I can tell the difference between the dream world and reality.

"Because I felt it," he admits.

Butterflies flood me. "I said the same thing to Julie."

"That it was magic?"

"Yes," I whisper.

Our eyes lock as the world freezes, and I fight the intense urge to kiss him again.

"Fuck," he hisses, and his hand is on my cheek as my fingers slide against the softness of his neck. Then I inch forward, closing the space, making the first move.

I don't care, I can't deny it, not when everything urges me to do it.

I don't care if he's a stranger, we'll get to know one another.

I don't care about anything, only him, only right now.

Our tongues slowly swipe together as the nuclear meltdown happens inside of me. My head spins and my body begs for more, for all of him. I may have started it, but I don't want him to stop as

I moan. His hand fists through my hair, gently tugging, and a low grumble releases from his throat as we grow desperate.

"Autumn," he whispers against my mouth between breathless, greedy kisses.

"I'm sorry," I say, gaining control as he pulls us back down to reality. I cover my swollen lips with my fingertips, trying to clear my clouded thoughts.

"Don't apologize. Unless you regret it."

"I don't," I mutter. "It was confirmation."

"For?"

"Just confirming I wasn't imagining things."

The silence draws on.

"I'm not sure what's going on with us," he admits. It's a confirmation.

"Me either." Butterflies swarm inside me, then I think about kissing him again, and he tilts his head and laughs.

We're undeniably explosive and every part of me is red hot with want and need.

"You're eye fucking me."

"And I've explained why," I say. "I can't help it."

"And now you're thinking very inappropriate thoughts," he adds.

"Get out of my head."

The conversation is easy and fun.

"Make me," he teases.

"Just avoid door number three. That's where the naughty thoughts are kept."

"About Mr. Dreamy?"

I burst into laughter, watching the crowd enter the festival. "I *almost* regret telling you."

"You wanted me to know, Pumpkin," he states, shooting me a wink, and then he grows serious. "Meeting you has already been my greatest pleasure."

I smile, feeling the same, but also shocked that he's the man who said my coffee tastes like shit. "It's been a long time since I've allowed *anyone* new into my life."

"You allowed nothing. You trespassed my personal space, so I fairly did the same to your boundaries," he says, rolling his sleeves up to his muscular forearms.

My body is on fire, too, but I'm relaxed.

The line to enter the pumpkin patch still snakes to the street, but we're in no hurry to join it. Once it calms down, we'll go in, too.

"I could've said no," I state.

"No wasn't an option. I'd have haunted you in your dreams."

I scoff. "You play dirty."

"Nah, just have an advantage. Thanks, Mr. Dreamy." He laughs, focusing on the crunchy leaves tumbling across the sidewalk.

The sizable crowd of people slightly dissipates. "I've decided to go to my father's wedding as long as you're joining me."

I grin. "Oh, I got approval earlier today to use some of my vacation days."

His face breaks into a wide smile. "Great. Maybe once I show everyone I'm fine, I'll finally get closure and the lies about me will no longer be perpetuated."

"What lies?" I want to know exactly what I'm walking into so I can be prepared. "As your girlfriend and future fiancée, I deserve to know."

"Future wife," he tells me with a smirk, then continues. "Everyone believes I'm an obsessive weird fuck who stalks Celine and that I'll never move on after she cheated with my now ex–best friend." He rolls his eyes.

"Is there truth to it?" I ask.

His brows furrow. "I've avoided them both since she broke up with me. I've ghosted the world."

"Hey, it was a valid question because I want to understand. I'd help my friends bury a body if they needed me to, okay?" Then I realize what he said. "Wait, you caught her cheating and didn't end it? She did?"

His jaw clenches tight. "My weakness is my heart."

My assumptions about him were wrong, and I twist to face him.

"What?" he asks, glancing back at the little boy catching a pumpkin frisbee.

"I think your heart is your greatest strength," I say.

Time freezes for a few seconds as the cool wind blows through my hair. If I don't walk away right now, my lips will be pressed against his again.

I stand and hold out my hand, hoping he'll take it. He does.

"Let's get through this stranger phase as fast as fucking possible," he mutters, interlocking his fingers with mine as we move toward the crowd waiting to enter the pumpkin patch.

"I agree." I want to know everything about him and his past.

Ten minutes later, we find the end of the line and wait.

"So what's our plan?" I ask, glancing over at the side-by-side towing a trailer with four bales on it. It's the first year I've spotted the miniature hayride.

"We're carving pumpkins for the porch of my haunted house."

His words make me laugh. "I'm down for that."

I grin and swing his hand in mine as we move forward. When we're almost to the gigantic arch constructed of hand-carved pumpkins painted by local artists. Spooky music floats through the sound system.

A smile touches my lips as I turn to him. "Visiting the patch on the first weekend is one of my traditions," I explain. "But there is one caveat."

"Yes?"

"Selfies by the entrance." I pull my phone from my pocket and guide him over to my favorite section of the archway. He ducks down behind me and I hold the camera, glancing at him on the screen. "Ready?"

He's a good sport and changes his expression from smirks, to smiles, to funny faces.

"Oh, I'll help you kids out," an older woman says. I don't have the heart to tell her no, so I let her.

Zane stands next to me, wrapping his arm around me, and I move close to hold his waist.

"Look at you cuties," she says, taking several photos of us. A minute later, she hands my device back.

I swipe through the images as Zane looks over my shoulder.

"Wow," I whisper, realizing we look like a couple. I tuck my lips inside of my mouth, losing my ability to speak, not able to ignore how goddamn gorgeous he is with his messy dark hair, bright blue eyes, and high cheekbones. He really is the man of my dreams.

"We should pick out our pumpkins before the good ones are gone," I say, shoving my phone in my back pocket.

He turns to me. "I've already picked my pumpkin."

"You better stop with that," I playfully warn.

"Just practicing," he says with a wink.

We enter the main path, our eyes scanning over the varying sizes strategically stacked at different heights. They range from tiny ones that would fit into my palm to some so large it would take a few people to carry them. The colors span from white to light orange to dark. His wrist rests on my shoulder and I keep my finger hooked in his belt loop as electricity floats through the air.

As we pass groups of people, I notice how they're drawn to Zane. All six foot two of him.

"Do people always stare at you?" I ask.

"Yes," he breathes. "Since I was a child."

I breathe in. "I really should google you."

"I'll tell you anything you want to know. The truth, even if it makes me look shitty," he admits, removing his arm from me. He walks toward a tall pumpkin with a curled stem and knocks on the side of it.

"It has character and would be perfect for carving," I tell him, then walk farther into the patch and stop when I find the one. It's round, the size of a basketball.

I bend over and lift it up for him to see. "I found mine too!"

He picks up his and we meet up on the dimly lit walkway.

"I'm a champion carver," I warn.

"How do you know I'm not?"

"Guess I'll be the judge of that," I say, and he grabs my pumpkin in his arm and somehow manages to carry them both. We move down the path toward the orange and black booths where we pay. No gourd leaves without a ghost sticker.

"Wait, I need a picture," I tell him, quickly snapping one.

A smirk plays on his lips and a silent conversation streams between us.

Fuck, I hope I don't fall in love with this man.

It would complicate our lives.

But then again, I thrive in chaos.

CHAPTER 14

Zane

After loading the pumpkins into the back of the Jeep, I open the door for Autumn and she climbs inside.

"You've got good taste," she says, sliding her hand across the smooth leather seats with neon orange embroidery and accents.

"I think so," I tell her as I climb in and crank the engine. I put it in reverse and we cruise the town before heading up the mountain blasting the oldies station. "Rich Girl" blares out and she laughs, singing along. Her hand is out the window and her hair blows in the breeze. Autumn is picture perfect, her laugh contagious.

"I haven't been in a Jeep since high school," she admits, looking in the back seat. "This one would be a lot easier to fool around in."

I tilt my head at her. "It was like that?"

"It's always the quiet ones," she warns. "Always."

"Mm. I'll have to remember you said that."

As I turn into the driveway, I scan in. The tall wrought-iron gate is exactly what I'd imagine would protect a haunted house.

She sits at the edge of her seat in awe as we slowly drive down the twisty road that leads to Hollow Manor. It's only wide enough for one vehicle and is surrounded by trees that hang above us. With no lights lining the pavement every five feet, it would be spooky as hell and I understand why the rumors about the manor began.

There is no one to prove the tale right or wrong, and with the distinct lack of life, the stories are more than plausible.

Hollow Manor has been a large, vacant house for over twenty years. Before I arrived, ghosts might as well have occupied it.

When I look farther ahead, the tree line fades and displays a sky full of twinkling stars. I drive to the back of the house and open her door. Autumn takes my hand, meeting my eyes before passing me. Fucking flirt.

I grab the pumpkins from the back and we move to the backyard where the lights are brightly lit, waiting for us, before I set them down. "Thirsty?"

"You have no idea," she tells me and follows me into the kitchen.

She stands beside me as I open the fridge, glancing over my arm. "Oktoberfest."

"You mentioned you liked it, so I got a case for us."

"You were listening?"

"Of course. And I remember everything you've ever shared with me," I say. "Maybe I'll write a book."

"Now that's something I'd love to read," she says, reaching inside and grabbing two bottles for us. She hands me one and we twist off the caps and flick them onto the counter, where they spin for a few moments before settling.

"Shall we toast?"

"To us." She grins, repeating what I said at Bookers last night. Flirt.

"*Always* to us," I repeat, clinking the glass bottle necks and taking a sip. The light hint of pumpkin dances in my mouth and I swish the liquid around before swallowing.

"What does your refined palate say?"

"It's great." I chuckle, glancing at the carving tools for two that are waiting on the center island. It's hard for me to believe she's inside my house again, hanging out and comfortable, like she belongs in my space. She does.

"Sometimes you look at me like I'll disappear." Autumn takes a drink of her beer.

"Everyone does, eventually," I state. "Don't they?"

"Not me. I'm not going anywhere. When you go back to wherever it is you live, I'll still be here. Hopefully not as a memory," she says.

"New York and Washington," I admit, wanting her to know where I am when I'm not here. "I split my time throughout the year depending on my mood."

"I love New York," she says. "At least I enjoyed the four years I lived there."

"And somehow we never crossed paths."

"Wrong time," she tells me. "Had I met you then, I wouldn't have given you a chance."

"So, you're saying I have a chance?"

She ignores my question.

"I was extremely focused. Nothing could distract me. Not even you."

"Hm. I disagree."

She rolls her eyes. "Cocky."

I shrug then drink. "I want to know you for more than just a season. But I always fuck up things in relationships—friendships, romantic, even with my family. I'm almost convinced I'm the problem."

"You're not," she says. "I don't get that vibe from you."

It's a relief.

"I don't trust my judgment because I've allowed horrible people access to me."

She looks at me with sadness swimming in her eyes.

"Don't feel sorry for me. I chose it."

"Then why am I here?" Autumn asks.

"Because the universe keeps linking us together. It's like I can let my guard down around you without worrying that you'll tell the world."

"I'll always keep your secrets," she offers, not moving away from me. "No matter what happens."

"Can I take that to the bank?"

"You can take it to the grave," she says. "And I never break my promises, that's why I don't give IOUs. Except for you."

The eye contact grows too intense, and I have to glance away from her because I'm five seconds from capturing her lips with mine. I change the subject. "So, pumpkin queen, ready to carve?"

"Ooh, do you have a large mixing bowl? We can throw the guts inside, then prep the seeds to cook afterward."

I open cabinets, searching until I find the one that's painted like a jack-o'-lantern. It takes me back to carving pumpkins with my mom and sister all those years ago.

"There you are," I say, pulling it out and setting it on the counter in front of Autumn.

She stops and stares at it. "We had the same bowl when I was a kid, over twenty years ago. They sold them in the home goods store in town. Was that left behind from the family that used to live here?"

"I guess you could say that."

A gasp escapes her. "It could be cursed."

"Stop." I try hard not to laugh because she's serious, but I fail miserably. "Trust me when I say, if there are any ghosts in this house, they're friendly."

She narrows her eyes, not convinced.

I cup my hands around my mouth and yell, "This is a message to all the spirits haunting Hollow Manor!"

My voice bounces off the high walls.

"No." Autumn immediately shakes her head. "Don't! You clearly haven't watched enough horror movies."

"If you're here, give us a sign!" I glance at her with a snicker. "Should I say Beetlejuice three times?"

Then, the light in the living room above the mantel clicks on and I freeze.

"What have you done?" Autumn asks, and I can tell she's freaked out. "Are you trying to scare me?"

I have to admit, it's weird as fuck.

"No. I swear. I didn't plan that." The smile fades from my face.

"Nope. I'm not doing this. We're leaving," she singsongs and grabs my hand, guiding me toward the hallway that leads to the backyard.

I pull her to me and place my hands on her shoulders and squeeze, forcing her to look into my eyes.

I can't allow this to continue on. "My family has always owned this house and this property. My mother designed every square inch and had it custom-built to her specifications over thirty years ago."

"But—"

"Listen," I say, keeping my voice soft. "We came here one spooky season through Christmas after my mom found out she had stage four cancer. She wanted us to create memories in Cozy Hollow before sharing the news with us. After the new year, when we returned to the city, she told us her diagnosis. No one was gruesomely murdered. No one died in this house.

"After my mother passed away, I tried to forget this place existed. When I turned eighteen, I inherited the house, but I had no reason to come back. It's stayed vacant until I returned at the beginning of September. Nothing bad *ever* happened within these walls. It was actually one of the few happy places I had as a kid. I promise."

Autumn covers her mouth and her brows crease. "Oh. I'm very

sorry. I was disrespectful. I had no idea. Zane, I'm incredibly sorry about your mom. I—"

I smile and lift her chin. "No, please don't apologize. My mother would've weirdly loved to know her dream house became the center of a fictional story about murders and it being haunted with ghosts. Even if it's unrealistic." I chuckle, glancing at the frames that are shining in the light as her feet stay planted in the kitchen. "She was a witchy hippie who adored summer nights, fall, and growing flowers."

"She sounds like sunshine."

"Mom was stardust. Sparkly and beautiful, but gone too soon," I say with a sad smile, walking past Autumn. "Come on."

She doesn't budge.

"Do you trust me?" There is a reason this happened and I want to find out what that reason is. Even though I know I've avoided these photos since I arrived, it's time to face them right now.

I glance back at Autumn, hold out my hand, and nod my head. While she takes it, she's hesitant.

"Don't you find this strange?" she asks.

"I do." I look around, noticing the living room is pitch dark other than the light from the kitchen leaking onto the floor, and the one above the mantel. None of it makes sense. "It's my mom, or maybe there's an electrical issue and it's a pure coincidence."

"Nothing is ever coincidental," Autumn says, her eyes scanning over the pictures. She spots one, and it's me and my sister posing at the patch with my mom.

"Wait. I think I met you when I was ten," she whispers. "How is that possible?"

"Sometimes it's as simple as being in the right place at the right time," I tell her, pulling the frame down and handing it to her.

"What's your sister's name? We hung out an entire day and got our faces painted with butterflies. I have a picture somewhere."

A lot has happened since then and the memories are too fuzzy. "When we were kids, we used fake names to hide our identities. She went by Lucy."

"Yes. *Lucy*," she whispers with a grin. "That was it. I couldn't remember for the longest time. And you?"

"I've always answered to Alexander and Zane."

"Do you have a preference?" she asks, and I adore how respectful she is. No one has ever asked me before.

"It's whatever you prefer. Depending on the setting, people call me different things." I kinda like hearing my first name come from her lips though.

"Interchangeable. I like that." She continues looking at the photographs. "This was your mother?"

Mom stands outside of the greenhouse with dirt on her overalls and a pair of cutting shears in one hand and some flowers in the other.

"Zane, she's holding coneflowers," Autumn whispers. "Did they come from her garden?"

"Yes. They were her favorites. I thought you'd like them too."

"Wow. That means a lot to me," she says, her voice cracking, setting the picture back down. "She's beautiful. You have her eyes and smile."

"Thank you. It's been a long time since someone told me that," I say, focusing on the photo as the letter comes to mind. "My mom is why I came back to Hollow Manor. She always said the mountains could heal anything. I came to find out if it was true."

My words get choked in my throat. Autumn carefully wraps her arms around me and I don't know how to react at first.

"What's this for?" I ask, allowing myself to relax.

"Because you looked like you needed it."

"Thank you." I hold her tighter, not sure if she knew I was building mental walls. When I inhale the sweet scent of her shampoo and close my eyes, the light clicks off.

"Friendly ghosts," she whispers, burying her head into my chest with a laugh. "I'm still scared."

"I won't let anything happen to you," I tell her, then lead her back to the kitchen. I shove the carving tools and some markers into the mixing bowl, then we wash our hands and return to the backyard.

As she moves to the picnic table covered with newspaper, I start the fire in the pit that I prepared for tonight. The wood immediately catches and cracks and pops into the night.

The string lights cast a warm glow against the soft, stubby grass. Autumn smooths her hand over the top of the table. "I'm starting to believe you really are a pro."

"Time will tell," I say, sitting across from her. I hand her a carving knife and a scoop.

She removes the cap to the marker and begins drawing. I try to steal a peek of her design but she's fast and twists it so I can't.

I pick up my beer, taking a swig. "Why'd you and Sebastian break up?"

I notice she tenses.

"You don't have to talk about it right now, but one day I want to know."

"Oh, it's fine. He came up with this wild idea that we both wanted to see other people. And told our friends that the breakup was a mutual agreement."

"Was it?"

She sarcastically laughs. "What do you think?"

"I'll have him fired," I state. "Tomorrow."

She stops drawing and glances at me. "He's one of the greatest instructors in the country."

"And?"

"A lot of business is brought to the resort because people want to ski with him."

I blink a few more times. "There are other celebrity snowboarders I can hire who are ten times better with less of an attitude. He's extremely replaceable."

"No. No." She reaches forward. "The best revenge is him thinking he lost me forever."

"Would you take him back?"

"Honestly?" She hesitates. "No. And what about you?"

"I don't give second chances once things are really over. It's a rule of mine. It ends for a reason."

"Who was she?"

"Celine Madison." I meet her eyes.

"The *supermodel*," she deadpans.

"You've heard of *her*, but not me?" I ask. Celine was obsessed with the spotlight; it's why she got with me. To use my connections to further her career. Good for her, it worked. "Actually, that checks out."

Autumn grows quiet.

"Why are you putting up walls?"

She finishes drawing, then carves the heart shape at the top of her pumpkin. She removes it, shoves the scoop inside, and starts scraping. "Not one person in your social circle will believe I'm her replacement. Get real."

"Are you fucking kidding me? Trust me when I say everyone on that island will want to know who you are while simultaneously trying to steal you from me."

A small smile plays on her lips.

"I wish I could show you what the rest of the world sees. If you really knew how goddamn gorgeous you are, you wouldn't say shit like that."

She swallows hard. "It doesn't seem plausible. Why would you choose me when you can literally have anyone?"

"You are anyone. Point?"

With one swift movement, she flips her hair over one shoulder and carefully follows along the outside of her line. I can't stop staring as she steals my breath away.

"You have nothing to worry about," I assure her. "Nothing at all."

She grins, plopping the pulp into the bowl. "I'll trust that you know your type more than I do."

I draw a circle around the stem then cut it out, wondering if I have a type. If I do, what's the similarity all of them have? Autumn isn't like anyone I've ever met.

"This is my favorite part." She stands, watching me wiggle it off. Seeds and guts hang down and she peeks inside.

I think about old memories, and how the last time I did this I was fifteen. I scrape the sides then throw the goop into the bowl with Autumn's.

"Have you ever made homemade pumpkin pie?" I ask.

"All the time. My gran has this world-famous recipe," she explains. "Won a few state fairs down in Texas."

"Really?"

"We should've bought an extra one. Actually, we can use mine."

"No, no. I'll take a rain check. You think I'll allow you to quit our contest so easily?"

Her head falls back on her shoulders and she laughs. "I was forfeiting for pie. It's what any respectable human would do!"

"We'll have plenty of time," I tell her. "And I'll make you my mother's famous oatmeal raisin cookies."

"Deal."

Once the pumpkins are emptied, Autumn picks up the bowl. "Let's prep these, then we'll come back and finish."

I stand and open the door for her, then follow her to the kitchen where she places the pumpkin guts in the sink. After it's full of water, seeds float to the top.

"This is part of the process?"

"Yep. Makes it easier to clean the gunk off. Do you have a colander?"

"Somewhere," I say, opening the cabinets again. Eventually I'll know where everything is in this house and I won't feel like a stranger living here. I find it in the back then rinse it before handing it to her.

"We need a baking sheet." She turns the oven on to 350 degrees and we work around each other as she strains and dries the seeds, then places them back in the bowl and seasons them. I take a step back, out of her way, watching her float in my space. After adding olive oil and mixing it with a wooden spoon, she lays them flat on the tray.

"Now what?"

"We drink. Fifteen minutes, turning them every five. When they're finished, we'll have a snack while I kick your ass at carving a pumpkin."

"Ah, well, if that's what we're supposed to do then I have the perfect beverage." I move to the liquor cabinet and grab the Clase Azul and set it on the counter.

She chews on the corner of her lip. "What is it?"

"Tequila."

"Ah, my kryptonite," she says.

"Another thing we have in common. Damn."

CHAPTER 15

Autumn

I take a step forward and Zane removes the plastic from the top of the exquisite bottle of tequila, then pops off the white cap. Pink flowers and vines intricately trail up the sides. It looks like it was once displayed behind a glass case. "Wow," I whisper, sliding my fingers across it.

"It's a handcrafted, hand-painted Talavera carafe. Extremely limited edition and all the proceeds go toward fighting breast cancer."

"You should save this for a special occasion," I offer.

"I did." There is zero hesitation in his voice.

He pulls shot glasses from a cabinet and fills them. "No lime or salt needed. It's smooth. I'm convinced it's hangover-proof. Hence why it's one of my favorite tequilas in the world."

"Oh, I wish you wouldn't have told me that. What if I hate it?"

"Then the fake engagement is off." He winks.

We shoot them back. It tastes incredible, refreshing in a way. Tequila like this will get me in trouble or naked. Fuck, maybe both.

"What does your palate say?" he asks.

"It's wonderful." I stare at the bottle. "Is it pricey?"

"Only five," he tells me, refilling our glasses.

"Hundred?" If so, it's the most expensive thing I've ever drank.

"Thousand."

"Seriously?" I nearly choke on the second shot.

"You're fucking cute." He pours himself another and I move my glass forward, allowing him to fill mine again.

"This is dangerous." I meet his eyes.

"It's as easy as drinking water."

"I'm not talking about the tequila," I say, and he fully understands.

"We forgot to toast." He smirks, holding up his glass. "To us."

"To *us*." I shoot it back and set it on the counter.

My body buzzes, and it's not from the alcohol, though that's helping. The five-minute alarm dings, pulling us away.

Zane grabs two mitts and flips the seeds, then returns them to the oven.

"Ten more minutes," I say, reaching for the bottle, contemplating drinking more.

"I'm keeping up with your pace. But at this rate, we'll both be shitfaced before we finish our pumpkins," he mutters with a brow flicked upward.

Fuck, I cannot handle him looking at me like that. But somehow, I keep my composure as his closeness drags me under.

"We should play a game," I tell him, smiling, even if my cheeks feel numb.

"Truth or dare?" he sarcastically asks.

"No. It's called twenty-one questions. We get to ask each other twenty-one burning questions. And you have to answer the ones you ask."

"Wouldn't that be considered forty-two questions?"

I chuckle. "Smart-ass."

"And what happens if one of us refuses?"

"Then a piece of clothing gets removed," I admit, making that part up. However, I'm curious to see what he's hiding under those clothes that hug his body.

A mischievous grin meets those gorgeous lips and he holds out his hand. "Deal."

I take it and we shake, sealing it.

"I have no limits," he warns. "I hope you don't either."

Fuck. I grab the bottle, knowing I need more of this. Another shot down. Now, how many are we in? Four? Five? More? There is no turning back now. I'm in too deep.

"Go first," he offers with narrowed eyes. It's a warning, a temptation. "Ask me *anything*."

I stare into his blue eyes, wondering about his deepest, darkest desires.

"Let me note, this is fucking exclusive. You're the only person on this planet who has *ever* had the privilege."

"Well then, I consider myself lucky." My alarm rings, but he takes care of flipping and returning the seeds to the oven. I hop up on the counter, swinging my legs, and he moves toward me as I admire every inch of him.

He's artwork in human form with his dark, messy hair and bright blue eyes. Not to mention his deep voice that nearly brings me to my knees. Yep, I'm drunk.

"What was your first love like?" I ask.

"Interesting question. Not what I expected you to start with."

"I'd like to know your origin story. I'm curious. *About everything.*"

Zane licks his lips and his eyes pin me in place. "I haven't thought about that in a long time. It was temporary. Fun. We snuck around my family's home in the Hamptons before I left for Princeton. I would've changed the trajectory of my life for her, but I was nothing more than a summer fling. She was almost twenty-three." He pauses for a moment. "What we had was obsessive, toxic love. I think all of my relationships have been like that, though. Fast, furious, and fleeting."

"Who was she?" I ask.

"My ex–best friend's older sister. Her name is Miranda."

"Scandalous." I can tell he's lost in a memory. "Wait, are you still in love with her?"

"No. Absolutely not." He laughs. "Miranda is happily married to a good man and they have three cute kids. I was young and didn't know how the world worked yet, but I learned my lesson quickly. Thirty-seven-year-old me knows I have to write my own rules and not give a fuck what anyone else thinks when it comes to my life and relationships."

"That's the way it should always be."

"It wasn't." Zane nods. "Your turn."

I'm brought back to memories I haven't thought about in fifteen years.

"His name is Teddy, and we were biology partners. Dissecting frogs made me squeamish, so he took it upon himself to make me laugh the entire semester. It was puppy love, the kind that when you look at them you're shocked that they're actually yours. He was smart, but also a football star, popular and completely out of my league. Everyone loved him, knew him, and still does. He plays quarterback professionally now, one of those MVP Super Bowl ring wearers."

"It sounds like it was great. Why did it end?"

I meet his eyes. "Long distance isn't for me and never will be. When I'm with someone, I'm *with* them. I was accepted at Columbia and he was attending LSU to play college ball. We set clear expectations, and after our final summer together, we broke up and went our separate ways. To date, it was the most adult relationship I've ever had. We still exchange Christmas cards and he comments on my social media posts sometimes, but that's about it."

"I'm sensing a type with NFL players and retired Olympians."

"Yes." I snicker. "The other man I dated, Antonio, played professional baseball."

"And what about Mr. Dreamy? What's he into?"

"*Me and only me,*" I confidently say. "In real life, my shining personality carries me a long way, just not down the aisle."

"Athletes are assholes, Pumpkin. They never appreciate what they have," he says.

"Then I'm glad you're not one," I tell him.

"Fuck, me too. Do you wish you would've tried to make it work?"

It's not a question I've ever asked myself, but I think about it, taking it to heart. The tequila helps with my honesty and I hope I don't regret spilling all my truths tomorrow. Hell, maybe we'll drink so much that neither of us will remember.

"I never imagined a future with him. We knew it was short term. I missed his company, but we were always better friends than lovers."

The silence draws on for a few seconds. "I'm impressed. Ivy League."

"And I graduated with a *perfect* GPA. I peaked in college, though. Look at me now."

He shakes his head. "Give yourself more credit."

"Did you like Princeton?" I change the subject, catching what he said earlier.

"I wasn't interested." He pauses. "I was a competitive snowboarder, and I'd placed to compete in the Olympics. It's all I wanted in life. During training before the trials started, I took a halfpipe and landed wrong and injured my knee and tore some ligaments, which took me out. Princeton was a backup plan because my father required it in case my *hobby* didn't work out. He never considered it a career. When I stopped snowboarding professionally, I continued my studies in world affairs and finance, and joined the family business."

It's hard to place his expression.

It's full of regret and pain, maybe sorrow too.

"I'm sorry." I want to hug him.

"It's how I know Sebastian. He was my replacement. Fucking asshole. And knowing he was with you . . ." He stops talking and shakes his head. "You deserved a million times better than him. I'm thrilled you're not together."

"It's personal with you two."

His gaze is distant. "Very fucking personal."

Before any more words are spoken, Zane pours another shot into his glass and I slide mine forward. The conversation went too deep already. Sebastian was an Olympian because of Zane's misfortunes. Their reaction to seeing one another makes more sense now. The tension was too thick.

"It's why you should follow your dreams if you are capable, Pumpkin. Some of us lost that opportunity and can never get what we want."

"You're right," I whisper, feeling guilty. Perspective does that.

I study his mouth, remembering what it felt like against mine. It was first-love magic. The logical side of my brain says that at least. The tipsy part begs me to take risks and fuck it all. It's like I have an angel on one shoulder and a devil on the other.

When the last timer rings, Zane removes the pumpkin seeds from the oven. He grabs an empty bowl and scoots the roasted ones inside. I enjoy watching him be domestic, and he catches me. After a brief second, he focuses back on his task at hand, but his sexy little grin isn't lost on me.

I reach forward, grabbing one and putting it into my mouth, then immediately regret it. I spit the seed back into my palm to blow on it. "I just burnt the fuck out of my tongue," I say with a laugh.

"You're impatient," he says.

"You have no idea." I pop it back in, loving the crunch and flavor.

He grabs the bowl and our shot glasses. "Grab the tequila. We have snacks to eat and pumpkins to carve."

"Hell yeah we do." I pick it up and follow him down the hallway. The fire barely flickers, so Zane adds a few more logs on top. I stand beside him, holding my hands out as the flames lick up toward the sky.

"I love it when it's like this outside. The briskness in the air makes me excited." I hiccup, a sign that I've drunk too much. "Oh no."

"What?" he asks.

"The hiccups. They mean I'm on my way to being fucked." I laugh. "Not literally. Just tipsy."

Laughter roars from him. "Pace yourself."

"Nah," I tell him. "Do you know what number question we're on?"

"Um. I lost count." He steals a glance. "But I think it's my turn. I wonder what I could ask that you'd not want to answer."

I flip my hair over my shoulder. "There isn't one."

His head falls back on his shoulders. "That's why you agreed, because you have no limits."

"Only with you. If you're willing to cut yourself open, then I will too. Secrets for secrets. I'll trade with you."

"Mm." His voice is velvety. "You might not like everything you learn."

"You might not either. I'm not perfect, but I'm not scared of you learning who I am. I have nothing to hide, either."

"Then what are you afraid of with us?"

I glance at him. "I guess that's a question I have to answer?"

A sly smile slides over his lips. I breathe in, tucking my hands in my pockets. "I'm afraid of growing attached then having to navigate a world without knowing you."

His face softens and I wonder what he's thinking.

"Your turn."

"I'm afraid of falling madly in love with you," he says.

"Zane." I search his face, and I think I stop breathing completely as I watch the stars disappear behind clouds. Then thunder claps and lightning strikes close by and we're both pulled out of this conversation. The rumble has me nearly jumping out of my skin as I slide my phone from my pocket to check the radar app. "We're about to get shit on."

He glances at the screen just as a few drops fall from the sky like torpedoes. The wind picks up and I realize we were enjoying the calm before the storm. Figuratively and literally.

"We need to get inside now," I tell him, looking at the growing red blob, knowing how these mountain storms work. They creep up randomly, even when there is a zero percent chance of rain.

I stand and I'm wobbly on my feet. Zane is too.

"Shit," I tell him, grabbing the pumpkin seeds and the tequila.

"At least you got what's important." When his arms wrap around both pumpkins, the bottom falls out of the sky. I pick up my pace, trying to sprint without tripping, but I'm already soaked.

When I'm on the porch, I turn, finding him right behind me. I glance at the fire that's sizzling then notice my phone is still on the table.

"Oh no," I say, then set everything down by the back door.

"I've got it." Zane rushes out, grabbing everything, including the pumpkin tools, then sprints back toward me. Fat water drops run from his hair and face. It sounds like a fucking freight train.

"My hero." I chuckle.

"You're awful with phones." He hands it to me.

"It's a bad habit I'm trying to break."

"Come with me." He holds out his hand, glancing back at the falling drops. "You're already soaked."

I take it and he leads me off the porch back into the rain. It's slamming against us and I look up at him, smiling, as he says, "Dance with me. I have a few things I promised my mom I'd do."

I laugh, taking his hand, and he sings "September." And I don't think I'll be reminded of anything else when I hear this song again, not considering the day is actually the twenty-first night of September. He spins me around as the drops sparkle down like glitter. Joy spreads over me as I join him when he starts the chorus. Zane grins wide, chuckling as I sing the high-pitched *oh oh ohs*.

Our eyes lock, and I've never wanted someone to kiss me more than I want him to right now. My lashes flutter closed and our lips move toward one another in slow motion. Before we touch, lightning cracks behind us, and Zane is taking my hand, pulling me away.

I shiver and notice his shirt is stuck to him, every inch and ridge of his body embossed in sharp relief. "We should probably change clothes," he mutters, grabbing the pumpkins again.

"Yeah." I carry the rest of the things inside. We set everything down on the counter before I follow him. Zane walks through the kitchen, flicking on the lights in the living room and upstairs. With each step we leave behind wet footprints.

"Will you give me an official tour?" I ask, joining him.

"I'd love to. Let's save it for tomorrow when the sun is up because you'll be able to better appreciate the design with how the sunlight leaks through the windows at different times of day. It's an experience."

"Wow. I can't wait," I say, my eyes scanning my surroundings, taking in how well the decorations flow together, knowing his mom designed it. At the top of the stairs, he takes a left, and I follow him to the end of the wide hallway. I stop and stare at the double doors that stretch from floor to ceiling.

"Is this your lair? Seriously, it looks like something from a castle."

"Good eye. It's what they consider Gothic Oak and is from a house that was built in the fifteenth century. French, I believe."

"It's beautiful." I smooth my hand across the dark carved wood, appreciating the history.

He pushes them open and we walk into a gigantic bedroom with high ceilings and two walls of windows that connect at a corner. In this room, he has the perfect view of the sunrise and sunset. "Wow," I say, taking a step forward.

"I was thinking the same," he says, but he's not looking at the room, he's zeroed in on me. Then he moves to a pocket door that blends in with the wall. He slides it open and waits for me to join him.

"You have a department store inside your house," I say with a snicker, amazed by his well-organized closet. Then I hiccup again.

Zane chuckles, moving to a tall dresser across the space that's as large as my loft. He pulls out a small stack of clothes and hands them to me. I'm more than ready to get out of this soggy sweater and jeans.

"The bathroom is right next door if you'd like privacy."

"Just turn around," I tell him, twirling my finger.

He does without question.

"What's a deal breaker in a relationship for you?" I completely undress, removing my bra and panties, which are soaked too. I glance at the T-shirt he gave me and notice it has his name written in the corner and a number 13 on the back. One of his childhood jerseys, no doubt. Soccer, if I had to guess. I slide the soft material over my body.

"Lying. I can forgive the truth and work through it with someone I love more than a lie. And you?"

"Cheating," I whisper. Old memories flood in about all the nights I thought Sebastian was with other women. However, it was never confirmed. During our final year of being together, I slowly became the insecure girlfriend he warned me I'd become, almost as if he planned it.

Sebastian stole my confidence, and with it, my creativity.

I slip on the pair of bottoms he gave me, seeing another number on the leg. They're too long and baggy around the waist but I manage. "I'm dressed."

He turns to me and grins wide. The corners of his eyes crease. "My clothes look good on you."

"I promise they'd look better *off* of me," I say, shaking my head with a laugh. "Sorry. That's the tequila talking. Ignore it."

"It's the devil's drink," he says, but his smile doesn't fade. Zane returns to his dresser. I turn my back, giving him the same respect he offered me.

Moments later, he walks past me with a black T-shirt in his hand. The performance joggers sit low on his waist and hug his toned thighs and taper at the ankle. Muscles cascade down his back and I lose my train of thought as I admire each inch of him. He is the man of my dreams, every part of him. "You're . . ."

"You're back to eye fucking me again, Pumpkin." He turns, catching me as he stands in the doorway before walking away. "You should really stop doing that."

He may have said it like a warning, but I take it as an invitation.

CHAPTER 16

Zane

I slide the black T-shirt over my body and wait for Autumn to recompose herself and join me in the bedroom. Eventually, she emerges, and it's cute seeing those clothes on her. I haven't seen them since the last time I was here, and there is no way they'd ever fit me again.

The rain still falls heavily outside, and she stands beside me.

"Can we go out there?" she asks.

"Sure," I tell her, sliding the balcony door open. The cool breeze whips around us.

"Do you still snowboard?"

"Occasionally, but never in the same capacity as I did. It's why I split my time between New York and Washington. I might trade the last one for Cozy Hollow." I turn to her and there is fire in her eyes. "Please don't look at me like that."

"Okay," she says, staring out into the darkness. "I won't. But I think you might be my new hobby. Are you sure you still want to be my friend?"

"I'm following this road that we're traveling down all the way to the end," I tell her, hoping she understands exactly what I mean.

A shiver rushes over her and I realize how cold it is. It has to be in the forties. "We can go back inside."

She leads the way, smelling so damn sweet. "That's where the magic happens?"

"It's where dreams turn into reality," I counter with a wink.

Her cheeks heat and she hiccups again. "Hardy har har with the Mr. Dreamy references. I could've predicted your comforter was black. Let me guess, the sheets are red?"

I narrow my eyes at her, walking to the edge of the bed and turning them down. "How'd you know that?"

"Because I've been here before with you," she whispers. "In a dream."

I cross my arms over my chest as I try to find words. "And what happened?"

She shakes her head. "Let's just say everyone was completely satisfied in the end."

Fuck. When Autumn walks past me toward the door, I adjust myself, wishing she would stop looking at me like that. If she only knew she was in control of this entire situation, and where this goes between us. But considering we're both broken in some sort of way, I'm not sure either of us is ready. Or maybe we could fill the cracks of our hearts with the sunshine the other brings.

There's too much push and pull. When we take the stairs, my stomach growls. Autumn grabs onto the railing, but I hold my arm around her, steadying her. Once we're in the kitchen, I open the freezer that was recently stocked full. "Hungry? Want some pizza?"

"God yes," she says, as I grab a baking stone, turning on the oven. I grab the packages of pepperoni and cheese from the fridge and add extra on top of the frozen pizza.

"I do the same. They never put enough on them," she tells me, snagging a pepperoni.

"What type of books do you write?"

With a grin, she sprinkles shreds of cheese into her mouth. "I don't."

"Oh, come on."

"Romance, but lately my specialty has been haikus. All love themed. Julie tricked me into doing it, and it's gotten easier, but she's also been pushing me to write about Mr. Dreamy."

My brows rise. "Now, that's a book I want to read."

"Pfft," she says.

"What if I paid you to write it?" I ask.

Her lips part. "You're not serious."

I laugh. "I'm dead fucking serious. Think of it as an advance. That's all a publisher would give you, right?"

"Plus royalties and distribution."

"What's your ridiculous dream price?" When the oven is preheated, I put the pizza inside.

She refuses to answer.

"Which piece of clothing are you removing?" My eyes slide over her, knowing she left her bra and panties on the floor of my closet. I saw them on her tiny pile of clothes.

She narrows her eyes. "You play so fucking dirty!"

"It's a house advantage," I state, leaning against the counter.

Autumn stands, twirling the hem of the T-shirt in her fingers and barely lifting it, showing her flat stomach. I wait, not taking my eyes from her until she pushes the material down.

"I don't know if I can put a number on it because I don't think I can deliver."

"Ten million," I offer. "You realize that's an author's dream advance."

She gasps.

"We can make it twenty?" I shrug, glancing at my nails. "I have more money than any person should. That's nothing."

"Zane."

"What if I said fifty million? Could you imagine selling your first publication for that much money?"

She shakes her head. "No."

"I have one stipulation, though. I want *every* fucking detail of Mr. Dreamy."

Her eyes are wide. "You're *serious.*"

"I'll put the funds in a trust for you this week. Oh, I'd also like it delivered in six months."

"Don't you think that's strict?"

"Not for the price I'm paying. Actually, let's make it before the new year. Up the ante a little."

"Are you out of your mind? I have finished no projects since I graduated with my MFA a decade ago. You're giving me fourteen weeks."

"Exactly."

She stares at me like I've grown a third head and then she scoffs. "You know what, I will take your offer."

I hold out my hand and we shake on it. "Every. Detail."

"It will make you blush," she says. "And you'll probably learn a thing or two."

A roar of laughter escapes me. "I look forward to it, Pumpkin."

When the word leaves my lips, she inhales and glances away from me.

"What other dreams do you have?"

"Well, I wanted to be married by thirty. No way you can make that happen, unless you have enough money to buy a time machine and we can go back three and a half years."

"Ah, unfortunately no. But marriage by thirty isn't a fail."

"Considering who I would've married, I'd say you're right," she says.

"Now that would've been tragic."

Autumn moves over to the pumpkins and carving tools. I grab a few dish towels and we dry off what we can, then I clean up the wet footprints we tracked into the house.

Afterward, we sit at the breakfast bar and continue with our conversation, returning to our pumpkins. We fall quiet as we work on our designs. It's a comfortable silence, though.

"Phew. I think I'm done. I win because I finished first," she says.

"Most women do."

"Mmhm. Unless she fakes it." Autumn snickers.

"Have you ever faked it?" I ask. "The truth."

She lifts a brow. "More times than I'd like to admit."

I chuckle. "I'm sorry for laughing."

"You don't think a woman has ever faked it with you?" She scoffs.

"Never."

"And how would you know?"

I lean in and lick my lips. "Let's just say I love confirming."

She chews on the inside of her cheek, holding back a smile.

The timer buzzes and Autumn gets up and removes the pizza since I'm still working on my pumpkin carving masterpiece. She sets it on the stovetop and I try not to watch her, but it's hard when she's right there.

"This looks incredible." Then she snags a pepperoni and the cheese stretches then snaps as she pops it in her mouth. "Hot, hot!"

Her mouth is wide open and she's waving her hand in front of her face. She hops between her feet like it'll help. A minute later, she swallows it down.

"Was it worth it?" I ask as I shake my head, finishing my carving. I move it back, making sure everything I cut out is straight.

"Yep."

"You're stubborn," I say, glancing back at her.

"But you already knew that." She reaches for another pepperoni.

I stand and grab the two battery-powered candles I got for our pumpkins then I walk over to her. I gently take her hand and set it in her palm. "We have a pumpkin reveal while it cools."

"Okay."

Her cheeks are pink and I realize how much I enjoy the tipsy version of her. Cute. Funny. Sexy. I study her face as she looks up at me.

"Did my eyes blink at two different times?" she asks.

I burst into laughter and my head falls back on my shoulder. "No, they didn't."

"Felt like it." She glances back at the pizza, snagging another pepperoni and repeating the process of burning the shit out of her mouth. I watch her. "You know your eyes give you away."

"Yeah?"

She nods. "They say they're the window to the soul, ya know."

"Shakespeare. Though, I have a feeling you're more of a Poe fan," I tell her.

"I enjoy them all for different reasons. I studied the classics but found their life stories more interesting than the fiction they wrote. Artists are wired differently, I think. My obsession with love is why I chose romance."

My brows furrow. "You're no longer obsessed with it?"

She shrugs as we stand in front of our pumpkins. "I think I need convincing after the relationships I've had. I can't write the end because I don't believe my characters will get a happily ever after."

"Because you haven't?"

I huff, but it's the truth. "Basically."

Silence streams between us. "I'm happy you'll be creating again soon."

"It will not be easy for me."

"Going back to something you almost gave up never is," I tell her, knowing what it was like to be back on the snow after I thought I might never ski or snowboard again. For weeks, I wasn't sure if I'd even walk again. "But it's just like training a muscle. The more you work at it, the stronger you become. I believe in you."

She meets my eyes. "You do?"

"Yes. I know you have brilliance up there. Just need some inspiration," I say, brushing my hand across her hair, pushing it from her face.

She swallows hard and I create space between us before I lose control and cross that line. It's something I won't do, not when we've been drinking. That's not fair to her, and I already have too much respect for this woman.

I clear my throat, removing the top of my pumpkin and placing the light inside. "And I selfishly want to read your fantasies about me because it's only something you can write. Can't really put a price on that."

She does the same.

"Okay, now close your eyes," I say, moving to the switch and flicking off the lights. We're in darkness other than the warm glow that's leaking from our carved gourds. I move beside her.

"Are your eyes closed?" she asks as I steal another glance at her pretty face.

"They are now," I tell her. "Now, on the count of three we'll open our eyes."

We count down together, then twist our pumpkins around.

Autumn giggles when she sees my buck-toothed, different-sized-eyes pumpkin. Then I see our initials in hers with hearts surrounding them. The fake candles shine bright enough light for me to see her.

"Okay, you win."

"Yes." She looks up at me and I almost fall into her trance.

Fall I Want **159**

"Food," I say, lifting her chin, not daring to slide my lips across hers again. But fuck, I want to.

I step back. "Pizza time."

I cut slices and put them on plates, then we carry them to the living room, leaving our pumpkins to cast their shadows in the kitchen.

"There is a remote on the table at the end," I tell her.

She snatches it up and clicks on the ultra large TV that takes up a huge portion of the wall above the mantel.

"Pick something," I tell her, taking a bite.

"Oh, what about this?" She stops on one of the Friday the 13th movies.

"Works for me." We're close enough that our legs touch, but she doesn't move away from me.

"Jason is the hottest," she mutters between bites. "Classic slashers are my thing."

"Really? I'd have guessed you're more of a Hallmark fall festival lover."

"Pfft. No. Freddie. Jason. Chuckie. Every September and October, I have a list of horror films I can't go a season without seeing. It's one of my secret obsessions and has been since I was a young teenager. Some girls cancel plans because they have to wash their hair. I have cult classics to watch."

She makes me smile. "Which is your favorite?"

"That's like forcing a parent to choose their favorite kid," she explains.

"You love horror and write romance. You're sunshine and darkness all rolled into one," I say.

"A good way to describe me."

The first scene opens with two men walking through a cemetery, carrying lanterns as violins screech.

"The music makes it creepier," she says, covering her mouth as she speaks.

Jason's grave is shown and the two guys dig as lightning flashes in the background. Thunder crashes in the distance on the television and in real life. The suspense builds as the guy asks his friend for a crowbar, and just as he lifts the casket lid, Autumn screams at the top of her lungs and grabs at my waist.

"Fuck!" I drop my slice of pizza and it smacks onto the floor, cheese side down, as she loses her shit with laughter.

"Aww, I'm sorry!" She chuckles. "I'll clean it up."

My heart races. "You scared the shit out of me."

"Are you ticklish?" She grabs my waist again and I wiggle away.

"Don't tell a soul," I warn, squirming, laughing, but also avoiding her hands.

Her face softens. "You were into it. I appreciate that."

"I'll get you back," I tell her, just as lightning reanimates Jason. "When you *least* expect it."

"Can't wait. I enjoy the thrill. Love to feel my heart pumping. Reminds me I'm alive," she admits, placing her fingers on the pulse in my neck. I lean over, stealing a bite of her pizza. I notice a bit of marinara on the corner of her mouth and stop to wipe my thumb across it, then lick it off my finger as she watches.

"Mm."

She moves closer to me and the mood in the room shifts. It grows intense as she meets my eyes.

"I want you," she whispers.

"We've had too much to drink," I say, studying her perfect, parted lips that beg for me.

Her eyes flutter closed and she waits. "Don't you want me?"

"It's the tequila talking, I promise."

"Answer the question or remove a piece of clothing," she states.

Autumn is beautiful, with long dark lashes and high cheekbones. Her tongue darts out and I want to capture it.

"Pumpkin." I place my thumb on her chin and lift her face, giving myself a better view of this gorgeous woman. I close my eyes, our mouths only inches apart, and contemplate crossing the imaginary line I've drawn as electricity soars.

I want to. Fuck.

We wouldn't stop, though, but it's hard to ignore the magic swirling between us, pulling us closer.

The attraction streams between us, and at this point of the night, if a line were crossed, we'd fully lose control.

If we're going to be together, it needs to be without lost inhibitions. Without excuses. Without the worry of consent. No regrets afterward.

Somehow, I fight the magnetic force that yanks me toward her.

She's hypnotic, and I almost fall under her spell. It's a recipe for either disaster or heartbreak. Maybe both. One of us has to be logical, and right now, I hate that it's me.

"I'm really sorry." My voice drops an entire octave as I move to her ear and breathe her in. "It's not rejection, it's respect. I promise." I run my fingers through her soft dark waves and gently tug. "I'm sorry," I say again before I stand, remove my shirt and toss it in the oversized chair.

I walk to the kitchen with my cock so rock hard that it aches. I give myself a minute, trying to calm down, knowing I could be a man-whore monster. Without a doubt, I could fuck Autumn right there on the couch and pretend like nothing happened the next day. My ex predicted I would sleep with tons of women after our breakup, almost as if she wished for it so she'd feel validated for cheating on me with my best friend.

After I adjust the monster in my pants, I grab several napkins and clean up the pizza smashed on the floor. I throw it away, then return, putting some space between us.

We speak in unison.

"Go ahead," I say.

"You first," she says.

"If I didn't care about you, I'd fuck you right now."

She laughs. "It's fine. I'm used to rejection."

"You're not fling material. You're the type of woman that men want forever with."

"Even you?"

"Even me." I'm not afraid to admit it. She deserves that at least.

Autumn looks away from me.

"And if we *ever* cross that line, it won't be when we're drunk." I grab her chin, forcing her to look at me. "Understand?"

She nods. "If you're one of those guys whose dick doesn't work when you drink, I get it."

I scoff. "I'd fucking break you."

"Hm. Guess we'll never know." Her gaze slides down to my bulging cock.

I give her a smirk, catching her as she gulps.

"Actually, I retract that statement," she says.

"Oh, I know." I move my attention back to the food and movie. My mind isn't on anything other than Autumn as she steals glances at me. I'm glad I'm seated because that sexy-as-fuck expression on her face makes me weak in the knees.

When we're finished eating, I grab our dishes and put them in the sink.

I return to the couch, sitting close, and she leans her head against me. I lift my arm, allowing her to rest on me, and we lean back together, watching TV. Halfway through, my eyes grow heavy, and I'm relaxed with Autumn in my arms.

I don't know how much time passes, but next thing I know, she's waking me.

"Zane," she whispers. "I think we fell asleep."

I grin, tucking loose strands of her hair behind her ear. "You're comfortable."

"You are," she says, yawning, but neither of us moves.

"Shall I call you a ride?" I ask, glancing at the clock. It's just past midnight. "Unfortunately, I'm not in the position to drive you home."

"Let me text Huber." She holds out her arms to balance, then laughs as she walks to the kitchen.

A few minutes pass and she returns to me on the couch. "He's not doing rideshare because of the rain. Apparently, the conditions are unsafe."

I meet her eyes. "I guess we're having a sleepover."

She immediately smiles.

"You can have my bed," I offer.

"And where will you sleep?"

I pat the cushion next to me. "Right here."

CHAPTER 17

Autumn

He stands, holding out his hand to me. "I'll tuck you in."

We take the stairs together and turn down the long hallway to the double Gothic doors, then I walk inside. Zane pushes the blankets down for me and I sit on the edge of the mattress.

"One second," I tell him, going to his closet and grabbing something out of my pocket. I keep it tight in my hand and move directly in front of him.

His brows are lifted as he watches me. "Happy birthday," I tell him, opening my palm and offering him my four-leaf clover.

He gives me a wide smile, showing his perfect teeth. "You remembered?"

"Of course. I found that when I was a kid and my mom had it laminated for me. It feels right for you to have it. I hope it brings you all the luck in the world."

"Autie. I can't take this."

"You can. I thought about what I could give the man who has everything. It's something money can never buy."

He wraps his arms around me and holds me against his chest. I inhale his bare skin. "Thank you. I'll treasure it for the rest of my life."

"Good. I didn't know how to sneak a cupcake in my pocket for you to have at midnight."

"Tomorrow, we'll have cake," he tells me, stepping aside, allowing me to crawl into his bed. The sheets are cold.

"Good night," he says, flicking off the main light and turning on the lamp.

"You can stay," I say, glancing up at him.

"Don't worry about me. The couch is super comfortable. I've fallen asleep on it once per day since I arrived. Plus, there are three extra bedrooms. This house has plenty of places for me to sleep."

"It's not that. It's just . . ."

"Please tell me the horror movie queen isn't scared." With a half grin, he shoves his hands into his pockets and I try not to admire his shirtless body.

Instead, I grab one of his fluffy pillows and toss it at him, but he's fast with his reflexes and catches it.

"Fine. I am! I don't want to stay here by myself in this big ole house knowing there is a ghost wandering around. Even if it's friendly."

Just as he opens his mouth to speak, the bedroom door snaps shut behind him. He glances at it over his shoulder and I grow more creeped out with each passing second. I nearly jump out of my skin.

"What the hell?" I whisper, my blood pumping faster as my adrenaline spikes. "*Please*, don't leave me."

I meet his eyes and his expression softens. Three steps later, he's sitting next to me on the mattress. "The doors are heavy, and if they're not closed, the draft in the house does that. It happens every day."

"Or maybe it's a sign that you shouldn't go?"

He sighs. "If it will make you more comfortable, but you have to promise to stay on your side of the bed and keep your hands to yourself."

I make a face. "You expect me to control dream me?"

"You'll have to or I'll move to the couch."

"Fine." I huff, closing my eyes tight and pressing my pointer fingers into my temples.

"What are you doing?"

I meet his gaze. "Telling my tequila drunk subconscious to behave, per your instruction."

The sound of his laughter is my reward.

"It's a good reminder for both of us," he says.

"I love to snuggle. You're denying me the best night's sleep."

"I'll deal with that," he tells me. "Which side do you prefer?"

"This one."

He slides under the blanket, letting me choose. He turns off the lamp and I stare up at the ceiling, noticing the autumn and winter constellations painted up above.

He lies back and stares up at them too. "It's incredible, isn't it? It almost seems real."

I turn to face him, the moonlight washing the room gray. "Falling in love with me wouldn't be the worst thing to happen to you, would it?"

"No. Losing you would," he says. "Good night."

Zane rolls over onto his side, his back toward me, and I twist away from him. I stare at the blank wall. Key moments from tonight are on replay and I can't get him out of my head, especially when he's this close. I inhale deeper, holding my breath at the top, then slowly exhaling.

"Go to sleep," he mutters in his low, sexy rumble, and I smile, knowing he's still awake too.

What is he thinking about? Me? Because he's the only thing on my mind right now.

"Hold me and I will," I say. "Ten minutes max and then you can go back to hugging the edge. I promise. It's just been . . . *so long*." It comes out desperate.

He stays frozen.

When I'm sure he's denied me, Zane moves toward me. He nuzzles his nose into my hair and gently wraps his arm around my waist. At first I tense, but I quickly relax against his firm body. I feel safe in his arms, loving how warm, rigid, and protective he is.

"Better?" he growls in my ear.

I arch against him, feeling how hard he is. "Mm. Yes."

The little devil that tequila creates dances on my shoulder.

"Behave," he mutters in my ear, his breath causing goosebumps to trail over me.

I suck in air, squeezing my thighs together, wishing for relief as I arch against him.

"Don't test me," he warns, lightly peppering kisses along my neck. "Or your payback will be a bitch."

"It's a game I'll beat you at every fucking time," I whisper, reaching between our bodies, rubbing my palm against his cock that I know would destroy me.

"Autumn." He grips my wrists tight, positioning himself behind me. I'm brought back to being in his library. He restrained me in the same way, tight, unmoving, until I was completely under his command.

My body is on fire and my nipples are hard. I desperately need relief and my breasts rise and fall with anticipation.

"You don't want me?" I ask.

"I'm scared I won't let you go," he admits. His hand snakes down my stomach and rests between my legs, adding the tiniest bit of pressure.

I stop breathing as I slowly buck my hips upward, feeling like I'll come by a single touch.

"Mm," he says, pleased. "You're so fucking wet for me."

"Please," I desperately pant out, nearly begging as I wait in anticipation for him to make his move. I'm too impatient as my heart rate ticks furiously in my neck. I swear he can hear the *thump thump thump* in my chest. Sober me wants a relationship; drunk me begs to be fucked by this man, leaving me unable to stand for a week. And based on the size of him that's currently pressed against me, that might actually be the case.

"The chase is the fun part." Then he moves his hand from me and creates some space, still keeping his arm roped over me, allowing me to feel how hard he is.

My mind spins and I don't know how much time passes, but I watch the moonshine travel across the room.

When I think it's safe, I roll onto my back. His strong hand stays resting against my bare stomach. My body sings with warmth knowing a few inches up and he could touch my peaked nipple. I stay still for another five minutes as I steal glances at Zane, checking that he's asleep and his breathing is steady.

Then I carefully slide my hand down my stomach, making sure I don't touch him, as I slip my fingers between my legs. I'm soaked and so damn horny that I have to do this, knowing he's right here, in the flesh. My eyes flutter closed as I slowly rub circles on my needy clit. My heart rate increases as I dip a finger inside, wishing it were him. Imagining it's him.

I bite down on my bottom lip as my muscles tense and I return to my needy bud. My pussy clenches and I know I won't be able to hold it back. I keep going, desperate, worked up and teetering on the edge. I keep a methodical pace that doesn't cause a lot of movement.

His fingers barely move across my stomach and it sends me over. I come violently and it's a goddamn miracle I didn't scream out his name. I feel as if I've been catapulted to a different dimension, and I see stars as my cunt pulsates with pleasure. I exhale a pant and he stirs.

I slam my eyes shut, staying frozen. He wasn't awake, his breathing was too steady and his face too relaxed. When I glance at him, I swear I see the ghost of a smirk on his lips. It's my imagination playing tricks on me like it's been doing.

Zane rolls onto his side and I follow, scooting close, pressing my breasts against his back. The only thing that's between us is the thin material of the shirt he gave me. Carefully, I wrap my arm around him, inhaling his scent that's a mix of pine and mountain breeze. Just as I'm falling asleep, I think I hear him mutter, "*My good fucking girl.*"

And those words have me tempted to do it all over again.

CHAPTER 18

Autumn

*I*t takes me a few seconds to remember where I am.

Hollow Manor.

In Zane Alexander's gigantic bed surrounded by windows.

The large T-shirt is up over my boob and I'm sprawled across the mattress like I'm at home. I reach over to his side and find it's cold to the touch. I'm not sure why I feel disappointed. I sit up, enjoying the view and readjusting my clothes.

I'm in awe that he gets to wake up to this daily. I can only imagine it with the snow-capped mountains and the slopes right outside the windows.

The visibility is fantastic on the mountain today and I can see the tall peaks in the distance. A smile touches my lips as my hand rubs across the silky sheets, and I lie back, staring at the constellations painted on the high ceiling, thinking about last night. He had me so turned on that I had to handle it myself. No more tequila around him needs to be something I enforce in the future.

However, I'm not ashamed. Imagining him pretending to be asleep as I got off to thoughts of him has me squeezing my thighs together again. Proof that he's buried deep under my skin already.

Had I taken one more shot, I would've begged for him, but I respect his no. Sometimes a girl just has to take care of herself.

Before I can think about anything else, my bladder screams out in protest. When I stand, I'm shocked I don't have a hangover, considering how much I drank. He wasn't joking. I actually feel great and *alive*.

My feet touch the cool black marble with golden flecks that look like fairy dust. This house feels magical and whimsical, with its hidden details and quirks. I could spend weeks in this house and never be able to take it all in. Everywhere I look, I notice something different. Care went into building and designing the manor. That much I know.

After relieving myself, I wash my hands, wishing I could brush my teeth. I glance at the leather toiletry bag with golden zippers and read *Tom Ford* in tiny letters, then I unzip it. Inside are normal things.

I open the cabinet under the sink and see an unopened package of toothbrushes. I swipe the orange one then open and squeeze a line of the spearmint toothpaste that I've smelled on his breath onto the end.

As I look in the mirror, a smile touches my lips, because for the first time in two years, I woke up somewhere other than my bed in my loft. I tuck hair behind my ears, trying to look somewhat presentable before going downstairs.

The curse feels broken, like today is a new beginning. The thrill of that rushes through me.

I walk out of his room, taking in the space and the sunlight through the windows. It shines against the paintings, naturally spotlighting them on the walls. Zane was right. The house is gorgeous in the daylight with personal touches that are often overlooked in spaces. At night, it's a totally different vibe, a little spooky when the lights are off, but I like them both.

I slide my hand down the smooth railing of the stairway, and at the bottom I see Zane in the kitchen. He's standing with a dark-haired woman, laughing. He hugs her tight. I stop, not wanting to intrude, and try to sneak away. As if he senses my presence, he looks up and pins me in place with his gaze.

His eyes trail down my body then back up to my face, and I notice the fire in his eyes as a sexy smile meets his lips.

"Autumn. There you are."

Escaping is now completely out of the question.

He lets go of the woman and I walk toward them, my palms sweaty. Is this his ex? The woman he said would never take him back. He waves me closer and I wish I could read his mind, so I could learn who she is. The last thing I want is a weird confrontation.

"I was just talking about you," Zane offers, then turns to the woman, who's watching us.

When our eyes meet, I immediately know who she is—Zane's younger sister—the girl I played with at the pumpkin patch over two decades ago. The last time I saw her she was with her mom and older brother. But I don't remember any details about them, just her.

My heart hurts knowing what happened after, not able to imagine how that must feel to lose a parent at such a young age. I can't comprehend it.

"I'm Harper, or Lucy, although, I don't go by that name any longer."

She holds out her arms and squeezes me in a tight hug. "I have very fond memories riding the carnival rides with you on bracelet weekend and playing a lot of games." She releases me.

"I think those pink bears we won are still at my parents' place somewhere," I say with a laugh.

"Really? That's awesome."

The two of us became best friends and then I never saw her again. The rumors about Hollow Manor crept up soon afterward, and I stupidly helped perpetuate them.

Zane focuses back on Harper and speaks up. "You should hear the story about the house and how we were all murdered in here. Now three ghosts haunt the quarters."

It's creepy how he easily strolls through my thoughts.

"Honestly, Mom would've loved that."

"That's what I said." He grins, and it's true happiness. It's a good look, one I hope stays.

"Ready to tell me what you're doing here?" he asks his sister.

"I came to tell you happy birthday, of course. I couldn't bear the idea of you being here alone on your special day. I wanted to surprise you and I brought your favorite cake." She glances at the black box on the counter. "The fact it made it here without me swiping my finger across the chocolate icing once is a miracle."

Harper glances at me and her eyes trail over Zane's name on my chest. I know how this looks, and I'm totally okay with it.

"But," she continues, "it seems like you didn't actually need me."

"Just ask," Zane finally says. "You want to."

"Okay. Are you two together?"

Zane wraps his arm around me and pulls me into him. I study his mouth before meeting his eyes.

"We're fake dating." There is heat behind his gaze and words. I could kiss him right here, right now, in the early morning sunlight, because when he looks at me like that, the world fades away.

"Uhh, I see nothing fake about this," Harper mutters, focusing on her brother. "Please tell me this means you're attending Dad's wedding."

"Only if Autumn joins me."

"And?" She turns to me, smiling wide, giving me the same doe-eyed expression as Blaire and Julie. She's already paired us together too. I can see it.

"I've agreed," I explain. "I'm not backing out now."

She laughs and interlocks her fingers. "I can't wait to see everyone's faces when you two walk in. Heads will spin."

"You think so?" Zane asks.

Harper confidently nods. "You *actually* found your forever person."

He holds up his hand. "Okay, you can stop now."

"The only reason I am is because I don't want to embarrass you in front of your future wife," she admits. "But during your wedding reception, I want you both to tell everyone at the toast that I predicted it, okay?"

Zane playfully rolls his eyes.

"You'll tie the knot before the end of the year," she adds. "I'll bet either of you."

"Confidence runs in the family?" I ask Zane.

"You have no idea." He brings me closer to him. My stomach growls loud enough for him to hear. "Hungry?"

I feel the carved ridges of his muscles through the T-shirt, and his breath grows ragged. "Starving."

"Now I feel bad for showing up unannounced. I messed up the morning after."

"No, no. It's not like that at all, trust me. No lines have been crossed." He glances at me, and I know the word *yet* hangs on the tip of his tongue. It pops into my mind like a whisper.

"Regardless," she says, grabbing her designer handbag from the counter. "I think I'll give you two some privacy and head to the resort. Can we meet for dinner later?"

I smile with a nod and Zane agrees, but only after I did.

"Great. I'll see you both tonight." Just like that, Harper wiggles her fingers then walks out the front door with her purse over her shoulder. "See you later, lovebirds."

When the door clicks closed, he lets out a sigh. "I'm sorry about that. I didn't know she was coming."

"No, it's fine. It's your birthday. You should hang out with your sister, even if she has jokes."

"About that," he says. "She wasn't kidding."

"Wait, she *really* believes we're getting married? Is she psychic or something?"

"Clairvoyant is the official term. I've seen it in action. The things she has predicted in my life are creepy."

"Like what?"

"Meeting you."

A chill runs over my arms.

"Right down to the detail of me forcing you to be my friend."

"What?" I study him. "What else happens?"

He smiles and shrugs. "I can't tell you. Unfortunately, you'll have to get your own prediction from her. It's just how it works."

I take a step forward and he places his hand against the small of my back. My face softens. "Do we end up together?"

"Yes. We get our happily ever after," he whispers, swallowing hard.

Between my dreams about him and his sister's premonition, I'm slightly freaked out. What if there is something deeper at play here?

"You believe her," he says. "I can see it on your face."

"What if it's fate? Two people shouldn't fuck around with that."

"How about we just take it one day at a time and see what happens?"

"Okay," I say, needing a distraction because I'm too lost in my head replaying the invisible string that has forced us together this past month. There are too many unexplainable things that have happened between us.

Zane lifts the lid to the cake. It smells sweet, and he swipes his finger across the icing before placing it in his mouth.

"How is it?"

"Delicious. Try it. The inside is strawberry cream. Best cake in the States."

I slide my finger across the soft sugar and taste it. Orgasmic—it's the only way to describe it, but the moan that releases from my throat does it for me.

His brow pops up. "Never been jealous of icing until now."

I chuckle. "It's yummy. But we should eat actual food."

I can't remember the last time I slept in, but I also haven't drunk tequila like that since I was in my early twenties. Yes, it's sleeping in, considering I'm up for work each day at four.

"Would you like to have breakfast with me? We can stop at your place so you can change into something more comfortable."

"And what if I wanted to show up wearing your clothes?"

"Do you?" He takes a step back, looking me over from head to toe. "I'm down for whatever you'd like to do."

My eyes slide down him. His head falls back with laughter. "Let's go eat."

"Let's," I say, and he rushes upstairs. Five minutes later, he's dressed, grabbing his keys and adjusting the baseball hat on his head. I snag my phone and then we leave.

I'm in awe, driving out of Hollow Manor in the morning. Fog floats and rolls across the road.

"Do you think Harper is right?" I ask as the gate slides open.

"I don't know." He glances over at me. "I just want your friendship. Nothing else. No expectations. Just me and you getting to know one another. Being each other's plus-one to the holiday stuff and having fun," he explains, making it sound simple.

"What if I meet the man of my dreams while we're pretending to be together?"

"The man of your dreams?" He kicks the Jeep into drive and we turn onto the main road that leads to town and his words aren't lost on me. "Bottom line is, I want you to do what makes you happy because that's what matters most."

He drops me off at my apartment and parks as I change into some leggings and a sweater, then I grab a baseball hat too. By the time I'm ready, he's crossing the street, meeting me on the sidewalk full of tourists.

The diner that serves the best breakfast is only four blocks away, so we walk. By some miracle, there are free tables when we enter. The host slides two laminated menus from the large stack of them then guides us to our table.

Zane's hand is on the small of my back as we move to the booth by the windows. All eyes are zeroed in on us and I look down, making sure there isn't something on me. I glance back at him and he pops his brows at me, smirking.

We slide in and sit across from one another. I read the menu, even though I don't need it.

"Is everyone staring?" I ask, scanning over the laminated paper.

"Yes," he says, not meeting my gaze.

"Do you know why?" I feel like there is a spotlight on our table.

"Who knows?" He shrugs. "It's like that everywhere I go."

Our server sets two mugs on the table and immediately fills them with coffee then leaves to give us time.

Zane shoots a wink to several older women beside us who giggle when he moves his attention back to me. The charisma he exudes without even trying. Damn. Men like him are why cults exist. I think I'd join.

"Did you just flirt?" I keep my voice low.

He licks his lips and opens his mouth, but before he can speak, it's time to place our order.

"An apple cinnamon waffle, bacon, and scrambled eggs."

Zane closes his menu. "I'll have the same."

When we're left alone, I get up and slide next to him. Instinctively, he wraps his arm around me and pulls me in close. "You smell amazing."

I smile, taking a hot sip of my coffee as his fingers trail against my skin. Goosebumps cover me and he glances down at them.

"Hm" is all he says.

"Autumn!" Mrs. Mooney yells, joining us. She grins wide. "Is this him?"

"I'm confused," I say, glancing at Zane.

"The man you had us put a love spell on. Alex?"

My face burns red.

"Actually, yes. It's a pleasure to meet you," Zane says, holding out his hand toward her. She gently takes it and he gives her a smile.

"Honey, he's cute. Total boyfriend material. I can't wait to tell your mama about him later tonight at our little shindig," she says.

"Mrs. Mooney," I say as my entire body catches on fire with embarrassment.

Zane chuckles beside me, picking up his cup of coffee. I can tell he's enjoying this conversation as I die a little inside.

I huff. "Please don't meddle. I want the right to tell my parents I'm with someone first."

"After last night, I think the whole town knows."

"What do you mean?" I ask, feeling like I don't have the full story.

She pulls out her cell phone, squinting as she types. Moments later, she turns and shows me the town's official private group on social media.

A picture of Zane and me kissing at the patch is pinned to the top. The text says: Someone add them to the Pumpkin King and Queen ballot.

I flick my finger down her screen and speed-read the comments. My name was dropped and everyone is calling Zane either Alexander or Alex.

I gasp. "This is bad. How do I get it removed?"

"You need to contact the admins."

Then I see the number of likes it has on it. Thousands.

"Anyway, I am gonna put you on the ballot. You'll be at the ball, right?"

"Yes," Zane says before I can even process, and Mrs. Mooney stands, wearing a large, toothy smile. "Our love spell worked!"

She walks away and I turn to him. "We have to go to my parents' house directly after breakfast."

"Why?"

"You have to meet my mom and dad before this spreads around town. I don't want them to think I've kept you a secret. They'll take it personally."

Our breakfast is slid in front of us in record time, considering how busy they are.

"Let's go, then. The last thing I want to do is piss off my future in-laws," he says, chuckling, picking up a crispy slice of bacon and biting into it.

CHAPTER 19

Zane

Knock. Knock. Knock.

Autumn lightly taps her fingers across the front door of the log cabin built on an adjacent mountain. A few hand-carved rocking chairs are on the porch and they look comfortable. Pumpkins line the railing along with autumn-inspired decorations.

No one answers and Autumn turns to me, glancing at the flowers in my hand with a grin. "They're probably in the back."

Her phone buzzes in her pocket and she reads a text message.

"The rumors are spreading," she says, showing me.

Julie
ALL HAIL THE PUMPKIN KING AND QUEEN!

Below it is the photo someone snapped of us making out on the park bench.

Autumn sighs. "By nightfall, we'll be the talk of the town."

"Great. Looks like our fake dating plan is in full effect." I grab her hand, gently pulling her back, spinning her toward me. Those walls that she's let fall are back in place. "What's going on? Tell me."

"This is happening fast."

She's right. I met her the first day of September and I already can't imagine a life without her in it.

"We can explain we're just friends," I offer. "No lies."

"After that photo was posted in the town group, no one will believe it, especially not my parents. I haven't dated anyone since Sebastian. I'm never caught kissing someone in public." She meets my eyes. "They'll think you're my forever person."

"I am." I chuckle and she playfully slaps me. I pull the four-leaf clover from my pocket. "I've got this. We'll be fine."

She glances at it and slowly smiles. "I bet you think this is a really stupid way to spend your birthday."

"There is nowhere else I'd rather be," I admit, glancing down at the picture of us on the phone. It was just us, and I replay the moment like a hazy dream.

She grabs my hand, pulling me from my thoughts, and leads me off the porch and around the house. In the backyard is a freestanding garage with the door open. Music drifts out of it as her parents dance and laugh.

I smile, seeing how in love they are, knowing this is the standard that Autumn stacks her relationships against.

"Mom, Dad," she says, crossing the grass as I match her stride.

They turn toward us, surprised, as they glance between us.

As soon as we're close I hand the bouquet to her mother. I required one stop in town before we drove over.

"My favorite," she says, smelling them. "Very thoughtful. Thank you."

"You're welcome."

"This is my *boyfriend*, Zane. He typically goes by Alexander," she says confidently. Hearing her call me that, like I belong to her, does something to me. By her tone, it sounds like she means it.

I thought she'd at least introduce us as friends. Their smiles widen as they glance between us.

"Nice to meet you, Alexander," her father says, and I catch the hint of a Southern accent. His handlebar mustache is intimidating, and I wouldn't be surprised if he rides a Harley around town during the summer months. As I take a step closer to shake his hand, I see the bike I imagined he'd ride. It has slick black paint, fat tires, and leather saddlebags on the back. It's the trophy in the room, surrounded by his neon signs. An outdoor pool table takes up the other half of the garage, along with a dartboard.

His grip is tight, his hands rough, and he oozes confidence. "I'm Daniel, but my buddies call me Danny. And this is my wife."

"Diane," she says in a friendly tone.

"It's an honor to meet you both," I say. "Truly."

"Welp, now you've all met. We can go," Autumn says, grabbing my hand, trying to escape.

"Whoa, whoa, whoa," her dad says. "Where are your manners, Autie? This is why we should've raised her in Texas. This attitude wouldn't exist."

"Would you like some tea?" her mom asks, quickly redirecting the conversation. Her smile and eyes are kind, just like Autumn's, who is a cookie-cutter version. They look alike with the same wavy hair, but her mom has slivers of gray.

"I'd love some tea," I offer, and Autumn lets out a tiny groan as her parents lead the way inside the house. In the back is a large kitchen with long windows that give a perfect view of the sunrise.

"Have a seat," Danny offers, and Autumn sits beside me as her mom places a kettle on the stove. Moments later, a plate of pumpkin-shaped sugar cookies are placed in the center of the table.

"You both help yourself," her mother basically demands, and we each take one.

She turns to Autumn. "How'd you and Mr. Dreamy meet?"

I chuckle and Autumn nearly chokes. "Mom."

"You told him, didn't you?"

"Yes, I know about him." I glance at her. "I walked into the coffee shop and Autumn took my breath away. Then I lied and said the coffee she made tasted like shit."

"Oh," her dad says. "Surprised she forgave you. She's very proud of her barista skills."

"It took some coaxing, maybe a little threatening," I say as she watches me. "But yeah, I knew right then and there."

"The same thing happened to me with Diane," her dad says. "Except Diane was a mechanic. When she slid from under that cherry-red 1970 Chevrolet Chevelle with grease on her cheek, I knew she was the woman I'd marry. She brushed loose strands from her face with the back of her hand and looked up at me with big brown eyes. When she smiled? Damn. The world stopped spinning. It was fate," her dad says, smiling as he reminisces. "Always said it was like magic."

Autumn gulps.

I smirk, and soon after, the kettle whistles. Diane pours tea into our cups and offers sugar cubes.

Her mom looks between us and laughs. "When are you two getting married?"

"Please," Autumn whispers. "We're trying each other on. That's it. Don't rush us."

"I predict we'll be married within a year," I say, and Autumn's cheeks heat. "If you allow it, of course."

"*Your* prediction?" Autumn playfully rolls her eyes, knowing Harper said it.

I pick up my tea and shoot her a wink. "Yep."

"Shall I put it in my calendar?" Autumn playfully pulls her phone from her pocket, then opens her app and types something into it. "Married by Zane's birthday."

"I look forward to the notification that will pop up," I tell her, wondering if Harper's prediction will be true. A part of me hopes it is. I can almost imagine the day when that reminder pops up, and she's my wife. A smile touches my lips.

It could happen. Anything is possible. At least that's been my experience since visiting Cozy Hollow.

"Oh, today is your birthday?" Autumn's mom asks. "Happy birthday!"

Her dad says the same.

"Thank you. We had breakfast this morning and plan to have dinner and cake tonight."

"That sounds like fun," her mom says as I sit in the kitchen and meet this beautiful woman's parents like she's mine.

When our cups are empty, my phone vibrates. I slip it out enough to see who it is.

My father's name flashes across the screen and my brows furrow. I reject the call. A minute later, it buzzes again and I hold down the side button, turning it off.

"Do you need to take that?" Autumn asks.

"No, I'm fine," I say, but she doesn't take her eyes off me.

"Well, it was great meeting you. Please join us for supper sometime soon," her mom says.

"He's *very* busy," Autumn offers.

"Actually, my calendar is clear. Any time, any day, just name it," I say as Autumn stands. I follow her lead.

"This was fun." Autumn hugs her parents and then they pull me into a hug, too.

"Don't be a stranger. Either of you," her father says.

"Okay," Autumn tells them with a grin, and I smile with a nod.

She takes my hand, pulling me down the hallway toward the front of the house.

The space is cozy and peaceful. The living room opens up to high, vaulted ceilings, and a gigantic brick fireplace stacks up the wall. Pictures of the mountain cabins in snow are hung around and an oversized rug is splashed across the dark, hardwood floors. Autumn glances back at me before she twists the knob to the door.

When we're outside, I stop walking and she turns to face me.

"Do you have somewhere to be?" I ask, noticing how she's in a rush to leave. Her parents noticed too.

"I want to go running," she tells me. "It helps me clear my mind. I have a lot to think about."

"Like?"

"Do you believe Harper is right?" she blurts out. "Stop avoiding the question."

I smirk. "Pumpkin, I could meet another woman tonight, the one I'm supposed to be with. I don't know. It might not be you."

To be clear, the thought of that hurt my fucking heart.

Her brows furrow and I think she's offended.

"Do you want it to be?" I ask.

"I . . . Uh."

"Until you know the answer to that question we'll take it one day at a time." I walk toward her, placing my hand on her shoulder, leading her to the Jeep. "Okay?"

She walks to the passenger side and I open the door for her. She climbs in and I stand in the doorway, then reach over and buckle her seat belt for her, but she's lost in her head.

We drive down the mountain with the windows down and the music plays low on the radio. She twists her long hair around her fingers, revealing the softness of her neck and her sun-kissed shoulder.

I find a parking spot a few blocks from her place. The traffic is too thick to pass through quickly.

"I want your sister to read me, or whatever it is she does. I want a road map for us, too."

"Is that what this is about?" I burst into laughter. "Scared I have the upper hand?"

"Yep." She smirks, and before she can reach for the handle, I get out and open the door for her.

"What about your dreams? That has to be some sort of advantage."

"It's not the same."

We make our way across the street and each time our fingers brush together, tiny sparks flood through me.

"Thanks for meeting my parents," she says.

"They were amazing. You're lucky to have them."

She nods and smiles.

"Dinner tonight with my sister," I say, and we awkwardly stand in front of one another. I take a step forward and hold out my arms, and we exchange a friendly hug.

She turns and walks up the stairs. I glance over my shoulder at her and smile before she goes inside.

On the way back to the Jeep, I turn on my phone. After I shove it back into my pocket, it buzzes. It's my dad's number. Part of me wants to reject it and send him to voicemail like I have since I left the city. Today is different.

"Zane? Did you actually answer?"

"How can I help you?" I breathe out.

"Happy birthday!" he says.

"Thanks."

"Where are you? I've been worried."

"Have you?" I ask.

"Don't act like an asshole. I called to check on you."

"Sure you didn't call to confirm I'd be at the wedding?"

"You're my best man. It would hurt if you weren't there."

The lump in my throat grows three sizes too big and the silence lingers for a few seconds as I watch the leaves roll across the ground. My mother would want me to attend, even though I don't feel like my father was there when I needed him the most. We grieve in our own ways.

"What happened between you and Celine wasn't right, and I hate that she's still around and you have to be subjected to her presence. I don't support their behavior, but son, listen to me when I say she did you a favor. I want better for you than—"

"Please, stop. Okay? I'll be there."

He lets out a sigh of relief.

"But," I blurt, "I want you to ensure that me and my date will be left alone. If my boundaries are crossed, I'll leave without saying a word to anyone."

"Whatever you need."

I unlock the Jeep and climb inside.

"Great. I can't wait for you to meet my girlfriend." It feels right calling her my girlfriend. *Mine.*

"You're seeing someone? This is news to me."

"I'm not discussing my private life with you." I end the call using the same words he gave me when I learned he was marrying my ex–best friend's mother.

He can do what he wants. I'll support my father because I love him, but there is a lot of hurt I haven't worked through. Therapy has helped some.

Once I'm home, I clean up the mess in the backyard, then go upstairs for a shower.

On the counter rests an orange toothbrush and it makes me smile.

The hot stream pounds against me and I close my eyes, succumbing to it. Remembering how Autumn's body felt molded to mine, knowing she was touching herself next to me.

My cock begged me to take her right there. She wanted me to, nearly asked me, but I know sex complicates things, blinds people. I won't cross a line unless we're sober. No excuses. No regrets.

The sound of her greedy pants plays on repeat and I grab myself, stroking. Goddamn.

I place my palm on the tile wall as I allow thoughts of her to flood me. I race to the end, my balls tightening as my breaths grow ragged. She meticulously teased her little clit until she spilled over.

"Fuck," I growl out, steadying myself, picking up the pace. My eyes slam shut and the orgasm quickly rips through me. My heart nearly beats out of my chest as I fall from my high. Once I catch my breath, I step out of the shower and wrap a towel around me.

After I dress, I go downstairs with Autumn in the center of my mind. This morning, when I woke up with her wrapped in my arms, I didn't want to leave the bed. However, a knock on the door forced me away. By some miracle, she didn't wake up.

My phone is on the counter where I left it and I notice a few notifications on the front, all texts from my sister.

Harper

> Is it okay if I invite someone to dinner tonight so I won't be an awkward third wheel?

Zane

> Feel free. Meet us at the resort restaurant at eight. Reservations will need to be updated.

The resort has a five-star restaurant run by a world-famous English chef. He's known for his assortment of puddings and beef Wellington.

Harper

> Fantastic. Btw . . . I like her a lot.

> **Zane**
> I do too.

Harper
See you soon! Hope you enjoy your cake.

> **Zane**
> Thanks for coming out. Love ya, sis.

Harper
Love you too.

I make a few phone calls and set up a limo to pick Autumn up for dinner. Tonight, I want her to have the time of her life. Maybe it will be a birthday I'll never forget. I guess we'll see.

CHAPTER 20

Autumn

I've really, really gotta go," I say to Julie and Blaire. We're on a three-way call and have chatted for the past hour while I got ready for tonight. Talking to them helped calm my nerves because I didn't know what to say when a Dolce & Gabbana dress showed up at my place this afternoon, not to mention the designer heels. Everything is in my size, and I'm not sure how Zane knew. Maybe it's a lucky guess, or he's paid more attention than I give him credit for.

"Promise to keep us updated," Julie says.

"I will," I tell them.

"You better," Blaire warns. "No details left out, either!"

"Okay, okay! Bye!" I grab the tube of red lipstick and drop it in the wristlet that was also gifted. It's just large enough to fit that and my phone. Right now Julie and Blaire are both living vicariously through me. If the tables were turned, I'd do the same.

Quickly, I glance out the window and see a slick black limo with flashers blocking the street. Vehicles stack behind it and some blow their horns.

"Shit," I whisper, then take one last look at myself in the full-length mirror in the corner of my room. The dress fits me like a glove, low cut and backless, leaving nothing to the imagination.

My nerves get the best of me, but I flip my bouncy, curled hair over my shoulders and take in a deep breath. After the quickest pep talk I can manage, I leave my loft.

As I descend the stairs, tourists stop and stare. My cheeks heat as a few teenagers take pictures of me. I'm getting adult prom vibes, and the driver waits for me by the door.

The door of the stretch limo opens and Zane gets out. He floats across the sidewalk, his eyes laser focused on me, and I can't help but smile. How is this my life?

Zane reaches out, giving me his hand before my high heel touches the ground. He leads me to the car, opening the door for me as my heart nearly flutters out of my chest. I take a step back, admiring him in his stark black suit and tie. His smoldering eyes stare at me like he's Mr. Dreamy in the flesh.

"Hi, beautiful," he says, looking like a fantasy.

"You're here," I say, sliding inside. I expected to meet him there.

"I couldn't wait to see you." He joins me, closing the door. Moments later, we zoom away.

"I've never met a man who's admitted that."

His brow quirks up. "You could've stopped that sentence after *man*."

A chuckle escapes me. "Unfortunately true."

I swim in his deep blues as he pours us both a glass of champagne. "You look . . . *gorgeous*."

"Thank you for saying that." A blush hits my cheek and I glance away from him, not able to maintain the intense eye contact for too long. "I can't remember the last time I went out."

"That changes now."

"What shall we toast to tonight?" I swirl the golden liquid around the edges of the crystal.

"To your exes."

My brows furrow

He continues, "For not realizing what they had."

We lightly tap our rims together and sip the sweet bubbly as my body blazes from the inside out. "Do you mean that?"

"Fuck yes I do," he states. "I speak what I mean, Pumpkin. Especially with things like that. Who has time for bullshit?"

"Is this real?" I sit in the moment, waiting to be ripped away and to wake up in my bed. Instead, we continue down the street in the back of the stretch limo.

"This time you're living the dream." He chuckles. Since meeting him, my life has been a whirlwind and my head is spinning.

Is this . . . is he too good to be true? I try not to think about that.

"It's that déjà vu feeling again," I admit.

By his expression, my admission pleases him. "Can't wait to read more about it."

I haven't forgotten his offer, but I also haven't shared it with my friends, either. It all seems a little unreal and will take some processing. Considering I've kept a journal with summaries of all my Mr. Dreamy fantasies, it shouldn't be too hard.

"If I can do it," I say, not completely convinced yet.

"You can." There is zero doubt in his tone.

"I'll try." That's all I can do. "No guarantees."

When the limo arrives at the resort, he slides out of the car, holding out his hand for me. I take it, my cheeks heating when I look up into his eyes. Once on my feet, I realize I'm a tiny bit tipsy, which I appreciate because it calms my nerves.

The gigantic fountain dances in the distance and the cool breeze whips around me, cooling me off. Which is something I need, considering my body is on fire. I glance back at Zane and notice him studying me from behind. He moves forward, his fingertips gently trailing down the center of my back, causing every inch of me to fully ignite. My skin singes where he touches and I don't want him to stop.

A man strolls past us and stares at me, but I ignore it.

Zane blocks me from view. "I don't like anyone looking at you like that."

I turn to him. "Jealous?"

"Mm. No. I know who you belong to."

I meet his eyes and I swear they darken. "Already staking claim?"

"Fuck yes. I absolutely am." He's confident, and I'd be lying if I said I didn't like the thought of that, of him taking ownership of me. Is that the champagne talking?

I grin, turning back to the fountain, and we finish watching the water and light show. It goes off every hour when the weather is nice. As a kid, I remember begging my parents to drive me to the mountaintop so I could watch it. It's comparable to the one at the Bellagio. One day I'll visit Vegas.

"Do you want men lusting after you like that?" he asks.

"After my dry spell, I don't mind. It's somewhat empowering, but I know it won't lead to anything." I turn and face him. "I'm kissable, just not fuckable enough. Everyone chickens out."

He focuses on me. "I actually love to hear that."

I groan. "It's been two years. I thought by now I'd have found someone who wants to spend time with me. I'm convinced I'm unwanted." My truths spill out.

He eliminates the space between us and tucks hair behind my ear. "Your feelings are valid, but I don't think that's true."

"I've tried."

He narrows his eyes. "Have you? If I recall, I had to threaten you with jail to befriend me. I can't imagine how you'd act had I mentioned wanting to date you. Actually, I can. I bet you would've told me to get fucked."

A small smile touches my lips. "Probably."

"You're fucking adorable." He boops my nose, then wraps his arm around me. "Let's go inside."

There is an unexplainable spark with a deeply rooted sense of understanding.

"Tell me one of your secrets," I say as we stroll down the sidewalk that leads to the five-star restaurant.

"Hmm," he ponders, glancing over at me. "You're the first person I've ever shared a soul connection with."

"A soul connection," I repeat. "That's one way to describe it."

There is an invisible rope that always pulls us together. The odd sense of familiarity, like I've always known him. We're strangers, I remind myself. Perfect strangers.

"It's undeniable," he admits. It's not one sided, even if I try to convince myself otherwise.

Butterflies flutter in my belly when he steals a glance. I don't know what to say, so we stroll in the comfortable silence.

Ground lights illuminate the path toward the restaurant and it creates a romantic ambience as music plays overhead. Muffled chatter surrounds us as couples walk in and out of the building. The lodge requires reservations months in advance, and most people who dine here come for special occasions.

Flames dance in the large lanterns on both sides of the entrance. When we're close, a man in a tuxedo opens the door and we're escorted inside. The room is low-lit, and a woman dressed in black greets us. Her eyes slide up and down Zane. I don't like the way she lusts over him, and I fully understand his earlier reaction when the roles were reversed.

"Hello," she says with a brow arched at him. She acts as if I'm invisible and looks straight past me. "Reservation?"

"For Alexander." Zane's tone is flat. Unamused.

"Alexander," the woman repeats, returning to the podium to open a leather-bound book. She speaks to him like he's a tourist.

Over the years, I've only eaten here a few times. Two-hundred-dollar meals aren't something I can afford on my barista budget, but the food is well worth it.

"*Zane Alexander,*" he snaps with annoyance in his tone, and I see recognition flash in her eyes as he gives me his full attention. I smile as he twirls a strand of my hair around his finger. "You're so pretty."

Moments later, when she approaches, her attitude is pleasant, but he's stand-offish and pretends like she doesn't exist. He makes her wait for two solid minutes before acknowledging her.

Once he's satisfied, he turns to her, narrowing his eyes, then checks his watch.

"Did you have issues finding it?" This man is intimidating.

"No, Mr. Alexander. Please, accept my apologies," she offers.

"If we could be seated now, I'd appreciate it," he snaps.

She fumbles with the menus as she leads the way.

"After you." He holds out his hand for me to go first.

Heads turn, watching us like we're royalty. When he notices, Zane pulls me closer toward him. Someone lifts their phone and takes a photo. The flash gives them away. Then I see another person do it, too.

"Zane Alexander," I hear a woman whisper, and more people notice us. He interlocks his fingers with mine, then slightly increases his pace enough for me to notice. The spotlight isn't a place I've ever stood and I don't think I want to.

He whispers in my ear, "Ignore them."

When she removes the private rope from the stairs that lead up to the balcony that overlooks the golf course and mountains, I almost gasp as I climb them. It's where celebrities and world leaders dine and it costs over ten grand to book. I've only dreamed about what it must be like to experience this.

Zane allows me to go first, and I glance over my shoulder at him. His brow pops and I smile, continuing to the next level. When we're close to the table, he pulls the chair out for me, then sits to my right. His hand rests on my thigh as leather-bound menus with gilded pages are slid in front of us. The display of candles in the middle flickers from the surrounding movement.

He glances over at me.

"Enjoy your visit, Mr. Alexander," the hostess states with a curtsy. He nods, giving her nothing else, and she immediately leaves.

"Did you have to be like that?"

"She was a bitch toward you. So yes, I had to be like that. Be grateful I didn't fire her on the spot." He says it nonchalantly.

I watch him, knowing he's serious. "Do they all greet you like royalty?"

"Yes," he says, focusing on the menu. "Even royalty."

My lips part, and maybe I'm just as guilty as the woman who sat us and I don't realize the magnitude of this man. "Who are you?"

"The heir of Xander Resorts and Enterprises. A total asshole. I'm also a brother. A son. A kick-ass friend. Oh, and a damn good lover."

He focuses on my mouth before meeting my eyes. "And a tease," I add.

This makes him laugh. "I don't want to rush anything. Especially not with you."

We both focus back on our menus. The next time I steal a glance at him, he catches me. It's nearly impossible to hold back a smile. Right now, I want to stare and admire.

Moments later, Harper approaches and sits in the high-backed chair in front of Zane. "You're early."

I realize the table is set for four.

"By five minutes. You know I don't like tardiness," Zane states. "Your date?"

"He's coming," she says, lifting her hand and waving. I focus on Zane, and over his shoulder I see the last man on earth I expected to find walking up the stairs: Sebastian. He's zeroed in on me, then he waves at Harper.

Zane hasn't noticed because he's staring at me. "You tensed. Are you okay?"

"I—"

"Hello," Sebastian states as he slides into the seat across from me. I study the menu as my heart rate increases. He shouldn't be here.

"Look who I ran into earlier," Harper states. "Oh, how rude of me. Sebastian, this is Autumn. My brother's girlfriend."

Zane wraps his arm around me, glaring at Sebastian. "Why are you here?"

"I invited him," Harper says, giving her brother a dirty look. "Where are your manners?"

"Manners?" He stares at her, and before anything else can be said, a server walks over carrying a bottle of Chardonnay.

"From management," she states as she pours it into the crystal wineglasses that are already in front of us.

I pick up my glass, overly aware that Sebastian is staring at me. Zane moves closer and whispers in my ear, "Say the word and we'll leave."

I smile, placing my hand on his thigh and squeezing. "I need to go to the ladies' room."

I need to escape.

"Okay." Zane nods and I excuse myself from the table. Seeing Sebastian in public is different from having to sit across from him during a dinner that I was looking forward to. He shouldn't be here.

In the past, I'd dreamed of having his attention. Now, I don't want it and it feels like a nightmare I can't escape from. I move into the stall, pulling my phone from my wristlet and I group text my best friends.

Autumn

911

Blaire

I'm here.

Julie

Me too.

Autumn

Our date was going great until Zane's
sister showed up with Sebastian!

Blaire

Uhh . . .

Julie

WHAT?

I sigh.

Autumn

So, if this was a choose-your-own-adventure,
would you choose option 1: go back and flirt
with Zane so hard it drives Sebastian insane or
option 2: go back and tell Zane it's time to leave.

Blaire

Option 1

Julie

Option 2

> **Autumn**
> See. You two can't even agree.

> **Blaire**
> So do both?

> **Julie**
> Yea! Flirt hardcore and leave before dinner arrives because you're sooooo DTF.

A smirk spreads across my lips. One hundred percent down to fuck.

> **Autumn**
> That might actually work. I'll keep you updated.

I shove my phone back into my tiny purse, then make my way down the hallway lit by hanging chandeliers. Moments later, my arm is gently being grabbed from behind. I spin around, not expecting to be face-to-face with my ex.

"Don't touch me," I say, pulling away from him and taking a step back.

His brows rise. "I'm sorry. I was calling your name, but you didn't stop."

"I have nothing to say to you."

His eyes scan me from head to toe. "I'm glad you received my gift."

"Excuse me?"

"Did the note not come with the shoes and dress?"

The world around me crumbles and my heart races harder.

"No," I state, freezing in place, unraveling what he said.

Sebastian sent this, not Zane. The low-cut slit at my back now feels too revealing.

"I had it made for you, Autie, when I was in Canada. I couldn't get you off my mind. And you know . . ." he says, studying my body again. "It fits you exactly as I imagined it would. Fuck, you look so good. I was hoping to be the man to peel it off of you tonight."

I want to disappear as I cross my arms over my chest, wishing I could rip every inch of expensive silk and beads off of me. Understanding I'm wearing the dress he sent me makes me sick to my fucking stomach. "I'm with Zane now."

"I don't see a ring on your finger." He takes a step forward, closing the protective space between us. "I know you haven't stopped thinking about me."

"Stop. You had your chance, and you royally blew it."

"It won't last," he says. "You and Zane. Pfft."

"You don't know what you're talking about."

"I know him better than you can ever imagine. He'll start ignoring you. Gets too busy. Then waits for you to cheat and blames you for not being satisfied. He's done it with every single one of his exes. You're next. It's just a matter of time."

"Hm. That actually sounds like what you do, except you do the sleeping around, if I'm not mistaken."

"Autie—"

"Don't use my nickname like we're friends. We aren't. Not anymore."

"That's why I want to talk to you in private, so we can work through it."

"Please, listen to me carefully when I say this: There is nothing left for us to repair. I begged you to go to couples' therapy. I wanted to marry you, but you wanted to see other people."

"We wanted to see others."

"No, *we* fucking didn't. Don't you dare try to rewrite history. I was there. You hurt me."

"I'm sorry." He shakes his head. "I know I messed up. But I deserve another chance to make it up to you. We were so good together."

"Were we?" I glare at him. I remember the times I made dinner and ate alone because he was too busy. There were so many canceled dates I lost count. After a while, I stopped making plans. The person I became when I was with him isn't who I am. Or who I ever want to be again. I don't know that version of myself anymore.

"I won't give up on us until you're married. I hope you know that. I'll be waiting for you and Zane to end it."

I narrow my eyes. The fucking audacity.

Moments later, a firm hand is on my waist.

"Hey, beautiful. Are you okay?" Zane asks in my ear, but I hear the concern in his tone. His fingertips brush the outside of my arm.

I turn and face him, wrapping my arms around his neck. "Much better now."

Then I gently press my lips to his. At first, he tenses as if he wasn't expecting it, then immediately reciprocates. Our tongues slide together and the world threatens to disappear as my bare back presses against the cool wall.

I hear Sebastian mutter something under his breath, and a few seconds later, we pull away.

Zane watches me. "What happened?"

"I thought you sent me this dress."

His brows furrow. "I—"

"Sebastian did."

With a clenched jaw, he exhales slowly. "Can we leave, please?"

"Yes, I'd very much appreciate that."

Zane grabs my hand, guiding me down the hallway. "Fuck him," he seethes.

I enjoy his protective side and that he even noticed.

"You're mine, Autumn," he confirms as an electric current hums between us.

"At least until January." It was our deal. The thought comforts me like a warm blanket in the winter, and I hold on to the time we've confirmed we'll be together.

We walk through the restaurant, past the host stand, then we're outside. I suck in fresh air, noticing the temperature has dropped ten degrees since our arrival. When the sun fully sets on the mountain, that happens. I shiver and Zane removes his suit jacket and places it over my shoulders, covering my bare back. It's warm and smells like him. I feel safe and my self-consciousness fades away.

The white suit shirt bulges at his biceps and hugs him around his tapered waist. Zane Alexander is what dreams are made of. Is that ironic?

As we stand at the pick-up area, instrumental music plays over the loudspeaker.

"This song reminds me of my teenage dirtbag years."

I chuckle. "I couldn't name it, but also, I don't believe you."

"There are pictures to prove I had a phase. Dance with me," he says, holding out his hand.

"Right here?" I ask with a chuckle, but I take his hand anyway, wanting the distraction.

He gives me a smile and pulls me in close, nuzzling his face into my hair as he inhales.

"I'd dance with you in Hell," he admits. "You're so damn beautiful."

Confidence drips from him as he spins me, bringing me back to his chest. My body relaxes and everything around us vanishes. Nothing matters. Not the dress, not my dumb-as-fuck ex. No, right now, it's just us.

I breathe him in, losing myself in the moment, wishing the song would last forever. After a few minutes, it ends. He twists me one final time and lets me go. He's charming and has it down to a science.

"Thanks for pulling my mind away," I say.

"Anytime." He unlocks his phone and types something, then shoves it back into his pocket. He reads me like a book and memorizes each page.

"How'd you know I needed it?" I whisper as he stands close.

"I could feel you shutting down. Don't push me out," he says, hooking his finger with mine.

And he's right. My head is still swimming.

"I should've walked with you."

"No, I don't need a bodyguard."

"Are you sure about that?" he asks with a brow popped. "Because I don't think I'll ever let you out of my sight again."

I grow quiet, squeezing my eyes tight for a brief moment.

"Zane," I hear from behind us, and it's Harper. She uses the sidewalk as her runway as she struts toward us like a supermodel. I'm blown away by how beautiful everyone in his family is.

"Are you not staying for dinner?" Harper asks, confused.

"No. I won't be around Sebastian Holmes and neither will Autumn."

Harper glances between us. "What piece of information am I missing? You two were friends. You competed together for years."

"That's Autumn's cheater ex. It's a hard fucking no."

My mouth slightly parts as I suck in air. "What? Is that true? Confirmed?"

Everything freezes.

Zane turns his full attention to me. "I'm sorry. Shit. I shouldn't have said that."

Old memories flood in. There were countless late nights when Sebastian came home and immediately showered, but I could still smell the alcohol on him.

Julie encouraged me to hire a private investigator, but I didn't. It was almost better not knowing, that way I could continue living in delulu land. What I don't know couldn't hurt me and my love for him made me pathetic.

Zane turns to Harper, straightening his stance. "I won't watch him eye fuck her all night."

How many lies had Sebastian fed me that I stupidly swallowed down?

"Can I give you a hug?" Harper asks, pulling my thoughts back to them.

I nod and she squeezes me tight. She smells like citrus and sugar. "I'm so sorry. Please forgive me."

"No, no need to apologize. You didn't know," I say, sucking in cool air, trying to ground myself.

She focuses back on me and I realize her eyes are the same color as Zane's. The color of their mother's. "Things are turning around for you, and soon you'll be happier than you ever imagined, so don't let this get you down, okay? Don't get lost in your head about the past. Your heart is on the correct path. You know what you want and what's right. Don't be afraid to fight for it."

"Is this one of your predictions?" I ask.

She grins wide. "Oh, Zane told you?"

"Yeah," I say, meeting her eyes, wanting to ask her a million questions.

"You'll know when it's the right time," she says.

"For what?" I ask.

"You'll know." Harper gives me a wink and then glances at Zane.

"I have zero doubt about you two," Harper says. "Anyway, I hope you have a happy birthday, big brother."

She takes a step forward and hugs him tight. "Can we get together at Dad's wedding?"

"Sure," he says as the limo arrives. "But no assholes are allowed."

"Sorry to ruin your night. I will settle this," she offers and turns on her heels.

Zane smirks. "I'd tell you to go easy on him, but—"

"We both know that won't happen," Harper says like she's going to seek revenge. "You two have an incredible night. I fly out in the morning."

"Text me," Zane tells her.

The door opens and I move inside first. Zane follows.

As we zoom away, I want to cry, but I'm out of tears. I'm fucking angry that Sebastian embarrassed me like that, knowing I have a boyfriend. Even if it's fake, he disrespected it. Moments pass.

"Are you okay?" he asks with concern in his voice.

"I am now."

CHAPTER 21

Zane

I'm sorry I've ruined your birthday dinner."

"Ruined?" I chuckle. "Not at all. I've had a great day full of adventure."

"Thank you for offering to leave." Her voice is soft and I can see she's turning inward, lost in thoughts.

"No way in hell we were staying. Anytime we are together and you ever feel an iota of discomfort, we go. Okay? Life is too fucking short to be in awkward or annoying situations."

She smiles but it doesn't quite meet her eyes.

The car slows and turns off onto the road that leads to Hollow Manor.

"You're not taking me home?" she asks.

"I think we need to talk," I say. "But if you'd rather go ho—"

"No, no, it's fine. I wasn't ready for our night to end."

I chuckle. "Not without cake."

We stop long enough for the gate to open and close. After a minute, we travel down the driveway. The car takes it slower than I do because of the curves and climb.

"I owe you an apology," I offer.

"You did nothing wrong." She glances at me.

"I should've never referred to Sebastian the way I did. I should've controlled my tongue, regardless of how annoyed I was knowing that he'd dressed you like he owned you. It was a dick move and incredibly disrespectful to you. That will never happen again."

"Zane, it was the truth, and I'll never ever fault you for being real. I prefer it because most people aren't." She moves closer to me and I can smell her hair and skin.

My mind eases anytime we touch and it sets me on fire.

I swallow hard and we sit in silence for a few seconds. "You mentioned you were together for six years."

"Yes," she mutters.

I do the simple math in my head. "I might fuck him up."

Autumn tilts her head at me, noticing how I tense. It isn't my place to say anything, however, guilt creeps over me.

She silently begs me to tell her and I shake my head, not wanting to discuss this any further. While I don't know many details about their relationship, I know he hurt her, and I won't be the one to twist the knife. Deep down, she knows he was a cheating bastard. There are always signs, little hints. It's how I caught my fiancée with my best friend.

"You saw him with another woman, didn't you?" Autumn breathlessly says. Can she read my mind? Were the words written on my face?

I don't have the heart to tell it was more than one.

"At the end of the day, does it matter?" I ask. "Will it change your current opinion of him?"

"He's at the top of my shit list. Wait, are you protecting Sebastian?" she accuses.

This makes me laugh because he's the last man on earth I'd ever help. "Fuck him. I'm protecting you and your heart."

After the stunt he pulled tonight, I'm tempted to fire him and ban him from all Xander premises.

"He made me believe I was insecure, jealous, and paranoid. I've never been any of those things in my life. Several times he asked me why I didn't trust him. I want answers."

I search her eyes. "Sweetheart, I don't want to hurt you."

"You won't," she whispers. "You're only confirming the suspicions I've had and giving me closure. I need this, please."

She nearly begs and I release a long breath. Autumn deserves to know the truth, but I fucking hate that I'm the one to deliver.

"At the end of the ski season, we always give our celebrity instructors a two-week all-inclusive stay at the private island resort as a thank-you. For the past decade, Sebastian has brought a different woman with him. None of them were ever you."

"Every *year*?" Her voice cracks and her jaw tightens.

"Please understand how sorry I am, Autie." I shake my head and interlock her fingers. "This isn't a conversation I expected or imagined I'd have with you. It's not my place."

The sadness on her face breaks my heart. I tuck loose strands of soft hair behind her ear. When a few tears stream down her cheeks, I wipe them away. I'm fucking livid that Sebastian is still hurting her, that he has the goddamn audacity to try to win her back after disrespecting her so deeply.

"You deserve better, Autumn. He's not worth crying over."

"I know," she states, but the silence lingers on. "These are angry tears. Years of pent-up frustration over being lied to. It makes so much sense now. He told me those trips were for end-of-season training. Fuck," she hisses, forcefully wiping her face. "I'm not a crier."

"Sometimes it's the only way the body can release the emotions." I open my arms, wanting and needing to hold her. "Come here."

My pretty girl falls into my chest and I hold her tight against me. She sniffles and I pet her hair, trying to comfort her in the only way I know how, by being here, by being close. The car hugs the final curve before taking the long stretch home. Neither of us moves until it stops. She pulls away and wipes her cheeks, forcing a smile.

She chews on the corner of her lip and I rub my thumb across it as she meets my eyes. I want to kiss her, tell her none of it matters, that she's fucking incredible, but I say nothing.

"You really shouldn't look at me like that." I smirk, rolling up my shirtsleeves because my temperature rises when her eyes lock on me in that way.

"I can't help it," she says.

"Would you ever take him back?" I ask, needing to know where he stands in her heart.

She glances down at her hands and I appreciate the time she takes to think about it. "No. Being alone with him brought back a lot of memories and none of them were great. Knowing he actually cheated on me and lied about it a handful of times . . ." She pauses. "The answer is no. I realize why my friends hated him. They saw through it. I'm so glad I went and got tested after we broke up. He could've . . ." She stops and shakes her head. "Tonight, he had the nerve to tell me he wouldn't stop pursuing me until I was married."

"You're kidding," I deadpan, not sure what kind of game Sebastian thinks he's playing. Maybe he thought she'd never find out about his sexcapades; bro code and all of that bullshit.

"He's trying to break us up," I say with a sarcastic laugh. "Fucking prick."

Her brows furrow and a hint of anger emerges. "He is. But it's not like we're together, so he loses anyway."

We both know what's going on isn't fake, even if the title is . . . for now.

The door opens and we exit. I give my driver a nod and fall in step beside Autumn as she leads the way down the lit sidewalk. There's a gentle breeze and it carries a crisp reminder that winter is coming. Our pumpkins are on the porch with their electric candles inside.

It makes her smile, and I fucking love to see it.

When we enter, a cool draft drifts through the space so I light the fireplace.

Autumn steps closer to the instant warmth. The flames cast a warm glow across her sun-kissed skin and my eyes trail down her body. From this angle, the material is see-through and clings to her. Her tiny nipples are hard little pebbles and poke through the silk. My eyes wander down to the thong sitting low on her hips. I knew the open-back design seemed familiar, but I couldn't place it until now. He's dressed every woman he's been with in something similar to mark his territory.

Sebastian made her a spectacle, after knowing she was mine. He didn't have the goddamn right.

Had I known he'd delivered it to her house today . . .

I fight the anger bubbling inside of me. Part of me wants to go back to the resort and beat the fuck out of him, something he's had coming for a long while.

Instead, I'll ensure the sorry bastard never has a chance to hurt her again.

"The rage I have when I see you dressed in that." My nostrils flare and I run my hand through my hair as she takes a step closer to me.

"I feel cheap," she whispers. "And used."

I remove the remaining space. Her warm brown eyes lock on me and I slide my hands under the thin sleeves. Then I firmly pull, wanting to destroy everything the material symbolizes. The silk splits in half and reveals her beautifully bare body.

Instinctively, I kiss her shoulder, trailing up the softness of her neck. Seconds later, the sparkly black fabric is in a pile at her feet. Autumn threads her fingers through my hair as her head rocks back on her shoulders.

"You'll never be his again," I mutter, sucking on her earlobe then tasting her skin. Our mouths crash together. We're desperate and dangerous, despite the alarms sounding in my head telling me to stop. Autumn urges forward, sliding her tongue against mine, moaning against me.

Her beautiful breasts are on full display and her nipples are peaked.

Fuck, I'm in over my head.

She tugs on my tie, removing it, then steadily unbuttons my shirt. I said I wouldn't pursue anyone else, not until I found my forever person.

She desperately pushes the material from my body, running her hands down my chest. Her hands trail around the muscles of my stomach and I'm hard.

"Pumpkin," I whisper, leaning my head against her forehead.

"Please," she whispers.

I study her, not knowing if I'm strong enough to keep denying her when she wants this, wants me.

"It's supposed to be you."

I run my fingers through her hair, bringing her ear to my mouth. "I want you to want me, and just me, not the idea of erasing someone else."

"You think that's what this is?" She studies me, shaking her head. "I want you to claim me."

"And what happens if I decide I don't want to let you go once this line is crossed?"

"You will," she whispers. "You have a life outside of Cozy Hollow."

I shake my head. "Wrong answer, Pumpkin. I don't want a fling. I need to know that you're ready for the possibility of forever."

"I can't guarantee the future. Just right now," she mutters, picking up the material and throwing it into the fire. She tosses the shoes in too, then we stand and watch them burn until they're nothing more than ash. Then she turns on her heels and walks toward the stairs in nothing but a thong. "I need to find some clothes."

Fuck.

I can't let her walk away from me, not like this.

Not ever.

CHAPTER 22

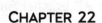

Autumn

$\mathcal{B}$efore I make it to the first step, I'm being spun around.

Zane pulls me close and our lips slam together.

"You have no idea how much I want you," he says between greedy kisses. Our mouths and tongues tangle and I'm breathless.

"Your eyes have always given you away," I say, threading my fingers through his messy hair.

Seconds later, he's lifting me into his strong arms and carrying me up the stairs.

Moon rays beam through the high windows, creating the perfect amount of light for me to admire how beautiful he is with his chiseled jaw and plump lips. He kicks open the large, historic doors to his room and sets me on my feet. I unbuckle his belt as he walks me to the edge of the bed. As he pushes the thong from my body, he never once takes his eyes from mine.

We hold a silent conversation. This is right.

His mouth is on me and he kisses up my stomach, between my breasts, until he's back to my ear. A strong hand rests on my ass as he whispers, "There is no uncrossing this line, Autumn. I don't fuck and forget."

"I want to take risks with you," I admit as his hand wraps around my waist and he turns me until my back is against his chest. I feel his rigid cock and think it might actually break me in two.

He gently guides me forward until my knees are on the mattress, then guides me down onto my palms. I'm on all fours with my ass upright as he stands behind me. I glance over my shoulder, catching a peek of him, and he smirks as he admires me.

"Arch that back for me a little more, Pumpkin, and show me that beautiful pussy I'm devouring tonight."

I do exactly what he says, spreading my legs, giving him views of all that I am, all that I'm offering. Typically, in the past, had I been in this position, I would've been timid, maybe shy. Not under his gaze, not when he smiles at me like the man in my dreams.

I crave him like I crave cooler weather, bonfires, and crunchy leaves. I need him at the core of my essence, burying himself deep inside me.

Seconds later, he's kissing, sucking, and biting my left cheek before moving over to the right. Sparks ignite, and by the stroke of midnight, he'll have burned me to the ground with his touch. His warm breath gently brushes against my skin.

My pussy clenches in anticipation as his fingers tease my clit. Then there I am, on all fours for this man that I want, that I need, that I've craved since the very first word he ever spoke to me.

"You're already so *fucking* wet for me," he says, rubbing my ass then barely dipping the tip of his large finger into my entrance. I grab onto the silk comforter with my fists, nearly crumbling by a single touch. It's been so long since anyone other than myself has touched me.

"Dripping fucking wet like a goddamn needy girl."

"*Your* needy girl," I say, my body springing to life with anticipation as he moves closer. I *am* needy, almost desperate for him. A part of me believes this is what his sister was talking about tonight. Maybe this is the right moment. It seems like it. My heart says it is.

A ragged breath releases from my throat when he kisses my pussy then slowly inserts his fat tongue inside me.

"Mmhmm," I hum and sink into him, the scruff on his face creating the perfect amount of friction.

"Fuck, I love the way you taste," he whispers against me, sucking on my clit.

"Oh yes," I moan out, nearly coming on his face, but he stops.

Unpredictably, he flips me over, sliding his hands under my ass to move me to the edge of the bed. When I'm there, he drops to his knees like he's ready to worship me. Tonight, he will.

"Zane," I whisper, and he looks up at me like I'm his. "No one has—"

I try to find my words and push my embarrassment aside. If we're doing this, I have to be honest with him. He deserves to know.

"No one has gone down on me."

He meets my gaze. "If you're uncomfor—"

"No, it's not like that. It feels *incredible*. It's just . . . no one has ever wanted me so intimately. Only you."

A fire erupts behind his eyes as he gently guides me back then parts my thighs, burying his face back between my legs. "Enjoy it, baby girl." He slowly licks down my slit to my clit and cunt, lapping me up.

"Oh. My. Fucking. God," I growl out, writhing against his face as my eyes roll into the back of my head.

His tongue twirls around my hard nub and flicks. My pussy clenches tight. He's working me up so fast and if he doesn't slow down, I'll come within the minute because I'm so damn horny for him.

When he reaches up and twists my peaked nipple, I can barely take the sensations coursing through me. It's never felt so intense, so incredible, like he knows my body.

I want him buried deep inside me. I need him to fuck me into oblivion until nothing is left but the two of us.

As if he reads my mind, he slides one of his fingers to the first knuckle, then the second. He curls them, adding the perfect amount of pressure as he slowly sucks and teases my swollen clit.

A guttural groan releases from me as my back arches with anticipation.

"I can taste how close you are," he whispers.

"Yes yes yes," I breathlessly moan, teetering on the edge.

"You want to come so fucking bad, don't you?" he growls, continuing the war he will absolutely win.

Words hang in my throat as I race toward the end. "Yes," I hiss.

His pace slows and it's agonizing. Sweet fucking torture.

"Then come for me." His voice is a sexy rasp as he adds another finger, stroking my G-spot.

"Please let me," I beg, knowing he has control as he teases me with his breath. My ass clenches as I rock my hips on his fingers. "I'm . . ."

I can't even form comprehensible sentences. Everything is tense, every muscle is seized and I just need more of him. I need it all and he's holding me at the edge, teasing me.

I'm suspended in the air waiting for the cards to fall.

My heart rate increases and I don't know how long he holds me back. Seconds, minutes, hours? Time doesn't exist with him.

"You're mine, Pumpkin," he growls, kissing my inner thighs.

"I'm willing to negotiate," I desperately plead. "If I can have you. All of you."

His mouth is back on my pussy and he smiles against my folds. "That's a damn good deal."

Then he peels me open with his tongue and gives me exactly what my body begs for. I run my fingers through his hair, holding him close.

And then the thread snaps and I come so hard I don't recognize the sounds that escape from me. The orgasm tears me to pieces and I'm nothing but shreds. He doesn't move his mouth from me, adding just enough pressure to my clit. He milks my G-spot as I pulse and throb.

Just when I think I've fully come down from my high, the intense pleasure creeps up again as Zane laps up every drop, like he's starved for me. And that's when I realize this isn't over.

Heat rushes through me. Coming once is a miracle, twice is an act of God. I'm convinced he is one.

"Mm, I want to worship this pretty little pussy all night. Be a good girl and come for me again."

"Za— Shit," I whisper, my back arching as I dig my fingers into the comforter.

This time he doesn't stop. Euphoria surrounds me and I feel as if I've been catapulted to another planet where Mr. Dreamy actually fucking exists.

"I need more of you," I beg.

He peppers kisses along my inner thighs then towers over me, shirtless, with a monster cock tight in his pants. Zane slides open the drawer and pulls out a foil wrapper.

I shake my head, pushing up onto my elbows to get a better view of him as he removes his belt and undresses. "Nothing between us. I'm on birth control."

He meets my eyes, staring me down, before setting the condom on the dresser. "Okay."

I scoot up the bed and Zane moves to me, hovering above me, kissing me as he patiently waits at my entrance. His thumb brushes across my cheek as we kiss. The anticipation is almost too much.

"I'm never in a rush with you," he says gently, sucking the softness of my neck, giving me another inch as I widen my legs to adjust to him.

"It's like time freezes," he mutters against my lips.

The pressure fills me so full that I think he'll split me in two. I want him to.

He nibbles on my shoulder as he gives me every last inch. Then we stay connected, neither of us moving as I suck in ragged breaths.

"You feel so good," I whisper, nearly drowning in the sensation of being with him. It's so damn right, everything about this. "Like . . ."

The words are on the tip of my tongue, but I feel them in my core.

"I was made for you?" he whispers.

"Yes," I say as he meets my eyes and finishes my thought. Goosebumps trail over my body and I can't explain the sensations swirling inside me. It's pure bliss, something I've never felt with any of my partners. It's too intense as I gasp for air, lost in the moment.

"Fuck," he says in a low growl. "You feel like you're mine."

His words exhilarate me as he slides in and out, so deep, but gently as he brushes against my G-spot. It's too much and I'm scared he'll split me in half.

"Oh, oh," I groan, scratching my nails down his back.

Zane moves to his knees, sliding his hands under my ass, easily lifting and guiding me on and off of his cock.

"Harder," I whisper, racing for more of this sensation. As I suck in more air, he grunts, fucking me so damn good.

"Zane, yes, cum in me," I breathe out, noticing how his muscles tense. He's close. "Please. I want all of you . . ."

My eyes roll into the back of my head and I'm flooded with heat as he pumps deeper, a tidal wave rushing through me. My pussy pulses around him and he moans out.

"You're squeezing me so tight," he huffs as my back flies off the mattress. We are nothing and everything all at once as our sounds fill the room. I'm breathless and my body is useless.

We stay connected and he kisses me. It's hard for me to imagine a time when I didn't know he existed. How do either of us come back from this?

With his eyes closed, he sucks in a ragged breath and nuzzles into my neck. "It's never felt like that before."

I swallow, blinking up at the ceiling and the constellations painted from one side to the other. "For me either."

Maybe, just maybe, Zane broke the curse, or our souls bonded. Either way, I'm convinced the entire world shifted on its axis and I'm already craving more.

I WAKE TO a heavy arm wrapped around my body and let out a content sigh. I squeeze my thighs together and I can feel everywhere he's been, like he carved the shape of him inside me.

"Good morning," he whispers, and I turn my head to look at him as our bodies stay molded.

"Morning."

He meets my eyes. "What did you dream about?"

I shake my head and stretch my legs. "It was wild. I had dinner with Mr. Dreamy and then, for some reason, my gross ex was there. But then we left and . . ." I waggle my brows. "All night long."

He laughs. "Sounds like one hell of a dream."

"It was *incredible*." That word doesn't fully cover it. Just thinking about it has me smiling wide.

His phone buzzes on the floor, temporarily pulling our attention away. Mine is still in my tiny designer purse downstairs where I left it last night. I can only imagine the text messages I have waiting for me, considering I never updated my friends.

"Ignore it. I want five more minutes just like this."

"Mm. Do you like to snuggle?"

"With you. You're warm," he says, eliminating the remaining space between us. His phone stops vibrating and he lets out a contented sigh. I close my eyes and almost drift off before the buzzing begins again.

This time, I roll over and face him, propping myself up on my elbow. A small, boyish grin touches his lips as he admires me. "I want to remember you like this forever; with a sleepy smile on your gorgeous face, and messy, wavy hair."

Zane reaches forward and wipes his thumb across my bottom lip, focusing on it before meeting my eyes. "You wake up pretty."

My heart flutters and I believe I've lost my ability to speak because Mr. Dreamy has said the same thing to me before.

"What?" I ask as he places his palm on my cheek and our mouths slide together.

I can't explain the electricity humming through my veins or the way I am magnetically drawn to him. He tugs and sucks on my lip. Want quickly takes over and I know where this is going. I want it to continue what we started because it all still feels like a dream.

Buzz. Buzz. Buzz.

"You should answer it," I whisper, knowing I have morning breath. "I'll brush my teeth and use the bathroom."

"Okay," he tells me, and I straddle him to take a shortcut and he digs his fingers into my hips. I'm still naked and his eyes trail over my body in the glow of sunlight. I grind against his hardness through his boxers and want to go for round two after I empty my bladder. But damn, he feels so good.

I gasp, my head falling back on my shoulders as his cock grazes my clit, creating just enough friction to make my heart rate increase.

"Shit," he whisper-hisses and we almost lose ourselves again.

I place my hands on either side of his head and hover above him. "I'm not going to disappear."

"I've heard that one before," he says. "But go pee."

He lets me go and watches me walk to the bathroom door. I'm sore from the inside out and will be feeling the evidence of his presence for days.

I glance at him over my shoulder and smile before I disappear.

Seconds later, he answers the phone and I try to listen to what he's saying. His tone changes and his voice grows mumbled before the main door to the bedroom clicks. Then I'm alone.

After I wash my hands, I search for my toothbrush and see it sticking out of the golden holder next to his electronic one. I sneak into his closet the size of my loft and look for some clothes.

I find a pair of running shorts and a T-shirt that doesn't look like it would fit half of him, then I head downstairs. I'm convinced these were his teenage clothes, but I don't mind.

Zane is pacing the kitchen in jogging pants. My eyes slide down the cascade of muscles on his back and he turns around and spots me. When our eyes meet, I smile and move closer to him.

"I'll talk to you soon," he says and ends the call with furrowed brows.

"Everything okay?"

He sets his phone on the counter. "I have to return to New York immediately."

The free bird he was this morning has vanished. Now he's back to the man I met in the coffee shop—all business.

"You should come with me."

My lips slightly part and I study him, like I'm waiting for him to say he's kidding. I don't think he is, though. The thought exhilarates me, but I don't think it's possible.

"I can't," I mutter, and it almost pains me. "I have to be at work and I'm using my last bit of vacation to attend your father's wedding."

"What if those things didn't matter?"

I pause, staring at his chiseled face. This man is unreal. He has to be a figment of my imagination and that's the only reason he's . . . perfect for me.

"There would be no question. I'd say yes."

He claps his hands together. "Great. After I pack I'll take you home so you can grab whatever you need."

"Zane," I say with a laugh, pulling him toward me. "I really can't."

He moves forward, lifting my chin upward so he can easily steal a kiss. "You said yes."

"Hypothetically, if those things didn't matter."

He smiles wide. "They won't. Can you text me the owner's phone number?"

It's almost easy to fantasize about going on adventures with him. Isn't this what I've wished for? "There's no one to cover my shift."

"Do you trust me?"

I smile and nod, then send him Julie's parents' contact information. "Good luck," I say.

He reaches inside his pocket and pulls out the four-leaf clover I gave him. "I've got all the luck I need."

CHAPTER 23

Zane

When I decided to spend the next quarter in Cozy Hollow, I stored my plane in the company hangar in case I needed to be somewhere fast. My pilots have been on standby for the last three weeks. After receiving the call, they made it to the airport, fueled up, and did the preflight check before Autumn and I arrived in Denver.

We make small talk on the way there, but I feel like she's walking on eggshells.

As we board the private jet, Autumn is quiet, and her eyes dart everywhere but to me.

"What is it? What are you thinking? Ask me," I finally say as we buckle.

"Why the sudden rush to New York?"

"I'm sorry." I turn to her, realizing I never said, but I have nothing to hide. Not when we're building the foundation of something bigger than us. "My father was rushed to the hospital due to a suspected heart attack," I explain, knowing my mind is slowly spiraling with what-ifs and unknown scenarios.

"Don't apologize," she says, lifting the middle armrest and wrapping her arms around me. "It's going to be okay."

I didn't realize I needed a hug until her warmth pressed against me. Whenever she is close like this, the ball that's wound tight inside me loosens. With each passing second, Autumn breaks down the wall I built to protect my heart and she doesn't even know it.

"When your demeanor shifted," she says with her head against my chest, "I knew it was serious."

"Most people wouldn't have noticed," I admit.

Can she hear the pitter-patter of my heart, the beats that skip because of her?

"I'm not *most* people." She chuckles, but it's an easy laugh. Not forced, not fake; nothing about being with Autumn is.

"You're damn right about that." I adjust my body, making it more comfortable for her because I don't want her to pull away, at least not yet.

"Are you worried?"

"Yes." I twirl a strand of her dark hair around my finger. "I'm concerned that something awful will happen before I can make amends. It would be one of the biggest regrets of my life because, while we don't always agree or get along, I love and care about him."

She nods. "Is there anything I can do to help?"

Her kindness warms my heart.

"Having you here is more than enough."

I keep my fingers in her silky strands to confirm she's real and that I'm not dreaming.

Her phone rings, grabbing her attention. She pulls it from her pocket and Julie's photo appears on the screen.

"You should take that. There's a conference room with privacy if you'd like." I point toward it.

"Are you sure?"

"Absolutely. Don't ignore your friends. I'm sure they're concerned, considering I captured you."

"I willingly joined you." She playfully rolls her eyes and unbuckles, then walks across the plane to the sliding door. I watch her walk away and our eyes meet as she slides the door closed. She grins.

I lean my head back on the seat, smiling wide. Her voice is muffled, but I can hear her laugh.

I pull my phone from my pocket to see if there have been any updates from Harper.

Nothing. Not a word.

Silence stresses me out more than hearing from my sister nonstop. It's never good when Harper grows quiet, and that plagues me. I try not to think the worst, though, and suck in deep breaths, trying to relax.

Eventually, Autumn returns. "They're already planning our wedding."

"I love that for us." I chuckle, enjoying that I have her best friends' stamp of approval.

She stares at me. "Julie said you paid off her parents."

It's impossible to hold back a smirk. I knew she'd find out. "You're worth it."

She playfully shakes her head but looks at me with stars in her eyes. "You're unbelievable."

"Like Mr. Dreamy?" I ask.

She glances past me out the window at the fluffy clouds floating as we soar through the bright sky. Then I see that familiar gaze, the one I've come to recognize.

"You're *living* the dream." I shoot her a wink, wanting to kiss her but deciding against it. I won't make the first move today, not after last night. But damn, right now, the urge to slide my lips across hers nearly overtakes me. I break the intense eye contact.

"Are *you*?" she asks.

"Yes. I'm having the time of my life," I tell her. "Truly."

We soar through the sky like a speeding bullet and I open my arms. Autumn comes to me without hesitation and I inhale the sweet scent of her shampoo as I hold her against me. When her breathing slows, I replay everything that's happened and try not to worry about the future. A future I can't predict. The past tries to flood in, but I push it away.

Last night, something inside me unlocked, and Autumn felt the shift, too. I saw it on her face, heard it in her moans, and knew it when she held me tight. I close my eyes, trying to get some rest, not knowing what emotional roller coaster I'll ride when we arrive in the city.

Hours later, the jet lightly touches down and the two of us wake when the cabin lights click on. My pilots grease the landing, but they're the best in the country and I'd expect nothing less. A blacked-out SUV waits for us once we taxi to the private hangar and deplane. We're escorted inside like I'm the president of the United States and are driven to the hospital across the city.

When I breathe deeply, Autumn grabs my hand and flips it over, stealing my attention.

"This is your love line," she says, tracing my palm. "But I don't know anything about it, you're out of luck."

I laugh. "Thank you. I needed that."

"I could tell," she admits.

Reaching forward, I grab her hand and flip it over.

"It's this one?" I trace her love line, going from the top to the bottom as she watches me.

"Wait." She places my palm next to hers. "They're almost exactly the same. Long lines with a forking branch at the end."

"Yeah," I mutter, and she doesn't let me go. I don't pull away either. I fucking love her touch.

"I was told it meant I'd have significant heartbreak, but overall, I'd find true, everlasting love. I guess it's the same for you."

"Hate knowing your heart was broken."

Her gaze meets mine. "You too."

"I'd endure it a thousand times to be here with you."

She chews on her bottom lip and it's too damn adorable. Just one kiss, I could steal it right now, but I won't.

Eventually, the vehicle slows in front of the hospital, the only one my father would go to in the city. I get out, and as soon as Autumn's feet are on the pavement, I hear the clicking of a shutter. As I turn my head, I spot the glare of the zoom lens on the camera across the street.

"Are you fucking kidding me?" I hiss, wrapping my arm around Autumn, keeping my head down and blocking her from view.

We rush inside, and when the doors close, she glances at me, confused.

"Photographers," I whisper, leading us to the reception area. "Gross that they'd do this under these circumstances. I'm sorry. I thought we'd have privacy here, or I would've nev—"

She places her finger on top of my lips. "You can only control yourself, no one else, okay? You don't owe me an apology. I said I wanted all of you, Zane. That means the good and the bad."

I tilt her chin upward, my expression softening. "Thank you."

"For what?"

"For being you. For being here. For understanding. For not being upset."

She hooks her finger with mine. "You're more than welcome."

Fuck. I'm incredibly lucky. It's all I can think when I look at her.

When we reach the counter, I give my father's name to the woman behind the glass window. She asks for my identification, then excuses herself and walks into an office in the middle of the room with its blinds drawn. She's on the phone, speaking to someone. Autumn glances at me and I shrug, but I also know my father more than likely has security around his room to stop unwanted guests from entering.

Moments later, the woman returns. "You're on the approved visitor list. You'll go to the twelfth floor and check in there. A nurse will lead you to his room."

"Thanks," I say, knowing where the elevators are. It's not the first time I've been here, but I hope it's one of the last for a very long time.

As I push the button, Autumn reaches out and grabs my hand. I glance over at her and my heart flutters when she smiles. Together, we step inside, and when the doors close, she moves forward and captures my mouth. Holding back is impossible as I greedily kiss her back.

I run my fingers through her hair, tugging it. The elevator stops and we pull away from one another, guilty with swollen lips as we move to the desk. Several nurses type on computers. In the distance, beeps ring and machines hum.

"I'm here to see my father. Last name is Alexander."

She nods. "Do you have the password?"

"One-zero-zero-two," I say, and she checks her records. Moments later, we're being escorted to the end of the hallway where my father's bodyguards sit in chairs outside of the room. They stand and greet me with handshakes as the nurse knocks on the door and enters.

"Please wait here," she says.

"Sure," I tell her, focusing back on the men who swore to take a bullet for my father. They've worked for him for at least a decade and he doesn't go anywhere without them.

"Has Harper been here?" I ask.

"Yes, she left thirty minutes ago," Christopher states. "She forgot her phone on the plane."

I shake my head. "No wonder I haven't heard from her."

The nurse cracks open the door and waves me in. "He's awake."

I reach out for Autumn, but she shakes her head. "I can stay out here."

"Absolutely not," I say. "I want my dad to meet the woman I'm marrying."

She bursts into laughter. "Stop with that."

"No way," I say with a grin. "One day, I'll remind you how you laughed when I said that."

"Remind me how cocky and confident you were too."

I lean in and whisper in her ear, "You fucking love it."

Her cheeks redden and it's the confirmation I needed.

We enter and the nurse excuses herself after she adjusts my father's pillows. He's awake, watching *Star Trek* on the tiny television hung on the wall.

"Son," he says with surprise in his tone. "I didn't expect to see you here."

"I wanted to make sure you were okay."

My dad's eyes wander toward Autumn.

"Dad, this is Autumn. My girlfriend," I proudly say. It feels natural and real. Have the lines already blurred too much? She agreed to be mine until January.

All I needed was the chance to prove to her that I'm actually the man of her dreams. She's giving me that now.

"Ah, it's a pleasure to meet you. I'm Ambrose. Most call me Alexander."

"Very nice to meet you," she says sweetly while smiling.

Dad glances between us, and I know he wants to say more but doesn't.

"How are you feeling?" I need to fill the awkward silence that draws on.

"Perfectly fine."

I meet his eyes. He looks exhausted. "Harper told me you had a heart attack."

"It was gas, nothing major. However, my blood pressure is high, so they're keeping me overnight to make sure I don't have a stroke."

"What?" Relief floods through me.

"Wedding jitters and beans. A painful combination, but not deadly." He laughs.

"I'm happy to hear that," I explain. I won't be taking over the company as quickly as I thought, which thrills me. I always imagined when I stepped up, I'd be much older, in my late fifties. As long as my father is healthy, he will not give up his position as CEO, and I support that.

"Can we talk?" my dad finally asks.

"I think that's a great idea. I think I need some coffee." Autumn grins.

"Hospital coffee?" I lift a brow, not wanting her to leave but knowing she will anyway. Determination is written on her face.

"Yeah, would you like some?"

I shake my head. "You know shitty coffee isn't my thing."

She shrugs and turns to my father. "Would you like a cup?"

"No thanks," he tells her. "Shitty coffee isn't my thing either."

"I see where you get it from." Four steps later, the door clicks closed.

I sit in the fake leather chair beside the bed and he stares at me.

"How have you been?" he asks.

"Surviving," I say. "About the interview—"

He shakes his head. "When I thought my heart was giving out, my life, along with my mistakes, flashed in front of my eyes. The biggest regret I had was how I'd treated you."

"Dad."

"Please, let me finish."

I nod.

"I realized I've treated you the way my father treated me, and I owe you an apology. I promised your mother that I'd always give you and Harper the choice to do things and not force you for the benefit of the company. I'd forgotten about that until I thought I was dying. I'm sorry."

"I'm sorry too."

"No, you've been through enough and I wasn't there to support you. In the future, if there is something you don't feel comfortable doing, then don't. That even includes attending my wedding."

"Thank you."

Whooshing and phaser gun sounds from the TV briefly pull our attention away. I glance back at my father as he grabs the remote and mutes it.

I glance back at my father. "I'll be there. I'm picking up my tuxedo on Wednesday and am flying out with Autumn that afternoon."

"You seem good for one another," he says. "Harper believes the two of you will get married. Seeing you together, I believe that too."

I smirk. "When you met Mom, did you know?"

He adjusts one of his pillows. "Yeah. The moment our eyes locked, it was intense. I didn't know anything about her and didn't care. True love."

"Like lightning in a bottle?"

"That's one way to describe it." He sucks in a deep breath. "Just because I'm getting married again doesn't mean I'm erasing your mom."

"I know," I tell him, knowing he waited nearly twenty years before moving on. "She would've wanted you to be happy."

"Yeah. I do wish things had been different though."

"We all do. But we can't change what happened. We can only move forward."

Dad grins. "You've always been smart. I'm proud of you, son. I don't say that enough. Your mother would be proud."

Before I can respond, the door clicks open and Autumn enters with a Styrofoam cup in her hand. She crosses the room toward me and sips it with a straight face.

"How does it taste?" I ask, amused by how well she's handling it.

"Great." She drinks more, but I can tell she's lying by how her lip slightly twitches. "Want some?"

"I'll pass." I smirk, watching her. She's a shit liar.

"You're both missing out." She shrugs, and it's convincing. To anyone not paying attention, it would seem like the truth. I know better.

A knock taps on the door and our heads turn.

"Zane. A pleasure to see you," Dr. Hanson, our family doctor, states. I stand and we exchange a firm handshake.

"Hi. How have you been?" I ask.

"Fantastic. Still snowboarding?"

"Have every season since the accident."

I turn back to my dad, knowing we should probably leave. "I'll see you this weekend. Please keep me updated. I love you."

"Love you too. Very nice meeting you, Autumn. I will see you again soon."

"Pleasure was mine. I look forward to attending your wedding."

I give him a nod, then we leave. Neither of us says anything else.

Autumn glances at me as we walk down the hallway and step onto the elevator.

"How is the coffee? Really?"

She chuckles. "It tastes like toilet water."

"I knew you were lying."

"You needed time with your dad. Alone. Did it go okay?"

"Actually, yeah." I smile. "Funny, a serving of beans was his wake-up call."

"Was yours too." She glances down at the liquid that looks like motor oil with a weird film floating on top. A sly grin slides over her face. "Scary you're this good at reading me."

"Eventually, we'll hold conversations without words," I say, cataloging every single one of Autumn's quirks as I learn them. Already, she's not like anyone I've ever met.

We step out of the elevator and she tosses the half-drunk cup in the garbage.

"Everything worked out," she says when we walk past the reception desk.

"It's because I have my lucky charm."

"The clover?" she asks.

"You."

CHAPTER 24

Autumn

The ride across the city is shorter than I anticipated. The door of the SUV swings open and we're let out at a building that towers above us. The name on the front reads: THE TOWER.

"You live here?" I ask. I remember hearing about the construction of this place.

"Only when I'm in the City." Zane places his hand on the small of my back, guiding me toward the tall glass doors.

It's been over ten years since I've been here, and while I love Cozy Hollow, nostalgia hits me. The sounds of distant honks and the chatter of random passersby surround me, and I realize I've missed New York. I breathe in the distinct smell, appreciating the cool breeze against my skin, then I turn my head, noticing Zane. The scene plays out like a black-and-white movie and it's as if we're moving in slow motion when his head turns to meet mine.

My Mr. Dreamy, I think to myself then smile. He returns the gesture like he knew what I was thinking.

Security stands outside, not allowing anyone to enter that they don't recognize. Zane gives him a nod. Inside are shiny slick floors, tall ceilings, high chandeliers, and it drips with extravagance.

He guides me to the hallway of elevators and I take in the space as we wait.

The door slides open and as soon as the guy spots Zane, he

breaks into a lighthearted laughter. They're friends. Close in age too. He has dark hair, bright blue eyes, and is the same height. Definitely not an athlete, though. I have a knack for picking them.

"Damn. Weston, I didn't expect to see you here," Zane says, giving him a brotherly hug.

He meets my eyes and immediately introduces himself. "Weston Calloway. And you are?"

"Autumn Travis," I say, holding out my hand, and he takes it, kissing my knuckles.

Zane's jaw ticks. "Stop flirting with my future wife, Calloway."

"If you decide you want someone better . . ." He laughs, knowing he's getting under Zane's skin.

"Someone better exists?" I ask, giving Weston a little attitude.

"Here I am. In the flesh." He shoots me a wink, then glances at Zane. "I like her. She's *feisty*."

"You have no fucking idea," Zane tells him, and I playfully scoff.

"Very nice meeting you Autumn Travis." Weston checks his watch and inhales. Zane and I step inside the elevator before it bolts upward without us. "You're staying at the Tower now?"

"Yeah," Weston explains. "I'm having a dinner party at my place tomorrow night. You both should come."

"Maybe," Zane tells him.

"You're coming. I'll text you the details," Weston says as the doors slide closed.

"Would you like to go?" Zane asks, glancing at me. "You can say no."

"I have nothing to wear," I explain.

"If there were no barriers, what would your answer be?"

"I'll go wherever you go," I say. "If you don't want to attend, you can say no too."

"Okay." Zane grins, grabbing my hand. "I'll think about it."

"Who is he?"

"He's a close family friend, but has been going through a messy divorce. I thought I had it bad with Celine, but then I met Lena. Poor Weston actually married his demon. It's been a long, drawn-out, super long legal battle. I haven't seen him at the Tower in years."

I can tell he's thinking about something.

"Did they sign a prenup?" I ask.

"Yeah. But he inherited a lot of money after they were married. His ex believes she deserves a portion of it. She's refusing to move forward with the divorce unless she's paid billions."

My mouth falls open. "Shit."

"I'd give her the cash to never have to speak to her again. Weston's too stubborn. He said he'll fight her in court for the rest of his life before he gives her a penny."

The metal box grows quiet and I glance up at the mirrored ceiling, looking at Zane overhead. He looks up and meets my eyes.

"Would you make me sign one?"

He turns to me with his head tilted. "If you were mine, I'd do everything in my power to make you happy. And if I failed, you'd deserve to take half of it all. I wouldn't care. I'd want the best for you with or without me."

"You should do a better job of protecting your heart," I state. "I could be a terrible person."

He bursts into laughter. "You? Tell me the worst thing you ever did."

I breathe in, trying to think of something terrible I've done. "I've said hateful things to people. And hurt them with my words," I say.

"You're bad," he deadpans. "It's a human response."

"I had sex in the back of my parents' car," I say. "I ate edibles before my college graduation."

"Did you?" He snickers. "Well, I also happen to know that you get with your mom's book club and sew blankets to be handed out to the homeless in New York every year. That once a month, on the first Saturday, you volunteer at the library and read to kids. And you created a fuck jar because Julie says it too much during your shifts and the pastor wasn't happy about it. You run fifteen to twenty-five miles a week, a habit you only picked up because Sebastard broke up with you. And if you didn't like to travel, you'd have five cats."

I chuckle. "Have you been in my head again?"

"People in Cozy Hollow love to share facts about you."

My head falls back on my shoulders as I laugh, not even embarrassed. "I can't imagine what else you know about me."

"A lot," he admits. "You're a good person. An American sweetheart. Everyone truly loves you and how kind you are, even if you pretend like you're a hard-ass. You genuinely care about people and that means something. It can't be replicated," he tells me just as the elevator stops. "It's what I appreciate most about you."

"Thank you for saying that," I say as I exit. He leads me down a wide private hallway toward the large oversize door. It reminds me of the one at Hollow Manor. Actually, the entire foyer does.

"This is familiar," I say, placing my palm on the wood.

"It came from the same castle," he says as he presses his thumb onto the pad. Seconds later, the doorknob clicks and he pushes it open, allowing me to enter.

"Okay, you never said *castle*! You mentioned it was French."

"Must've forgotten." He shrugs. "I'm not a bragger."

"I've noticed." As soon as I'm farther inside, I see the glass staircase and large window walls that surround the place. I move to the edge, amazed at the view that overlooks Central Park. Leaves on the trees have turned yellow and orange, the first indication that fall has arrived.

The door clicks closed and locks, then his footsteps stop behind me. I turn and glance at him over my shoulder as he rolls his shirtsleeves to his elbows.

"This is incredible," I whisper.

"I have one of the best views in Manhattan," he says, but he's focused on me.

I want to kiss him again, especially when he looks at me like that, like he sees something I don't. Maybe he does. Before I cross that line, I force my attention back to the park. Zane moves beside me, his fingers brushing against mine as the sun sets in the distance.

The surrounding buildings glow gold and I think I could stand here for hours, watching another day fade to night.

"I have something for you." Zane pulls something from his pocket and hands it to me. It's a black credit card with my name etched on the bottom.

I'm confused, and before I can ask questions, he speaks. "I had you added to my account."

"I can't accept this." I try to return it to him, but he shakes his head.

"If I recall correctly, this was part of our negotiations. I always keep my end of the deal."

I make a face, unsure what he's referring to.

"You agreed to be mine through the holidays if you could have *all* of me." He glances down at it. "Now you do, Pumpkin. You have me physically, mentally, emotionally, and financially."

"This is not what I meant." I tap the metal card against my fingers, wishing he would take it back, but he's stubborn.

"Time is one of your most valuable commodities. I don't want you to worry about anything while we're together. Focus on the good, and on the things that make you happy. Money won't."

I stare at it, feeling a cyclone of emotions, not knowing how to respond.

"You're fucking adorable." He bursts into laughter.

"I'm in shock."

He takes a step forward, reducing the space between us. He gently tilts my chin upward until I meet his eyes. "Buy whatever you want. You'll never be able to spend it all."

"You say it like money is unlimited."

"It is," he says without skipping a beat, then he leans in and whispers in my ear, "Try me, Pumpkin."

"What if I want a new car?"

He nibbles on my earlobe. "We'll shop for one tomorrow."

"A new wardrobe?" I whisper, wrapping my hand against the back of his neck.

"I'll call my personal tailor."

"A house?" I mutter.

"I know a few builders." His hot breath is on my skin.

"And what if all I want is you?" I finally say.

He pulls away, meeting my eyes. "You have me."

I stand on my tiptoes to capture his lips, needing him like a fire needs air as an inferno swirls inside of me.

Our tongues twist together and he rests his hand on my waist, moving me backward until my back is pressed against the cool glass window. We're lost again, floating into the abyss. Material things don't matter.

His fingers thread through my hair and warmth pools in the pit of my stomach. I tug on his bottom lip and he places his hands on either side of my head, blocking me in, surrounding me with him. It's a brief moment of clarity, enough time for me to realize I lost control. He does that to me, though. I grab his shirt in my fists, pulling him back toward me, not wanting the space, as unspoken words float heavily in the air. We're breathless, with swollen lips.

Zane swims in my brown eyes. "I already want to give you the world."

His voice is a deep husk as he leans in and kisses along my neck.

"I'm falling too fast," I desperately whisper.

Zane grabs my wrists in his large hand and holds my arms above my head.

"Do you have regrets?" he asks, peppering soft kisses wherever he can.

"Zero," I mutter, the truth setting me free. My breasts rise and fall with anticipation of having him again, knowing I'm risking my heart again.

He smiles against my skin, tightening his grip, and I squeeze my thighs together just like I did all those weeks ago when we were in the library. Dominance, I crave his. I look up into his eyes, giving him full control of me.

"I want to do very bad things to you right now," he growls, and it's music to my goddamn ears.

"Please," I beg, fully submissive as he lets me go.

Zane loosens the tie around his neck. "Undress for me, Pumpkin."

He pins me in place with his gaze as I peel off my shirt, dropping it to the floor. Then I kick off my flats and wiggle out of the dark-washed jeans. I don't break the intense eye contact as I reach behind my back and unclip my bra. My breasts fall free and I watch a devious smirk slide across his perfect lips.

When he focuses on me like that, I nearly go weak in the knees.

I hook my fingers into my lacy pink panties and slip them off. His eyes trail down to my perky, pebbled nipples, down to my pussy, then back up again. I stand on display for him, confident, loving how he looks at me with want, need, and intense desire. His thick cock is straining against the material of his suit pants; proof that he wants me just as much as I want him.

"Damn," he hisses, adoration in his gaze. "Come here."

With my head high, I nearly float over to him. As soon as I'm close, our mouths gravitate together. "You're fucking beautiful," he whispers. "Do you know that?"

"Because I was made for you," I say as his hand slides down my stomach. His fingers lightly brush against my clit and slide into my slick slit.

"Wet for me," he mutters, dipping a finger inside my aching pussy. I grab on to his shoulder, a whispered sigh releasing from my throat.

"Always." I'm breathless, even though he barely touches me and I swear he could make me come on command. "I've wanted you all day."

"Mm, I love that for me." He pinches the soft skin of my neck between his teeth as he returns his finger inside of me and curls it while his thumb circles my needy clit. I rock against him as he memorizes my body. Then he slowly drops down to his knees in front of me. I run my fingers through his hair as we hold a silent conversation.

"I have to taste you," he says, lifting my leg over his shoulder. My back presses on the cool glass window and I let out a moan. Zane dives face-first into my pussy. His tongue and mouth focus on my clit as his finger slides deep inside my cunt.

My breathing grows ragged.

"Please fuck me," I whisper. "I need to feel you again."

There is zero hesitation as he grabs my hand, pulling me down to him. He unbuckles his belt and pants and allows his cock free. I push myself up on my elbows, watching him stroke himself a few times, admiring the thick veins in his cock. Zane guides me back, kissing me gently, before slamming into me. It's like he knew what I needed as I scream out, feeling as if he'll split me in half as he gives it to me hard.

"Zane," I pant, the intense sensations putting me in a choke hold. I'm his. Every part of me, every inch. "I . . ."

A flood surges through me and I have an out-of-body experience like I'm desperately chasing my next fix. I'm addicted to him.

"I'm falling for you, Autie," he whispers, his eyes closed, as he tenses. I'm teetering on the edge, knowing any minute the thread will snap.

"It's mutual," I breathe, and he slows as goosebumps trail over me. Zane holds himself up on his elbows, brushing loose strands of hair from my face. His cock fills me full as he soaks in me, our ends meeting.

"I can't imagine a life without you." The words fall from his lips like a prayer.

"Then don't," I tell him, my back arching when he picks up his pace, capturing one of my nipples in his mouth. Immediately, my orgasm rebuilds, and my body begs for release. But before I come, I somehow roll him onto his back. Then I slowly slide down on him, placing my palms on his chest, trying to steady myself as he watches me. Once I take him all in, my eyes move to the city lights surrounding us. It's the only light in the room.

"You feel good," Zane grunts as I rock up and down on him. His thumbs are dug into my hips and he thrusts upward, giving me more of him.

"Fuck," I moan out, my muscles tensing.

And then it happens, my pussy clenches around him and I come hard. It's one of the most intense orgasms I've experienced, almost too much when every muscle tightens. I'm on my back again and he fucks me into oblivion.

"You're mine," I say, meaning it, claiming him as I hold him, kissing him. "Mine."

"Yes," he says, pumping hard as he empties inside of me.

Eventually, with our eyes still closed, he slowly pulls away, as if he's fighting against losing the connection. Once he's pulled away completely, I open my eyes and sit up, spotting the puddle on the floor. Our eyes meet.

My mouth falls open. "I did that?"

"Have you ever . . . ?"

"No," I say, almost embarrassed.

He leans forward, pressing his lips to mine. "So fucking sexy."

Zane stands and reaches out his hand to me. I take it and he leads me upstairs into a large bathroom, where he turns the faucet. "Will you join me?"

"Yes," I say, wanting the warm water to soothe my sore muscles. My legs and thighs are like gelatin, especially after last night.

Zane lights a few candles and pours capfuls of something from a golden bottle into the tub. Bubbles immediately form. I dip my toe into the warmth before submerging myself in the depths. He positions himself behind me, moving my hair to the front. His hot breath is on my neck as I relax against him and his arms snake around my waist.

"Did you mean it when you said you couldn't imagine a life without me?" I ask, leaning my head on his shoulder.

He presses his lips against my cheek. "Can you?"

I try to picture a world in which he doesn't exist before focusing back on him. "No. You'd haunt me in my dreams for the rest of my life."

He holds me tighter. "Guess I do have the upper hand."

I laugh. "Asshole."

He chuckles against my neck. "I'm not going anywhere, Pumpkin."

"Is that a promise?" I ask, turning my head enough to meet his soft eyes.

"One I'll keep for a lifetime," he whispers.

CHAPTER 25

Zane

The next morning, I wake to the sound of a distant hum. I reach beside me and the bed is cold where Autumn is supposed to be. Sitting up, I glance out the window, spotting Central Park far below. Runners in bright-colored clothes jog the path. A part of me expected mountains and pumpkins. It's almost disorienting being here, considering how quickly I escaped this concrete jungle.

I slide on a pair of joggers and grab my phone. There are a few notifications from Harper and Weston, but I'll respond later.

When my feet touch the bottom floor and I catch a glimpse of Autumn, I stop. She stands at the espresso machine wearing nothing but one of my oversized T-shirts and white panties. Her messy hair is flipped to one side as she reads the buttons. I take her in as the early sun sparkles through the windows.

I want to always remember her like this.

I enter the space and she turns toward me. "Good morning," she says with a smile. "Coffee?"

"That would be great." I wrap my arm around her, then slide my lips across hers. She's breathless when we pull apart.

"What was that for?" she asks with her eyes still closed, our mouths only an inch apart.

"Just kissing my girlfriend," I say, confirming that she's real. I can't help but notice the way her mouth turns up like she's pleased. "How'd you sleep?"

"Perfect, but only after you snuggled me. And you?" She pulls away from me when the maker stops brewing.

"Best rest of my life," I admit as she hands me the fresh shot of espresso then makes another. With a push of the button, it automatically starts the process of grinding the beans.

I blow on the top of the cup, watching the crema. A minute later, she grabs hers and moves closer to me as I lean against the counter. After she inhales the chocolate notes of the beans, she takes the tiniest sip.

"Well?" I ask, not able to take my focus from her.

She's fucking gorgeous. She's mine. Isn't she?

"Tastes like shit." Autumn barely gets the words out before she bursts into laughter.

"You suck at lying. Now, the truth."

"It's delicious. Smooth. No harsh aftertaste. If I had to guess, Italian. Medium roast."

"Mm. Impressive." I take a sip, snickering.

"What?" she asks.

"You're a coffee snob."

Autumn rolls her eyes. "You are too."

"Oh, I'm aware. Just glad I found someone who understands that life is too short to drink shitty coffee. One of our final arguments was over that machine."

Autumn glances at it.

"She wanted me to quit caffeine because it was the only thing I looked forward to each morning. Every cup became an act of rebellion."

"You're kidding." Autumn sets the cup on the counter. "I can't imagine having to fight for coffee."

I shoot her a look.

"Are there any redeeming qualities about her?" she asks.

I think about the question for a minute. "Actually, no."

"At all?" Autumn deadpans.

"She was one step away from shitting on my pillow and blaming it on her dogs," I explain.

"Wow. I'm really sorry," Autumn says.

"I spoiled the mood, didn't I?" I ask, shooting back my espresso. "It's this place. Too many of the wrong memories were made here."

"So sell it." Autumn drinks hers down, too.

"Sell it," I repeat.

"Is it sentimental?"

I know she's asking because Hollow Manor is.

"No. Just a few embellishments that will be removed if I leave. I don't have any personal ties. I just enjoy the view."

"There are other penthouses, some with even better views," she says.

My face cracks into a smile. "You're right. And since it was your idea, I'd like you to help me find a new place. Something you'd like."

"Was this her space?" she asks, glancing around.

I chuckle. "Hell no. I've had this penthouse for over a decade, and purchased it because I need to see grass and trees. Also, I have friends who live in the building. Lately, I haven't felt like I'm meant to live in New York," I admit, something I've never shared with anyone. Not even my sister.

She reaches forward, grabbing my hand. "Then where will home be?"

"Wherever you are." It falls out like a confession. "You ease my mind."

"You'd move to Cozy Hollow permanently?"

"Yes," I say. "No fucking barriers, Pumpkin. Not when it comes to us."

Autumn's expression softens as she glances away, smiling. "We can always make new memories here, too," she suggests.

"Okay, I fucking love the sound of that."

Before I can say anything else, my phone vibrates and I unlock it. I read the email notification containing an itinerary for the day I planned for Autumn. I quickly check the time. "I thought we had a few hours together this morning."

"Huh?" she asks, standing to rinse our cups, then drying her hands. It's almost like she's meant to be here.

"Oh, right. You mentioned needing a wardrobe, so I called my sister and asked for a favor on her day off. She agreed to be your personal stylist if I booked the both of you for mimosas and massages."

"No way." Autumn moves forward, wrapping her arms around me. "You're too good to me."

"No. You've just never been treated the way you deserve. This is the bare minimum, Pumpkin."

She captures my lips and the kiss deepens. My head is hazy as I swim in the taste of the mint of her toothpaste and espresso. Words vanish, but I somehow speak first. "What was that for?"

"Was just kissing my *future husband*."

"Hell yes," I say against her mouth as her hands move down my body. Her fingers hook on my joggers and she slides them down, freeing my cock that's been at full attention since the moment I saw her in my kitchen.

Autumn drops to her knees, bowing before me. "Please?"

"Fuck," I say, nodding, lifting her chin as she parts her lips. Need dances with want as she slowly takes me into her hot, greedy mouth.

I groan, gripping the counter hard as she forces me to the back of her throat. My eyes roll into the back of my head as she cups my balls then strokes me down my shaft. I ache for more of her as she enjoys having complete control of me. Her tongue traces my tip and she licks down my thick vein.

"Mm. My good girl."

She moans with her lips tightly sealed around my cock. I grunt as she works me, varying her speeds.

Right now, I want to satisfy her. To allow her to feel just as good. My body hums with desire, with the need to please this beautiful woman who can command me with a single look. Autumn has no idea how much power she has over me. Or maybe she does.

Pre-cum glistens on the end and she licks it off, humming with anticipation as she tastes me.

"I'm addicted to you," she says, kissing and sucking as she gently massages my balls.

"It's mutual." I repeat the same words she said to me last night.

She continues to stroke, and I thrust into her hand and tight throat. I'm surrounded by Autumn as she works me into oblivion. Guttural groans and grunts boil up from my chest and push past my lips, the sensation almost too intense. Her mouth is too hot, her eager moans too sweet.

"Come for me," she whispers as my body tenses. "I need you."

I thread my fingers through her hair as my balls tighten. With a moan, she sucks and strokes until I crumble to nothing. She milks every last drop of pleasure from me. I throb and pump inside her greedy little mouth.

She stands, licking her swollen lips, wearing a proud smirk. "You taste good."

"Let me return the favor." I adjust myself.

"You can owe me one. I need to change." She twirls around in my shirt and I slide my hand under her silk panties to grab her bare ass.

"Now I regret planning a day of you being away from me," I admit.

"Aww, will you miss me?" she teases.

I pop a brow. "Too fucking much."

She grins and I tuck loose strands of her hair behind her ear.

"Oh, you like knowing that?"

She nods. "Because you mean it."

My phone buzzes and I pull it from my pocket. "Fifteen minutes."

She slowly pulls away from me. "Stop distracting me."

"Never."

Autumn nearly skips to the stairs and takes them with a pep to her step. Before fading out of sight, she glances at me over her shoulder.

I shake my head, then follow her to change clothes. The water runs in the bathroom, and I can hear her listening to music as she gets ready. I remove my joggers, slip on some jeans and a T-shirt, and grab an old baseball hat.

The door opens while she brushes her teeth and her eyes slide over me. "You look delicious."

"And how'd I taste?"

"Like I want more." Heat simmers behind her gaze, and I'm tempted to lay her down on the bed. My sister can hang out with Autumn later.

She leans against the doorway, watching me.

"I think I'd like to attend Weston's party tonight. So get a dress," I say, wanting the world to know I've finally found the real deal.

She nods. "I look forward to meeting your friends and learning all sorts of juicy details about you."

I don't miss the excitement in her tone.

"It's been a long time since I've hung out with anyone, especially them."

She moves back into the bathroom and rinses her mouth. "If it sucks or if it's awkward, we'll leave. Okay? No pressure. We've been going nonstop for days."

"You're too damn pretty," I tell her from the doorway as I check the time. She pulls her hair into a low ponytail and applies pink to her lips. Then she turns to me.

"When you look at me like that, I feel special."

I hook her finger with mine, pulling her toward me. "You are."

She tastes like spearmint.

On the way to the bottom floor, I can't help drinking her in, convinced she's my other half. I really will miss her, but I also understand how important it is for Autumn to have the proper clothes for the events we're attending. My father's crowd is intimidating on a good day and snobbish on all the others.

Once outside, my driver greets me with a nod and I open the door for her.

"Have fun today. Please don't let my little sister corrupt you too much."

She steals another kiss. It's greedy and desperate. "I'll miss you too," she admits.

I brush my thumb against her cheek. "I love that for me."

Limos and blacked-out SUVs stack on the street. Autumn notices.

"Purchase an entire store if you'd like," I tell her.

"You're serious."

"If it makes you happy, I encourage it." I close the door, tapping the top of the car.

Seconds later, it zooms away, and I watch until they turn at the next intersection. I pull out my phone and text my sister.

Zane

Please be on your best behavior.

Harper

Pfft. I was friends with her first.

Zane

I wondered how long it would take
for you to bring that one up.

Harper

It's the truth!

I flick to Weston's message and read the invite he sent me last night and his text this morning.

Weston

Are you coming?

Zane

I'll be there. I also have a really big favor to ask.

Weston

Anything you need. You're like a brother.

Zane

Can you meet me at my place?

Weston

I'll be there within the hour.

Back in the penthouse, I let out a deep breath and smile as I glance around, knowing this place isn't my home. Cozy Hollow is.

CHAPTER 26

Autumn

I officially feel like gelatin," I say to Harper in the changing room at the spa. Three mimosas and a ninety-minute hot stone massage later and I'm ready to crawl into bed. My body hasn't been this relaxed since . . . now is not the time to think dirty-as-fuck thoughts about Zane.

"Me too." Harper smiles as she puts ChapStick on her plump lips. The woman makes athletic wear look like it should be on a runway.

Once I'm dressed, we walk toward the front of the building as Zen music floats through the space. "Before I forget, we're attending a dinner party. Zane mentioned I need a dress."

"Oh, when?"

"Tonight. Weston Calloway is hosting."

"What?" She scowls. "And he didn't invite me!"

"Crash it," I say with a grin. "I'm sure he wouldn't mind. He seemed very . . ."

"Flirty?" Harper grins mischievously. "He is, but unfortunately unavailable to anyone who tries. Tonight, I'd rather wear stretchy pants and eat chocolate-covered peanuts while watching old seasons of *Project Runway*."

I burst into laughter. "That actually sounds perfect."

We climb into the SUV that's parked and waiting for us.

"About the other night . . . I'm sorry for inviting Sebastian."

"It's fine. I'm not sure certain things would've happened had he not been there," I tell her, leaving out the details.

"Oh, really? That's great, then. I did talk to him after you two left." She hesitates. "He seems to be very much in love with you still. But I told him he was shit out of luck because my brother was marrying you."

I chuckle. "He's shit out of luck because he's a cheating bastard."

"That too. So, we need clothes for the island, a dinner party, and a few dates. Anything else?"

I think about it. "What about a ball gown for a charity formal I'd like to attend in Cozy Hollow?"

"Absolutely. That sounds fun. Any boundaries? Certain materials or styles you dislike?"

"Nope. You have complete control."

"Just how I like it. This will be just like dressing my Barbies." She's legitimately excited. "I do have to prepare you for some things, though."

"Huh?"

"Zane's ex. I don't want you to be blindsided by her on the island and I'm positive he hasn't shared much about her."

I shake my head. "Not any redeeming qualities, at least."

"She has none." Harper is direct with her statement.

"He said the same thing."

"It's the truth. She doesn't want my brother, but she also doesn't want anyone else to have him either. Celine is a mean girl."

I suck in a deep breath. "I'm dreading this."

"Please don't. You're the perfect partner for Zane." She glances at me. "I haven't seen him this happy in years." The car slows in front of a high-rise building. We step out and I follow Harper.

"Ms. Alexander," the woman at reception says. "We didn't expect you in the office today."

"Hi. Just stopping by for personal matters," Harper states with a wave as she makes her way toward the elevator. It's midday on a Monday and there are tons of people around. She's kind and says hello to each person we pass. We ride up to the sixteenth floor and she escorts me into a room with mirrors and tape measures.

A man enters with a smile.

"Harper," he says. "What a pleasure to see you."

"Hello, Gentry. This is Autumn. She's dating my brother. Anyway, I thought we could grab measurements then start with a few dresses and pantsuits. I'll need them completed by the end of day Thursday. I'll send an email with the styles I'd like made, along with the delivery address. Overnighted."

"Absolutely." He leads me to the platform and measures every inch of me, from my inseam to my waist to my head. Nothing is left unmeasured.

Once we're finished, Harper takes me farther up the high-rise and unlocks a door. The room is full of clothes on racks, coordinated by color and season.

"I believe everything in here will fit you, but based on your body shape, I'd like to handpick some items." Harper moves through them, pulling out outfits and draping them over my arm. It's fascinating watching her work and being in her element.

"If there is anything that you see, feel free to add it to your pile."

"Okay," I say, giddy with excitement. She gives me cashmere, silk, and cotton in beautiful shades of the rainbow. Harper is a godsend.

"Oh, this for tonight." She holds up an elegant dress that screams class. "These clothes were pitched by designers and worn at shows we've hosted. If you let me dress you, you'll become a style icon."

"You're my fairy godmother."

She snorts. "Now that would be a fun job. Bippity boppity booping women and making their fashion dreams come true."

More clothes are added to my arm and it's heavy.

"It's also a test, too. I have a theory that Celine is a chameleon and imitates the personalities of the ladies my brother falls for."

My brows furrow. "What the hell?"

"She was friends with the woman Zane dated prior to her, Diana. At times, it was hard to tell them apart and I thought they were sisters. So when the end came, Celine was there, forcing herself into his life. She copied my brother's personality to trick his best friend. Bottom line: she's manipulative and a fucking problem. I don't want her alone with Zane. Please don't let him leave your side at the resort this weekend."

"Should I be scared?" I ask. "Is she dangerous?"

"I think she's just obsessed," Harper explains.

"I mean, I get why," I tell her with a laugh, trying to lighten the mood. "Your brother is great."

She nods. "And I think you're the only woman he's been with who's recognized that."

"How is that possible?"

"Because he's actually himself when he's with you."

She flicks her fingers through a few more racks, handing me sweaters and high-waisted pants, then leads me to the corner of the room that opens up into a hallway with doors. "Let's focus on finding you something to wear for tonight first."

"Perfect." I'm genuinely excited as I hang the fine fabrics on the hooks in the oversized dressing room.

Knowing actual models have stood back here has me shaking my head. How am I here right now, hanging out with Lucy, the girl I became besties with on a random October weekend?

I unzip the back of the first gown she handed me and wiggle inside. The sheer sleeves of the midi dress give the style an elegant look with a hint of sexy from the split that reveals the upper thigh.

Details are cut out under the bust. It's classy and fits like it was personally made for my body. I stare at myself in the mirror, spinning around, amazed.

"Let me see," Harper says.

I step out and give her my best mock runway strut. I catch a glint of the mesh material sparkling in the bright overhead lights.

"Wow. Yes, you absolutely have to wear this tonight. Oh, hold on."

She runs to the other side of the room and returns with a pair of black high heels. "A nine?"

"Yeah," I tell her, sliding my feet into them, which will make me three extra inches closer to Zane's mouth.

"That's the outfit. A total showstopper. Heads will turn when you enter. My only regret is not being there to witness it," she says with a grin. "Don't try to talk me into it. Season four of *Project Runway* is calling my name."

I change in and out of dresses and jumpers, loving every single thing she gave me. "These clothes were practically made for you. Geez, I want to put you on the runway."

"Oh, stop. You're just being kind."

After one final sweep, Harper and I load everything into garment bags, then she gives the driver several addresses. For hours, we enter stores with crystal chandeliers hanging from the ceiling and thirty-thousand-dollar dresses on the walls.

Harper helps me pick out a few bathing suits too. It was a miracle anyone had stock, considering October is right around the corner. She doesn't allow me to pay for a thing, even though I offer Zane's card.

When we're done, I'm ready to drop, but we make one last stop. It's not a department store or a high-rise building either, it's a mansion on a street of beautiful homes.

"I called in a favor," Harper says, unlocking her phone and

checking the time. "Makeup and hair from one of the best in the city. You have exactly three hours before Weston's party starts. I told my brother you'd meet him there."

"I just got super nervous."

"Do you trust me?" she asks.

"I do," I tell her, because I have no idea how to navigate this world that I've somehow slid into. "Will you give me a rundown of what I need to expect? I feel lost."

She gives me a sweet smile as she leads me down the cobblestone sidewalk. The door swings open and a beautiful man with gorgeous eye shadow appears.

"Harper, sweetie." They exchange kisses on the cheek and Harper steps aside.

"Oliver," she says. "You smell great. What is that?"

"Just a new scent that hasn't been released yet. One of my clients dropped it off," he says.

Harper grins wide. "This is Autumn. My future sister-in-law."

"I'm Oliver." His mouth falls open and he smiles wide, showing his perfect teeth. "Girl, you're fucking beautiful. Those cheekbones and lips are to die for. What a canvas!"

I laugh and immediately feel comfortable.

"Right?" Harper agrees. "Even I'm jealous."

"Stop," I tell her with soft eyes, and she shoots me a wink.

"If Zanie-poo doesn't marry you, maybe I will. Who am I kidding? I'm too gay for that. But I thought about it for a few seconds. That counts for something. Come on, don't want the paps getting too many photos of you two," he says, stepping aside and allowing us into his house.

"This is my bestie, April. She'll take care of your hair and I'll do the face," he explains.

"Hello," April says with a kind smile. Her hair, glasses, and lipstick are hot pink. It suits her.

The room is set up like a salon with mirrors and chairs, and there is even a sink in the corner. There are pictures of Oliver with countless celebrities—Oprah, Adele, Beyoncé, every Kardashian, and the list goes on.

"This is my trophy wall." He watches my eyes slide over the selfies he's taken with beautiful people. "Speaking of."

Oliver snaps a photo of me, him, and Harper on his phone. After a click of a button, a tiny printer on the counter beside his tool chest of makeup spits out a picture. He peels the paper from the back and slaps us right beside Kylie. "Now, let's get to work."

April leads me over to the washing station and puts a thick robe over my body. Once I'm comfortable in the chair, she gets down to business. The water is loud and I can't hear anything Oliver and Harper are saying.

With my eyes closed, I think about Zane and wonder what he's doing today.

After my hair is washed and rinsed, April works her magic on my mop. The blow-dryer is loud too. I'm not sure how much time passes, but when she's done, I know my hair has never looked this good before and probably won't ever again.

"Wow. You're so talented," I whisper, running my fingers through my silky strands.

She laughs. "Thank you."

"Ready for your face?" Oliver asks. He has everything set out and has already matched the foundation to my skin.

"Yes," I say, and Oliver gets to work. Harper sits on the counter, swinging her legs as he asks me questions.

"So, what do you like to do for fun?"

"I run a lot. Watch horror movies. In the winter, I do some snowboarding."

"You snowboard?" Harper asks, intrigued.

"How do you think I met Sebastian?" I ask with a smirk.

258

"You really are perfect for my brother," she says, looking at me with amazement. "The actual real deal."

I blush.

"You are. Start believing it."

If she keeps it up, Harper might convince me it's true.

Once my foundation is in place, Oliver draws fat lines on my face with a contour stick, then adds lightener. After he blends it all, I catch a glimpse of myself in the mirror and my mouth falls open.

"This is artwork."

"It's the canvas, not the paint," he says, lifting my chin upward. "Now close those eyes."

"Have any predictions for me?" Oliver asks Harper, and I hear her giggle. "A deal is a deal," he says.

"I have to focus," Harper tells him, sucking in a deep breath. I'm not sure how much time passes; it feels like five minutes.

"You'll meet someone who will change your life in unimaginable ways. Financially. Spiritually. Shit, you're going to fall madly in love."

"Please tell me he has a huge dick. I'm tired of mediocre men."

"Same," I mutter.

Harper bursts into laughter. "I can't predict penis sizes."

Then it grows silent again. Oliver stops working on my eyes and instructs me to open them. When I do, Harper stares at me, but her eyes are unfocused.

"You're scared," she says. "But you'll say yes and it will be the greatest thing that's ever happened to you. You're his queen, the only woman who can sit beside him, not only as his wife, but as his equal. You've been waiting for confirmation that he's the man in your dreams. He is and always has been. Twin flames. Mirrored souls."

I glance at Oliver and his eyes are wide. This prophecy isn't for him, it's for *me*. Now I'm freaked the fuck out. I never told her about my dreams. Did Zane?

"Sweetie," Oliver says, taking a step forward, and places his hand on Harper's shoulder. She focuses back on him, smiling like nothing happened. "You good?"

She studies him. "I can't tell you if his dick is huge. Sorry!"

Oliver looks at me. We both heard what she said, but Harper has no recollection.

"Do you know about Mr. Dreamy?" I finally ask.

"No. Is he hot?" She shakes her head, confused.

I rub away the chill bumps that form on my arms.

Harper glances between Oliver and me. "I said more, didn't I?"

"Yes," we whisper in unison.

"Shit. I really need a vacation," she sighs, as if this is normal.

CHAPTER 27

Zane

I don't like the idea of showing up to Weston's party without Autumn, but my sister insists we meet there. When Harper gets like this, it's easier to go with the flow than to argue. Her intuition is never wrong, so this time I'm trusting her even though I'm an anxious mess.

The event started and I haven't left for Weston's because I know Autumn won't arrive until thirty minutes after it starts. I'm trying to bide my time because as soon as I walk into that room, my old friends will bombard me with questions; ones I'm not sure I'm ready to answer yet.

Celine isolated me from those who meant anything to me. It was slow at first and then one day I realized I had no one else in my life but her. My family, my friends, I'd cut off everyone. Depression took hold and she had me exactly where she wanted me—a shell of myself.

While I have some extra time, I stroll through the penthouse. I see a small Moleskine notebook on the bedside table. I stare at it, curious as to what's inside, wishing I could see straight through the cover and read what's on the pages. But I leave it in place.

Harper

We'll be there soon. Are you at Weston's?

> **Zane**
> Almost. Are you sure you're not coming?

Harper
Nah. I've got some things to take care of.

> **Zane**
> Is there something you're not telling me?

Harper
You need to arrive alone without a safety net. It's your first time in a public setting since the breakup.

She's right. I've avoided everyone from my past thanks to the shame I've felt. I ignored those who cared about me. There is no excuse for how I treated people when I was with Celine.

I tuck my phone into my pocket and make my way to the elevator. Weston's penthouse is several floors above mine and has a much better view. However, he was given the opportunity to purchase it first or I'd have chosen his place. Or his brother's. The Calloway family has connections I wish I had. Then again, that goes both ways.

The elevator is fast and I barely have enough time to think before the doors open to his private floor. As soon as I step out, I'm greeted by a bodyguard who looks me over.

I'm handed a drink before entering. A pianist sits at the grand piano, playing songs from the 90s. The lights are low and the city buildings twinkle in the distance. A server with a tray of wine-glasses walks through the crowd, passing them to anyone empty-handed.

I take a sip, glancing around the room. Half the people I know, the others I don't, but I feel like a spotlight beams down on me. I ignore it, trying not to give a shit or let it grow too awkward. No one approaches me.

I try to think back to the last time I hung out with Weston. He had recently married Lena. That was four years ago.

In a blink, time passed. Days transformed into years.

As I finish my first glass of wine, a strong hand grabs my shoulder.

"You made it," Weston says, wearing a cheesy grin.

"I needed to be seen," I say. "Show proof of life."

This makes him laugh. "Where's your pretty girlfriend?"

"On the way."

"Ah."

"She'll be here," I confirm.

Weston stares at me, meeting my eyes.

A server hands me another wine. I don't gulp this one down.

"To be in love." Weston sighs. "Lucky bastard."

I chuckle.

"In love?" a familiar voice from behind says.

I turn to see Billie Calloway, with her jet-black hair and crimson lips that move up into a gorgeous smile. Weston's baby sister has always been a cocktease, unavailable, and absolutely not my type. She's a ballbuster and obsessed with her work. Men are nothing more than commodities, and she makes it known.

"Zane Alexander, in love? How did this happen?" She wraps her arms around me and hugs me.

"Surprised Harper didn't tell you," I say. Billie and Harper are business partners. The two of them stepped away from billion-dollar family businesses to do fashion, and they're making waves.

"I haven't seen my bestie in two weeks," Billie says, finishing the last bit of wine in her glass. As she swallows it down, another is being handed to her. The empty glass practically disappears. "I've been in Paris, negotiating."

Weston grins. "Oh, Paris. So fucking fancy."

Billie elbows him in the side.

"So who is she? The woman you're in love with."

I think about Autumn and smile.

Billie's eyes widen. "Shit. You just had the look. You're going to marry this woman."

Weston chuckles. "That's what I said."

"Her name is Autumn Travis. She's smart, pretty, and down to earth."

"Feisty as fuck. Don't forget that one," Weston adds. "But it's obvious she has a kind heart. Super protective of this old asshole. She reminds me of Lexi."

"Who?" I ask, glancing between them.

Weston pats my shoulder. "My brother's wife."

My brows lift. *"Wife?"*

"You haven't been around in a while, but to be honest, it's a new development. They're grossly in love, perfect for one another. When they're together, it's just like . . . wow, you know?"

"And you like her?" I ask Billie. She's always had the same issue that Harper has with my dating choices.

"I love her," Billie says. "Lexi saved my brother. He's the happiest he's ever been."

I nod, a chill rolling over me. "Will they be here tonight? I'd love to give my congratulations, considering I didn't get an invite to the wedding."

The Calloways have been close family friends for as long as I can remember.

"So happy you brought that up," Weston says, shaking his head, and I see Billie's jaw tighten.

"Yeah, well, we didn't get invited either. They eloped. Just up and fucking left and got married and told us afterward."

I burst into laughter.

"It's not funny. He robbed our entire family of those memories." Billie is serious.

I shrug. "In a way, I understand it though. Who wants a spectacle made out of a ceremony that's supposed to be sacred and special? We deal with that enough, don't you think?"

"He could've had a very small party tucked away somewhere remote where at least we had the chance to witness something so beautiful." She turns to Weston. "If you do the same thing, I swear I'll disown you."

"Is that a promise?" Weston asks. "Because I might make it happen tomorrow."

Another elbow goes straight to the gut.

"What else have I missed?" I ask, knowing a lot can happen in six months.

"Weston has a girlfriend too," Billie says.

"Really?" I ask, curious as to why he didn't tell me earlier. "Then why were you flirting with mine?"

"I don't have a girlfriend. We're friends."

"For now," Billie adds. "You have the same fucking look in your eye that Easton did. The same one that Zane has. It's gross."

"So, have you spoken with Nicolas?" Weston asks, quickly changing the subject.

"He's dead to me. The first time I'll see him will be at my father's wedding next week."

"The whole Calloway family will be there," Weston says. "My dad has talked about it nonstop."

"Or maybe tonight," Billie states.

"He's not supposed to be here," Weston confirms. "I asked him directly."

"Thank fuck," I say with a sigh. "And thanks a lot, Billie."

"Just making Harper proud." She chuckles. "Your face though. You were *stressed*."

I narrow my eyes. "You're actually worse than your brothers."

"Who do you think trained her? But anyway, I have a few rounds to make. Go easy on him?" Weston says to Billie with a grin.

She rolls her eyes then smiles when he's out of sight. "How are you, really?"

"Happy," I say. "Fucking ecstatic the trash took itself out."

"That's the Zane Alexander I remember. Glad you're back. The last time I saw you, I was worried. I'd seen the same thing happen to Weston. You're both too fucking stubborn to ask for help."

"When you're in too deep, it's impossible to break out of it until you have an awakening," I say, taking a sip of my wine. "Glad I woke up."

"That sounds intense. Speaking of that documentary: Wow. You must've gotten under Celine's skin for her to make up all those lies about you."

I glance out the windows, not wanting to relive it, but I prepared myself to talk about it. "Wait, you know it was bullshit?"

"Anyone who knows you knows everything she says isn't reality. Are you kidding? She's been boycotted by the most influential families. No one trusts her. All the party invites you got her? Revoked. Celine isn't welcome anywhere and your ex-bestie, Nicolas, doesn't have the same influence as an Alexander."

"You're joking." Laugher escapes me. "I hope she gets what she deserves, whatever that may be."

"It looks like karma was your personal assistant," she says, lifting her wineglass. "Cheers to that."

I clink mine against hers and drink. "Thanks for telling me. Harper hasn't mentioned it."

"Harper doesn't know. She warned me that if I brought up Celine one more time, she'd quit. That girl is not a fan."

"I know," I say. "No one has ever hated Harper either. Should've seen the red flags."

"It's because Harper saw straight through Celine's mask," Billie says. "It's a great quality to have around. One bad vibe, and Harper is like, *hell no*. That alone has saved us from making million-dollar mistakes with total fucking pricks. But yeah, Celine only gets pity invites or crashes parties these days."

It's impossible to hold back my smile. "I think you just made my night. Thanks for that."

"I'm just glad you didn't do something stupid like a tell-all interview," she says. "Career killer that screams desperation. When you don't explain yourself and let people think whatever they want, everyone stops caring. It keeps you relevant, or in your case, mysterious."

I stare at her. *"Fuck."*

"What?"

"That's it. I'm firing Roxane."

"She's worked for you and Harper for decades."

"She secured a prime-time live spot for me to share my side of the story when it came to Celine. At the last minute, it felt wrong, so I skipped it."

Billie's mouth falls open. "Do you think it was a setup?"

"Yes. Anyone else manipulating me that I'm not aware of?" I ask, my nostrils flaring as I shake my head. "Why didn't I see this sooner?"

I think about the last five years and the whirlwind of shit I've gone through. Roxane was eager to help, but nothing she's suggested lately has had results.

"Instead of extinguishing fires, she was starting them," I mutter.

Billie studies me as if she's recalling the past too. "Oh my God. If there isn't anything for her to do, she doesn't have a job, and you're the least problematic person there is."

"Do you think . . . do you think she was one of the anonymous sources in that documentary?"

"Anything is possible." Her brows are squished together.

"I trusted her," I say, feeling betrayed by the realization.

"I'm sorry," Billie tells me. "When everything was going on with Weston and Lena, our team gave him that very direct advice. Look at him now. He's America's Playboy. Shit, you are too."

She chuckles and smiles with soft eyes. "Maybe I need a scandal. Hmm."

"I do not recommend it. Zero out of ten stars," I tell her, but she doesn't respond. Her gaze fixates over my shoulder.

Then I see the people behind her do the same.

I turn my head and my eyes immediately meet Autumn's. She's like royalty; an elegant, classic beauty. All she's missing is a crown as she flips her long brown hair over her shoulder. Our gazes lock and everything around me disappears.

"Who is that?" Billie asks with awe in her tone.

I smile wide. "My future wife."

CHAPTER 28

Autumn

I walk in and search the room for Zane. There are too many tall, dark-haired men dressed in expensive suits and beautiful women in well-fitted cocktail dresses. Harper knew exactly what she was doing when she put this gorgeous gown on me.

I stare at who I think is Zane. He's wearing a black shirt and gray slacks. One hand holds a glass of wine and the other is tucked into his pocket. The Mr. Dreamy stance is correct along with the messy hair. As if I summoned it, he turns around and his bright blue eyes lock on me.

A boyish grin slides over his lips and I immediately smile.

There he is.

He says something to the woman he was chatting with, then walks toward me. It's like we're the only two people in this crowded room. My heart rushes with excitement and appreciation as his arm wraps around me. Then his mouth captures mine and we're lost in the moment as the twinkling of the piano plays behind us.

"You're so goddamn beautiful." He smiles against my lips. "I really fucking missed you."

"I missed you," I tell him, pulling away, and that's when I realize the entire room is staring at us.

"Don't be embarrassed," he says, whispering in my ear. "It's been a long time since they've seen me."

"I'm not," I say, looking up at him, glad I won't wake up this time.

I adore the sweet smile that sweeps across his face. A glass of wine is handed to me and I take it with a smirk.

"We should leave," Zane mutters, running his fingers through my hair.

Next thing I know, Weston approaches and pulls Zane into a hug. I smile at him when they pull away.

"So are you going to introduce me?" he asks.

I furrow my brows, and before I can ask him if he's drunk, another version of him steps up wearing a cheeky fucking smirk. My mouth falls open as they stand beside one another.

"There are two of you? And you dress the same, too?"

"Great to see you again, Autumn. And yes, we're twins," Weston says.

I blink between them and it's unsettling how I can't tell them apart.

"And that reaction never gets old," Weston offers, proudly.

"I'm Easton," the other one says, holding out his hand. He's openly agitated with Weston. "I don't try to dress like him. The bastard has a camera in my closet."

I try not to laugh. "Autumn Travis. Very nice to meet you."

"It's a pleasure," he tells me.

"This is my girlfriend," Zane offers, softly. His eyes sparkle when he glances at me.

"They're getting married," Weston says.

"Congratulations," Easton happily adds.

"It's not official yet," Zane tells him, but doesn't deny it. "Soon."

I grow giddy thinking about a future with him. Then I realize that I was able to imagine something I haven't imagined with anyone else—ever. As the three of them chat, I'm lost in my thoughts, imagining our happily ever after. Us being together is crystal clear in my mind, as if my subconscious manifested this perfect man.

Another few sips and my wine is gone. I'm immediately given another glass.

I study Zane as he talks, randomly stealing glimpses of me, shooting me little winks and smirks. Flirty as hell, but I enjoy it, knowing each time our eyes meet I have him. His gaze doesn't lie.

"Well," Easton says, looking at his watch. "I've gotta go. Just wanted to stop by and check out the shindig. I've had a very long, exhausting day. Nice meeting you, Autumn."

Another polite head nod and then he's walking past us.

"Your brother is nicer," I say to Weston.

"Ah. You don't know him," he warns. "Easton is a bigger asshole than Zane and . . ."

His words trail off and a smile fills his face as a pretty woman in a cute dress approaches him.

"Carlee," he says, his voice softening. "You made it."

I glance at Zane and he looks at me, then pulls me away. The pianist continues playing.

"Dance with me?"

I glance around. "No one else is."

"Who gives a shit?" He holds out his hand and I take it. His strong hand is on my waist. "How was your day?"

"Fun and exhausting."

"I hope you got everything you wanted."

"Everything except you," I say.

"Ah. I almost forgot about the IOU from earlier."

I smirk. "No you didn't."

"You're right." He whispers the rest in my ear. "I've been thinking about you sitting on my face all day."

When he pulls away, he locks me in place with his smoldering gaze. "And what if I said I wanted to leave?"

"Then I'd tell you to lead the goddamn way."

A mischievous grin dances over my lips and I grab his hand,

pulling him away. He tugs me close to him, kissing me, brushing fallen hair back.

"You're giving everyone a show."

"No, Pumpkin. Right now, it's only me and you. No one else here matters."

I slide my hands behind his neck, desperately kissing him as he laughs. I feel like a teenager again, skipping prom to make out in the hallway. The pianist nods as we move past him, and when I turn back to the room, I notice more couples are dancing.

"They just needed a leader," I say as he wraps his arm around me.

"They usually do."

We walk through the crowd and I steal glances of this beautiful man. Needing, wanting him, not caring about the party or the clothes or the people.

As we move to step out of the door, Zane pulls me closer to him. I pass a woman in a red dress who glares at me with crystal-blue eyes. Familiarity washes over me. It's her. His ex.

He walks past her, seeing straight through her, pretending she doesn't exist.

It's cold.

Zane doesn't tense, and when I look back over my shoulder she's staring at me, anger and jealousy radiating from her like death rays. I want to scream at her that she threw him away.

"Zane," she says as we walk toward the open elevator. He keeps ignoring her and places his hand on my hip as he guides me inside. His fingers dig into me and I wrap my arm around him.

"Hey," I say, brushing my nose against his, wishing he'd talk to me. Just like that, he slips into his shell, a protection mechanism.

"Zane," I whisper.

He kisses the top of my head as we travel down to his floor. "I'm so glad we're leaving. It's like . . . everything was perfectly planned."

"Are you okay?" I ask.

"My sister took care of me," he tells me. "It's like she knew what would happen tonight. Divine timing." He smiles, taking a step toward me, his eyes sliding down me. "You look like you break hearts for a living."

Butterflies flutter throughout me. "I used to. I don't give many people a chance anymore."

The elevator doors slide open, and as soon as they do, we exit, nearly stumbling on our own feet. His mouth is on mine, greedy and desperate like we need to destroy the other. I want my IOU and I want it now.

Zane unlocks the door, pulling me inside. He's hard and thick and has me pressed against it. "Who was the woman you were chatting with?"

He pulls away and places his hands on my hips. "Are you jealous?"

"I have trust issues," I state. No use denying it, because Zane knows what Sebastian did to me.

"Babe." His face softens. "It was Billie Calloway. She's Harper's best friend and business partner. Don't you worry about that with me. There is no one else. There are no secrets. Not with you. I have nothing to hide. Right now, there is only one woman on the planet who I want." He kisses the softness of my neck. "And she tastes . . . so . . . fucking . . . good."

I pant out a breath, exposing my neck further, wanting him to lick every damn inch of me.

"It's only you, Autumn," he confesses. "It will only ever be you."

"Promise me," I say, nearly begging. "Promise me that's true."

"I fucking promise with all of my being, Pumpkin. On every memory I still have of my mother. You were made for me."

"Mirrored souls," I whisper.

"Twin flames," he says, then both of our eyes bolt open.

"Did—" I tilt my head at him. "Did Harper tell you that?"

"Did she tell *you* that?" He crosses his arms over my chest, watching my breasts rise and fall. His cock is so fucking hard in his pants, and I trace the outline of him. My body aches for more of that. All of him. He's made me a sex-crazed monster.

"Ah, I know that expression," he tells me.

"Which one?" I ask, laughing.

"It's the Alexander addiction look. You're wondering how you'll live without me."

"In a roundabout way," I tell him, not daring to mention his dick is basically plastered on a centerfold in my mind. A dirty thought I've replayed at least a hundred times.

"You'll never be satisfied," he warns. "I'll make sure you'll always want more of me."

"That sounds like a threat," I say, arching a brow at him. "I'd be willing to bet you're more addicted to me."

"Fuck yes, that's true," he says. "I don't want this to end, Autumn. Not in January. I do want to make you my wife. To take the risk. I want the whole goddamn world to know you're mine, and more than anything, I want to take care of you and go on adventures with you. I'm already bound to you, somehow. And I don't understand it at all, but in my heart, it's you. It will only ever be you."

My mouth is on his. "Just ask me."

Zane drops to his knee as if I commanded him and reaches inside of his pocket. He pulls out a black box and opens it.

"Wait. You planned this?"

"Not planned, just prepared. Autumn Travis, please spend the rest of your life with me. It's a wild request and I know we're practically strangers, but my heart knows you're my other half. If it's too soon—"

I kiss him, deeply. My heart wants this too. It's insane, but it feels right. "Yes. Absolutely. Yes." I nod. "I'll take the risk with the man of my dreams."

He grabs my finger. Kissing where the ring will go before he slides it on.

"It fits," I say, then I realize Harper had every inch of me measured today. Even my fingers. I smile. He's smart. I'd thought nothing of it.

"This is my mother's ring. I had Weston help me resize it for you."

I move toward him, wrapping my arms around his neck. "I can't accept this."

"It's meant for my wife. I've never even *thought* about giving it to anyone until I met you."

I grab his face, kissing him, drunk on the taste of sweet red wine on his lips. "You really want me to be your wife?"

"Fuck yes, I do," he says.

"I want to be her too," I admit. It feels right and I can't say no, not when I'm in this deep. It's a risk, but one I'm willing to take.

"You are," he says, lifting me into his arms and carrying me upstairs. Zane carefully unzips the back of the dress from my body and it falls to the floor in a puddle around my feet. Then his mouth is on my shoulder, sliding up to my neck, and then on my lips.

"Fuck," I whisper, the glow from the city lights just bright enough so I can see his face. "You're mine."

"For fucking ever," he confesses like it's a prayer as I slowly unbutton his shirt. I push it off his broad shoulders, then reach behind my back and unclasp my bra, allowing my breasts free.

He tweaks my nipple with one hand while capturing the other in his mouth. I run my fingers through his hair, the sensations overpowering as he sets me on the edge of the bed.

I shake my head. "Earlier, you mentioned me sitting on your face."

His eyes darken and a smirk slides across his face.

"I thought we might try that, considering."

His brow pops.

"Considering I've never had the pleasure of riding someone's face."

"Fuck, Pumpkin. Let me clear you off a place to sit."

Zane brushes his hand over his face and I watch him as he undresses for me, revealing his beautiful muscles, then lies back on the mattress. I crawl toward him and chew on the inside of my cheek. "Which direction?"

"This is your fantasy, sweetheart. Whichever fucking way you want. If you face the headboard, I'll get to watch you come all over my face. The other way, I get a close-up view of your beautiful ass. Either way I win."

"I want you to see me," I whisper. "See what you do to me. The look on my face when you make me come."

"Fuck yes. Come here," he says. "Straddle my face."

His hands grip my cheeks, scooting me farther down onto his lips. I glance down at his smoldering eyes, running my fingers through his hair as he tongue fucks me nice and slow. Then his mouth is back on my clit, sucking and flicking, but not too fast. He's playing with me, leading the way as I gently rock my hips.

The scruff on his face feels so good on me and I want to pick up the pace. Whimpers crawl from my throat, and when I look into his eyes, he growls against my pussy.

"Zane," I whisper. "You make me feel so good."

"Mm." He kisses me, lightly licking. "You're close."

"Yes," I say, my mouth falling open as my breaths come in desperate pants. The climb is slow and treacherous. "So. So."

Then the orgasm takes hold and every muscle in my body seizes up. Life itself feels as if it comes to an end as I come apart on his mouth, riding out my orgasms on his tongue and lips as he smiles beneath me. "Will you fuck me?"

"Thought you'd never ask," he says, taking one final lick of me as I move off of him. I scoot to the edge of the bed, my ass up in the air.

Zane moves behind me, kissing my ass cheeks, then slides his mouth down my crack. His palms gently open me as he licks around my tight hole. I moan out, never having been licked there before.

"Shit, that feels amazing," I whimper, swallowing hard. My pussy pulses and I don't know how it's possible for this man to get me so worked up so quickly. I want him inside of me. Right now.

As if he reads my mind, he grabs my hips, lining his cock up with my cunt, teasing me with the tip. I try to fall back on him, but he clicks his tongue. "No patience."

"Not when it comes to you."

Zane shifts forward, slamming inside of me, and I think I see stars. "Yessss," I scream out, clenching the fluffy comforter in my fists as he fills me so full.

Zane reaches around, adding just enough pressure to my clit to set me trembling beneath him. He knows what I crave and I slam against him, our bodies crashing together.

"Are you gonna be a good girl and come on my cock?"

"Only if you keep fucking me just like that," I moan out. His thrusts grow more intentional and my body lets go. I arch my back, his hands on my ass as I take him from behind, nearly crumbling to dust as he loses himself.

As he's moaning out his orgasm, the doorbell rings. We're sweaty and breathing hard and I just want to hold him under the skyline.

I roll over onto my back, staring at him, his cock still at full attention. "Should you answer it? What if it's Weston or someone?"

"No," he whispers, glancing at his phone. "They'd call or text."

"Zane," a woman's voice calls out, and his jaw tightens.

"Who is that?"

"Who do you think?" he asks.

I slide out of bed, grab the dress shirt he was wearing then button it.

Zane follows me across the room. "Autumn. Don't."

I hold up my hand. "I'll handle it."

I skip down the stairs, two at a time, then move to the front door, opening it, knowing what I look like. By the expression on her face when she sees me, she knows we've been fucking too.

Good.

I smile. "Hi. Can I help you?"

She stares at me. "Who the fuck are you?"

I grew up with mean girls just like her. I push my perfect hair back from my eyes with my left hand. The ring sparkles in light. "Oh, I'm Zane's fiancée. Autumn. And you are?"

She rolls her eyes. "You know who I am. I'm Celine."

"Who?" I ask. "I'm sorry, he's never mentioned anyone named Celine."

This frustrates her and she grows more agitated.

I blink a few times. "So, how can I help you?"

"I'd like to speak to him. Now."

I give her a sad smile. "Eek. I'm really sorry, it's just not a good time. He's really tired right now and is in bed waiting for me to return. Maybe another day, Celeste."

"It's *Celine*."

"Okay, sure. Anyway, have a good night. Great dress," I say, then close the door in her face and lock it.

Zane stands at the stairs, watching me with his arms folded over his chest. But he's smirking. "Wow. I didn't realize you had it in you."

"Don't underestimate me when it comes to what's mine," I say, remembering I made a promise to Harper. No way in hell will I allow that woman to be alone with him.

"No one has ever treated her like that. She might have a melt-down on the island."

"Can't control anyone but ourselves. But it's the audacity for me. Does she think she can break us up?" I ask.

"Yes, just like Sebastian thinks he'll convince you to leave me. But he's mistaken with his marriage bullshit because I'd marry you tomorrow."

"Then do it."

"Wait." The mood shifts. "You'd marry me tomorrow?" He tilts his head, watching me.

"We're already in too deep. What's the difference between tomorrow and next year? You're convinced this is happening. Why not now?" I shrug, but I'm smiling.

"What if you decide you can't love me?" he asks.

"I don't think you've got anything to worry about. Mr. Dreamy has home field advantage and has since I was eighteen."

A smile meets his lips. "Call everyone you want to invite and send them to my travel agent. All expenses paid."

Zane kisses me, pulling me close. We're giddy, ridiculously happy. "Where do you want to get married?"

"It's super kitschy," I say.

"Ah. Vegas?"

"Yes!" I squeal. "I'm so excited."

"Your parents knew I would propose."

"You asked my dad?" I'm surprised my mom was able to keep that from me.

"It's the proper thing to do," he says.

I wrap my arms around him. "Do you think we're making a mistake?"

"Not at all. I've never been more sure about anything in my life."

"I'm trusting you."

"Good." He grabs my ass. "Pack a bag. We leave tonight."

"Seriously?" I ask. My head is spinning, but I'm on cloud nine.

"Fuck, I can't wait to spoil you."

"You already do."

CHAPTER 29

Zane

I wake with my hands on Autumn's hips as she rides me with the Las Vegas skyline sparkling in the distance.

"Good morning," I moan, realizing how hard I am and how wet she is. I'm buried deep inside of her.

"You started this," she says in a sleepy tone, taking full control, fucking me like our lives depend on it.

"Uh, fuck," I groan, sliding my palms onto her ass, thrusting upward as she comes down, adding more friction. I don't know what time it is, not that it matters. Autumn is the only thing on my agenda from now until eternity.

"Feels so good." She flips her long, straight hair back, placing her palms flat on my stomach. I reach up, tweaking her pebbled nipple, and she lets out a few high-pitched moans.

"Autumn." My eyes roll into the back of my head as she fucks me into the mattress. I don't want this to ever end.

"Yes, yes," she whispers, shining in the glow from the Strip through the glass of the penthouse I borrowed from Weston. A guttural groan surrounds us as she topples onto me, capturing my mouth as she clenches around my cock. I rock inside of her, chasing my end, rolling on top of her and slowing down my pace.

She smiles at me and I smile back at her, biting her bottom lip and tugging it with my teeth. She sighs out, "How is this real?"

"It feels like a dream," I admit, not knowing what I did to deserve her, but I'm thankful.

"It's not," she says. "I'd have already disappeared."

We make love in the light of the glowing skyline to the sounds of passionate gasps until we're both fully satisfied.

I smile against her neck as she runs her fingers through my hair, inhaling the sweet smell of her skin. I want to say it, I want to tell her that I'm falling in love with her so hard, as if I base jumped without a parachute.

I roll onto my back and Autumn moves over to me. "I could use a slice of pizza."

"I know of a place," I say. "I was visiting one time and randomly found it."

"Is it a secret?" She chuckles.

"Actually, yeah, but I know the way," I say, nuzzling into her neck. "It's down a long, dark hallway."

"Seriously?" she asks, rolling over and picking up her phone, showing me her beautiful ass.

I run my hand across her. "What time is it? I think they close at four."

She smiles wide, sliding out of bed. "Ooh. Goodie. It's only two."

I slide on some jeans and a T-shirt, grabbing a baseball hat. Autumn puts on some leggings and a sweater that hangs off her shoulders. "What?"

"You're perfect," I whisper as we leave the room. I grab her hand and we move toward the private elevator. When we step on, I steal a glimpse of her. "How do you like your pizza?"

"There's only one way," she says. "Pepperoni. Mushrooms. Extra black olives."

"You know what they say about women who love black olives, don't you?"

Her brows furrow.

"They're fucking freaks."

Laughter bursts from her chest and her head falls back. I enjoy seeing her laugh like she's truly happy. It's something that's too hard to fake. "I hope I always keep you like this."

She stands on her tiptoes, kissing me. "Me too."

The doors slide open and a couple steps inside. The two of us move to the corner, allowing them in.

"See, honey? That's the way you used to look at me."

They exit and I chuckle. "How do I look at you?"

"Like . . . you'd figure out a way to rope the moon if I wanted it."

My eyes soften as we step off the elevator and make our way outside. We take the sidewalk toward the Cosmo, walking hand in hand. I glance up at the moon that's high in the sky. "Just say the words."

She lightly chuckles as she leans against me. "I don't know what you see in me, Zane, but I hope it stays that way forever."

"You're the magic, Pumpkin. Just always be yourself. That's what I like about you the most."

As we walk past the Bellagio, I check the time. "They don't play it after midnight."

"Dang, it was on my bucket list," she says.

"Really?"

"Yeah, it's one reason I wanted to visit."

I grab her hand. "Perfect. We'll get you a water show, then."

"Huh?"

I wrap my arm around her. "Whatever you want."

"It ended at midnight," she repeats back to me.

"And? There is a button to turn it on somewhere."

She narrows her eyes.

"You doubt my skills?" I chuckle, straightening my stance and removing my hat before handing it to Autumn. I run my fingers through my hair and walk to the front counter like I own the place. The manager walks toward me as Autumn stands to the side.

"Hi, good morning," I say. Then I glance over my shoulder at my girl. "I'd like for the water show to be played."

She chuckles. "Sweetie. It ended at midnight."

"I'm aware. However, I believe it will be in your best interest if you call the GM to approve it."

This woman is not taking my shit and I try not to get offended. She is just doing her job.

"I'm not calling him to do something that's against protocol. Who do you think you are?"

I smile. "I thought you'd never ask. I'm Zane Alexander, future CEO of Xander Resorts, son of Ambrose. If you don't want to call Charles, I'll be happy to reach out to him myself, but I thought I'd allow you the opportunity first. It won't be good if I reach out to him directly. Trust me."

Charles Oliver is a grumpy old man just like my father. If it weren't for Xander, a lot of these buildings wouldn't exist. I've never once pulled rank or requested anything, and I know he will go for it.

The sarcastic grin on her face falls away. "Mr. Alexander, I cannot break the rules for you."

"Make the call," I say directly. "I'll be back in thirty minutes, okay? Please, make sure it begins at the top of the hour."

The woman glares at me as I turn around.

"Three o'clock," I say, tapping on my watch, then grab Autumn's hand as we walk out.

"You think that will work?" she asks, swinging our hands as I lead her into the other hotel.

"Without a doubt," I say. Then, just as promised, we meet the end of a line down a long, dark hallway with pictures hung on the wall.

"You're serious about this?"

"Yeah, it's Secret Pizza. So fucking good too." I check the time. "We should move to the front so we don't miss the show."

"We can't cut," she whispers. "Be patient."

The line is moving, but not fast enough. I tap the shoulder of the guy in front of me. "Hey. Can I pay you a hundred bucks to have your place in line?"

"Fuck yeah, man," he says, and he's tipsy, just like most of the people here. I hand it to him and Autumn giggles as I continue to pay off everyone until, eventually, we end up at the counter.

"What can I get ya?" the guy says.

"A whole pie. Pepperoni, mushrooms, a fuck ton of black olives."

"And a slice with pineapple," she says.

"Wedding is off," I say with a laugh.

"You're taking a bite just for that," she warns as the guy slaps it in the oven to warm it up. I go to the cash register. "And I'd like to pay for everyone in line."

The guy looks at me like I'm crazy. I step out and count how many people there are really fast, then I hand him ten grand. Whoever orders for the rest of the shift, let them have whatever they want."

The manager comes over and the guy explains while holding a stack of cash. Autumn is shocked.

"Who do I have the pleasure of meeting?" the manager asks with a smile. Dough flour is caked on the front of his shirt.

"Zane, sir," I say with a firm shake.

"Thanks, Zane. Appreciate that. You're gonna make a lot of hungry people happy," he says.

"Great. That's what I want to hear."

A minute later, our pie is being removed from the oven and the box is handed to me. "Hope it's good."

"Always is," I say, grabbing a stack of napkins.

Autumn smiles the entire walk down the hallway. When we're out in the open, she steals glances at me.

"What?" I finally say once we're halfway through the resort, hustling as we make our way to the water show. We have ten minutes before it starts.

"You really don't care about money."

"Some call it irresponsible. But every day, I make millions off of the interest alone by doing absolutely nothing. If I gave away a hundred thousand dollars a day, I'd barely notice. So I try, knowing that one act of kindness could completely change someone's outlook on life."

Her face softens. "How are you this normal?"

"My mother. She deserves all the credit. She was raised by blue-collar workers back in Oklahoma. My mother was an incredible interior designer and model, and when she met my dad it was history."

We continue walking and I lead the way as we turn down another corridor.

"When Harper gave you your prophecy, did she remember what she said?"

"Not at first," I explain. "What did she say?"

"Twin flames," she mutters, as if she's recalling every single word my sister said.

"Mirrored souls," I finish, remembering exactly what my sister said to me. "It's why, when you said my aura was red and I reminded you of a flame, I thought it was interesting."

She'll walk into your life when you try to escape. She'll speak of the dreams she had about you. They are you. Astral projections of yourself to your twin flame. Mirrored souls.

She gasps. "You're right."

"Harper has never been wrong," I explain as we move to a bench in front of the show. During the day, this area is bustling with tourists trying to get a good view of one of the most spectacular attractions in the city, if I do say so myself.

Autumn takes a bite of her pineapple pizza. "Mm. So good. Your turn."

"Only because you want me to," I say, tasting it. "It's okay."

"My favorite is better," she says, opening the box of pizza and exchanging it for a pineapple-free slice. She folds it in half like a true New Yorker and takes a bite. "This is the good stuff."

"It's great," I say, handing her a napkin and snagging a piece for myself. Just as the minute hand hits the top of the hour, the lights come on.

Autumn's eyes go wide. "They're actually doing it."

"Of course they are," I say, almost wishing I could've heard that conversation. "They understood the assignment."

"You could be dangerous with all that power."

"But instead, I use it for good," I say. "Enjoy, Pumpkin. This is just for you."

The pool drains a couple inches and when the first cannon goes off, Autumn nearly drops her pizza. The booms clap against the walls. During the day, it's not quite as loud.

We eat until we're full, and have a ton left over for later.

Random people stop and stare, noting the time. It's unusual, I have to admit, but worth every string I had to pull to make it happen. I'm sure my father will have some strong words for me tomorrow.

Autumn watches in amazement as the water shoots up a thousand feet into the air, dancing across the way like elegant ballerinas to classical music.

"Wow," she says as the colored lights change. After the final show, the display goes dark, like it never happened.

"That was incredible," she tells me. "I always wanted to see that and never got the chance. The one at the resort in Cozy Hollow, it's almost identical. Other than the scale."

"Yes, because I've been fascinated with it since I was a kid. So, when my father announced opening a state-of-the-art restaurant, my mother required a miniature version to be added just for me."

"Aww," Autumn says. "That's special."

We walk back to the penthouse, and I scoot the gigantic box of pizza into the fridge. It's nearly impossible, considering it was freshly stocked for our last-minute arrival.

Autumn yawns.

"Let's go to sleep," I say, and she leads the way upstairs.

We remove our clothes down to our underwear and slide under the cool blankets. I wrap my arm around her and press against her, our bodies molding together.

I let out a contented sigh.

"Viva Las Vegas," she whispers, and I glance at the ring sparkling in the low-lit room. Screens from the surrounding buildings splash different colors across the space, even though they're distant.

I smell her skin then whisper in her ear, "I love you, Autumn. You're my everything."

"I love you too. I can't wait to marry you." A smile touches her lips before she turns and kisses me. I don't want this moment to end, even as exhaustion takes over.

"Thank you for loving me," she whispers.

"Thank you for allowing me to." I hold her tighter, never wanting to let her go. Tonight, I'll fall asleep with a smile on my face. Tomorrow, this woman will be my wife, the first day of forever.

CHAPTER 30

Autumn

*T*he penthouse is full of family and friends. Harper walks through the place like she owns it, carrying a garment bag with glasses on her face. When she arrived this morning, she dropped off her bags then left to take care of planning everything. Zane insisted it was low-key, that we already had the venue secured—because money can literally buy anything in Sin City—and that she didn't need to fuss.

As soon as she's close, she guides me away from Zane. I nearly spill my martini but save it at the last minute. In less than five hours, we will all take limos to the little chapel to get married by Elvis.

I glance at Blaire and Julie, who are chatting with my parents. With a nod of the chin, they're breaking away and following us.

"I invited my friends," I tell Harper.

"The more the merrier." She grins, leading me to the oversized bedroom.

Julie and Blaire enter and shut the door behind them.

"I was able to find a dress that I think you'll love," Harper says. "Vivie and I are close, and she had this in your exact measurements. She had it flown to me." Harper does a wiggle and rubs her arms. "Sorry, it gave me chills again. It's like it was made for you."

My best friends stand beside me as Harper sets the dress on the hook on the back of the door. She unzips the front and reveals the pearl-white fabric that shimmers in the light. The three of us gasp and an overwhelming sensation floods through me. My emotions run wild, and though I'm smiling, tears stream down my face.

I'm living a fairy tale.

"Harper . . ." I can barely speak, the words stuck in my throat. "It's beautiful."

"Right? It's totally you," Harper says. "When I saw it, I had the same reaction. It's Bagatelle. Off the shoulders. Internal bone corset with a super cinched waist. Plus." She reaches forward. "Pockets."

"Wow." Julie exhales and she's crying along with Blaire.

"Oh my God, if the three of you don't stop, I'll lose my composure too," Harper playfully warns. "Sometimes it sucks being an empath."

"It's just . . ." I suck in a breath. "It feels like a dream come true." I wipe my cheeks.

Harper places her hand on my upper back. "You're the one, Autie. The *only* one. This was meant just for you—my brother, the dress, the intense burning love. You were made for one another. And I'm so thrilled for both of you."

A knock on the door steals my attention. Harper cracks it open and I hear Zane's voice, as if talking about him somehow summoned him.

"No, you absolutely *cannot* come in here," Harper states, her tone firm and mildly terrifying.

He slightly peeks in and sees us crying.

"What have you done?" he accuses.

Harper scoffs. "I didn't do anything."

"No, no," I say, moving forward, switching places with Harper. "It's fine. Just happy tears."

"Not getting cold feet on me?" His tone drops an octave and he shoots me a sexy smile.

"Never," I whisper. "Are you?"

"Fuck no."

Our mouths magnetize together and we nearly lose control.

"Okay, okay, that's enough," Harper says, pulling me away, giving him the evil eye.

"We're wedding planning, got it?"

He chuckles with swollen lips and checks his watch.

"We're gonna kick your ass if you don't go away," Julie threatens with her hands on her hips.

I meet his eyes. "She means that."

A chuckle rumbles through him. "I know."

I steal another kiss before Blaire pulls me away, and Harper pushes Zane out. The door locks and she turns to me.

"Before we were *rudely* interrupted, I was going to suggest that you try it on just to make sure it fits," Harper says.

Julie and Blaire agree.

Harper removes it from the garment bag. I'm in awe, holding it as the bright sun shines in the windows, making it shimmer like a pearl.

"Shit, I have shoes too, one moment. They're in my suitcase." She leaves the room, allowing me alone time with my besties. It's the first time I've had the chance to talk with them without everyone around and I'm thankful for the time.

Harper is one of the most thoughtful people I've ever met and pays attention to social cues. Even Blaire.

Julie smiles wide. "You're *actually* marrying Mr. Dreamy!"

Blaire claps her hands together. "So glad I did that love spell."

Julie turns to her. "Yeah? Well, it didn't work for me. You gave Autumn the entire potion, apparently."

I burst into laughter. "I don't know how this is my life."

"It couldn't have happened to a better, more caring person. You're proof dreams come true," Blaire confirms.

Julie gives me a sweet smile. "You've made me believe in love again."

"Jules," I say, hugging her tight. "You'll find love."

"I know, I know. Now, please go try it on before I force my ass into it first," Julie says, but she's smiling.

Reaching forward, I grab both of their hands. "I love you two. Three Musketeers forever."

"I'm just waiting for you to tell Julie I'm your maid of honor," Blaire says.

Julie crosses her arms. "Hell no! We will fight right here."

"Can you two figure it out and just let me know?" I ask.

I move to the bathroom and slide out of my clothes. I step into the material, pull it up, and glance in the full-length mirror. Happiness and excitement swell inside me.

I am marrying the man of my dreams, and I can almost imagine our entire life together. Not wanting my emotions to take over again, I blink hard, inhale a deep breath, and catch a glint of the beautiful ring on my finger.

A knock at the door pulls my attention away.

"Are you okay in there?" Harper asks.

"Yep, fine. Want to help me zip her up?"

The door clicks open and Harper walks inside. I meet her eyes. She covers her mouth with her hand, then walks forward and zips it the rest of the way.

"Do you like it? You can say no and I'll find other options. I just thou—"

"It's what I would've chosen. I'd marry your brother in a T-shirt and shorts." I pull her into a hug. "Thank you for saving the day. It's like you knew."

"I'm happy you're going to be my sister," she says, and we let go of one another.

"We want to see!" Julie says from the bedroom.

Harper nods and moves out of the way as I walk by. As soon as I step out, the bedroom door swings open and my sister enters.

"Autie! Holy shit." Winter is speechless. So are Blaire and Julie.

Harper grins wide. "You're a showstopper, babe!"

My sister immediately bursts into tears and hugs me, pushing hair out of my face. "You're beautiful. Look at you."

"I missed you," I tell her. The last time I saw her was two years ago. She's been busy with school and work. "I'm glad you're here."

"Yeah, well, I kinda quit my job to be here," she says.

"Winter, no." I shake my head. "Please tell me you're kidding." My sister has worked her ass off to be where she is.

"You'll only get married once." She grabs my hand. "No way I'm missing it."

"Well, shit, there goes our maid of honor title," Julie says. Blaire snort-laughs.

"Can you go get Mom?" I ask Winter.

She nods and walks away. I spin around, placing my hands in my pockets. Harper puts the shoes on the floor and I step inside the two-inch heels.

"Taylor does four-hour shows in that brand. You could run a marathon in them," she says. They give me the perfect amount of height for where the dress falls on the ground. "I'm good at this."

"You are," I say with a laugh. "My fairy godmother."

A minute passes and there's a light tap on the door. Harper walks over and cracks it open, then steps to the side to let my mom in the room. As soon as she sees me, she rushes over and hugs me tight.

"Autie. Wow. My beautiful daughter. I'm happy for you. Zane is a *good* man." She meets my eyes and tears well again. She lets me go and reaches into her pocket to pull out a black velvet pouch. "They were your gran's, that she wore on her wedding day, and that I wore on mine. It's tradition."

My mother hands me a pair of earrings and I put them in, then she places the matching necklace around my neck.

"Thank you, Mom," I whisper. She smiles brightly. It's true happiness for me.

"Okay, now, if we don't stop with all this, I'll cry the rest of the day and I probably shouldn't do that."

"And we have makeup and hair, so please, kindly change. I'll make sure your gown is at the chapel waiting for you."

I nod and excuse myself. Harper unzips me halfway, knowing I'd need the help, and after I'm back in my jeans and T-shirt and the dress is on its hanger, I return.

"Oh, almost forgot to tell you, Oliver and April are already at a salon close to the venue." She checks her watch. "You have to arrive within the next thirty minutes to be ready in time."

"Seriously?" I ask.

"Should probably get going." She glances at her phone.

"Already?"

"Yep. Now. Don't want to be late. Too many moving pieces."

I nod. "Thank you."

"The next time we see you, you'll be saying 'I do,'" Blaire says.

"All of you have to promise me you won't drink too much, okay?" I ask as Harper guides me out of the room.

"We'll save it for the after-party," Julie says, and Winter laughs.

Harper's hand is on my back and Zane follows us. As soon as I'm close, he cups my palms in his hands and kisses me. "You have to go now, don't you?"

"Yes," I say. "I'll see you there."

"One moment, I owe Harper something." He smirks.

I already know where this is going.

"Excuse me, excuse me." Zane meets the gazes of our closest friends and family. Weston, Easton, and Billie Calloway must've arrived while I was trying on my beautiful gown. "I just want you all to know that Harper predicted this entire thing, and she's the *greatest* sister in the world." Everyone laughs and smiles fill the room. He turns to her. "I fulfilled my promise."

"Thank you," she says. "Is this a good time to mention how many kids you'll have?"

My eyes widen. "Nope! Not ready for that yet!"

She shrugs. "Fine."

"Did you say five?" My voice goes up an octave.

"I said fine. F-I-N-E."

"Oh, thank God!" I'm relieved.

Zane chuckles.

"Wait, do you know?" I ask.

"I requested no more spoilers."

Harper's phone vibrates. "Car is downstairs."

"I'm going with you," Zane says. "No way I'm letting you out of my sight."

"Great, you should probably get going now," Harper says, pushing us both toward the door.

Once we're in the hallway, our mouths collide. Zane steps forward until my back touches the door, and I moan against him. "Fuck," I whisper.

"I've wanted to be alone with you all day," he tells me, kissing my neck, nibbling on my ear.

"We have forever," I say, smiling. Our noses brush and I'm breathless.

Zane places his hand on the small of my back and once we're outside, we slide into an SUV that's parked at the curb. We zoom across town and I don't think I see his smile fade once.

"What?" I ask with brows raised.

He shakes his head. "Are you truly happy?"

I nod. "Only because of you."

"I wrote you something." He pulls a folded piece of paper from his pocket. "This is my last chance to see you until later. Please read it right before you walk down the aisle. Not a moment sooner."

"Okay." I tap it in my hand then meet his gaze. "The anticipation might actually kill me."

"You'll survive. Don't cheat," he warns.

"I won't. I promise."

The car slows, then comes to stop. The door opens and I realize we had less time together than I thought.

"I can't wait to marry you," I confirm, stealing a kiss. His fingers brush softly across my cheek and he steals my breath away as he pours all that he is into me.

"Today is the best day of my life," he whispers against my mouth, and I need him like I need air.

The driver doesn't rush it, but Oliver does.

"Autumn, you better get your ass in here so we can get you wedding ready." He leans against the door of the salon they rented for the entire day.

I turn back to Zane, sucking in a deep breath.

"What is it?" He searches my face. "You can tell me."

"This isn't right," I whisper.

CHAPTER 31

Zane

*N*o, not like that," she says, climbing back into the SUV. The door closes behind her and we sit silently for a few seconds. I study her, not sure where this is going, but my heart might lurch out of my chest. Had I misread her intentions? Or the entire situation? Is this where she walks away?

"Zane," she whispers, gently placing her hands on my cheeks, forcing me to look into her eyes. "Don't ever doubt the way I feel about you. I'm not going anywhere. *Ever.*"

"Okay," I say with a relieved breath, and she slowly paints her lips across mine, pouring every part of herself into me. "Please explain."

"Las Vegas isn't where we're supposed to be. It feels all wrong."

I breathe out with a nod.

"Why didn't you speak up?"

"Because I want you to be happy, Pumpkin. I would marry you right here. I don't care."

I stare into her golden-brown eyes, tucking loose strands of hair behind her ear. "Where do you want to go? Anywhere in the goddamn world."

After a soft sigh, she closes her eyes. "Cozy Hollow."

I give her a sly smile. "I had a feeling you were going to say that."

AUTUMN AND HER family took my father's private jet because it was larger, and I took mine.

Harper plops down next to me, drinking a whiskey on the rocks. "Go ahead and say it."

I shake my head at her.

"Oh, come on, you know I predicted where you and Autumn would get married down to the location." She shoots back the whiskey. "But you doubted me."

I exhale. "I did."

"Did you doubt she was the one?"

"No, I just doubted your prediction being one hundred percent correct."

She laughs. "You should be glad I booked the helicopter service for you just in case. You'll have to owe me one."

I roll my eyes. "And what would've happened if we hadn't used it?"

"It would've cost you." She shrugs. "You're good for it."

"Thank you, though. I'm not sure we could've pulled it off at the last minute."

"It helped tremendously; the resort had no one scheduled for mountain tours today. It worked out like it was destined."

"And you found someone to officiate?"

The thought takes hold of me and wraps me like a warm blanket.

"Yep, I booked three hours for Autumn's hair and makeup for a reason. Gives us enough time to fly to Denver, then helicopter to the little chapel on the hill at golden hour."

"And the flower bouquets?"

"Chopped and wrapped in pretty ribbon. They'll arrive with the pastor. Not that you needed any convincing, but it's flowing so naturally that I have zero doubt that she's The One," Harper confirms. "Autumn is the real deal."

My sister smiles then excuses herself. Seconds later, my father sits in the empty chair next to me. My soon-to-be stepmother, Silvia, is asleep a few rows up.

My dad has two glasses of whiskey, one in each hand, and offers me one. I take it.

"I'm thinking about canceling my wedding."

"What?" My voice is a hushed whisper.

His voice is low. "Watching you willingly shift gears without hesitation for Autumn made me realize I haven't budged on our wedding plans. She doesn't want to get married on the island."

"Ah. Locations aren't important, Dad. Only the way you feel. I'd marry Autumn in a back alley. All that matters is spending the rest of my life with her. It doesn't matter how we get there."

"I can tell how deeply you care for one another." He sips whiskey and leans his head back on the seat. "I remember what it was like to be young and in love like you are now. I was obsessed with your mom and would've burned down the world for her. Two weeks. That's how long we knew each other before I proposed, knowing she was the love of my entire life. Never wanted to let your mother out of my sight and vice versa." He sighs. "She felt like home."

I nod, remembering how in love they were until the end. Afterward, my father grew cold. For the first time, I deeply understand why he turned inward. If I lost Autumn, I'm not sure what I'd do.

"I'm really sorry," I tell him.

He shoots back the rest of his whiskey. "Don't be."

"No, I get it now. I didn't before."

"Do you forgive me?"

"There is nothing to forgive." My thoughts linger like a ghost, realizing my father was in pain for two decades, refusing to move on. He wasn't obsessed with work; he escaped into it. "Do you love Silvia?"

My father glances at me. "Yes. She makes me feel whole again. I wasn't for so long."

"You should ask her what she wants. I switched venues in hours. You have days to figure it out. Take a risk. Who gives a fuck? I'll be wherever you are."

"Thanks." He chuckles. "You inspire me to be a better man."

My heart pounds a little harder. "Autumn changed me."

"No. She just reminded you of who you truly are."

CHAPTER 32

Autumn

I deplane in my wedding gown, hair and makeup done. Zane and I took different planes, our version of not seeing one another before the wedding. The three hours away from him might kill me.

"Elegant," my mother says, whispering as we load into the limo. From here on, I have no idea where we're going, but I'm looking forward to the surprise.

"You're all wearing orange." I gasp, glancing around.

"Of course we are. Zane requested we did," Mom says.

My parents, sister, Blaire, Julie, Oliver, and April slide into the car.

A few minutes later, it zooms away.

"Are you excited?" my sister asks, pulling the champagne bottle from its bucket stuffed with ice. Blaire passes out glasses to us.

"Understatement of the year." I gulp the vanilla-flavored bubbly. It's delicious, and I wonder if Zane chose it for me.

"I can't believe we're back home," my mom laughs. "My head is spinning."

"It feels right, though." There is a sense of excitement surrounding us. I am Cinderella in this story. The thought makes me smile.

My sister's phone buzzes and she turns it off. I make a face, wondering what it could mean. When our gazes meet, she slightly shakes her head and glances at our parents.

She hasn't told them about her job.

As if she reads my mind, she leans in close.

"I'm trying to find a good time to drop the news." Her voice is a whisper.

"I won't say a word. What will you do? Stay in California?"

"I was thinking I'd move home for a little while. I miss it a lot."

"Selfishly, I think it's a great idea."

"Staying with Mom and Dad for longer than two weeks sounds like a nightmare," she admits.

"You can have my place. Take over my lease."

She laughs. "Oh, that's right. You're getting married." Her words trail off. "It seems like it worked out, doesn't it?"

"An intelligent woman once told me it always does and that we shouldn't stress about things that haven't happened yet."

"Are you nervous?" Winter asks.

Calmness washes over me. "No. Every day I'm with him, I'm living a dream. He has a good heart that should be protected at all costs. Earlier, he thought I was going to call this off. The expression he had . . ." I shake my head. "I never want to see that look again. It nearly destroyed me."

"Because you love him."

"Yes," I whisper. "And I keep asking myself how it's possible, how I can feel this strongly and deeply about someone so fast."

"Hey." She squeezes my hand. "Time is irrelevant when you've waited a lifetime for love like this. There isn't a rulebook to life, sis. You've been obsessed with it for as long as I can remember. It's why you wanted to write romance books. You found it, though. Some people never get to experience what you have. Don't question it, embrace it."

Ten minutes later, the car slows. When the door opens, a helicopter awaits us on a pad.

"This way," the driver says, leading us across the path. The eight of us climb on board, putting on the headsets and buckling ourselves into the leather seats. It drips with luxury and extravagance.

My sister sits beside me and rests her hand on my shoulder as we lift off. I grab her hand like we used to when we were kids. Her fingernails are cut short, which is usually a sign that she's stressed.

Time is passing fast and we'll be in Cozy Hollow quicker than I anticipated. It's almost like having the wedding here was the plan all along.

Oliver, April, Blaire, and Julie take shots. My parents are focused on the view on the opposite side of the cabin.

"I'm glad you're here," I say to her.

"Me too." Winter smiles, and we grow silent as we fly over mountain passes past the highway. The sun hangs low in the sky as wisps of clouds float in the distance. My thoughts go to Zane, and I wonder what he's doing right now and if he's thinking of me, too. Being apart is hard. Once we return from his father's wedding, we're not leaving the manor for a week.

I want to be with him and only him.

An hour later, I realize where we're going—the secluded one-room chapel and white steepled church at the top of the resort, which is only reserved for the most notable events. White folded chairs with bows face the staged platform.

In my dream, when I married Mr. Dreamy, it wasn't at the Chapel of Love in Vegas. It was . . . *here*. I gasp, covering my mouth.

Winter bumps my body with hers. "How are you?"

"Happy," I whisper.

The helicopter pads, where we land, are housed on the other side of the property. Once we're back on the ground, I watch someone walk across the grass like it's a runway. By the gait alone, it's obvious it's Harper. When she is close, she smiles wide.

"Wow," she says. "My brother won't be able to hold it together when he sees you. And vice versa, he looks handsome."

I blush. "I had a dream he was wearing a steel-gray tuxedo."

"Recently?" She tilts her head at me and narrows her eyes.

"No," I laugh. "Years ago."

"Ah. I guess we'll see." She scans my face. "Makeup is still good. I told Oliver to make sure it was waterproof. He guaranteed you could go swimming and still have a face."

I chuckle. "I'm grateful."

"It's the least I can do."

We continue walking toward the staging area for me and find my father standing patiently in place, waiting for me. The sound of warming string instruments drifts quietly in the chilly mountain air. Harper checks her watch. "We're right on time. Are you ready?"

I shove my hand in my pocket and feel the letter Zane gave me. "I will be in just one second. I have to read this."

"I'll give you some privacy," she says as I unfold the paper and turn my back. My eyes scan over the handwriting, which looks like an elegant script.

Pumpkin,

My beautiful bride. How is this my life? It's a question I've asked myself since the moment I saw you.

While you were sleeping this morning, I wrote this for you. Right now, you're lying between the silk sheets, breathing softly, with your hair splayed across the pillow as sparkling sunlight leaks through the windows . . . I wish you could see how fucking gorgeous you are.

> When our eyes meet, I know you're the woman I'm
> supposed to be with for an eternity. Things are moving
> fast; I don't care. I've waited a lifetime for you.

I try not to cry, not wanting to ruin my makeup. "Harper. I'm sorry, do you have a tissue?"

"Of course," she tells me, pulling a package from the pocket of her burnt-orange dress with a swoop in the front. "I never attend weddings without them. Five minutes," she says with a wink. "Time to get you hitched, sis."

I nod, soaking up the tears that threaten to spill and continue reading.

> Unfortunately, Harper's prophecy was wrong for once.
> She said that I'd marry the love of my life in Cozy Hollow.
> This will bother her for an eternity, and I won't ever let
> her live it down. I hope you don't either.

"What?!" I say out loud, rereading his words. *"Harper."*

"Yes?" she singsongs.

I turn to face her.

"You knew I'd change my mind?" I study her, goosebumps covering my skin.

"Of course. How do you think all this happened so flawlessly? Booked it all on a hunch. I was waiting for you to wake up and realize it."

"How?" I burst into laughter.

She shrugs. "Sometimes when you know, you just know. And oh, God, there is tons more to come."

"Good stuff?"

She smiles wider. "Wonderful, beautiful, incredible, life-changing things. I'm fucking excited for you and my brother. Now, you have to speed-read so you can exchange vows at the perfect time."

"Okay," I whisper, trusting she knows how this should go.

I'm sure Elvis will be great. I'm most excited about hearing him sing "Can't Help Falling in Love." It's my motto. I've repeated it to myself every day since we danced in the rain together. I fell for you like raindrops fall from the sky.

You're my one true love, and I'm madly, deeply, obsessively in love with you. I've never been able to give anyone the real me until you. Autumn, you have me without barriers. No one else has ever made me feel safe. No one has ever made me feel seen. No one has ever loved me with all of themselves. I see it in your eyes and your heart. It's in mine, too. Love like this has only been reserved for you, my good luck charm.

My mother once told me to be known is to be loved. You know me. And I love you, Autumn. I love you like I've known you for a lifetime.

Thank you for making me the happiest man alive.

Your soon-to-be hubby,
Mr. Dreamy

CHAPTER 33

Zane

*T*he orchestra finishes warming up and the pastor steps forward. A photographer floats in and out of my peripheral, taking photos. Thankfully, Harper took care of everything before we arrived and had already informed him of what was happening. My father stands beside me, wearing a tux with a burnt-orange bow tie.

A minute later, Harper approaches, smiling wide. She gives me a thumbs-up and sits next to the Calloways. Easton's arm is wrapped around his beautiful wife, Lexi, whom I met when the helicopters landed. The two of them are perfect together, obsessed even.

I have the same type of love.

Autumn's mother is beside Silvia, and they're giggling about something like old friends. Meanwhile, Julie and Blaire glance at me and smile from the front row. I return the sentiment and look forward to getting to know them better, especially since they're Team Zane. Winter is the maid of honor. The three drew blades of grass because they couldn't decide who should get the title.

My father gives me a grin and a nod. A minute later, the string quartet begins, grabbing my attention.

It's time, I think to myself. Finally, I've waited an eternity for today.

Winter casually holds a bouquet of coneflowers that I had cut from my mother's garden for the occasion and delivered here.

Her sister offers me a sweet smile and steps to the side.

Anxious excitement takes over. Knowing I'll be married to Autumn in less than an hour has me smiling wide.

The wedding march plays, and I wait with bated breath to see the woman who was made for me.

A butterfly flutters in front of me and I glance at it. Harper noticed, and my dad did too. A chill runs over me and I try to push back my emotions.

Thank you, Mom, I think, believing she'd love Autumn. She has to be the reason for this.

The small crowd stands, and seconds later, Autumn and her dad walk down the cobblestone path.

"Wow," I whisper in awe, realizing I'll spend the rest of my life with someone beautiful inside and out.

My other half, my twin flame, my wife.

We focus on one another, and my gorgeous girl glows as a playful grin meets her lips. I inhale a deep breath, overcome by emotions. This is real. Tears form in the well of my eyes. Several fall down my cheeks as her dad lets her go.

Autumn takes the step, moving in front of me.

"Hi," I say, leaning in and mumbling against her ear. "Is this how you dreamed it?"

Her eyes slide over my gray suit and burnt-orange tie, and she grins. "Yes."

The pastor smiles and begins. "Good evening. Today, we're gathered here to celebrate the union of Zane Alexander and Autumn Travis. I'm honored to be a part of your special day."

"Thank you," I whisper. Autumn glows golden like a daydream. It's a moment I never want to forget.

I pull my phone from my pocket, wanting to cherish this forever.

"Sorry, I have to capture this. I know we have a photographer, but this is personal," I explain, interrupting the ceremony, knowing the way she looks right now will be imprinted on my mind forever. I open my camera app and take a quick snapshot of Autumn and her devious little smirk.

"Uh, no selfie?" Autumn asks, and I stand beside her, holding up my phone. My dad and Winter move into the background, so the people we care about the most are seen. I take a few and realize the pastor wasn't in our photos. We rectify it.

"That was fun. I think it should be a requirement at every wedding. Now, where were we?" he says softly. "Ah, yes. These two beautiful people have written their own vows."

I grab and unfold the cream paper, then meet Autumn's warm eyes, taking a moment, drinking her in as the sky glows golden.

"Autumn. Autie. *Pumpkin.* My breath was stolen the first time I saw you, and I didn't know if I could speak. I felt like I'd known you a lifetime or in another life." I smile, muttering, "Do you remember what I asked you?"

She nods, swallowing hard, tears streaming down her cheeks. I pull my orange handkerchief with a pumpkin embroidered in the corner from my pocket. Autumn laughs when she sees "for my pumpkin" beside it.

"Prepared."

"Always." I shoot her a wink. "That day, I asked if we'd met, because it was like we had. I knew right then that you were the one for me. That's when you took my heart. I was always told I'd know when I found true love. I didn't know what that meant until you. You brought me back from the dead and made me feel alive again. And each day since meeting you, I've woken up grateful and have asked how someone so perfect for me can exist. You were made for me, Autie. When I say I'm the luckiest man in the world, I mean it."

She licks her lips, smiling so wide, and I want to capture her mouth right now, but I fight the urge.

"I promise to *always* be by your side, support your dreams and visit a few, protect you, make you laugh at the most inappropriate times, and love you for the rest of my life. Being with you is the only place I want to be on Earth. You make me believe in prophecies. My mom told me in a letter that she hoped I still believed in magic. You are the magic, Autumn, and I love you so much. You're my other half, and I can't wait to grow old with you."

She sniffles and chuckles as she wipes her eyes. "Fuck."

As soon as the word leaves her mouth, her eyes widen, and she glances at the pastor as Julie howls with laughter.

"Whoops," she says, laughing a little harder as she pulls her paper from a pocket in her pretty dress. "Zane Alexander. Before you, I'd given up hope. I no longer believed in fairy tales or that happily ever afters existed. The world was a dark place once, where I was only surviving. Before you, I didn't understand what it was like to be comfortable, to be myself, or to have true friendship in a relationship. An incredible, awe-inspiring man once told me, 'To be known is to be loved.'"

My mother's saying. I breathe in, smiling, taking in every word, knowing she wrote them just for me.

"You're kind. Passionate. Respectful. The stars aligned for us, and I'm complete for the first time in my life, like finding you was my destiny. Zane, you are the man of my literal dreams and the love of my entire life." She meets my eyes, smiling.

"I love you," she whispers, studying me, her face still perfectly lit. "And I will always love you with my whole heart."

Autumn's mother cries and I glance around, seeing everyone tearing up. There's not an inkling of doubt on this entire fucking mountain.

I don't wait for the pastor to give me permission to kiss her. Our lips crash together, and it doesn't matter that we've done things out of order. It's our lives, our journey, and we'll write our story however we want.

She grabs my cheeks. "I love you."

"I love you," I say, stealing one final kiss.

"How about we exchange those rings now?" the pastor says, and I'm grateful he's keeping us on track.

"Zane," he says.

"I give you this ring as a symbol of my love," I say, sliding it on her finger.

"I give you this ring as a promise to love, cherish, and respect you," she says.

A wide grin takes over as she puts it on my finger. The silent conversation we hold nearly takes me to my knees. Autumn is my life.

"May you be blessed with health, happiness, and everlasting love. By the power vested in me, I now pronounce you husband and wife." He nods at me. "*Now* you may kiss your bride."

The orchestra plays "Can't Help Falling in Love" and Autumn laughs as I pull her into my arms, then we dance.

"You got your song," she says, kissing me.

"Dreams come true," I whisper, desperately capturing her mouth. Our friends and family applaud. We smile and take a few shots with the photographer. Five minutes later, I lead her away.

"You can fly that?" she asks as I walk her to my private helicopter pad.

I smirk. "Yeah. Easton delivered it for me."

"What else don't I know about you?" She laughs.

"Ask me anything," I say. "Want to play forty-two questions?"

"We suck at keeping count, but I'd love to play." I open the door for her and she climbs in.

I reach across her, pulling the harness over her chest, then meet her eyes. "I can't wait to take this dress off of you."

"Mm. It's what I'm looking forward to the most."

I buckle her in.

"Where are we going?"

A smirk touches my lips. "On our honeymoon."

CHAPTER 34

Autumn

*T*he moonlight reflects off of Lake Tahoe, casting beams across the water. I stand at the oversized windows, taking it all in. It's still and quiet, other than the crickets.

"You own this place too?" I ask. Every single one of his homes has the best views.

"*We* do." He moves toward me, wrapping his arm around my waist and pulling me close. I crave his warm mouth and take what I want, but I take it slow.

His lips are on my neck and he peppers kisses upward. He traces the shell of my ear with his lips, inhaling me. "You smell good."

I grab his shirt with my fist and pull him closer to me. "You do too. I need you."

He smiles, takes my hand, and we dance by the light of the moon.

"Did you know I didn't want a reception?" I ask.

"I did," he says, spinning me around.

"Thank you for marrying me," I whisper.

"Pleasure is mine."

"Am I awake?" It still feels like a dream, a fairy tale that I'll be ripped away from. Every day, I'm worried I'll wake up in my loft, dreaming of a life I wanted to live. I want to keep these precious memories with him for a lifetime.

"Yes," he says, kissing me. We break apart, and it's easy to imagine what the outside looks like covered in snow. I've only ever seen photos of this place online. Now I'm here.

Zane grabs my hand, leading me up the wide, log stairs, lifting me into his arms and carrying me up them. We say nothing, not even when he kicks open the door.

He sets me on the edge of the bed, dropping to his knees, then disappears under the silk and tulle.

"Mm," he hums and rubs his scruff against my bare pussy.

"That feels amazing," I say breathlessly as his tongue darts out. My eyes slam shut as he lifts my thigh over his shoulder, allowing himself better access. I want him, need him closer.

"More. Please," I say, building up too fast, greedily racing to the end even though he's barely touched me. It's always been like this for us since the beginning. I can't get enough and never will. This man is my fantasy, my dream, and I'm insatiable for him as he devours me like I'm his sustenance. Like I'm the only thing that can keep him alive.

My back arches and the orgasm threatens and builds like a summer storm in the mountains. Two fingers slide deep inside me and a groan releases as heat swirls. I need this bad.

He smiles against my pussy as if he can read my thoughts. "You're so fucking close."

"Yes." I'm not sure I even spoke. It's hushed as he rolls his tongue across my clit.

"Enjoy it."

Zane Alexander is my ecstasy, the man of my dreams; now he's my husband.

"My *husband*," I whisper. My body trembles, the thread snaps, blinding me. As I say his name, I fall into the abyss, completely lost with this man. He continues teasing my bundle of nerves as my pussy pulses.

"Fuck, Autie." He moves my dress, sucking his fingers before licking his perfect lips. "I need you so damn bad."

He leans forward, and I taste my release on his mouth, loving how eager he always is to please me.

"Please always want me like this," I say, and he pulls away.

"Pumpkin, this is the ground floor. We're only going up from here," he growls, pressing himself between my thighs, slowly kissing me like we have eternity. The ring on my finger and the love in my heart tell me we do.

We're the real deal. I sigh, relieved that he's mine.

"I finally found you," he says, sounding like Mr. Dreamy. "I'm not ever letting you go now. That's a fucking promise. One I'll keep until my last breath," he says, nuzzling against my neck.

He looks at me like I'm the stars in his night sky. I smile, clasping my hands on his cheeks, moving his face closer for one more kiss.

"I love you. Every inch of you inside and out," I say, grateful and overwhelmed by the emotions swimming through me. No more crash landings, not with Zane.

When he smiles, my heart flutters. "I love you, Autie. Today, tomorrow, and forever."

He stands and pulls me up to him. He takes a step back, admiring me. No one has ever looked at me the way he does.

"Love you too." I lick my lips, turning my back. "Unzip me halfway."

Zane sucks and nibbles on my neck as his fingers trail up my arm to the zipper. I turn to him, reaching forward to remove his tie as he watches me. I throw it on the bed and he lifts a brow.

Carefully, I untuck and unbutton his shirt and push it off his shoulders. Stepping forward, I kiss down his body, licking the curves of his muscles. I unbuckle his belt, then toss it on the mattress.

"Tonight, no boundaries."

"Be careful what you ask for," he growls, threading his fingers through my hair. Our tongues greedily massage each other.

"I want you to unravel me."

He tugs my long strands, forcing me to look up at him. "I will have you begging."

"I can start now if you'd like. Fucking please," I say more desperately, removing the dress from my body.

"Damn." His eyes move down my breasts to the crotchless lace panties I'm wearing. "How are you mine?"

"Because you chose me," I say.

"Because *you* chose *me*," he counters, sliding his hand down to my ass cheek, grabbing a handful.

"I would a million times over." I pull him toward me. "Is this where I start begging?"

His laughter is light as I kiss him. Seconds later, he has my wrists, twisting me around like he did in his library. Hot breath brushes against my skin as he trails kisses up my neck. "Is that what you want?"

"Since the first time," I hiss out as he tightens his grip, restraining me more.

"I saw you first in the library. I watched you from the corner of the room for at least five minutes. I'd been thinking about you before you appeared like a figment of my imagination."

"You manifested me," I whisper.

Zane spins me around, capturing my lips. "I think it's the other way around, Pumpkin."

He glances at my throat, then at my mouth. "Tonight, I want to make love to you."

"I'll take an IOU, then. One where you don't hold back," I say as he steps forward, gently guiding me onto the bed.

"It's a deal." Our mouths slam together. He gives my body time to adjust to him before picking up his pace, and it doesn't take long before I'm floating like a feather with him. High on his touch, the taste of his skin, and everything he has to offer.

I WAKE UP to Zane's cock pressed into my back, and I arch against him. We make love to the early morning sunlight peeking over the horizon. Afterward, we stand on the balcony, watching the fog drift over the water.

"How is it here in the winter?"

"Beautiful. You'd love it," he tells me.

I imagine it covered in a soft white powder as snowshoe hikers take the trails.

"We'll come back," he promises with a yawn. "Coffee?"

"That's the magic word."

The chill in the air creeps along my exposed legs and I shiver slightly.

Zane grabs his phone, shoves it into his pocket, and leads me downstairs. He places logs in the fireplace and lights them. "Oh, the real deal."

He grins. "It's nostalgic."

I smile because it reminds me of scribbling down stories about ponies and cute boys.

"What?" Zane asks.

"I remembered a childhood memory of writing by the fire."

"I can imagine that." He moves into the kitchen and begins his search for an espresso machine. He opens a cabinet and pulls out a French press.

"Do you have grounds?"

"Hm." Zane moves to the pantry with his joggers sitting haphazardly on his waist. I admire every inch of him, knowing my lips were pressed against his skin. "Right here."

I move toward him.

"Have a seat. I'm making you a cup this morning."

"Great. I'll sit here and enjoy the view."

Zane shoots me a wink and fills a kettle with water, placing it on the stove. "What do you want for breakfast?"

"You choose."

Our lips touch, softly, but communicating all the desire still burning between us. "You?"

"I think we can make that happen."

A yawn escapes me.

"After coffee and breakfast. I need you nourished for the rest of our day."

"I fucking love the sound of that."

Almost on cue, his phone dings. He unlocks it and reads the screen.

"My father has decided to cancel his island wedding," Zane says.

"Oh no. Are he and Silvia okay?"

"They're great." He smiles. "Silvia wants to get married at the resort in Cozy Hollow. They're loving it there." Zane laughs.

"Really? When?"

"Tomorrow."

I take a few steps forward. "So that means I get you to myself for the rest of the day without interruptions?"

He nods. "That's a fucking promise."

I pull the Moleskine notebook from my travel bag and sit at the bar top as Zane pulls eggs and bacon from the fridge, then makes me a perfect cup of coffee.

I start by adding the date to the corner of the page, then I write.

How did this happen?
I married Mr. Dreamy.
I'm so damn lucky.

Smiling, I shut the book and set the pen on top. I haven't missed a day of writing poems about Zane and never plan to. Not for the rest of my life.

"Can I read them one day?" he asks, handing me a cup of French pressed coffee.

"I'll trade you. One haiku in exchange for reading one of mine."

He laughs. "You should've never told me that. How many do I need to write to catch up with you?"

"A lot."

"Guess I better get started, then."

CHAPTER 35

Zane

*A*fter twenty-four hours of uninterrupted time, Autumn and I travel back to the resort at Cozy Hollow. When we arrive, luxury vehicles fill the valet parking lot. Autumn is wearing a gorgeous brown dress, and her hair is pulled half-up. We hold a silent conversation as we walk down the sidewalk. If this weren't my father's wedding, I'd lift her over my shoulder and carry her back to the car.

The thought makes me chuckle. She lifts her brow as I open the door for her and we move toward the ballroom.

"You're telling me later," she whispers as we pass security.

"I'll show you," I warn.

She chews on her bottom lip and I grab her hand as we enter the chapel at the resort, which is just for weddings.

I suck in a ragged breath. Autumn stops me. "Are you okay?"

"Yeah, why?"

"You tensed as soon as we entered."

No one else would've noticed or cared. It's how I know it's different with Autumn. She wraps her arms around my neck, kissing me. I pull her closer to me, holding her tight. "Mr. Dreamy once told me the only way to make a ghost disappear is to acknowledge them. Or maybe it was my sister." She chuckles. "Or Blaire."

My mouth parts. "That makes a lot of sense. Face your fears."

"Wow, that's deep." She shrugs. "And if it doesn't work, I'll be your Ghostbuster."

Immediately, I relax because it's another solved piece of the prophecy puzzle. Harper predicted Autumn down to this very moment.

Your dream life begins when you face your fears. Don't hesitate. It will finally be over, and you can move on with your beautiful life with your wife. It all happens in Cozy Hollow.

It wasn't only facing Hollow Manor, but everyone from my past who will be here tonight.

"You promise you're okay?" she asks, studying me.

"With all my heart. I had an epiphany, that's all."

I hold her chin between my fingers, painting our lips together.

"It's the look," she says. "The one on your face right now. It's the prophecy, isn't it?"

"Autumn."

"It is." She grins. "I triggered something. Don't worry, I won't ask. But will you tell me after it's done?"

"Yes." I steal another kiss. "It's for us."

She grins up at me with hooded eyes. "Going to grab a seat now. You need to see your dad."

"No." I pull her to me.

"I'll be fine," she says as Billie walks past us.

"Hi, you two. How's married life?" She looks like Audrey Hepburn in that dress.

"Perfect," Autumn says, and I'm tempted to kiss her again.

"Zero complaints."

"Harper was right. You are grossly adorable."

I laugh. "Thanks. I'll take it as a compliment."

"Go," Autumn says, shooing me away. "It will be less than an hour. We'll survive."

"I'll take care of her," Billie confirms with a nod, and I trust her as much as I trust my sister.

"Have you seen Harper?"

Billie shakes her head. "Not yet. What about Nicolas?"

Hearing my old best friend's name makes me grow cold. I've avoided hearing or saying it for weeks. "No. We only just arrived."

Autumn pulls me in for the kiss I was tempted to steal minutes earlier.

"See you soon," I mutter before pulling away, giving one last nod to Billie. The two of them stroll down the hallway with dressing rooms. I twist the knob of the one marked GROOM. Inside, my dad is chatting with Frederick Calloway. They've been old friends for as long as I can remember and our families used to vacation together. It's why he's the only other man standing with my father today.

"Zane. My fourth son," Frederick says, and I give him a firm handshake.

"Hi, Mr. Calloway."

"Always polite. Congratulations on marrying the love of your life. It's a big deal with the right person. Trust me on that one. Divorce sucks," he says. Years ago, he divorced and traded in his old wife for a new one, a model. They recently had a child. I believe their son, Connor, is almost three now.

The older I become, the more I notice how fast time passes.

Frederick sets three whiskey glasses on the minibar and pours us each a hefty shot.

I glance at my father. "What do you want to drink to?"

"To happiness," he says.

"And family," I add.

"To happiness and family," we repeat, clinking them before tossing them back. The whiskey is smooth and goes down like water. I need it, though. I've been on edge since the plane landed, knowing

I'll run into Nicolas. Even thinking his name makes me want to punch him out.

"How's retired life?" I ask before I get too lost in my thoughts.

Frederick chuckles. "Boring. I'm going stir-crazy. Easton has told security not to allow me in the building unless he gives an okay."

"Sounds like it was the only way to keep you away," I say.

"It was."

"And that's exactly why I'm never retiring. I'll be put in the grave first," my father confirms. He's addicted to work and always has been, but I know the truth. It's how he ran from dealing with the death of my mother. Maybe Silvia can make him stop and smell the roses as they dance through life together.

"Morbid. But I'll drink to you running the business until you're ninety-five. I might have a little heir to take your place by then and skip the CEO thing," I say as I pour another round.

Dad laughs. "Don't tease me with grandchildren."

The thought of starting a family with Autumn brings me so much joy I can hardly contain it. Though, we haven't discussed it yet.

I make a mental note, but it does not matter. As long as I have her, I'm fucking happy.

"I'm still waiting," Frederick says. "But Connor is a handful. Can't imagine the trouble he'll get into when he's grown. He's nosy. Into everything. A little smart-ass too."

"As are all your kids." I chuckle.

"You're damn right about that." Frederick sets our glasses on the bar as a light knock taps against the door. I glance over my shoulder as it opens.

"Ten minutes," Silvia's sister, Alice, says.

I give her a nod and she leaves. Frederick returns to us, hugging my father before wrapping me in one too. "I'll see you both out there."

We're alone.

My father adjusts his tie in the mirror and I watch him from the side, just as I did as a young boy.

"Nervous?" I ask, wondering. Even if he was, my father is too hard to read. He's a pro at tucking his emotions away.

"No." He smiles. "I'm happy for the first time in a very long time. Thank you for being here. I know you di—"

I place my hand on his shoulder, meeting his eyes in the reflection. "I'm sorry for being a dick. Hurt people hurt people. I wanted someone to be angry with when I learned about Nicolas and Celine. You were an easy option, and I'm very fucking sorry about that. After some perspective and finding the love of my life, I realize they don't matter. Love you, Dad. I'm happy for you."

"No need to apologize. I understood where you were and just wanted to support you how I could. I'm bad at this emotional stuff." Then he turns and hugs me firmly, holding me tight. "Love you too, son. Seems like we've finally found our way."

"We have," I confirm, letting him go.

He laughs, a sound that brings me back to a happier time. "Mom would be so happy and proud of you," I tell him.

For a brief second, he chokes up but pushes it away. "She'd be proud of you, too."

"I believe she somehow had a hand in my happiness." I smile.

"The day you were injured on the slopes, I always felt like it was my fault because I wasn't there," he confesses.

I shake my head, remembering that day. He'd called me an hour before I was supposed to hit the slopes and said he was tied up at work. It wasn't a lie, but I'd hoped he would make it. That day meant a lot to me. If my mother were alive, she'd have been in the stands screaming at the top of her lungs like she always did when I was a teenager. I'd hear her at the bottom.

"I wasn't in the right headspace, but I didn't have a choice. It was either compete or lose my place."

"You almost lost your life," he says. "I know you think I never supported the idea of you competing. That wasn't true. You were the best and I was proud of you. But I was afraid to lose the only parts of your mother I had left; you and Harper, along with the memories and pictures, had become my everything. I missed it, and when I got the call that you'd be transported . . ." He stops talking. "Well, I don't think I'd have survived losing you, son."

Tears well, threatening to spill over as I choke up. "I'm here. Mom always told me that things happen for a reason, whether I agree or not. The dominoes had to fall for me to find true happiness. Discovering how fragile life is, was a lesson I needed to learn. Before then, I was fearless. It all worked out."

"It did," he says.

We hug one last time and I let out a deep breath, trying to gain control, before I walk toward the door.

As I reach for the handle, I stop. "Oh, before I forget to mention it, I fired Roxane this morning after I learned she wouldn't be in attendance. So did Harper."

"Why? Please tell me you didn't let her go just because she couldn't make it."

"No. She was manipulating us. And I'm in control of my life and image now. No one else. Same goes for Harper. We can handle ourselves."

"I'm so fucking proud of you," he tells me, and I know he means it.

"Thanks. I'll meet you out in the hall." I leave the room to give him a few seconds to himself. And I selfishly need a minute, too.

As I stand in the hallway, waiting for my father to exit, I slide the Moleskine notebook that matches Autumn's from my pocket. It has the same number of pages, and we promised one another that we'd trade when they were full. Eighty pages, front and back, 160 haikus. The theme? Each other.

> *My beautiful wife.*
> *You are all I think about.*
> *You give me purpose.*

When my father emerges, I return the book to my pocket. "Ready?"

"More than ready."

CHAPTER 36

Zane

My dad and I walk down the hallway beside one another, our strides and gaits the same. I glance over at him and he grins. As we round the corner, my father nearly runs head-on into Nicolas.

Our eyes meet, and he looks hollow inside, like a shell of himself. I feel pity for him, knowing Celine hollowed him into nothing. A puppet. He hesitates, and I think he may speak, but he doesn't. As I continue, my father exchanges a few friendly words with him.

I stand on the side of the stage until my dad eventually catches up with me. We say nothing because it's a pointless conversation right now when the ceremony will begin soon.

"I'll meet you out there, okay?"

"Yeah," he tells me. I move to the staging area. The itinerary with a map was emailed to me this morning.

I walk down the steps and pass Autumn, sitting in the audience beside Billie. She perks up as we focus on one another. An overwhelming amount of joy floods me—this woman is mine. When I'm close, I bend toward her, devouring her lips. "I've missed you."

"I've missed you too."

"It's been twenty minutes," Billie says, checking her elegant wristwatch.

"It only takes seconds before it sets in," I explain with a laugh. "We're about to get started."

"Okay," she whispers. Her eyes slide over me, the hunger behind them barely restrained.

"Behave," I playfully warn, and she smirks.

I hear my sister's contagious laughter from the back of the room. I excuse myself from my wife and allow the sounds to guide me to where I need to be when I enter the room, where Harper passes tequila shots between Weston and Easton.

With a tilt of her head and a wide smile, she hands me one too.

"It's my kry—"

"Tonight, you're Batman, because you might need it to fight the Joker later," she says, pouring me a double. Harper has always despised Celine.

"No one is fighting anyone tonight. Okay?" I shoot it back. "Dad doesn't need that."

"It's time to line up," Frederick tells us, glancing between his sons.

"Mr. Calloway," Harper says, pretending she's not buzzed. Easton and Weston leave the room and sit beside Billie, Autumn, and Lexi. There is someone else with them that I don't recognize.

When Harper walks out, I ask her.

"Oh, that's Carlee, Lexi's best friend. I think she's dating Weston. He denies it, for now."

I give her a look.

"They end up together. I was hoping I could drink the prophecies away today. No such luck."

I inhale deeply when I hear the piano music begin. Soon, the pastor emerges.

Harper stands beside Frederick.

Moments later, someone moves in close next to me, and when I glance over, I see the woman who took my virginity all those years ago. Miranda smiles. I knew I'd be walking down the aisle with her because she's Silvia's only daughter. It's the only thing that makes sense.

"It's been a long time," she mutters, keeping her eyes forward.

"It has. I believe it was your wedding," I say.

"It was. And you refused to speak to me."

"Ah. I did. Sorry about that." I shrug. "What did you want to discuss?"

"I wanted closure," she whispers.

"This is a joke, right? *You* called it off."

"I wanted you to fight for me. You didn't."

Harper must've predicted I'd need the booze, so she carried it. Tequila makes me not give a fuck. All inhibitions disappear. This conversation would've made me anxious, but right now, I feel nothing.

"We were always in different places. I'm sorry I ignored you."

"It worked out exactly how it was supposed to. I love my husband, and every step I took led me to him. Seeing you like this . . . Zane, I would've never been able to make you as genuinely happy as you are right now."

"I'm not sure how to respond to that," I tell her.

"I'm happy for you. That's all. So. How was it? As personal and private as you always wanted?"

"Actually, yes," I admit. "It was a dream come true."

I meet her eyes. "She's very lucky."

We exchange a friendly smile. "I'm the lucky one. Now. Are we ready?" I ask, stepping forward.

"Yep," she tells me. One ghost down.

Cameras snap and my eyes lock on Autumn. She turns her head as I pass, sitting up taller. I mouth "I love you," and she mouths it back. I move up to the raised stage and stand beside my father.

Moments later, Silvia comes into focus with Nicolas escorting her. He looks like utter shit.

I glance at Harper and we hold a silent conversation before focusing on my father. My heart warms, seeing a happiness he hasn't had in twenty-four years.

The thought takes over and I search for Autumn in the crowded chapel. She's watching me with kind eyes and a smile that lights the whole fucking room. A grin touches my lips.

"Ladies and gentlemen, thank you all for being here on this beautiful evening. It feels like we were all doing this together not too long ago," the pastor says, grinning. I nod, glancing at Autumn, and she winks at me. If anyone in the room didn't know I was married, they do now.

My father and Silvia stand in front of one another, repeating their vows of love and forever. There are smiles and tears. Throughout the ceremony, I steal glances at Autumn, who hasn't taken her attention away from me. Soon, I'm passing over Silvia's ring to him, and they seal their promises with a kiss. I've managed to narrowly avoid falling under the spell of my beautiful wife and pay *just* enough attention to the ceremony to fulfill my role.

The room erupts into applause as the photographer snaps photographs. Once my father and his bride have exited the room, I move toward Miranda and escort her out.

"It was nice seeing you," Miranda says.

"Same."

The pastor speaks over the microphone. "The happy couple invites you to celebrate in the main ballroom."

I glance at my sister, who shakes her head.

"You know what's going to happen tonight." It isn't a question.

"So what?" She grins, pulling a flask from the pocket of her dress. "Trust me when I say you'll need more tequila soon."

"Shit, probably." I take it from her, swigging it back.

A chuckle escapes her and Autumn's arm wraps around me. I kiss her hair as she smiles up at me.

"I'm ready for cake," Harper says. Autumn takes the flask, swallowing down two gulps.

She does a little wiggle. "Tequila?"

"Dangerous," I whisper, thinking back to the last time we drank together. I wanted to cross the line so many damn times.

The thought makes me smile. She notices.

"What?" Autumn whispers, chuckling.

"Reminiscing."

We enter the dimly lit reception area. Silk hangs from the ceiling and a live band has set up in the corner. In the middle of the room is an ice sculpture of a heart. Autumn's eyes widen as we walk past it, moving toward the open bar.

"What would you like?"

"Vodka and cranberry," she says.

"Tequila, dressed."

Autumn leans forward. "I'll take the same. Plus my other, thanks." She turns to me as the bartender makes our drinks. "Do you plan on fucking around and finding out tonight?"

"Hell yes," I whisper, and she snuggles against me.

"Here ya go," the guy says.

I place a tip in the jar and Autumn and I move out of the way to a high cocktail table. She lifts the tequila. "To us."

"Forever."

We lick the salt and shoot back the liquid before biting into the lime.

"Eh. I think I'm getting too old for that." Autumn does a little wiggle and I notice her nipples at full attention. I swallow hard, my eyes sliding back to hers as the band introduces my dad and Silvia. We watch them dance together as husband and wife, smiling and laughing. My dad kisses and spins her around and it warms my heart.

Autumn gulps the other drink. "You're so fucking sexy," I whisper in her ear.

There is a massive line at the bar as most attendees dance to the slow song that plays out.

She turns to me, running her fingers into my hair. I lean into her, kissing her arm.

"Will you dance with me?"

"Always."

She finishes her drink and I lead her to the middle of the room. With my hands resting on her hips, we lose ourselves in a sea of people. Some faces are familiar, but many aren't. We slowly dance together and my eyes flutter closed as our mouths drift together.

"Fuck," I growl against Autumn's mouth, growing desperate. Fairy lights overhead cast enough brightness for me to see the desire in her eyes.

"Come on." She takes my hand, leads me down the hallway, and opens a storage room full of extra decorations. Immediately, she locks the door and I push her against it.

"Now who was prepared?" I ask. Our lips crash together as waves of passion take us under.

"Me," she says, thrusting her fingers through my hair as I desperately lift her dress, sliding my fingers between her legs. No panties. She removes her dress. No bra, either.

"Very prepared." I obsessively eye fuck her perfect body as I unzip, remove my coat jacket, unbutton my pants, and step out of them. I lift Autumn's leg, holding it upright as I slam inside of her warm, wet pussy.

"Yes. Zane," she moans out, and I slam my mouth into hers.

I whisper in her ear, thrusting deep into her tight cunt. "Shh. Don't want anyone to hear me fuck your brains out."

"I don't care," she hisses as I pump into her, hard. Autumn is so fucking tight for me. I think I see stars. With a firm hand, I grab her ass, jerking her against my hips, filling her greedy little pussy with every ounce of force I can muster.

She kisses me and steadies herself with her back pressed on the door, pinching and twisting her perky little nipples. Her eyes roll into the back of her head as she greedily chases that orgasm, the one I've been thinking about giving her since we arrived.

"That's all you have?" she quips, and I guide her over to the table. With one sweep of an arm, the extra decorations are on the floor. I press her titties onto the cool wood and fuck her from behind, giving it to her how she wants—hard and slow.

She arches her body and I reach out, rubbing gentle circles on her clit.

"Zane," she hisses.

"Mm. Can't take any more?" I ask, continuing, noticing her precum on my cock. My girl is so horny, so fucking turned on, and I love teasing her when she's this close. Her breathing increases and she rocks against me.

"Fuck me," she begs.

"Did you say stop?" I try to pull away, but she grabs my wrist and moves my hand back to her.

"I'm dripping wet for you," she says.

"You always are." I pull away, dropping to my knees and devouring her pussy from behind. Sliding my tongue from her clit to her deep hole to her ass. Her precum is on my tongue, and each time her moans increase, I slightly pull back, edging my girl until I'm ready for her to come.

"Fuck me," she whispers, and I do as she requests, taking her from behind with my thumbs digging into her waist.

"Yes, yes, yes." She seizes, her pussy clenching against me, and then she squirts all over my cock and the floor, screaming out my name. I slap her ass. "Good fucking girl."

She inhales ragged breaths, gripping the table's edge as I increase my pace. I'm so fucking close, and any second I will lose control. Autumn rocks her hips, creating more pressure, then I slam deep inside her, filling her full.

I collapse onto her, trying to come down from my high as I throb inside of her. We stay connected for minutes, and I soak in her.

Up-tempo music quietly drifts into our little slice of heaven, breaking the spell and reminding us we're not, in fact, the only people in the world. The reception is still going. We've been gone for too long. But I'm not sure anyone will notice.

When I pull out, my cum drips down her leg and I smile. "What a fucking sight to see."

Her lips are swollen and her hair is a mess. Everyone will know where we've been. I help her clean up, giving her my undershirt.

"I'm glad you took off your pants. Not sure how we'd explain it." *Her squirting.*

"I'd have proudly worn you out there." I steal a kiss, playfully twisting her pebbled nipple.

She moans out, tugging me toward her. "I can never have enough of you."

I lick my lips, studying her. "One day, I want to watch you please yourself."

"Ahh, want to see the only way I used to come before you?"

I smirk. "Yes."

I move over to my clothes, re-dressing as Autumn returns to the table and lies back on it.

"I don't mean now."

"I'm still so turned on." She moves her hands down between her legs. "Like this?" she asks, her mouth falling open when she grazes her swollen clit.

"Fuck yes," I say, tucking my shirt into my suit pants.

"It's so sensitive." Autumn gently thrusts her hips upward before sliding two fingers inside. "Many nights, I've imagined this is you."

She places her fingers into her mouth. "I taste us."

I move toward her, bending down and kissing her. When our tongues swipe together, I taste our passion. Taste our love. "Keep going," I encourage as she returns to her clit.

"Mr. Dreamy wanted to watch too," she says, eyes on me.

"Of course he did."

She closes her eyes, writhing against her hand, and it's a beautiful fucking sight as she teases herself. "No one has ever watched me."

"Do you like me watching?"

She bites her bottom lip so hard I think she might draw blood.

"Yes," she hisses, sliding one finger inside and guiding her other hand back to her clit.

"Were you awake?" She lets out a moan. "The first night."

"Yes," I say, smirking, and she looks at me with hooded eyes.

"I hoped you were," she confesses. "I could've used your help. Oh, oh, fuck."

"Come for me like a good girl," I demand. "Let me see that pretty pussy wink when you do."

With my words, she grows more aggressive, increasing her speed, and her body quivers, her back flying off the table as she moans. "Fuck yes, yes, yes. I'm still . . . coming."

Autumn opens her thighs wide, showing me all of her, and I take the opportunity to face dive between her legs. Licking and sucking up every drop of her, not letting any of her go to waste.

She's breathing hard, and when she stops throbbing against my tongue, I try to pull away, but our mouths collide together.

"Now, come on before I suggest we leave the event and go home."

"*Home*," she says with a grin. "I love the sound of that."

"I've missed the manor," I admit.

"I have too."

Autumn dresses and I meet her eyes.

"How do I look?" she asks, adjusting my tie and hair. It's no use.

"Fucking gorgeous and guilty. But there's nothing you can do about that, babe."

She presses her fingertips across her lips. "I guess you're right about that."

I unlock the door and lead her back to the reception with our fingers interlocked.

We move to the far side of the room, giddy, like teenagers in love.

I notice many people are staring, but I try to ignore it. We don't look disheveled enough to stop a crowd, do we?

"Is my butt hanging out or something?" Autumn whispers, glancing behind her.

I look too. "Nah, your ass of mass destruction is put away."

"For now," she says, and we both laugh.

The bartender approaches us.

"I'd like a gin martini. Extra dirty." She eyes me.

"Make it two." I lean over and whisper in her ear, "Keep looking at me like that, and we will leave."

She smirks. "I love how it sounds like a threat. I know better, though."

Just as we're handed our drinks, we turn to a commotion. Across the room, I notice Nicolas and Celine arguing against the wall. Autumn sees it, too, and glances at me over the rim of her glass.

Other people start to notice, too, because she's raising her voice. I scan the room, searching for my sister as Celine reaches forward and slaps Nicolas.

"Okay, that's enough," Autumn says, her nostrils flaring. She glances at me.

Celine's voice echoes across the room. "I never loved you. I'm still in love with Zane."

Gasps sound throughout the room and I see my father and Silvia's heads turn.

"We have to get them out of here." Autumn steps forward, but I grab her hand and pull her back to me.

"This is part of the game, babe. Ignore it. Pretend she doesn't exist. She's searching for attention."

"Handle it," she nearly begs, and I can see how uncomfortable she's growing. How uncomfortable every person in the room is. Eyes traverse the room from us to Celine and Nicolas then back.

"Okay. Stay here. I'll be right back."

She nods and I place a kiss on her cheek. When I move away from her, I wear a frustrated scowl. When I'm fifty feet from Celine, I see my dad and sister approaching.

"You need to leave," my father says.

"Now," Harper demands, like a little bulldog. She's always been intimidating.

"No!" Celine yells. Her anger is now directed at me. "You were supposed to marry me! Me! You promised me!" she cries out, her throat raw. "It's over, Nicolas. It's over! You'll never be as good as him. Ever!"

Autumn moves beside me, wrapping her arm around me. "And you'll never be me," she says.

Celine tries to attack Autumn.

Easton's bodyguard, Brody, grabs her and holds her back.

"No," he says.

"You're a fucking bitch!" Celine screams at Autumn before turning to Harper. "And so are you."

My sister's brows furrow and I step forward, stopping Harper. "It's what she wants," I say to my sister.

"It's what I want too," Harper says.

Billie comes over and takes Harper's hand, pulling her away. Tequila is her kryptonite, too.

"Zane," Celine says. "You lied! You said you'd always love me." I gave her a million chances when she wanted a million and one.

"Get her out of here," I demand, crossing my arms over my chest, refusing to listen to her act.

Easton rushes over. "What the hell?"

Security splits through the crowd, taking Celine from Brody. She fights against them, screaming at the top of her lungs. I've got to give it to the band because they keep the music going and try to capture the crowd's attention, but it's too late.

Celine screams, making a scene until she's escorted out of the room. The crowd applauds when the door clicks closed.

I turn to my dad. "I'm really sorry."

"This isn't your fault," he seethes, glaring at Nicolas. "Enough is enough. She's banned from all properties and is never allowed in my presence again."

As he walks off, he shakes his head. "So fucking glad you didn't marry that one. A nightmare."

"Fuck, me too," I say, wrapping my arm around Autumn. "Oh."

I pull my tiny notebook from my pocket.

> *I found my daydream*
> *She helps me fight my monsters*
> *My wife, forever*

A wide grin meets my lips. "That one was good."

"I can't wait to read it," she says. As she opens her mouth to say something, I hear my name from behind me.

"Can we talk?" Nicolas asks.

"No. I'm not having this conversation here. Respect your mom's day."

He glances at Autumn, then at me, then walks away defeated.

Autumn turns to me and she doesn't even have to ask. It has been a lot in a short amount of time.

"We can leave," I say, capturing her lips. It's one of our rules: if we are uncomfortable or bored or want to go for any reason, we go together. Pulling away, I study her eyes, ensuring she's okay. She notices me reading her and smirks.

She snakes her hand around my waist and a sexy little smile touches her lips.

"I'm ready for dessert," she whispers as we move toward the exit.

"You're a dirty girl."

"You like it," she quips as soon as the fresh air hits our cheeks.

"No, Pumpkin. I fucking *love* it."

CHAPTER 37

Zane

The next morning, after I eat Autumn for breakfast, we go downstairs, where I prepare the batter for a batch of pumpkin pancakes.

Autumn sits at a high bar stool in the kitchen, looking so pretty in one of my old T-shirts and plaid pajama pants.

"This smell reminds me of the coffee shop in the fall," she says.

"Do you want to return to work?" I ask. Her vacation isn't even over for three more weeks, but it's not something we've discussed in depth. Whatever she wants to do, I will support her. It's her decision. The deal was she would go back on November first. I selfishly don't want her to.

"I think I want to try to write again and decide later," she tells me confidently. "You inspire me so much."

"I'm so fucking proud of you." I drop the spatula in the bowl and move to her, sliding my fingers through her hair to kiss her so damn softly. "Stay right here. Okay?"

"What? Why?"

"It's a surprise!" Quickly, I jog up the stairs and enter the closet, pulling out a gift bag. When I return to the kitchen, she's grinning wide as I hand it to her. She pulls the tissue out and unwraps the golden paper.

"A new laptop."

I nod. "The best for my pumpkin. I've waited a month for this moment."

She sets it down on the countertop and stands to hug me tight. "Thank you."

"I'm already your biggest fan," I say, smiling and kissing her. So damn happy that she's taking the steps to go after her dreams. "Think you'll make that deadline?"

"It depends on how *inspired* I am." She waggles her brows.

I reach around, grabbing a handful of her ass, capturing her lips. "Mm. I look forward to helping with that."

She laughs against my mouth, pulling me to her. "You do without even trying."

This pleases me. "Fuck, I love you."

"I love you too," she says, reaching forward and slipping her hands into my pajama bottoms. I'm already hard for her again.

I swallow as she strokes me. Her eyes twinkle with want and need. My wife craves me.

"If you keep it up, I'll fuck you right here on this counter," I growl as she peppers soft kisses along my stomach. I fist my fingers in her hair.

"You'd be a whole lot cooler if you did," she mutters against my lips as I pull down her bottoms. Autumn lifts her shirt, nipples hard as pebbles. With my arm around her waist, I move her closer, capturing her nipple and flicking it with my tongue. She moans out as she continues to stroke me, then she drops to her knees in front of me.

My perfect girl opens her mouth wide, taking me in.

"Careful," I warn when she shoves me to the back of her throat. She looks up at me, greedily working me with her hands and her hot mouth.

"Show me," I say, and she removes her shirt completely. Her

titties bounce and I place my hand on the back of her head, gently guiding her down farther.

"Fuck," I growl. If she keeps it up, I will fill her throat full of my hot, sticky cum. I desperately need inside of her.

She works me to the brink, and right before I come, I pull away, her lips popping. With hooded eyes, she bends forward, licking at the pool of pleasure that leaked from my tip.

"Not like this," I whisper.

"It's like you know what I want," she says as she stands, wiggling out of her pants. When she touches her toes, she wiggles her perfect ass for me one more time.

Moments later, Autumn is bent over the counter with her bare titties against the marble as I tease her with the tip.

She whimpers, wanting me inside of her, but I tease and play in her juices. I love that my wife is always ready and wet for me.

"Zane," she says, reaching between her legs and cupping my balls. I give her what she wants, slamming from the tip to the base of my rigid cock in one swift movement. I soak in her warmth, buried deep inside as she pulses around me. I let her body adjust as I stretch her wide.

When she rocks against me, I know my wife craves more, so I lift one of her thighs. I bite my lip, steadying myself on the counter.

She gets worked up so fucking fast, rocking her hips, chasing her high like a greedy addict. When I fuck her from behind like this, she squirts every single time, and I love that I help with that.

"You fill me so full," she whispers as her tight little pussy squeezes around me.

I groan. "I'm going to ooze out of your beautiful fucking cunt."

"Yes, yes," she screams as we fuck like animals. Greedy, desperate. The sounds of pleasure echo through the quiet house.

We're ravenous and addicted.

Leaning forward, I reach around, rubbing circles on her needy little clit as her tight pussy swallows me whole.

"How much inspiration do you want?" I tug on her hair and she arches into me.

She moans out my name. "As much as you'll give me."

"You want more?"

She nods. "I'll never have enough of you."

I sink my teeth into her shoulder and her breathing increases. "Come on my cock like a good fucking girl."

She's on her tiptoes, like she's suspended in the air as she tips over the edge, squirting all over my cock as I fuck her with fervor. Deep grunts release from her throat as her pussy pulses. She's still coming, enjoying every second, and when I'm close, she arches her back. I empty deep inside of her, holding myself up on the counter, nearly going weak in the knees as the mind-blowing orgasm shatters through me.

Neither of us moves. We're breathless and completely wrecked.

"I love how you feel," she breathes out, catching her breath as I wrap my arms around her stomach.

"You were made for me," I whisper against her neck, softly kissing the thundering pulse point.

"I believe that," she admits.

We break apart and she's amazed by the mess we made. I'm not. Quickly, we clean up and she sits on the stool watching me.

"Coffee?" She smiles.

"Oh, right," I say, completely forgetting we were in the middle of breakfast. I turn, pressing the button for the coffee.

She's perfected putting me in a daze.

I set the first cup of joe in front of her before turning to make my own. On cue, she picks it up and immediately sips the hot-as-fuck liquid.

"You'll never learn."

"I was ensuring it didn't taste like shit." She shoots me a wink as I go back to mixing.

A howl of laughter releases from me as I click on the stovetop, heating the iron skillet. When it's sizzling, I turn down the flame and put a spoonful of butter in the bottom. When it's melted, I carefully pour the batter into palm-sized circles. Then I wait.

Her eyes are on me. I can feel her gaze like it's burning holes in my back. I glance over my shoulder at her. "Yes?"

"Seeing you cook for me is sexy," she admits, her chin resting on her propped-up fist.

"Is it like a dream?" I ask, wondering.

"Every day with you is."

When I'm finished, Autumn bursts into laughter at the leaning stack of twenty pancakes I prepared and somehow balanced.

"It's too many!" she says.

"Have to keep my wife bred and fed. Butter and syrup?"

"Mm." She nods, glowing. I take a second to admire her in the early morning sunlight as she loads her plate with pumpkin discs.

"What?" she whispers.

"You wake up pretty."

A hint of a blush meets her cheeks as I move to the fridge and pantry, grabbing what we need.

"Fork?" she asks.

"You didn't want to eat with your hands?" I ask, opening the drawer and snagging two.

"I did that about fifteen minutes ago."

"Mm. Maybe we can do that again?"

As Autumn pours syrup on top of her pancakes, a knock sounds from the door.

"Expecting someone?" she asks.

"No," I say, wishing I could see through the door. "Stay here." I cross the living room, and when I twist the knob and pull it open, my smile fades.

"Nicolas." His name comes out colder than the steadily dropping temperatures.

"This a better time?"

I breathe out, pushing the door closed and turning to Autumn.

"Sure," she whispers with a cute shrug. Whatever I want, she'll support, but it's too fucking early for confrontation.

"Come in." I step to the side and his gaze immediately meets Autumn's.

Autumn turns to him with bright eyes, swollen lips, and messy morning hair. She beams like a fucking angel. If it weren't for Autumn . . . I don't want to think about where I'd be.

"Oh, I'm sorry. Am I interrupting?" Nicolas asks, glancing back at me. The smell of pumpkin pancakes and coffee floats through the air. Happy energy encapsulated the house until he arrived.

Autumn shakes her head, sipping her espresso with a kind smile. "Not at all. Are you hungry? We have too many pancakes. It's like fate," she says.

"I wouldn't impose," he admits.

"Oh, come on." She's too nice. He doesn't deserve her kindness. Or mine.

"Fine." She shrugs. "Missing out."

He glances at me. "I'll come back later when you're not in the middle of breakfast."

"It's okay. Let's solve this now," I tell him, wanting to get this over with now so I don't have to deal with him again.

He sits at the end of the bar. It's awkward, the tension thick.

"Coffee?" I ask.

"Uh." He hesitates, and I hand him the cup I brewed for myself. "Fuck her. Drink the caffeine."

Nicolas and I bonded over coffee a lot. It makes sense why

Celine would force him to give it up, too. I see the cogs turning, the PTSD surrounding the mug.

"It's delicious," Autumn says, knowing exactly what kind of manipulation he went through.

Reaching into the cabinet, I grab another mug and make another. As the next shot brews, Autumn focuses on him.

"I'm Autumn." She offers her hand, but he barely takes it. Smart, because I'll break off his fucking fingers.

"My friends call me Nick. Or they used to."

Autumn notices me tense and calms me with her soft gaze. She knows me. She can read me. It's something she's reminded me of a thousand times. While she seems too good to be true, she's not.

It's a dig at me, one that's deserved. He should be glad I'm even speaking his name because I didn't for a long time. This is the best I can do for now.

Awkwardness swells, but Autumn spikes it away.

"Nice to meet you, Nick. So, how do you two know each other?" Autumn is a sly little thing, knowing he'll answer whatever she asks.

"Zane is—was—my best friend. Our parents were old friends and we went to boarding school together. Shared a lot of memories. The loss of our parents. Snowboarding. Frat parties. Corporate life."

Before he takes a long-ass stroll down memory lane, I stop him. "We shared *a lot*, apparently."

He glances at the coffee in the mug. "I'm sorry."

"Is that what you wanted to say? Needed to give me an apology so you could feel better about your fucked-up choices?"

Nicolas shakes his head. "I hurt you. I betrayed my brother. And for what?"

"For mediocre pussy," I remind him.

Autumn sucks in a deep breath and picks up her phone.

Moments later, mine buzzes. I roll my eyes, pulling it from my pocket.

Autumn
It's hateful to kick someone when they're down. Be thankful he did this. You would've never found me.

I sigh. So she types more.

Autumn
You wouldn't have. Timing is everything!!!

Shit. I can read her firmness in the three exclamation points. I don't respond and keep my exhales to myself as I allow her words to sink in.

"I'm sorry. I have a lot of pent-up frustration and anger toward you. My therapist has been helping, but it still doesn't mean I don't want to slam my fist into your fucking face," I explain, grabbing my cup of coffee and sitting between him and Autumn.

"I deserve that."

"No one deserves to be treated like shit," Autumn says, meeting Nicolas's eyes. "Are you keeping score, too? Is that what she does to men?"

She glances at me and it triggers a memory of us, one of the first ones we shared on the park bench. And she's right. My anger is warranted, but violence is never the answer.

He's living in his own personal hell. I can see how she destroyed him. It's how she destroyed me, ruining how close Nicolas and I were.

"I don't expect you to forgive me. I wanted to tell you that I'm really fucking sorry for hurting you. You were my best friend, and I lost you in the worst possible way. No one was worth our friendship and I didn't realize it until it was too late," he says.

I take a sip of my coffee, amazed that he apologized, considering how goddamn stubborn he usually is. It's not something I ever expected, and I know it took a lot for him to do that.

"Acknowledged and appreciated. But you're right, I don't think I can forgive you. And I don't have to. Maybe one day I'll be able to look back with fond memories, but that day isn't today." I'm firm in that decision. I have more to work through. Autumn doesn't push anything, but she grabs my hand and squeezes it gently, respecting me.

He downs the liquid caffeine, and I wonder how long it's been since he had a cup. "Thanks for giving me some of your time. Appreciate the coffee. Glad it didn't taste like shit."

"You're welcome," I say as he stands and moves toward the door, a little less broken than he was when he walked in. And he leaves.

Silence lingers.

"I'm proud of you," Autumn says, turning and wrapping her arms around me.

"Why?"

"Because you respectfully protected your boundaries."

I kiss her forehead. "For a second, I thought you would tell me to forgive him."

"That's your decision. I don't care if you do or don't. You can be respectful and firm at the same time," she admits. "So he's a ristretto man, too?"

"You guessed it."

She grins. "Can we eat now?"

"Mm." I bite on my bottom lip.

"Pancakes."

Our knees touch as we cut into the warm bread, then take a big syrupy bite.

"Thank you for supporting me."

"Same," she says, glancing at the laptop. I know she's thinking about her book, the one she was convinced a month ago she couldn't write.

"What changed?" I ask.

She smiles. "I fell in love with you."

CHAPTER 38

Autumn

*A*fter breakfast, Zane finally gives me a full tour of the house. There are so many beautiful, hidden elements and images carved into every nook and cranny. The house is a testament to his mother's love, and I think she designed it for him, knowing it was her last gift.

It's fun strolling through the house with him and walking down memory lane. I can see how much joy it brings him to open up about his past and share parts of his heart that are covered in dust.

"And last but not least, the library," he says, opening the curtains, and the light burns bright in the room. My mouth falls open and a chill runs over me as I look at the storybook shelves, which have different fairy tales intricately carved into the wood.

"It's . . . beautiful," I say.

"My thoughts when I look at you." He leads me from one side of the room to the other.

"The story starts here." He points to the far left shelf. "A picture tale."

A woman dances alone through fields, across mountains, over the ocean, even in space. She dances through the forest and stops to pet animals like bunnies and foxes. The seasons change and the woman continues to dance, spin, and pass up festivals and parties. She travels and travels.

My eyes devour the carvings like a movie as I scan up and down the shelves.

And when we're halfway across the room, the hand-carved woman runs into a man. He holds out his hand to her. Then they spin through the world together. It's happiness: they're surrounded by butterflies, birds, and rainbows. It rains on them, but the sun always returns. Happiness always returns. They take time to stop and smell the flowers together. They buy bread and share it with the animals. The pair continue to spin and music notes splash out of their mouths as they sing. Or maybe it's an announcement.

Two small children appear, and then the four of them dance together. Happy. In the end, storm clouds, rainbows, and butterflies. After that are three figures: the man, the little boy, and the little girl. The rest of the shelves are bare.

I burst into tears.

"Sweetheart." He searches my eyes. "Are you okay?"

"It's sad."

"Every carving in the house. On the stairs. In the pantry. They're how my mom told her life stories. You can look at it like the shelves are bare, but I like to think that they're waiting for a new love story."

He wipes at the tears with his thumbs before kissing them away.

Where the carvings end, there is a gold copy of *Pride and Prejudice*. At this angle, it shines and sparkles in the light like a diamond. I pull it from the shelf and flip through the pages until a folded note falls out.

I pick it up and Zane grins. I try to hand it to him.

"Read it to me."

I carefully set the book down. Then I begin.

My smart, beautiful, talented son,

Hi! It looks like you found a letter that I left you. I wasn't sure you'd ever find this one, so the fact that you did it is a miracle. Deep down, I know you'll find them all, eventually. Were you looking at the carvings on the bookshelf? I used it like a finish line.

If the curtains are open and it's midday, this book shines from a certain angle. Is that what caught your attention? I wish I knew the answer.

"Zane. Is this from your mom?"

He chuckles, kissing my forehead. "It is."

"Are you sure you don't want to read it later?"

"Please," he urges me to continue. "Nothing is a coincidence, remember?"

I recently had a dream about you as a grown man who is married and happy. I woke up crying because witnessing it was so beautiful. It felt real, and I woke up with goosebumps. Your wife was gorgeous, funny, and had a contagious laugh. I loved her. So did Harper. Everyone did. That pretty girl loved you without boundaries—your perfect match.

It was so vivid. The two of you were married on the mountain, at the little chapel on the outlook. It was your favorite season. I remember how orange the leaves were.

You exchanged beautiful, heartfelt vows at my favorite time of day when the sun makes the world shine like gold. I was there with you, and we were a happy family.

When you do get married, wherever you are, I will be there with you in butterfly flutters. I promise.

Goosebumps trail over my skin. Tears stream down my cheeks, and I don't know if I can continue reading.

Zane wipes his face and I wrap my arms around him, holding him so fucking tight, like he might disappear if I let him go. It's too raw and deep.

"How did . . . ?" I ask, inhaling him, listening to the steady beat of his heart as he holds me too.

"I'm not sure."

The embrace is safe and comforting.

"Fuck, you feel like home, Pumpkin."

I pull away, meeting his sparkling eyes. "I love you."

"I love you." He slides his lips across mine. "Continue, please."

I nod, swallowing hard. The emotions on the page are almost too much. But I do it for him and his mom.

So tell me, are you in love right now? Have you found The One yet? Whoever you choose to spend the rest of your life with will be so special. Your heart is so kind and loving. I know hers will be, too. I hope she reminds you of who you are and who you will always be . . .

My thoughtful son who forgives quickly and doesn't hold grudges.

My hopeful son who believes in magic and wishes on stars.

My hungry son who can eat an entire stack of pumpkin pancakes alone.

My loyal son who isn't afraid to stand up for what's right.

My happy son who loves the snow and still makes snow angels.

My generous son who gives and shares with those who need it most.

My adventurous son who faces his fears head-on.

My sweet son who wears his heart on his sleeve and loves with his whole self.

Please don't ever let the world harden you, Zane.

Remember, everything happens for a reason, and sometimes, we don't know what that reason is, or don't agree with it. All we can do is go with the flow, take what life gives us, and continue forward with a grateful heart.

No matter how hard life gets, it's better than the alternative. You still have another chance to right your wrongs and make a difference.

Life is so precious and beautiful and fragile.

There was a time when I didn't know if I'd find true love, and then randomly, I met your father. The moment our eyes met, I knew I'd spend the rest of my life with him. Oh, how I wish it were longer. But then again, five hundred years wouldn't be enough. In a way, I'm glad I'm going first because I wouldn't have survived heartbreak like that.

Your dad will. You will. And Harper will, too. Your sister has the two of you to remind her that life goes on and the world is still beautiful even though bad things happen to good people.

Now, I do have some marriage tips for you when that time comes.

1. Kiss each other good night every single night. Tomorrow isn't promised.
2. Never go to bed angry. I don't care what happened.
3. Laugh until your stomach hurts. It's healthy for the soul.

4. Say I love you as much as you can. One day, you might not be able to.
5. Take a ridiculous number of pictures together. It's the only way to turn back time.
6. Be each other's best friend. Because together, you can conquer anything.
7. Share secrets and communicate. And never repeat what's said.
8. Forgive easily. Sometimes, it's the only way to move forward.
9. Love one another without barriers. Because then it's limitless.

I decided today that I'm leaving my engagement ring for you.

When you were close to four years old, there were many nights when you'd twist it around my finger and tell me how pretty it was. The light would catch it at a certain angle and it would shine like a diamond in the sky. You loved it. Please don't feel pressured to use it, but I wanted you to have it for your special person. And you'll know who it should go to when the time comes, deep in your heart.

I have many wishes in this life. One of them is that you find your forever person sooner rather than later. Time is too precious to waste.

I could probably write you a novel about love and how incredible it is when you truly find it. Fifteen-year-old you would groan loudly when I talked about these things. I hope adult you appreciates it.

If you find this letter before your big day, please come

back and reread this when the time comes. Perspective makes old things seem new again.

> Sealed with my everlasting love,
> Mom

P.S. I've written thirteen letters for you and hid them in different places at Hollow Manor because you always loved a scavenger hunt. What number is this? Ah well. Happy hunting!

I fold the letter and hand it to Zane, glancing down at the ring on my finger. He twists the diamond around.

I look up, meeting his soft eyes. "All this time, I thought I manifested you, but I actually think your mom manifested me."

He laughs, squeezing me a little tighter. "I love you so damn much that it almost hurts."

"I love you too." I meet his gaze. "You're *all I want* in life."

"You've got me, Pumpkin. For eternity."

CHAPTER 39

Autumn

One Week Later

"How's married life?" Julie asks me as she bites into her chicken sandwich.

Blaire grins wide. "Yep. We want all the details."

I laugh. "Life is incredible. Every day, I'm convinced I'm living in a fairy tale."

They swoon, as I chat about everything that's happened.

"Wish he had a brother," Julie says. "Or a hot, single best friend."

I shrug. "Sorry. Both of his friends seem very taken. There is his ex-bestie, though."

"Yeah?" Julie asks.

I shake my head. "He's a red flag. A giant one."

"Red is my favorite color," she tells me, smirking. "Maybe I can help him?"

"Now you sound like me," I tell her.

"Exactly. It worked for you," she says with a laugh.

Blaire reaches forward and grabs my hand. "Let me know when we can look at cottage designs."

"Oh shit," I say, my mouth falling open. "I almost forgot. The love spell. Shit."

"I'm officially eight for eight," she brags. "Just waiting for this one's spell to work."

"Is there a time limit on it?"

"Three moon cycles," she explains. "So we have a month to see if I have a perfect record or not."

"The pressure," Julie says, lifting her margarita. "You're fucked, Blaire."

I look between my besties and smile wide.

"Why are you looking at us like that?" Jules asks with her head tilted.

"I love you two. Thank you for always being my best friends."

"Oh goodness," Blaire says. "Please don't cry. If you do, I will too."

I laugh. It reminds me of Harper.

"I realized when I was in the worst place of my life you were both always by my side, no matter what. Through thick and thin. Through my moods. Neither of you cared and still loved me the same, supported me. Not everyone has that. Some people have to walk through the fire alone." I think about Zane and his life experiences. "I never had to, and I'm so damn grateful for that."

Blaire and Julie wipe tears away.

"Okay, you're not supposed to cry. But having perspective changes things." I pick up my napkin, thinking back to the beautiful letter Zane's mother wrote him.

As Julie opens her mouth, a deep voice says my name from beside me. I look over to find Sebastian.

Julie and Blaire give him a death stare.

"Autumn. Can we please talk?"

I glance at my friends and they shake their heads. Then I remember how Zane acknowledged his ghosts; maybe it's time to do the same for mine.

"Okay," I say, sliding out of the booth.

Julie shakes her head.

"It's fine. Five minutes," I tell them, then turn to Sebastian. "Five minutes."

"Okay," he tells me, and I move across the room toward the hallway by the bathrooms. I pull my phone from my pocket to note the time.

"Go ahead. You've got my attention," I say.

"Congratulations."

I look at him like he's lost his mind. "That's it?"

"Yes. And I genuinely mean that from the bottom of my heart. At first, I was frustrated and angry. Mainly with myself because I realized how badly I'd fucked up. Seeing you with Zane drove home what I already knew—that I'd lost you forever. I knew he would never let you go because he doesn't take good things for granted."

I swallow hard.

"I wanted to make a scene at his father's wedding, knowing I could ruin it."

"Thank God you didn't. You'd have embarrassed me." I'm brought back to how desperate Celine was and how she'd already accomplished that with no help.

"It's the only reason I didn't." He breathes out slowly. "Zane Alexander is one of the greatest men I've ever met, and I've always hated him for it. He's always been better at everything. Again, I'm in second place."

I open my mouth to say something, but he shakes his head. "I chose it, Autie. And I'm not fighting for you because you should have someone who can truly love you the way you deserve. Ego aside, I saw the way you two looked at each other, and there's no way I could make you that happy. I'm really fucking sorry for hurting you and for cheating and all the stupid shit I did and said when we were together. I didn't realize what I had until it was gone. This is me saying I hope you have a beautiful life with the man of your dreams. Love like that is what the rest of us wish for."

I let out a soft laugh. He remembered my stories about Mr. Dreamy. "Thank you."

He opens his arms and I hug him. It's odd to experience no emotions when I was stupidly obsessed with him for so long. We pull away, and he walks toward the exit. When he's out of sight, I replay what he said, not wanting to forget a word. Julie and Blaire are staring at me so I take a deep breath and return to the booth.

"What did he say?" Blaire asks.

"He apologized and told me congrats. Not in that order."

They look as shocked as I feel.

"Yeah." I repeat what he said about Zane.

"Maybe he isn't such a bastard," Julie says. "He gave the ultimate sacrifice in a way. His heart in exchange for your happiness."

"Oh, please tell me you're not getting soft for him."

"If I'm choosing a toxic man in your life, it won't be him. Love you, but don't want your sloppy seconds or small dicks."

I burst into laughter.

"However, Zane's ex–best friend?" She tilts her head. "What does he look like?"

Blaire playfully rolls her eyes.

"Uh. Actually, hold on. I'm friends with his mom on social media." I unlock my phone and go to Silvia's profile. "It's not the best photo."

She drops my phone. "Are you fucking kidding me? I think I just fell in love."

Blaire snickers. "Let me see."

Her eyes widen too.

"I need you both to repeat after me: red flag," I say.

"Have you met him?" Julie asks.

"Yes. Briefly," I admit.

"And? What was he like?" Blaire asks.

I think back to when he showed up at the manor. "Sad. I could tell he was harboring a lot of regret."

"I can see it in his eyes," Julie mutters. "He looks destroyed."

"Yeah." I take my phone back and lock it. "For mediocre pussy, apparently."

Blaire nearly spews the sip of margarita she was drinking. She coughs a few times as she laughs.

Julie sighs, and I think she might actually feel sorry for him.

"Look, I'll make you a deal. If he's *ever* allowed back in Zane's life and you're still single, I'll play matchmaker. Not because I think you'll fix him, but because you'll break him down and rebuild him properly."

"Promise on it." Julie holds out her hand and I take it.

"Promise."

"Ooh." Blaire rubs her arms. "I just got the chills."

Julie grins. "And so it begins."

I tilt my head at her. "What does that mean?"

She smiles. "Harper."

"Wait, she gave you a prophecy?"

Julie nods. "But you know the rules."

Blaire looks between us. "What? Someone fill me in."

"It's almost impossible to chat in detail to anyone about it, except Harper. Or until after the thing she predicted happens." I touch my throat.

"The words get caught in your throat," Julie explains. "Like it only fully lives inside you."

Blaire pokes out her bottom lip. "I want a love prophecy!"

I laugh. "You'll get one eventually. Everyone close to her does."

"Give me a hint, at least," I say to Julie.

"It was something about The One becoming brothers with someone I trust, who has the most valuable thing in my life. I think she was talking about you because our friendship means everything to me. And Zane did just acquire, through marriage, a very hot brother."

"That's the only thing that makes sense." Blaire pauses.

Goosebumps cover my arms. "Tell us after something happens, okay? I know you'll be able to share then."

"I will," she confirms.

"Now I'm invested!" Blaire says.

The three of us are lost in our heads as I contemplate her prophecy and what it could actually mean.

A fresh basket of chips and salsa is set in front of us. "I have some good news. I think I'm going to start writing again."

"This is the best thing I've heard all week," Jules says.

"So happy for you," Blaire adds. "You found yourself."

"Zane found me." An overwhelming sense of happiness and calmness takes over as the curse that's smothered my creativity vanishes. "I'm finally ready."

My phone vibrates in my pocket, and when I see his name, it's like I summoned him.

"Go ahead and answer it," Julie says. "You want to."

I grin wide. "Are you sure?"

"Yes," they both tell me. "You know what to do."

My cheeks heat. "All answered calls get put on speaker."

I close my eyes and answer, turning down my volume and leaning in to listen.

"Hey, Pumpkin."

Julie holds her hands over her heart.

"Hey. I was thinking about you."

"I was thinking about you too and had a weird feeling."

Blaire's eyes are wide and she rubs away her goosebumps. She mouths "That's twin flame shit."

"I'm fine. Just eating chips and salsa."

"Hi, Julie and Blaire."

They laugh and greet him as well.

I clear my throat. "There's something I need to tell you."

"Okay?" I can still hear the smile in his voice.

"I spoke with Sebastian."

"And?" His tone is still light. "Do I need to drive to Bookers and beat his ass?"

"No, no. Julie is here. She's a black belt in karate and has been asking to destroy him for years. I was safe, I promise. I was confronting my ghosts," I say. "And I felt like he wouldn't leave me alone until I let him speak."

"And what did he say? Let me guess, he's madly in love with you and his dumb ass is going to try to steal you away from me even though we're married?"

"Pfft," Julie says.

I quietly explain what happened. Julie and Blaire give me every expression under the sun when I relive it again, this time, not leaving out any details of what Sebastian said.

"He said you were one of the greatest men he's ever known and that you're the only person who can make me happy."

The line is quiet for a long time.

"Hello?" I ask.

"This is where you say you're joking."

"No. He offered a heartfelt congratulations," I admit.

"Wow." He sighs and I can imagine him running his fingers through his dark, messy hair. "It's true, though."

I snort-laugh, and my besties do too. "Of course it is."

He chuckles.

"Told you I was a Ghostbuster," I say as our entrées arrive. I move my phone, taking it off speaker. "I love you."

"Love you too. Thank you for telling me. I'm kind of relieved."

"Me too," I say.

"I think that's everyone, Autie. We confronted all of our ghosts."

"How does it make you feel?" I ask.

"Light as a feather."

CHAPTER 40

Zane

Two Weeks Later

"Can I remove this blindfold now?" Autumn impatiently asks as she stands in our bedroom at Hollow Manor. "It's my birthday and I should be able to do whatever I want."

"Keep it up and I'll have to deliver those thirty-four spankings I promised right now."

"Mm. Don't forget the one to grow on."

I chuckle, admiring how fucking beautiful my wife is without even trying.

"I want to know what you have me dressed in. It feels very . . . *fluffy*."

"You're an impatient little thing."

Her brows lift. "You have no idea."

I close the space between us and place my hands on her hips, guiding her into the bathroom. Carefully, I untie the blindfold. Autumn covers her mouth when she sees her reflection.

"Am I Cinderella?" she asks, noticing what I'm wearing. "Prince Charming."

I grin wide. "We have a ball to attend and some crowns to win."

Laughter escapes her. "Why are you perfect?"

"Only in your eyes," I mutter, stealing a kiss. "Finish getting ready. I'll meet you downstairs, okay?"

"How much time do I have?"

I check my watch. "Thirty minutes, max."

"Just need to put on some lipstick and pull some hair back," she tells me, grinning. "Be down in twenty."

I hold her face in my hands and sweetly kiss her. "You're fucking gorgeous, Princess."

"I'm grateful you're mine," she says in a whisper, and I taste her lips.

"Looking forward to taking that dress off you later."

"Don't tempt me," she warns.

My girl is insatiable, never satisfied, always wanting more of me. I feel the same. No matter how much time I spend with Autumn, it's not enough, and I'm not sure it ever will be. I want more than a lifetime with her. It's how I know she's my one true love.

I take the stairs with a hop to my step. All of our friends and family are in costume, hiding downstairs.

"Is she coming?" Julie whispers loudly.

"Not yet. Twenty minutes," I explain.

Silvia and my dad are sitting on the couch, chatting with Autumn's parents. Our folks are dressed like queens and kings.

Harper claimed the fairy godmother title, but her outfit is completely sequined.

Moments later, the door cracks open and Weston appears as the Grand Duke. It's fitting, considering our friendship has only strengthened since our get-together in New York.

"The pumpkin and horses are waiting where the road curves," he explains.

I check my watch, knowing in fifteen minutes, I'll return upstairs. "Fantastic, right on time."

Carlee, the woman who was his plus-one at my father's wedding, enters. She's wearing a light pink dress that looks like it fell out of a Jane Eyre novel.

"Everyone, this is Carlee."

Billie sweeps in behind her. "My brother's girlfriend."

"Shh. Autumn has excellent hearing," I whisper.

"See? No one cares," Weston says. "You're making a big deal out of it."

"You know, Zane, no one has ever been able to successfully throw Autumn a surprise party," her mom quietly says.

"She told me." I grin. "I'm on a mission to change that."

Her father smiles at me. "Is that Autumn's laptop on the counter over there?"

"Yeah," I explain. "She started writing a few weeks ago."

Julie and Blaire give each other a high five.

The front door cracks open and Winter quietly enters with a wide smile, wearing a dress very similar to Carlee's but purple.

"You made it after all," I say. Winter has hung out with us a lot and even took up running with Autumn. Last week, she officially moved into Autumn's old apartment. Well, now it's ours. I purchased the building and told the vinyl record shop they never had to pay a penny of rent again. The owners couldn't believe it and thanked me at least a million times.

Harper walks over and pulls her into a hug.

"Thanks for sending the costume," Winter tells her. She's become great friends with my sister. Everyone has. But Harper has always had a knack for making fast friends with everyone she meets. Her kind personality is one of her superpowers. Our mom was the same.

"Oh God, are we the evil stepsisters?" Winter says, glancing at Carlee, Blaire, and Julie, who find it hilarious.

"No, no," Harper says. "Think of it as being a cast member in *Bridgerton*. That came from the set. I asked for a favor."

Blaire's mouth falls open. "Seriously?"

The four of them discuss how it all went down. It's a story I haven't heard yet, but because she's in fashion, she knows tons of people in Hollywood. She and Billie have designed red carpet looks for the most elite.

"How are things?" my father asks.

We make small talk until the fifteen-minute mark. As if I can predict Autumn's moves, I turn to Harper. "Do you have the final piece?"

She nods and returns with a pair of clear high heels that were made for my wife. A few seconds later, I hear the thick bedroom door snap closed.

"She's coming," I whisper, holding the shoes behind my back. "Hide."

They scatter around and Autumn rounds the corner, grinning. Our eyes immediately meet and she pauses, taking me in before she approaches. I stand a little taller. "Hi, beautiful."

"Hi," she says, lifting her dress to show her bare feet.

"There is one problem," she explains.

"What's that?" I ask.

"What shoes do I wear? I tried on every pair I have."

When she's in front of me, I drop to my knees, revealing her glass slippers. "Will they be a match?" I grab her ankle, then put one shoe on and then the other.

"You've covered it all." She laughs, looking down at them. "Perfect fit."

"Meant to be." I wrap my arms around her and our lips slide together.

A confetti cannon goes off and Autumn jumps. I hold her tighter against me as her eyes widen.

"SURPRISE!" everyone shouts, jumping from their hiding places.

"Oh my God," she says, holding her chest. "I was fucking scared!"

"Curse jar!" Julie yells.

"How'd you pull it off?" she asks. "I didn't hear anyone coming or going!"

"Magic," I tell her. Harper walks over with a single cupcake and a candle. I take it from her and move closer to Autumn as our closest friends and family sing her "Happy Birthday."

"Make a wish, Pumpkin," I whisper when the song ends. She meets my eyes before closing hers. The candle lights her face, and then, with a single whoosh of breath, it's out.

She smiles.

"Was it a good one?" I ask as the lights flip on.

"The best," she tells me, swiping her finger across the chocolate cream. She places it in her mouth. "This is from that bakery."

"Cakes from that place are a tradition. One my mom started. Harper always delivers it by hand, no matter where I am in the world. Gifting sentimental things that mean something to her is her love language," I explain as everyone approaches us.

Autumn finishes licking the icing from the top, and it's fucking erotic as she looks into my eyes as she does it. I slowly shake my head and she grins like a little devil. As Autumn exchanges hugs with friends and family and compliments everyone's costumes, I take a step back and snap photos of smiling faces.

When we're eighty, I'm sure we'll talk about how young and in love we were. I never want to forget these moments. They're the ones I cherish the most. Champagne glasses are passed out and several bottles are opened.

Her dad holds up his flute. "Happy birthday, Autie. We love you."

"Happy birthday." I wrap my arm around her waist. "Are you happy?"

"The happiest," she says, grinning.

When everyone's glass is emptied, Harper claps her hands,

always keeping everyone on schedule. "We should probably get going! There is a ball we have to attend."

I guide Autumn to the front door.

She steps outside and freezes at the sight of the white horses pulling a golden pumpkin carriage.

"Surprise."

The coachman greets us with a nod as I step off the porch and open the door for her. She moves toward me.

"Living the dream," I whisper, and she smiles, stepping on board. Our friends and family load into the limos that pull into the driveway.

"We'll meet you there," I say, climbing inside with Autumn.

"Thank you," she says. "This is . . . I'm speechless."

I grin wide, grabbing the Moleskine book to write my poem for the day.

> *Happy Birthday, Love.*
> *Hope the wish you made comes true.*
> *Tell me when it does.*

Then I scribble below it.

> *(I love you!)*

As she tries to peek over my shoulder, I snap it shut. "No peeking."

"Not even on my birthday?" She playfully pouts.

"Rules are rules."

She pokes out her bottom lip. "What if I begged?"

"Keep looking at me like that and I might have to christen this pumpkin carriage."

"Mm. I think I decided what I want for my birthday."

Fire flashes in her eyes and she chews on her cheek as she scans down my body. I glance out the small back window, seeing the limos slowly following behind us. The driver is in the front, secluded away from us. It's fully private.

"What's that?" I ask.

"You," she whispers.

"Your wish is my fucking command."

CHAPTER 41

Autumn

*H*is lips crash into mine and we grow more desperate with each passing second. "I'm serious," I say, glancing down at the bulge in his pants.

"Me too," he tells me, grabbing my chin and meeting my eyes. "But we're going to play the quiet game."

I playfully narrow my eyes at him. "And if I get loud?"

"Control yourself, and I'll reward you like a *good fucking girl* later."

"When I receive my bare-ass birthday spankings?" My breathing grows ragged as it always does when he looks at me like he wants to unravel me. Over and fucking over again.

Zane licks his lips. Shit, I can barely handle how sexy he is and the fact that he's my husband. He may have a four-leaf clover, but I'm the luckiest woman alive.

"Now." He moves to the floorboard of the carriage and gets on his knees in front of me. I stare into his ocean-blue eyes and his eyebrow slightly quirks. "How many orgasms do you want, birthday girl?"

"How many can you give me before we cross city limits?"

"Hmm." His mouth parts. "What's your current record?"

"You're already holding the first place spot in Autumn's World

Records for everything," I say, parting my legs for him, leaning forward to capture his lips. He steals a glance at my breasts.

"Show me your gorgeous tits, wifey," he says, then I notice the tiny clasps on the material. Did they magically appear?

Then I remember I was blindfolded when he dressed me tonight. I don't know the inner workings of the dress I wear other than my pockets.

"Mmhm." He smirks, confirmation that it was by design.

I unsnap one side of the top and reveal myself to him.

"Beautiful," he whispers, moving forward, sliding his body between my legs, capturing my nipple in his mouth as he tweaks the other with his fingers.

"Yes," I say, my head falling back, loving the pressure of him against me.

"I guess we're living one of your fantasies right now?" I question as we desperately kiss. His strong hand slides up my thighs until he brushes down my wet slit.

"Apparently, we're living yours too," he tells me, placing his fingers in his mouth and licking my arousal from them. "So. Fucking. Good. Now, put those perfect tits up for me and enjoy the pretty colors. Remember, *quiet*."

Quickly, he moves my ass to the edge of the leather seat that's only big enough for the two of us. Zane pushes my thighs wider apart, then dives between my legs, slowly kissing and sucking my clit.

I gasp, leaning my head back, noticing the beautiful yellows and oranges as leaves flutter in the breeze. His warm mouth is almost too much because I'm so turned on.

"Mm," he hums. His scruff feels incredible against me. "So good."

He enjoys every single second of having me this way. I'm under his spell, and he can do whatever he wants. My body is a prisoner to him and all that he gives.

A quiet pant whispers through the small space as I rock my hips. His hot tongue darts inside. A moan escapes.

"Shh," he says, his breath tickling my most sensitive parts.

My mouth falls open as I sink farther onto his lips.

"Zane," I whisper, knowing he's urging me to let go. Minutes is all it takes for the first orgasm.

"Count for me, Pumpkin."

"One," I hiss out as he slowly returns to my swollen bud, not giving me too much pressure or too little. Sometimes I get a finger or two, and sometimes I don't. It doesn't matter.

He has my body memorized, knowing what I need and want. This man worships me like I'm his religion, and I come so many times that I almost lose count. But he asks after each glorious, heart-pounding release. Zane gives me enough time to recover before leading me back to the cliff, where I free-fall. Nothing is at the bottom but him.

I shiver and the last orgasm I think I can manage bustles through me like a runaway train, casting me to a different reality.

"Seven." I gasp out. My body wants to shut down. The euphoria, the head high, I've never experienced anything like this.

I fist my fingers in his hair as he sucks me clean.

"We're about to be at the bottom," I whisper. "No time."

He sucks on his lip. "We'll stop at lucky number seven."

His mouth is on mine and I can taste myself as our tongues twist together. "How was it?"

"The best I ever had," I whisper, my heart steadily pounding. I reach down, feeling how damn hard he is. "Let me."

"I'll take an IOU."

"Fuck, that's seven I'll give."

He holds out his hand and we shake on it with a soft laugh, then he moves my dress down over my body. Zane wraps his arm around me, kissing my forehead, completely satisfied.

"To be known is to be loved," I say.

"Thankfully, I have you memorized."

"How do I look?" I double-check my top, making sure it's fully clasped. The last thing I need to do is flash my boobs at the Pumpkin Ball. My best friends would never let me live it down.

Zane reaches out and smooths my hair down in the back.

"You already know the answer to that question," he mutters with a flirty tone as the carriage enters downtown Cozy Hollow.

"Good," I say, completely okay with it.

I glance out the side windows and Zane reaches up and slides open a sunroof. With shining eyes, looking like my personal Prince Charming, he smirks, lifting his hand for me. I take it and he pulls me up with him.

Kids are on the street with jack-o'-lanterns and candy bags in their grasp. They're giggling, skipping, and high on sugar as the trick-or-treaters stop by the local businesses.

"It's Cinderella and Prince Charming," one little girl says, pointing. "Look!"

People watch us pass by. We wave and smile, and I'm giddy as we create a traffic-stopping parade on the way to the ball.

"Mommy! It's them!" another kid says.

Zane watches me, smiling. He leans forward and kisses me so passionately that he steals my breath away. "Happy birthday, Pumpkin."

"It's been the best one I've ever had," I admit.

"Until next year," he says, wearing a boyish grin.

I shake my head. "I don't know how you'll top this one."

"I'm up for the challenge," he says as we enter the venue parking lot. Those walking into the ball stop and stare at us. Everyone is shocked, even the valet.

The door opens and Zane takes my hand, picks me up, and sets me on the ground. I take a step back, snapping a picture of us with the carriage in the background.

"Truthfully. After that, I don't think I'll ever be able to look at a pumpkin carriage or the cartoon the same way."

"Fuck, me either." He smirks with swollen lips and gorgeously messy hair that I want to thrust my fingers through again. He lifts a brow, catching me. "It's that look again."

"I'm not sure what you're talking about." I grin, grateful he's mine.

The limos unload and our friends and family enter together. As soon as we do, all heads turn toward our entourage, then the room bursts into applause. The president of the fundraising committee that hosts the ball is at the end of the red carpet, which leads to a bejeweled throne.

Each guest must approach the king and be officially welcomed in. I also think it's how they mark us off the guest list. Zane and I drift forward, capturing the room's attention.

When we're close, the presenter grins wide and stands to grab a microphone.

"Ladies and gentlemen, I'm proud to announce Zane and Autumn Alexander as this year's Pumpkin King and Queen."

I meet the eyes of everyone who loves and adores me. "Did you know?" I ask Julie and Blaire.

"We kinda became your campaign managers."

Mrs. Mooney and the women from the book club proudly waltz over with their chests out. "We manifested this!" she claims, and Zane laughs as pictures are taken. A sash is thrown over my body and Zane's. Moments later, we kneel to accept our crowns in front of the entire town.

"Ladies and gentlemen, this year's Pumpkin King and Queen have arrived. All hail."

Joy and laughter pour out of me as pumpkin-shaped confetti falls from the ceiling. It glitters and floats around us. Our eyes meet, and when he slowly kisses me, it's like magic. We danced around the world searching for one another, and I'll continue to twirl in his arms until our story ends. This is our fairy tale.

When our gazes lock, I smile wide and it fucking hurts.

Zane leans in, his thumb brushing against my cheek. "You'll always be my Pumpkin Queen."

"And you'll always be my Prince Charming."

EPILOGUE

Zane

I've never watched the ball drop in real life," Autumn explains as we grab a glass of champagne. A pianist plays in the middle of the room and the lights are low.

"Not even when you lived in thee City?" I ask, my eyes sliding over my wife.

"I avoided the area. Like a true New Yorker."

I chuckle. As I take a sip of the bubbly, I see Nicolas move onto the balcony. He stayed to himself all night. It's weird to coexist and not speak.

"Talk to him," Autumn says. "You want to. I can see it in your expression."

I sigh. "I know what it's like to be alone in that doom spiral. I believed everyone hated me when I hated myself. You saved me."

Her eyes shine as she wraps her arms around my waist. "You needed a friend."

"I needed *you*." I steal a kiss. "Five minutes?"

"Billie and Harper are here. Fashionably late. I'll come find you, okay?"

"Love you," I whisper.

"Love you." She smiles. When she approaches Harper, I refill my glass and make my way outside.

He turns and glances at me when the door snaps shut. I stand beside him and the frigid air brushes against my cheeks.

"A lot of people down there." His eyes glide over the crowd. Across the way is the stage where Anderson Cooper is filming.

"Been snowboarding this season?" I ask.

"Not once," he says. We used to be thick as thieves and would rule the slopes together. Nicolas was like my brother. Now that our parents are married, we're not even friends.

Awkwardness streams between us.

"I don't know what to say right now," I admit. "But you don't have to go through this shit alone. No one hates you."

"You do."

"I did." I drink my champagne. "But there isn't room in my life for that anymore. What you did to me was abhorrent, but we were pawns in a scheme that was bigger than both of us. I don't have to remind you of that. It spins around in your mind constantly. I know it does because you have a fucking conscience."

"You're right," he says, swigging back the rest of the amber liquid in his glass.

"I've forgiven you. It's what my mom would want me to do."

He sucks in a deep breath. "I miss her."

"We all do." I look at him. "Come to Cozy Hollow and ride the slopes with me."

"You mean that?" There is hope in his tone.

"Yeah," I say with a nod. "The mountains can heal anything."

We focus back on the crowd cheering below as someone walks onstage. I think it's Snoop Dogg.

"My mother hid letters around Hollow Manor for me to find—thirteen, to be exact."

He studies me as I down the rest of my champagne.

"I found the third one recently in my old bedroom, and you were mentioned several times. I'm willing to give you a second chance."

I meet his furrowed brows.

"Are you fucked up right now?" he asks, shaking his head.

Laughter roars out of me. "No. I'm in a really happy place in my life, and if it wasn't for all the bullshit, I'm not sure it would've happened. The dominoes had to fall."

"I wouldn't give you one if the roles were reversed."

"You've always been a grudge holder. I'm not."

A server steps onto the patio and takes my empty champagne glass, handing me another.

I continue. "However, if you touch *my wife* or even look at her the wrong way, I'll break your fucking fingers off, then shove them down your throat." I smile sweetly.

Now he laughs. "Almost thought you'd gotten soft."

"You're not stupid enough to make the same mistake twice."

I glance through the tall windows and watch Autumn laugh with Harper. My wife is so pretty in her elegant black dress. As if I summoned her attention, her eyes zero in on me and she lifts her champagne glass, grinning. I nod, ready to focus on her tonight.

"I can tell you're genuinely happy," Nicolas says. "You give me hope and make me believe maybe love does exist for assholes."

I chuckle. "You'll find someone. And when you do, you'll know. It won't be superficial, fake bullshit."

"Thank you," he mutters.

I hug him hard and pat his shoulder. "I won't let you drown."

"I'm sorry for letting you sink," he says.

"No more apologies from here on out. We move forward. Not backward." I let go of him and turn toward the sliding door. "Oh yeah, and I didn't sink, Nick. I fucking *soared*."

He grins, and it's the first time I've seen him smile in a long time. We exchange a nod.

I walk inside, moving directly to my wife. She studies me, her eyes asking a million silent questions.

"It went fine," I whisper in her ear. "I'll tell you later."

Harper laughs. "And when I bent over, my dress was tight, and it ripped the seam. Now there are pictures of my cute-as-fuck panties in the tabloids."

Billie is practically crying from laughing. "You always said never leave home without them."

"I knew there was a reason. The lingerie company called me today and offered to send me every color and cut. Their sales have tripled overnight because of my cute ass," Harper continues.

I lift my brows. "What conversation have I walked in on?"

My sister is tipsy. "TLDR version? My ass can sell anything. Might start taking advertisements out of it."

I wrap my arm around Autumn as Nick walks inside. My father stops him.

"You were hugging," she says.

"I invited him to snowboard with me."

Long lashes flutter closed. "Harper gave Julie a prophecy. She mentioned your brother."

I look at her with the same alarmed expression and then laugh. "You think Nick and Jules will get together?"

She sighs. "I promised I'd play matchmaker if you welcomed him back into your life."

I shake my head. "Autumn."

"Before this all happened, he was a good guy, right?" She searches my face. "I don't believe you'd be best friends with someone who wasn't."

"He was a great person," I explain. "Respectful, caring, and fun. He has a good heart. Or at least he did. He's not the same though."

She smiles. "Based on what Harper has shared, you aren't the same as you used to be either. You found your way and everything worked out."

"Better than I ever could've predicted. Only because I found you."

"Mr. Dreamy promised he would," she whispers, her mouth sliding against mine. We move onto the balcony of my father's penthouse when there are two minutes left.

My dad has hosted a huge New Year's party every year for the past decade, and I've skipped each one. Even if it's not my usual crowd, I'll never miss another one. Having Autumn by my side is my new tradition. After news spread of what Celine did at the wedding, she was banned from all events that anyone in my family could attend.

"Ready?" I ask when the gigantic clock begins the countdown. Music and chatter roars from the street. When the clock strikes midnight and confetti falls from the sky, I pull her into my arms. We are teeth and tongue and want and need. A mixture of fire and passion so hot I nearly crumble to ash. When we break apart, we're breathless.

"Happy new year, wifey."

"Happy new year, hubby," she says, grabbing my hand and leading me through the large living room as the pianist plays "Auld Lang Syne."

"Where are we going?" I ask.

The party would last all night, and my father offered us a room.

"Sit on the bed," she demands.

"Oh, it's going to be like that?"

She shakes her head, then pulls a gift wrapped in silver paper from under the bed. It's heavy.

"I didn't get the memo that we were exchanging gifts," I mutter.

"Open it," she urges.

I rip off the paper and lift the box. Inside is a stack of papers bound together with metal rings.

My eyes scan across the middle.

ALL I WANT
By Autumn Alexander

"This is what you've been working on?" I whisper, searching her eyes.

"Yes," she proudly admits as I pull out the stack.

I flip to the second page and read the dedication.

To my loving husband.
Thank you for inspiring me every single day.

Then I see thousands of words that she's written. I gently return the thick stack to the box and eliminate the space between us. Our lips desperately crash together, and I sweep hair from her face.

"I'm so fucking proud of you, Autumn." I pepper kisses on her mouth and her forehead. "So fucking proud. I knew you could do it. You finished your book."

Happy tears stream down her cheeks, and I kiss them away.

"It's *our* book."

Autumn

I sit on one end of the couch with my Moleskine notebook and write my poem for the day.

If this is a dream
I don't ever want to wake
Yours, eternally.

I reread my poem.

"I'm getting pretty good at this," I say as an engine lightly revs outside.

"You've had a lot of practice. Can't wait to read them." Zane chuckles as he reads my book by the window in the midday sunlight. I love how his messy hair curls at the ends as his eyes sweep over the pages.

"Is it him?" I ask, still shocked that Zane invited Nick to stay with us for a week because the ski resort is booked until March. It has been since the first snowfall. Not even the future CEO could pull enough strings to make it happen, so he offered him a room here.

"Not sure, but there is supposed to be a storm rolling in later today." He glances out the window before returning to the pages.

I walk over to him and sit in his lap. He wraps his arms around me, kissing my shoulder as I sink on top of him. "What chapter are you on?" I ask.

He's had the book for three days and has taken his time reading it.

"Fifteen. The one where they dance in the rain."

I smile warmly, looking back at him as he kisses my neck. "Oh, that's one of my favorites."

"Mine too," he mumbles. "I love reading your heart, Pumpkin. I can feel you in your words."

I turn to him, capturing his lips. "You believed in me when I didn't believe in myself. That's why I dedicated it to you."

"I'll always cherish this," he says, setting the large stack beside me. "Always cherish you."

A light tap on the door pulls our attention away.

"He's here," I whisper.

Zane nods. "He tries to make one move on you, and I'll fucking murder him. And he knows as much."

I chuckle. "You have nothing to worry about. Trust me."

Zane answers the door, swinging it open with a smile. "Need some help?"

"Yeah, sure," Nick says as Zane wheels an oversized suitcase inside.

Nick's ski and snowboarding gear is in an awkward-sized large zipper bag. He moves straight to the mudroom in the back and sets it down. Then it occurs to me that he's been here before.

"How have you been?" Nick asks with a polite smile, glancing at the Christmas tree we haven't taken down yet.

The lights twinkle and dance, casting a warm, magical glow up the large wall and ceiling. I might keep it up all year.

"I've been great. How about you?"

"Better," he says. "Better now that I'm here."

"Which room would you like?" Zane asks. "Your choice."

"I'm not picky." Nick smiles, and they head up the stairs together, talking about anything and everything to keep the conversation going.

My eyes scan the page Zane's currently reading and I smile. Dancing with him in the rain is a memory I'll never forget. It was magic. The fancy tequila *definitely* helped.

A few minutes later, they walk down the steps and laugh. At first glance, I could almost see them as brothers. Same height. Same demeanor.

"So I hope you don't mind, but I invited a friend to join us for dinner tonight," I say.

Nick meets my eyes. "Are you trying to set me up?"

"No, no, nope. Absolutely not." I immediately deny it as my cheeks burn red.

"Is she always a bad liar?" he asks.

"Yes," Zane confirms, meeting my gaze. "We can try her Cajun chicken pasta recipe after Nick leaves."

"Okay," I say, pouting, knowing my best friend is going to murder me. "Let me text her and cancel."

Nick checks his watch. "What time is she supposed to be here?"

I unlock my phone. "Less than twenty minutes."

"Please don't cancel your plans. I want a shower first, then I'll join you."

I smile, happy he's placating me even though I can tell he's not thrilled about the idea. "Great!"

After a quick nod, he takes the stairs. When the door closes, Zane crosses his arms over his chest. "Told you he'd see straight through it."

"I have to keep my promise," I explain. "It's important to me."

He leans forward, kissing my forehead. "You can't force things."

I take a step back. "Excuse me, Mr. *I'll have you arrested if you don't give me an IOU. You* forced *me!*"

His laughter is contagious. "It was a part of the prophecy, Pumpkin. You know that."

"I wouldn't change anything."

Gently, he tucks loose strands of hair behind my ears. "How do you think it will go tonight?"

"Not sure." I blink up at him. "Are you nervous?"

"No. Harper gave me some insight. You're too damn pretty." His fist is in my hair and our mouths collide. The only thing that pulls us away is the sound of light knocks on the door. "I want an IOU."

"Any day of the damn week," I say, pulling him back to me.

"I love that you only give them to me."

"IOUs?" I ask as I move across the living room.

He pops a brow. Ah. *Orgasms.*

"Ready for my bestie to meet your *brother*?"

"By marriage only." He smirks.

I open the door and the chilly draft whooshes inside. My best friend shivers and her red, sassy lips turn into a smile as she holds the pasta dish tight in her hands. I move to the side, allowing her in as snow falls in the distance.

Zane takes the dish from her hand and carries it to the kitchen.

"Thank you." Julie shakes off her coat, stuffing her gloves in the pockets as she hangs it on the coatrack. She pulls her dark red curly hair from her beanie and shakes it out.

"How's the weather?"

She presses her ice-cold hands on my arms and I yelp.

"I almost canceled because I didn't know if I'd make it up the mountain. It was an actual miracle."

Zane sets the glass pan on top of the stove and I move to the kitchen, removing plates from the cabinet. We work around each other as Julie watches, completely fascinated.

"Can you read each other's minds?" She glances between us. "You hold conversations without speaking."

Zane chuckles as Nick moves down the stairs.

His black button-up shirt is tucked into his slacks and his dark hair is still damp.

Julie notices us both staring and glances over her shoulder.

When their eyes meet, he briefly pauses, studying her. Nick's gaze slides from her head to her toes. The electricity streaming between them is so intense my arm hairs stand on end. I glance at Zane, knowing the last time I felt an energy like this was the day I met him.

Nick clears his throat, never taking his eyes off my best friend, then he shoots her a sexy smirk. "Jules? This is a *very* nice surprise."

Can't get enough of Autumn and Zane? Turn the page for the exclusive, extra cozy bonus scene,

Snow Day!

CHAPTER 1

Autumn

I follow behind Zane as we climb the stairs that lead up to the attic. We're setting up the Christmas tree while the quiche is baking in the oven. Today, we're transforming the manor into a winter wonderland.

"I don't remember the last time I decorated," I admit.

He glances over his shoulder and meets my eyes. "Same. I didn't have a reason to celebrate until you."

My cheeks heat when our eyes meet, and those warm fuzzies brush over me. I love it when he looks at me like I'm his everything.

"You're wearing that expression again," he says. "Did you dream about this?"

"Not this time." I laugh. "I was thinking how I want to snap off every button on your flannel."

"Mm," he hums in his deep timbre, and it almost sounds like a growl. "Keep that up and we won't reach the top step."

He stops walking and moves toward me, pressing my back against the wall.

Zane slides his palm up my shirt and tweaks my pebbled nipple. I desperately want his mouth, want him, *my husband.*

"You negotiated these terms. You said no quickies: food and tree first," he whispers as I capture his mouth.

"Because I want to stay in bed with you all day." A ragged

breath releases from me. "You know how greedy I am when it comes to you."

His hand dips inside my pajama pants and into my panties. Soft fingers rub against my clit, and my eyes roll to the back of my head. "Always so wet for me."

"Yes," I hiss, my mouth falling open as he kisses down my jaw.

He dips his finger inside, and I go weak in the knees. Seconds later, he removes his hand and places his finger into his mouth. "You taste so good. But if I don't get an orgasm, you're not getting one, either. A deal is a deal."

I glance down his body and see how hard he is. I press my palm against his cock that's straining against his matching pajama bottoms. "At least he's on the same page."

"You love the chase."

"I love a man who has complete control, who can restrain my advances even when he doesn't want to," I say. His lips are on my neck, and he inhales my skin as he peppers kisses along my jaw.

"I'll have you begging me later," he whispers, leaning his hand against the wall above me. I look up at him like he's a figment of my imagination. In a way, he is.

"I can start begging now?" I chew on my lip, capturing a kiss.

"You're a temptation." He grabs my hand and leads me the rest of the way. He steps aside, allowing me to push open the door. His hand slides against the wall until he finds the switch.

It's overcast outside, and the lights burn bright.

"Wow." Inside is a treasure trove of stacked storage containers filled with glittery decorations. "This space looks exactly like the attic in *Beetlejuice*," I whisper.

"Mom hired a crew to ensure it was a replica."

I gasp as I step forward. "You even have the town model."

He clicks on the miniature lights. "Now, this is the original prop."

"In your attic?" My eyes widen.

"It's in *your* attic too." He shoots me a wink.

"This house is incredible. There are so many secrets and surprises." I'm shocked as I study the graveyard in the town model. My hair falls into my eyes, and I tuck it behind my ears.

"You're beautiful," he says, watching me with his arms gently crossed over his chest. "So fucking beautiful without even trying."

I move toward him, pulling him in for another kiss. "Thank you."

"Thank you," he mutters across my lips. "Being this happy feels illegal."

I chuckle as we break away. He strolls across the space, and I glance out the window to watch the snow fall from above. Everything is blanketed in white.

"Found it," Zane says, moving to the corner of the room where a gigantic red-and-white box with wheels on the bottom sits.

I walk to stand beside him. "What is it?"

"The tree."

My mouth falls open. The container is large enough to fit a body comfortably. "In there? How big is this tree?"

His brow quirks upward, and he smirks. "It's a fifteen-foot aspen fir."

"Thankfully, you're tall."

"We'll still need a ladder." Happiness radiates from him. With his hands on his hips, he glances around the room. "Let's carry this down first. Then I'll grab the decorations."

I nod, seeing at least twenty tubs with labels on the side: ornaments, lights, tinsel, mantel, Christmas town. "Sure, which ones?"

He places his hand on my shoulder. "All of them, silly."

"You're rewarding me so damn good."

"Oh, I absolutely am," he promises, smacking a kiss on my cheek as he grabs the handle and wheels it across the wooden floor. We quickly descend the first set of stairs, then the second. It's heavy as fuck, but I lift it without issues.

When we're in the living room, I stretch my arms over my head. "I have a plan for the decorations. You should take everything from the attic to the second floor, and I'll meet you and bring it down here. That way, we're both only climbing one set of stairs."

He leans in and kisses me. "You're so smart."

"Nah, I'm just sore from the ten miles I ran yesterday on the treadmill. Not to mention last night." A sly grin washes over my face as I replay fucking on the balcony as the snow fell around us. It was cold, but my body was on fire.

"Last night was incredible."

I steal glances at Zane in his element, happy as he passes me tubs of ornaments on the second floor to take down to the living room.

"What?" he asks, catching me.

"I'm lucky you found me."

He grins. "I wouldn't have stopped searching until I did."

"Still feels like a dream."

He puts down the box to wrap his arm around my waist, pulling me closer. "I hope it always does, wifey."

I steal another kiss, elated that the man of my dreams found me, just as he promised he would.

After I drop two more tubs beside the couch, I check the quiche in the oven. "Think we can get this done in forty minutes?" I yell.

"I think we can do it in thirty," he says, followed by his footsteps. We go back and forth, up and down the stairs, like worker ants. I'm tempted to start my smartwatch to track my cardio.

As Zane predicted, we finish within thirty minutes, but we're glistening with our sleeves rolled up our arms. "I need to grab the ladder from the garage."

"Perfect," I say, watching him walk down the hallway. As if he feels me staring, he turns and glances at me, grinning with that perfect smile. The door opens and closes, and I move back to the living room and stand in front of the fireplace.

The mantel is full of old photographs from his childhood. Many include his mom. Then my eyes scan over one of him standing in front of the gigantic Christmas tree in the living room, holding a peace sign and sticking out his tongue.

I laugh, understanding why this is so important. Knowing he's remaking these new traditions with me makes me feel special.

The door opens and closes, and I hear his footsteps down the hallway. When he comes into view, he's still smiling.

"I guess the tree is going over there." I hold up the photo, knowing it was taken close to where I stand.

"Yeah," he says, leaning the ladder against the wall. "Or wherever you'd like to put it."

"It's the perfect place," I tell him.

When he's close, he glances at the photo. I set it back on the mantel where I found it.

"I forgot about this picture." He reaches and touches the silver frame. "I had no idea what was in store for me."

"None of us did at that age."

He nods. "You're right. So that's where you want it?"

"Absolutely," I confirm.

"Oh wait, I have a box of ornaments in my old bedroom," he says. "Be right back."

In less than five minutes, he's carrying a wooden container. Zane opens it and pulls out several pages of folded cream paper. His name is scribbled on top.

"Is that a letter from your mom?"

"Yes," he whispers. I move closer, wrapping my arm around his waist.

"Do you want to read it now?" I ask, allowing him to navigate this however he pleases.

He hands me the letter, and I suck in a deep breath. "Will you read this one to me, too?"

"Yes." I unfold the paper that's soft to the touch. It almost feels like linen. When I see his name at the top of the page, I stop and meet his deep blue eyes. "Thank you for sharing this with me."

"It's the only way you'll ever get to know her. Words hold power, babe. You know that."

"You're right," I say, clearing my throat.

Zane. My son. My pride and joy. My miracle baby.

How are you? Are you setting up the Christmas tree? If you randomly found this letter in your box of ornaments and weren't planning on it, I'd encourage you to go for it.

Listen, I know it's hell to carry down the stairs. Yes, it sucks climbing up the ladder to decorate half of it. But do you remember how happy the twinkle lights made you and the warm ambience that filled the living room when it was gloomy in December?

You loved making a pallet on the floor and reading by its glow. If you were searching for a sign, here it is. Set up the damn tree and leave it up year-round if it makes you happy.

I look up at him, and he's wearing a gentle smile as he reminisces. "You liked to read by the tree light too?"

"Loved it," he says, kissing my forehead. I continue.

Yesterday, I called Silvia and checked in. She said Nick was having a hard time adjusting to the loss of his dad and mentioned your friendship is what's helped him the most. It made me so proud to be your mom. I know how caring of a friend you are.

Losing a parent is hard, maybe one of the hardest things I've ever had to do, other than this. Just remember that when the tears come, it's nothing but love leaking out of the eyes. It means you had something worth missing, and I know it's hard, but we have to be grateful for the time we had and not mourn the time we lost. Honey, it's so hard, and healing takes time.

Nick is a good person; he will be beside you when I'm gone, remembering what you did for him. I hope you can keep your friendship with him for a lifetime. You're like brothers and have been through so much together. You'll both make mistakes, but what defines you is how you forgive one another. Everything is forgivable. Except cancer. Fuck cancer.

"So now my mother is convincing me to give him another chance?" he interrupts.

My nose squishes. "It seems like it."

"Should I?" he asks, searching my face like I have the answer.

I lower my arms, studying him. "It's a decision I can't make for you, but I will support whatever you decide."

He moves to the couch and sits on the edge of the cushions. I follow him, plopping down next to him.

"Would you forgive Julie if she slept with your fiancé?"

I tilt my head, glancing at the fire. "Eventually. After I wasn't so hurt. We go way back, like kindergarten. She only has my best interest in mind, so I know she would never cross that line."

He exhales. "Yeah, I thought the same of Nicolas."

"I'm sorry," I whisper.

"Me too," he says. "Please continue."

I almost shared my diagnosis with Silvia today, but I decided to keep it close to my heart for now. I don't want to acknowledge it's even a thing until January. It's not easy breaking devastating news to someone who is already grieving. My friend just lost the love of her life, and now she'll lose me too.

I worry about her in the same way that I worry about your father. In a perfect world, they'd end up together and happy. I love your father so much, but he needs to move on after me. He needs to find someone who gives him purpose again. I hope it's sooner rather than later and that he finds someone you and Harper love and enjoy. He will. He's a good man. Your dad loves you so much!

"Wow," I say. "Are you sure your mom wasn't a witch?"

He bursts into laughter. "Shit. Maybe she was. Look."

Zane lifts his arm, showing me the goosebumps that trail along his skin. I show him mine.

"She wanted Silvia and your dad to get together," I whisper.

"And it still took them over twenty years."

"Ah," I say. "I know where you get your stubbornness from."

"It was my mother. Trust me."

I chuckle, and then I continue.

Anyway, I'm rambling again. Put up the tree and let it bring you joy. Christmas is always so magical, especially when the first snow falls. I hope that you keep celebrating and keep our traditions alive. And because I'm sure you'll forget, I wrote the recipe for my grandmother's famous gingerbread cookies on the following pages. Yes, I even gave instructions for the icing. It was your favorite part.

Hang the mistletoe. Kiss under the moonlight. Dance in front of the fireplace. Play holiday music as loud as you want. Make tons of snow angels and have snowball fights. But never forget to tell those you care about that you love them. I love you, son, with all my heart. Merry Christmas! I hope it snows nonstop the entire season.

Merry Christmas, ya filthy animal,
Mom

P.S. If this is the first letter of mine that you've found, know there are thirteen total hidden throughout the house in different places. I can't wait for you to find them all. It may take you years, but I think they'll find you when you need them the most, not the other way around. Have you found any yet? Or is this the first?

"I love you," he says to me.

"I love you," I repeat, flipping the page. I read the ingredients of the cookies along with the icing.

"We're making these after you get lost between my thighs," I tell him.

"Hell yes. Do we have everything?"

"Yep. I randomly picked these things up yesterday when we went grocery shopping."

He laughs. "It's like it was meant to be."

"I think your mom planned it."

CHAPTER 2

Zane

The oven beeps, and I grab the mitt, setting the quiche on the stovetop.

Autumn follows me, wrapping her arm around me. "This looks incredible. Are you sure you didn't buy this from the grocery store?"

"I'll take that as a compliment. It needs to cool first."

She reaches forward and breaks off the edge of the crust, then pops it in her mouth.

"Mm. That's delish!" She blows air from her mouth because it's still scorching.

"Patience is a virtue."

She giggles, grabbing my ass. "Patience is my middle name today."

I set plates and forks on the counter before turning to her. "The wait will be worth it."

"Based on what I negotiated," she says, leading me into the living room. "Tree and food. Sex until sundown and cookies for dinner. I'll wait."

"You added the last part."

"Oh, we're making your great-granny's cookies tonight. Right after you sugar mine." Autumn opens the tree container that's stuffed full of branches. I'm brought back to the last time it was pulled out of the box, and I laugh.

"When we set it up, it was a total disaster. My mom's cat climbed the tree and knocked it over. All the glass ornaments fell off and shattered all over the floor. The next day, we went to the home goods store and bought every plastic ornament they had."

"That's hilarious. But also, that poor cat." Autumn places the base where it sat all those years ago. I snap the first row of branches inside it, and then we both drop to our knees to adjust the needles.

"This thing is a monster," Autumn says, separating each cluster like a pro.

"Honestly, I don't remember it being this big."

"That's what she said," Autumn mutters, waggling her brows.

As she continues with the branches, I grab the next section and stack it on top. When I glance down at her, she's on her knees, looking up at me with big brown eyes. I brush my thumb against her cheek, taking her in. "Fuck, you're gorgeous."

She stands, grabbing my cheeks in her hands. "I was thinking the same."

We are tongue and mouth and teeth as I run my fingers through her hair. I hear her stomach growl, and I laugh against her lips. "You're hungry. We should eat."

"Yeah, because at this point, you're going to edge me all damn day."

She flips her hair over her shoulder and glances at me as she walks to the kitchen. I love that cute little smirk she's wearing as she cuts into the quiche.

My phone sits on the counter, and I click on some Christmas tunes as the snow falls outside. Autumn hands me a plate, and we sit across from one another on the bar stools. "Oh, coffee?"

"Yes, please," she says. As the beans grind, then the coffee pours, I stare out the window.

"Want to go snowboarding tomorrow?"

She tilts her head at me. "You know I snowboard?"

I laugh. "I did my research, babe. People in town were very happy to spill the tea and tell me everything about you. Plus, I saw your board tucked in the corner of the garage."

"I'd love to go tomorrow." She holds the mug in her hands and sips. "Shit, that was hot."

I shake my head, joining her when my coffee finishes. "When my vacation ends, I told my father I'd like to stay in Cozy Hollow and work remotely."

"Yeah?" She searches my face, taking a bite.

"He agreed. I'll just need to fly to New York once every quarter."

Her mouth turns up into the biggest smile. "This is amazing news! I was just thinking about what would happen on January third when you were supposed to return. I wanted to focus on what's important."

"Your writing?"

"You," she whispers, smiling. "I love spending time with you. It's happiness. The real deal."

I study her, asking myself how I got so lucky. "I feel the same. You're my comfort. The only time I can freely be myself: emotionally and physically."

"I love you," she says.

"Love you."

She grins, taking another bite. "What do you want for Christmas?"

"You. Wrapped in a red bow."

"Mm. Depends on whether you're a good hubby for the rest of December."

"I guess we'll see, then." I shoot her a wink. "Would you like to watch the ball drop at my dad's penthouse in Times Square? He's throwing a party and has the perfect view."

She gasps. "Yes. I've always wanted to see it."

"Great," I say. "Nicolas will probably be there. If the opportunity presents itself, I might talk to him."

"I support your decision if that's what you want to do. Only you know how deep your relationship goes. You'll do the right thing."

"Thank you."

We finish eating and I pick up our plates, rinsing them in the sink. Autumn returns to the tree, and I meet her moments later, the music still playing.

"Have you ever had roasted chestnuts?" Autumn asks.

"Once. They were soft, like a potato, and somewhat sweet. We should do it."

"I would love that," she tells me, handing me the third part of the tree, which I easily stack on top.

"I'll order some for us." I step off the ladder when "Merry Christmas Baby" plays. I pull her into my arms, and we dance around the living room. I grab her ass, holding her close against me, my mouth against her ear. Her fingers thread through my hair, and she gently tugs.

I slide my lips across hers.

"Is this real?" I ask.

It's her usual question.

She softly smiles. "You're living the dream."

I lift my wife into my arms and carry her toward the stairs. Right now, I need her more than I need air.

"We haven't finished putting up the tree." Her brown eyes sparkle as she studies me.

"I'd like to renegotiate," I say. "I need you, Pumpkin. The tree can wait."

"And I still get my eight orgasms?"

"Today, our goal is double digits."

"Damn, I love snow days," she whispers.

"Me too."

Acknowledgments

Wow. First of all, thank you for reading *Fall I Want*. I truly hope it was everything you've wanted in a fall book.

Big thank-you to Erin Branscom for inviting me to be a part of this shared world. We're fall queens and I'm honored to be a part of something so personally rewarding. There will never be enough pumpkins, crunchy leaves, or sixty-degree-weather days.

Thank you so much to Enni Amanda for creating such a beautiful cover, omg. It's what romcom authors dream of having. I'm honored to have my name on this.

To Nora Everly, Piper Sheldon, and Laney Hatcher, thank you for being so kind and fun. I've never been involved in something that's been this easygoing. It's been an honor to get to know you!

To David Michael, welp. We did it. LOL! Thank you for having eagle eyes and for making this enjoyable.

To Ali, I always wanted a proofer who could tell the difference between *stationary* and *stationery*. Thank you for enjoying my words and for making this diamond shine!

To my Beta Bishes (Thorunn, Mindy, Lakshmi, Brittany), in my literary life, I've always wished for a team of fun, kind, loving ladies who elevate the process. Sometimes it's SO hard to do this, especially under a deadline. And deadline mode seems to be the state I'm constantly in. Thank you for loving and fighting over Zane. It honestly brightened my day and encouraged me in all the right ways. You came in like fairy bookbishes and I'm forever grateful that you gave my words a chance.

Thank you to my incredible assistants, Meg Latorre and Erica Rogers, for helping me with this book. I couldn't do it without you and appreciate you so freaking much!

To all my fall queens and kings, thank you for allowing me to bring a little autumn magic into your life. I am so grateful for every single one of you. This journey just wouldn't be the same without readers. You make this all possible, and I promise I will continue to give you my all. I promised that if you showed up, I would. And just like my characters, I never break my promises.

Last but not least, a big thank-you to the hubby Will (deepsky-dude) for inspiring me and reminding me that when I want to trash the book, it's just a part of my process and it always works out. Also, thanks for talking me through my plot issues and reminding me that I can do whatever I want.

I've fully found myself and my voice again, and it feels incredible to genuinely enjoy the process. There's so much more to come!

LYRA PARISH is a hopeless romantic who is obsessed with writing spicy Hallmark-like romances that always take place in a small town. When she isn't immersed in fictional worlds, you can find her pretending to be a Vanlifer with her hubby. Lyra's a Virgo who loves coffee, the great outdoors, authentic people, and living her best life.